STRICKEN

Lysabella Barrett

To order additional copies of this book, contact:
Xlibris Corporation
1-888-795-4274
www.Xlibris.com
Orders@Xlibris.com
63772

Contents

DEDICATION . . .

To *my* 'pack',
Desi, Moui & Marschall, Zoë,
Brenna, Elliott, Dillon, Anna & Kelley,
Carrie & Sally.
Thank you for saving my life.
To Noanie & my Daddy,
for inspiration and support.
But mostly to my husband ~Eric~
His own light & dark struggle laid the
foundation for this story. May he overcome the
curse that plagues him, before our historical
love ebbs away . . .

FORETHOUGHT

Could the essence of being; be trapped in our blood? Or is experience what makes us who we are? What is at the core of our development, and what truly lies in our hearts when all is said and done? Can we be inflicted, like Jekyll & Hyde, so easily or do we have more control over our demons than we admit? Are we just giving in or making excuses? I guess it all depends, really. It all boils down to choice. I guess the real question is,

Is a good man, still a good man, even when he is a beast?

The Beginning

It should have been like any other track and observe mission. It should have been fun. It should have been safe. It should have been over when they left.

It just should have been . . .

But the air was dank, and a low mist had settled over the lake. The cool moon cast its impression along the water and reflected a calm peacefulness to the observers that had settled themselves there. It was soothing, and serene, and deceiving. It was a perfect night for research biologist Thadeas Thayer and his friend and assistant zoologist Liam McConnell to study and film the timber wolves they had been tracking for the past three months. Tad loved these kinds of nights. It settled his nerves and comforted him. It made him think of Halloween.

Tad and Liam had received a research grant to track and study the lifestyle and behavior of the North American gray timber wolf. So they leased a cabin and a few acres of land in an isolated part of the lush woods of Montana's Big Belt Mountains and began their study. Luckily it was a wellspring of wildlife, including a pack of wolves that had become accustomed to their being there. The study was going well and the lake had become a popular meeting place for both wolf and man.

The lake was a perfect backdrop for the type of field study the guys were doing as they had incorporated film into their agenda, and as a bonus, the lake wasn't very far from the cabin. Maybe a city block's length so it was within walking distance and they didn't have to drag the Jeep out and disrupt the quiet serene of the forest. In fact, the cabin was only a few miles from Great Hope, the little one horse town this part of the mountains wrapped around, and only about 45 minutes to the next city out. So when they needed anything they weren't very far from a place to get it.

Tad and Liam were staked out on opposite ends of the lake, hidden within some of the shrubbery that surrounded it. Liam had set up the camera on the end facing the clearing on the other side, so when the pack came to refresh themselves, he would get a good clear view with the camera. They also knew the full moon would add a nice backdrop to their film, as well as give them plenty of good clear nighttime light to work with. It was a great photo-op for some still shots as well. So Liam loaded the still camera while Tad loaded his gun.

Tad always carried a .44 caliber revolver in a shoulder holster on every track & observe trek they did. He didn't want to use it, but he felt it was just wise to have it. You never knew what kind of trouble could find you out here in the deep dark woods, especially on a full moon night. He had only had to use it one time before. He was just out of college, and he had been on a track and observe trek to record the nocturnal habits of bats in Mexico. He was there with two of his colleagues when a couple of locals decided to have a little fun taking potshots at the bats as they flew out of the caves. Tad had used the gun to protect the bats and the team. Some people just didn't have enough respect for animals. Not like Tad did.

Finally the guys were all set up. Now all they had to do was wait. So Liam got comfortable next to the camera and loaded the tranquilizer pistols while he waited. The tranq guns were also just a precaution. They would always much rather sedate a charging animal as to have to kill it. Tad was busy adjusting his nocturnal binoculars just across from him on the other side. He picked up his comlink and buzzed over to Liam, just to make sure everything was working fine. It was.

They weren't waiting too very long before the wolf pack made it to the party. The Alpha male strolled in first to assess things and make sure it was safe for the rest of the pack. He put his nose to the air and breathed in a few sniffs. He looked over in Liam's direction and then to Tad's. He knew they were there. Actually, he probably caught their scent well before he got there. Wolves have an incredible sense of smell. The olfactory area of a wolf's skull is roughly fourteen times as large as a human's, and they can smell prey from up to 300 yards away. But they weren't really afraid of Tad or Liam so much anymore. They had grown accustomed to the men's presence over time. They still didn't completely trust them, but they no longer saw them as a threat. The Alpha turned behind himself and made a few short "Woofs" to let his pack know it was safe, and then out they came, two, then three, and then four. Finally the whole pack of eight was at the lake drinking. It was positively beautiful to observe. This was the part of Tad's job that he loved the most. He smiled big as he watched from behind the noc-binocs.

But as the guys watched the wolves, something else was watching them. The pack sensed its presence first. They had been unusually edgy and cautious tonight. They suddenly stopped drinking and came to attention. They began sniffing the air, tails stiff, ears pricked, totally silent and alert. Tad began looking around them. He could tell they were alarmed, but didn't hear or see anything yet. Then something moved in the bushes behind them. It grunted and huffed. The animals jumped and growled and started surrounding the bushes. The hair was standing up all over their backs and tails, making them appear larger and more ferocious. They were certainly spooked, and whatever it was that spooked them was just across the lake from where the guys were situated.

Liam buzzed Tad's comlink, "What do you think it is?"

Tad answered back, "I'm not sure."

"Can you see it?" Liam asked.

Tad re-adjusted his night vision binoculars. "Might be a bear, or a cougar. Only another predator would cause them to react like that. They're frightened."

"Gotcha." Liam said, "I'm going to up the dose in my tranq gun."

"Good idea. Don't forget, I've got the revolver if we need it."

The wolves were really getting revved up now. They were barking and growling ferociously in the bush's direction. Liam holstered his tranq gun and turned the camera towards the bush. He adjusted the lens to try to make out what was in there. Then he caught the shadow of something very large. He buzzed the comlink again, "Hey, Tad."

Tad answered back, "Yeah?"

"I'm not so sure it's a bear."

"What do you think it is?" Tad asked. He was getting a little apprehensive now. The pack was really going crazy. He reached into his holster and took the safety off his gun.

"I don't know. Something bigger. I don't like the sound of it." Liam finished, "I've turned up the volume on my camera mic and I don't think I've ever heard anything like it. Can you hear it from your spot?"

"No. All I'm getting is the wolves."

Deep, guttural sounds were coming from the bush. The pack was going nuts. All of them were howling and growling and acting extremely agitated. If it was a Grizzly the pack could handle it. It wasn't uncommon for wolf packs to take down Grizzly bears in defense of their families. Slowly it edged farther out of the bush. It had a wolf-like form that Liam could make out perfectly from the zoom lens on the camera. He buzzed Tad, "Tad," he sounded a little panicky now. His voice was shaky. "Tad, I think it's another wolf. A really big wolf."

"Are you sure?" Tad asked, "All I can see from here is a big shadow. The wolves are dancing around so much in front of the bushes I can't really tell much else."

"Oh shit, Tad." Liam was getting very panicky now. "Can you see it now?"

"Holy shit." Tad whispered as he realigned his binoculars. He could see it now. "Holy shit!" He stood from his position to get a better look. The pack went crazy as it moved all the way out of the bushes and into the clearing in the moonlight. Tad and Liam could see it *very* well now, and it was clearly sub-natural. "It's a freak of nature." Tad commented to himself. Then it stood. It stood up on its hind legs and rolling its fists back beside its waist, it leaned down and roared at the pack, lighting them into frenzy. Tad took a few steps backwards and nearly fell down. "Oh my God." He whispered.

"Holy Mother of God!" Liam shouted, completely panic stricken now. He backed up from the camera and fumbled for his tranq gun. This thing was huge! It looked like it was 7 or 8 feet tall. Liam didn't know for sure, but if you had asked him, he would have said it was a werewolf.

The pack surrounded the beast and one and two at a time attacked it from all sides. It pulled and flung them off. Tossing them yelping to the ground. They continued to charge at it, ripping and tearing at its flesh. But it didn't stop the huge creature or even slow it down.

Tad feared the worst. If the pack couldn't bring it down, then he and Liam didn't stand a chance. He tossed the binocs to the ground and grabbed the .44 out of its holster and cocked it. Liam was frozen to the spot. Tad knew they needed to get out now while the pack had it distracted.

All at once, the worst happened. The wolves gave up and retreated back into the forest, and the beast immediately turned its attention on Tad and Liam.

"Liam!" Tad yelled, "Don't move! Don't provoke a chase! I'm coming your way!" Liam was too afraid to move. He was still frozen to his spot behind the camera shaking and sweating. As Tad began to edge his way to the right toward his friend, the creature threw its head back and howled.

"What the Hell is it, Tad?" Liam yelled petrified.

"I don't fuckin' know, pal!" Tad answered. He continued to inch toward Liam, his eyes never leaving the abomination in front of them. It just stared at him, watching him move, its eyes gleaming in the moonlight.

"Just stay still! I've got the gun! I'm on my way!" Tad tried to reassure his friend though he had little hope for them if the thing charged. He knew he'd have to hit it square between the eyes if he hoped to stop it at all. He reached Liam. They watched the beast turn and start to move toward them slowly. It looked as though it was grinning at them. Liam was sweating profusely now and shaking all over, "It looks like,"

Tad stopped him. He knew what he was going to say, he had thought the same thing, he just didn't want to hear it out loud. "I know, man."

"It looks just like," Liam sputtered again. It kept moving toward them, walking on its back legs. They kept moving back.

"Don't say it, Liam! I know what it looks like!" Tad snapped at him. Even though he shared Liam's thought, Tad was trying to keep a realistic focus on the situation to keep his own fear at bay, and he didn't want to hear about movie monsters now. "Move slowly, man." Tad advised his terrified best buddy, he knew if it charged, they probably couldn't outrun it. If they had brought the Jeep they would at least have somewhere to go. The cabin was too far and he knew it. It still had to cross the lake to reach them, and he hoped that would buy them a few minutes.

It stopped in the lake and threw its head back and howled long and hard. Liam just about shit his pants. He was holding the tranq gun and shaking it all over the place. He let out a little yelp of his own, "Aghhah! Oh damn, man!" Liam was all but crying. Tad grabbed his hand to steady it and they kept moving backwards. It kept moving forward.

They both wanted to run. Instinct told them to run, but their experience with animals told them it would provoke a chase. Tad tried to stay calm, he was trained not to panic, but he could have shit his pants too. He had never feared animals before now. He was still trying to convince himself that's what this was, just a freak of nature type of animal. Some radio active coyote. But he really knew better.

Suddenly, it stopped at the edge of the water and leaned down and roared at the men. Just like it did at the wolves, then like the shot of a gun, it charged across the water with lightning speed. Despite its size it had unbelievable stealth. "Oh fuck!!" Liam shouted and ran backwards as fast as he could without turning around. He wanted to keep it in sight.

Tad opened fire on it. He stood shakily in one spot and sweating, he fired the gun. It was a loud and powerful weapon, and Tad was a good shot. BLAM! BLAM! BLAM! He sent three rounds directly into its forehead. He knew he hit it, but it just kept coming. It came out of the water on two feet. It was running like a man and bounding up on Tad quick. BLAM! BLAM! BLAM! three more, into its chest. It kept on coming, unfazed by the shrapnel splintering its flesh. It barely even flinched as the bullets hit it. Before Tad could blink the sweat from his eyes, the beast was on him. It swung out and slashed his chest wide open, ripping through sinewy muscle and cracking through his ribs. Then it swung again, across his throat, sending his blood air born, spreading it all over the ground. Tad, gurgling on his own blood, went into shock and fell limp to the ground.

Liam was in shock and almost couldn't move. He was trembling in one spot. He tried to aim the tranq gun at it, knowing it would do no good. It walked slowly toward him. Liam tried to pull the trigger but he was just too petrified and shocking over watching his best friend die. He knew he wasn't going to make it either. The creature approached him and took the tranquilizer pistol right out of his hands and tossed it to the ground. It had hands! Huge clawed fingers and hands! Liam watched with astonished anguish at the marvel about to kill him. Tears streamed out of his eyes. He couldn't believe what he was seeing. He knew it was the last thing he would ever see. It was horrendous. It *was* grinning. It reached out and wrapped its fingers around Liam's throat and began to pick him up off the ground with one hand. As Liam's feet left the ground he reached out and grabbed the beast's wrist and struggled to free himself. He couldn't just give up. He had to fight it, even if it was futile. He was soon dangling about three feet off the ground. He kicked at it and pulled at its fingers, but it just held him there, *grinning* sadistically at him.

Liam looked into its eyes. He had never seen such eyes on anything before. He was almost hypnotized by them. They were cold, intelligent and merciless. Liam gasped for air as the beast tightened its grip slowly. Then it reached up with its other clawed hand and with one of its talons it tore an opening in his throat at the base of his neck. It twisted its clawed finger slowly back and forth into Liam's flesh. As he choked and coughed, and writhed from pain, the beast smiled with pleasure at his distress. He could feel a deep burning sensation and then the warm blood trickling down his chest. It was torturing him and it was grinning about it. Its expressions were human. Liam could tell it was enjoying this. It leaned in slowly so as to terrify him further, it squinted its eyes as if it were going to kiss him and then it slowly licked the warm blood off the hole it had placed in his throat. With its eyes still closed, it pulled back and made an unnatural sort of throaty growl, "MMMMMM," it growled and resumed smiling.

After it enjoyed Liam's suffering for a minute or two more, it began to squeeze and apply slow deliberate pressure to his throat. Liam could feel the blood pressure in his head throbbing. He could feel his lungs pleading for air and burning. He could feel the creature's claws digging into his throat, and then he could hear the bones in his own body snap and crack as the beast kept applying slow pressure to his neck.

Liam was losing consciousness. He knew he was dying. He knew he was dying from the moment he had seen the beast rage across the lake at them. Then, just before he blacked out he heard gunshots. They were loud, even above the ebb of his pulse in his ears. Suddenly, the beast released its grip and Liam dropped to the ground.

Just before he passed out, he could just make out the forms of men in what looked like Gortex jumpsuits with helmets firing at the beast and netting it. He heard its roars. He heard the men yelling at it. More gunshots. Then all went black.

~~~~~~~~~~~*~~~~~~~~~~~

Two days later Liam woke up. He opened his eyes. His vision was very blurry. He reached up to feel for his glasses. Where was he? Everything was very disorienting and fuzzy. He was in a bed. He squinted and looked around. It looked like a hospital room, but he wasn't exactly sure because everything was so blurry. He suddenly remembered what had happened. He reached up and touched his neck. It was bandaged. It really did happen. But how did he get here? Had he been rescued? The Gortex poachers! They must have saved him! Or was he dreaming? Was he really dead?

He rolled over on his side and felt around on the nightstand for his glasses. A hand reached out to open the drawer for him and startled him.

He hadn't noticed anyone come in. He jumped and pulled back into the bed. He could barely make out two people-like shapes, and then a voice.

"It's O.K.," the man said, "You're alright now."

The man sounded a lot like Anthony Hopkins, with that same kind of Austrian accent. The man reached into the nightstand and pulled Liam's glasses out of the drawer and handed them to him. Liam immediately put them on.

"You've been through quite a shock." The man said. Now he was coming into focus. He looked a little like Anthony Hopkins as well.

"Thank you." Liam thanked him for the glasses. He blinked still trying to get the dryness from his eyes and focus. "Where am I?" He looked at the man. The man was a doctor, Liam supposed. He was wearing a lab coat, and this was definitely a hospital room. Liam was wearing a hospital gown and his wounds were dressed. Putting two and two together, this man had to be a doctor.

"That is not important." The man said, "What is important is that you are alive and doing very well. May I?" He asked as he pulled a penlight out of his coat pocket and showed it to him. Liam nodded. He cooperated as the man did a light examination removing his glasses and shining the light into both eyes. Liam put his glasses back on as the man finished with the light and returned it to his coat pocket. Then he held Liam's wrist and checked his blood pressure. When he was done he stepped back and talked to him. "You are a very lucky young man." He pointed briefly at Liam, "You are in superb good health after your ordeal."

Ordeal? It *did* really happen. "Where am I?" Liam asked him again.

"You are safe. Don't worry." He answered all of Liam's questions sort of indirectly, but in a way that made you overlook it. "Some ranger scouts rescued you from a Grizzly that was attacking you and brought you here to our facility."

The image of that Hellish creature's face suddenly popped into Liam's mind. It was still very vivid. He squinted his eyes tight trying to back down the fear that was rising in his chest just from the thought of it. He opened his eyes again and looked directly at the good doctor, "That was no Grizzly, and just where is "here"?"

"We are a research facility. We are located at the top of the mountain just West of your cabin in the valley."

"Wait. How do you know where I live?" Liam asked, his faculties returning rapidly now.

"Enough questions Mr. McConnell. You must rest for now. I expect you to make a full recovery."

"How do you know my name?" Liam asked him. He was getting a little edgy about this guy knowing so much about him, and what about this "Research Facility?" Who were these people and where did they come from? Liam wanted answers.

The man reached into the drawer again and pulled out Liam's wallet and handed it to him. Liam tapped it against his other hand and whispered "Oh."

"Get some rest Mr. McConnell. As I said, I expect you to make a full recovery." The man said as he walked toward the door. "I will be sending in a nurse to take some blood. I just want to check your white cells once more before you leave."

Liam nodded in agreeance, "O.K." Before the man walked out the door, Liam suddenly remembered Tad.

"Hey," Liam asked, causing the doctor to pause for a moment. "My friend, Thadeas." Liam was finding it hard to ask, he paused trying to find a way that didn't make him sick inside, "Where?" he tried again, "Is he?"

The man interrupted him and nodded, "Relax, Mr. McConnell." He reassured Liam, "You are *both* very lucky young men." Liam smiled with relief as the doctor continued, "He is resting in the next room. You can see him tomorrow. His wounds were quite a bit more extensive than your own."

Liam sighed again. What a nightmare! The man started to close the door, "Buzz if you need anything." He pointed to the hand bell, "The nurse will bring it. Try to rest, Mr. McConnell."

"What if I just want a nurse?" Liam joked under his breath then he lay down, he just wanted to sleep. Thank God, he thought, we both made it out alive.

~~~~~~~~~*~~~~~~~~~

After a fitful night of lucidly violent nightmares, Liam awoke the next morning to a beautiful nurse nudging him awake. "Mr. McConnell." She prodded him some more, "Mr. McConnell?"

He finally stretched and yawned and rubbed his eyes. Then he reached for his glasses and put them on just in time to see the man approaching.

"Good morning!" the man greeted him. "We're going to remove those bandages today. You should be back to almost 100%."

Really? Liam thought, after what happened to me just a few nights ago? He wondered what doctorate of medicine this guy really had. But, then again, he did feel fantastic! He was also feeling a bit friskier than normal. He smiled at the nurse as she handed him a pill and a drink of water. She smiled back at him. She smelled really good, he thought, but her perfume was on kind of strong. He turned back to the doctor, "You really think I'm doing that well?"

"Oh, my, yes." The man smiled at him, "You should be up for almost anything."

"Great," Liam grinned, "Do you think after this I could start with a sponge bath?" He flirted with the nurse. She liked him, he could tell. She kept smiling back at him, and he could sense her intrigue of him. Liam couldn't quit smiling. What the Hell was wrong with him? He was feeling a little randy, actually *alot* randy, and for some reason he wanted to bite that nurse. She snickered at him. She *wanted* him to bite her. He just knew it. Should an injured man feel this good?

The doctor answered him, "Ahh, ha," The man grinned as he sat on the edge of the bed and prepared to remove Liam's bandages, "I said *almost* 100%, Mr. McConnell. Let's give your other primal needs another day or two."

Liam smiled at what the man said like some kind of teenager. He couldn't stop it. Why did he feel so damn good? Were they slipping him mickeys or something?

"I'll try." He grinned wide and winked at the girl again. He was still smiling. It was like that silly smile was painted on his face. He was normally very even-tempered, but today he felt positively spastic. He was very handsome with his shiny black hair slicked back and bright blue eyes and black-framed glasses. He was very striking, all the nurses thought so. They all loved his dimples. He knew that. Women always loved his dimples.

The man took the bandage scissors off the tray the nurse had sat on the bed, and slowly began to trim away the tape that held the bandages shut. He unwrapped it layer by layer. As the bandages came off and his neck was revealed, the man smiled. He grinned like he was in on a secret that Liam wasn't privy too. Then he asked, "What do you remember about what happened to you, Mr. McConnell?"

"Why? Is it bad?" Liam suddenly got serious. These people acted way too strangely and he could distinctly remember the sound of his own bones crunching. He knew it had to be bad. Then again, why wasn't he dead? For all rights and purposes he shouldn't even be breathing.

"Just humor me for a moment, Mr. McConnell." The good doctor continued and then asked him again, "Now. What do you remember?"

"I remember," Liam paused for a moment and got lost in thought, "I was being choked to death. This," he paused again, "Creature. It was crushing my neck." He closed his eyes tightly, finally serious for a moment, and a clear recollection came over him. He could see it happening all over again. Like a horror movie playing in his head with him and Tad as the first to die. "It killed Tad. At least, I thought it killed him. He shot it, but . . . it didn't stop it."

"Yes, yes," the man interrupted impatiently, "But what happened to you?"

Liam stared at the foot of the bed as he relived his latest nightmare for the doctor, "It held me off the ground, and it pierced my throat. It licked me." Liam squinted with disgust at this memory. He paused and then looked in the man's face, "Like it was tasting me." He said it almost with a question mark, "Then I heard gunshots and it dropped me. I passed out and woke up here."

The man exchanged glances with the nurse then he looked back at Liam. He picked up a hand mirror from the tray and held it a minute before handing it to him. Liam thought he was just trying to ease him into what he was about to see in that mirror.

"Sometimes," the man began, "Our memory can play evil tricks on us in moments of extreme trauma or fear. It's the way our mind helps us cope with what is happening to us at the time. Sometimes it lapses time and even erases an event from our memories all together and replaces it with vivid dreams, or disorienting images that appear to be memories. It is a sort of sensory blocker, an image association factor that sometimes makes it far worse than it actually is. Much of what you remember must have been what you dreamed when you were unconscious. You were out of it for two days, after all." The man smiled.

Then he handed Liam the mirror and let him get a good long look at himself. Liam was shocked at what he saw. There were no scars, no bruises, nothing. How was this possible? Liam touched his neck all over. He was baffled. He couldn't find a single trace of an injury, and certainly nothing he could associate with the attack. He looked at the man in disbelief. The man smiled and calmly took away the mirror.

"Now you can surely see why I think your recollection of events is just a bit hazy?" The man looked over his glasses at Liam and waited for a moment. "You can go home now, Mr. McConnell."

Just then, the door opened and Tad entered the room, two nurses of his own were guiding him and he was already dressed. He smiled at Liam, "Hey, pal."

Liam still felt overwhelmed and hazy, like he was dreaming, but he was so excited to see his best friend alive, that he jumped up out of the bed and ran across the room and flung his arms around Tad tightly and hugged him. Tad hugged him back.

"I thought I lost you, man." Liam whispered, "I'm so damn glad to see you alive! I watched you die, Tad! I watched you die!"

"I know. I'm glad to see you too, my brother." Tad smiled and patted his back. Liam couldn't let him go. They had always been tight, like brothers.

It was an extremely touching scene. But from behind them there was giggling, because from their point of view, all the nurses could see was Liam's ass peeking out of his hospital gown.

~~~~~~~~~~*~~~~~~~~~~

The ride back to the cabin was a quiet one. Neither Tad nor Liam wanted to talk about happened three nights before, and they certainly didn't want to talk about it in front of the two strange chauffeurs driving them home. The drivers said nothing to them and they said nothing to the drivers. So much of the way home the guys just stared out of the windows into the beauty of the forest, their minds racing. Trying to cope. The research facility that had rescued them, had provided them with this ride back down the mountain to their cabin in the valley, and since the guys still didn't know enough about any of this, they opted to keep quiet.

They were both feeling pretty strange though. They had very heightened senses now, and it was as if they could read each other's minds.

The ordeal they had suffered was a powerful one and its residue still clung tight to their psyche. It would be a long hard road to recover from and they both knew, without confirmation that it really wasn't over yet.

Once they arrived at the cabin the men both got out of the Suburban and opened the doors for them, still not saying one word or even cracking a smile. They both seemed a little nervous and a little too serious. They were dressed in gray uniforms and they were both wearing what looked like some sort of strange laser-tag weapons on utility belts. The whole stay at that place was very strange. They were locked into their rooms. They had been put in separate rooms on different floors, and the man that treated them never told them his name or offered any explanations.

As Liam was stepping out of the truck he noticed a card on the floorboard, he reached down and picked it up without the driver noticing and quickly put it in his pocket. As soon as the guys stepped out of the truck, the men quickly got back in without saying a word, and backed quickly down the gravel driveway.

Tad half waved back, "Thanks." He slurred, "I think." He turned and looked at Liam. They exchanged glances. They each knew what the other was thinking. 'Weird'. Then Liam turned his attention to the card he had put in his pocket. He pulled it out and read the front out loud.

"F. A. P. R." he showed it to Tad. "Federal Agency of Paranormal Research." That's all it said. They looked at each other not quite sure what to think of all of this. First off, what the Hell attacked them, and how did they survive? Who were these researchers and just what were they doing hidden up there in the mountains? More importantly, what were they researching? The card did say "Paranormal", right? It was like an episode of the X-Files. Tad finally spoke up.

"What do you think, Liam?"

Liam looked him straight in the eyes and then answered, "The same thing you think."

~~~~~~~~~~*~~~~~~~~~~

Meet Cassidy

It was one month later. The night was clear and chilly. It was a few months till fall but the weather at night was starting to get a little nippy. Cassidy liked weather like this. It was his kind of season. He reached into the pockets of his leather jacket searching for his cigarettes. He found them and lit one up. What kind of Hell could he raise tonight? He was standing outside of a little tavern that all the locals loved to haunt. It actually was about the only tavern this little town had to offer. He noticed there were an awful lot of motorcycles lined up in front of it tonight. That looked like possible trouble. He'd have to go inside and see what he could stir up.

Cassidy was always looking for trouble. Any kind would do, but fighting was his field of expertise. Quite the formidable pugilist, he averaged several fights a year. Many that would land him in jail and some that almost got him a life sentence. He had a good solid build, all muscle, and he was quick. If he had applied himself earlier he could have been a champion prizefighter. He was highly skilled in the art of fisticuffs. But it was mainly just unbound violence that he loved. He was smart, very smart in a diabolical sense, and there was nothing he loved more than living life on the edge. So into the bar he went.

It was pretty raucous in here tonight already, he thought as he strolled on inside and found a place at the bar. He looked around to assess the averages. The bartender approached. "What'll it be?"

Cassidy turned to him, "Rum. Straight." That would get him started. He smiled at the bartender in way that let the man know he would be trouble later.

"Don't get any shit started in here tonight O.K., Cassidy?" A voice came from behind him. He recognized the voice. It was the owner, Webber, and he knew Cassidy well. Cassidy slammed his drink and whirled around in his seat.

"I can't make any promises." Cassidy smiled at him.

"Well try!" the man put emphasis on his words and gave Cassidy a dirty look, "If you do I'll call the law. I promise."

Cassidy smiled even bigger, "Now whose making promises?"

"Prick!" the man shouted before he huffed off. Cassidy just laughed and spun back around in his seat. He stood and leaned in on the bar. "Hey!" he shouted at the bartender, "Two more." He waved two fingers in the air and the barkeep nodded and brought them over. Then it happened. The moment he had been waiting for. A pretty redhead approached. She stepped up to the bar right next to Cassidy. He moved to give her room, seemingly a gentleman. She asked the barkeep for two more drinks and change for the jukebox.

"What do you like?" he asked her. She turned and looked at him. He was grinning from ear to ear like a Cheshire cat. He was good looking and he did know how to be very charming when he wanted to be. He was tall, dark, handsome & mysterious, every woman's lure. She decided he was cute and smiled back.

"I don't know," she said, "Maybe you should come with me and help me choose."

The bartender handed her the drinks and her change. She politely took the money and one of the drinks. Cassidy offered to help her with the other one.

"Here," he smiled, "Let me get that." He reached over and slammed his two drinks, then picked up hers. She seemed impressed. She smiled widely. "Wow!" she said, "You must have an iron gut!"

He grinned and asked her, "Where you sitting?"

"Over there," she pointed in the direction of the bikers.

Perfect, he thought, and a huge grin came over his face. "Ladies first."

She led him toward a booth in the corner where another girl was sitting waiting for her. The girl smiled big once she saw Cassidy. They were college girls. Probably from the next town over, looking for a little trouble of their own. This town frequently got a lot of traffic from the neighboring city.

He sat the drink down and introduced himself. "I'm Cassidy."

The girls both giggled. The red head sat down and extended her hand to him, "Thanks for the help, Cassidy. I'm Gina." He kissed her hand.

"Great." He looked at the other girl, a blonde.

"Oh. I'm Trinity."

He kissed her hand as well and smiled, "How nice."

"Hey" Gina said, "How about that jukebox?"

"After you." He followed her to the jukebox. They scanned the selections for a minute. Then he looked over to his right. The owner was sitting in a booth with a couple of his bouncers looking back at Cassidy. He made a gesture with his fingers to his eyes to let Cassidy know he was watching him. Cassidy could give a shit less. He frequently came in this tavern and tore the place up. The man still never kicked him out for good. Maybe he was queer, Cassidy thought, who knows? He looked back at the jukebox. Gina had already chosen a couple then Cassidy picked one. "How about this one?" he asked her. He was pointing to a Meatloaf song, 'Paradise by the Dashboard Light'. She agreed, "Sure, why not. Is it good?" She was too young to know this one. "Oh, it's a great one." He grinned.

Webber leaned in to one of the bouncers. "Maybe he's just here for a piece of ass tonight."

The music started and on the way back to the table Cassidy ordered two more drinks. He slammed one at the bar and carried the other one back to the girl's table and waited. There was a very low average of women to men in here tonight, and a very high percentage of bikers and alcohol. The way he figured it, it wouldn't be long before the bikers decided to hit on the girls. Then he'd have his fun. He made sure to make it a challenge for them. He continued to laugh and flirt loudly with both the girls; so as to keep the attention of the two heavily lit bikers seated just a few tables across from them.

It didn't take long for just what he thought would happen, did. The two drunken bikers walked up and hit on the girls. They were quite drunk and quite bold. They were also quite large. Perfect. Cassidy thought. The girls stuttered to find the right way to turn them down without getting anything started. Unlike Cassidy, they didn't want that kind of trouble. Cassidy sat back in the booth and just smiled. He stretched his arms out behind the girls. The bikers acted as though he wasn't even there, and through the most slurred of dialects, one of them spoke.

"How 'bout you girls come over and waste your time with some real men?" One of them said. "The name's Roy, and this here is Cowboy. Come on, this punk can't satisfy two woman's as fine as y'all."

The girls didn't know what to do. Cassidy was enjoying this. He kept smiling. Gina spoke up. "Uh," she stuttered, "No, Thanks. We're just fine with this punk."

Cassidy kind of laughed and stared at them. "You heard her." He started, "She doesn't need a greasy tub a lard like you lickin' all over her, so why don't you fags just go hump each other and leave the girls to me?"

The bikers took a second to look at each other in stunned disbelief. Like they couldn't believe what they were hearing. Then Roy laid down the law.

"Listen up, you som'bitch," Roy warned him, "You better shut your punk ass mouth, and get the fuck on outta here before you get broke in two. Ya got me, Moth'r Fuck'r?" he slurred and swayed.

"Let me ask you something, Roy, is it?" Cassidy stood up and the girls decided now would be the time to scoot out of the booth and slip out the door. As soon as they did, Cassidy kicked the table out of the way and stood nose to nose with Roy. "Does Seigfreid know you two pussy's jumped the cathouse to be here tonight?"

"All right, boy." Roy yelled, "It's on! No buddy calls me a pussy and lives."

Over in the opposite corner the owner stood up on his bench to try to see what was going on. "What is it? What is it?" he said as he tried to get a better look, "It's that damn Cassidy, isn't it?" He sat back down, picked up his cell phone and immediately called the law. "That son-of-a-bitch!" he growled.

Everyone had moved and the bouncers were on their way to the other side of the room, but they were too late. Cassidy just smiled as Roy swung to hit him. He dodged it then threw his own punch landing it square in Roy's face.

Cowboy grabbed Cassidy by the shoulders so Roy could get a few in. Cassidy absorbed the blows, the whole time never losing that sadistic smile on his face. After Roy swung a couple, Cassidy used Cowboy's body as a counter-weight for leverage and reared up and planted both feet into Roy's face. By the time the bouncers got to them the whole place was lit up. Everybody was fighting everybody, and Cassidy loved it. He cut loose on the bikers with an unrivaled ferocity. Every time he tied up with one of them, he beat them senseless, and they were men who certainly knew how to throw down and take and deliver a punch. The bar was in upheaval. The owner was in a panic and the girls had made it outside unscathed. They decided to wait outside for Cassidy. They hid in the car and waited, they hadn't counted on him going to jail.

Finally, the law arrived. In this town the law consisted of the county Sheriff, and his Deputy, both of whom were accustomed to these kinds of calls. They were greeted in the parking lot as soon as they pulled up by the owner. Before they could get all the way out of the squad car he was on them.

"It's that God Damn Cassidy!" he shouted, "I warned him! I told him he would go to jail tonight if he started anything! He didn't give a shit!" the man screamed and followed them to the front door, "He so much as told me that! I want his ass in jail tonight!"

The deputy officer reassured him. "Just calm down there Webber. We'll make sure and get the bad guy. You just sit out here and calm down."

They reached the front door and the minute they opened it a beer mug came flying through it. The Sheriff dodged it. "Son-of-a-bitch!" he yelled. He was pissed off now. He stepped inside and pulled his gun out and fired it at the ceiling. BLAM! BLAM! The crowd immediately ceased to a halt. Except for Cassidy. He continued to beat the living Hell out of one of the bouncers he had pinned backwards over the bar. "Stop it!" the Sheriff hollered at him. He fired the gun again. BLAM! BLAM! "I said stop it now!" He headed toward the bar. The deputy was already making his way through the crowd to Cassidy. "The rest of you just stay where you are!" the Sheriff shouted at them. Everybody was at attention, even the bikers. None of them enjoyed the idea of spending the night in jail. The bouncer and Cassidy had their hands around each other's necks and fell over and behind the bar.

The deputy, Patti Leason got to the bar first and jumped up and over it. Cassidy was on top of the bouncer still punching him in the face. The man barely had any swing left in him; he was primarily trying to block the psychopath's blows.

Patti was used to dealing with Cassidy's shenanigans. He got behind him and wrapped his right arm around Cassidy's neck and locked his hands to apply enough pressure to make him let go. In his past dealings with Mr. Caine the deputy had learned you had to completely disable him to get him off of someone. He imagined you could probably beat him with a lead pipe and he'd still keep swinging. You had to use brute force with him whenever he got this revved up to bring him down.

"Ease off, Cass." The deputy warned as he pulled him in a headlock up and off the other guy. It still didn't stop him from kicking the man hard a few times on the way out. Sheriff Milligan met him on the other side of the bar as the deputy pulled him off.

"Come on shithead." The Sheriff said as he locked the cuffs around his wrists. Patti kept his arm tightly locked around Cassidy's throat until the cuffs were on and the Sheriff had a good hold on him. "Let's go." They each grabbed an arm and proceeded to drag Cassidy out of the bar. Before they left the Sheriff made an announcement to the rest of the drunks. "The rest of you people lighten up and help the owner straighten up this joint!"

As they dragged him out to the squad car Webber approached them. "You little bastard!" he shouted and waved his fist in Cassidy's face, "If you ever come in here and do this again, I'll shoot ya!" Cassidy just laughed at him and that sick smile flashed back across his face. He still didn't kick me out for good, he thought.

"All right, that's enough Webber." The Sheriff said, "Keep mouthin' threats and I'll have to let you spend the night in jail with him."

"Oh!" the man huffed flagging his hands at them, and then he went back inside.

The girls jumped out of the car and ran over to the squad car as they put Cassidy in the back and shut the door. They waved at him through the window and blew him kisses. Cassidy smiled like a snake from the backseat.

"Oh, bye Cassidy!" Trinity waved. "Maybe we'll see you later, O.K.?" He just kept on smiling, blood all over him.

The Sheriff turned to them, he had had enough, this just pissed him off, "Now you two girls need to go on home and don't be comin' back here to fool around with this one, you don't want to be a part of what he's about, you just think you do. He ain't so cute once you get to know him. Now move along home, and don't go back into that bar!" He snapped at them and then he and Patti got in the cruiser and cranked it up. The girls continued to wave. You'd have thought they just met a rock star.

"What is it about young girls and hoodlums?" Sheriff Milligan asked his deputy.

"You got me." Patti laughed, "Especially you." He said as he turned to look at Cassidy.

The ride to the station was no picnic either. Cassidy cursed and kicked the back of the cage just to be annoying. Patti turned around quickly and pointed his finger at him.

"Cut it out you fuckwad. You've done enough for one night. Don't make me taze your ass."

Cassidy thought it was funny. "Just my ass?" he laughed.

Patti threw his hands up. This trip promised to be loads of laughs, he thought. The station, like everything else in this small town, was out in the middle of nowhere. There was a long stretch of road from the town that led out to the jail and that was where they were. They weren't far from the station when the Sheriff suddenly slammed on his brakes. It caused Cassidy to fly forward and then back. "Holy shit!" he yelled.

"What the Hell is that?!" Sheriff Milligan exclaimed. He was referring to the very large figure standing in the middle of the road. The moonlight was to its back and its silhouette was enormous. He flashed his high beams on it, and what they saw caused the blood to rush from their faces. It just stood there breathing at them. It was only what they could have described as a werewolf.

"Oh my God." Patti whispered. Cassidy leaned forward in the seat and pressed his face to the cage. Thank God he was a little drunk and tired, or he might really have to worry about this. He got a good look at the beast in front of them and his heart stopped beating for a minute or two.

"What should we do?" Patti asked his superior.

"Hell if I know." The Sheriff answered, "But I'm not gonna get out of the damn car to arrest it."

"Have you ever seen anything like it before?" Patti was horrified.

"Only in the movies, son."

"Should we call the city station for back-up?" Patti asked him.

"And tell them what?" The Sheriff asked.

"Run it down!" Cassidy offered advice from the backseat of the car. "Shoot it! Do something you bastards. Don't just wait around for it to eat us!"

"You just shut the fuck up!" Patti yelled at him, "If we hadn't had to come get your ass we wouldn't be here right now!"

The creature made sure its presence was known, it threw its head back and howled. It was the most spine-tingling sound any of them had ever heard. It was deep and chilling, and it came out of the beast with a double octave pitch. Then it lowered its head and began to slowly walk toward the squad car on its haunches.

"Give me the keys to the cuffs, Pat!" Cassidy yelled at the deputy. Patti looked at his superior. The Sheriff nodded, "Give 'em to him. Just in case."

Patti took the cuff keys off his utility belt and pushed them through the holes in the cage. They fell to the floor of the cruiser. "Shit!" Cassidy yelled as he reached into the floorboard to find them.

"Well why the Hell didn't you catch 'em? We cuffed you in front, you bastard!" Patti griped at him.

"Why don't you go fuck yourself, Patti?" Cassidy bitched back.

The Sheriff interrupted, "I'm gonna ram it." Sheriff Milligan had decided their best bet was to take Cassidy's advice and run into it and hopefully kill it. Without any further warning he put the pedal to the floor and built up some RPM's then took his foot off the brake and let it rip.

Cassidy, still searching for the cuff keys, was suddenly launched back into his seat. "Damn it!" he yelled.

The creature was a few yards ahead of them at best, so he knew he'd have to build up some speed to hit it full force. It stood as if in defiance and roared at the cop car. As the cruiser plowed up on it they got a good look at its face. It was definitely a werewolf however unbelievable that sounded; they had to accept that that *was* what it was. They hit the beast hard and sent it flying over the roof of the car. Cassidy watched through the back window as it fell out of the air and hit the ground behind them. He could see it lying there through the red glow of the taillights.

"Good! Now let's get the Hell out of here!" he suggested.

"No sir." The Sheriff said calmly as he put the car in park and took the safety off his revolver, like he dealt with this sort of thing all the time, "We have a duty to serve and protect and that's what we're gonna do. Now, I'm not sure what that thing was, but I'm gonna wait right here with my foot on the gas pedal until I'm sure it's dead."

"What?!" Cassidy yelled, "Are you fuckin' nuts? Don't you ever go to the movies?"

"Sir," Patti said, "With all due respect, I have to agree with Cassidy. Maybe we should go on back to the station and call for back-up, or get silver bullets or something."

"Are you suggesting that beast really is some supernatural creature?" he asked his deputy. "If that was really a werewolf, do you think we would have been able to kill it this easy?" He was clearly in denial, his mind trying to figure a way around the facts. He had seen it too, how else could he explain it?

"No sir. I mean," Patti stuttered, "Yes I am. Didn't you see it?"

The Sheriff and deputy argued back and forth, temporarily distracted by fear and dissention. Cassidy was busy watching it from the backseat. He had seen enough horror movies to know how this shit worked.

"I saw a large mutant animal. That's what I saw, and that's what we're all going to say we saw. Got it?" Sheriff Milligan turned to Cassidy, "Mr. Caine?"

"If you say so." Cassidy answered without turning around.

"You turn around and look at me when I'm talking to you, boy." The Sheriff snapped at him. Cassidy turned around and flipped him a bird, causing Sheriff Milligan to seethe with rage, "You show some respect, you son-of-a-bitch." The Sheriff growled. Then the arguing exploded between all of them. Their fear was making them scattered and illogical.

Suddenly Patti turned white as a sheet and stopped talking, his eyes got as big as saucers. Cassidy noticed his expression, shut up and turned to look in the same direction. He could feel himself turn white. He sat back in the seat and scooted as close to the door on the opposite side as he could. The Sheriff was afraid to turn around. He knew by looking at them it had to be right outside his window. He heard a 'TAP, TAP, TAP' on the glass.

Patti and Cassidy were pale and their eyes were as big as planets. Sheriff Milligan knew it was bad. He turned slowly and what he saw froze him to the spot. The wolf's face was inches from the glass in the cruiser's driver's side door. It had gotten up while they were distracted with argument and snuck up to the car, and now it was tapping on the glass with one of its long clawed fingers and it was grinning at them. Its smile was big and toothy. Its unnatural eyes were gleaming and reflecting the light of the moon. It had the face of a wolf, but the expressions of a madman. It was enjoying scaring the Hell out of them. The Sheriff was trying to scream, but nothing was coming out, and before they could react it made a fist with it's huge grasping claws and broke the glass, then it grabbed the Sheriff around the neck and began dragging him out through the window. Patti suddenly came to life and pulled his gun. He had to be careful not to hit the Sheriff. He didn't realize he would have been doing the man favor if he had. He leaned over in the seat and shot it twice in the forehead. BLAM! BLAM! It growled and flinched but it didn't back down.

Cassidy jumped at the gunshots and moved to the floorboard. He had to find those keys! It was so dark out he couldn't see anything on the floor. He gave up on the keys. The beast had pulled the Sheriff halfway out of the window. He was struggling against the monster and trying to reach his gun. Patti decided to open the door and go outside the car for a better shot. It was against his better judgment but he felt he didn't have a choice.

"Don't go out there!" Cassidy yelled at him.

Patti ignored him and did what he felt he had to do. Once he was out of the car he reached over and opened Cassidy's door. "Run!" he yelled at him, "Go! Now!"

Cassidy poured out of the car onto the pavement. He quickly got to his feet but he couldn't run. What good would it do, he thought? He knew he couldn't outrun it. He was already horrified. He'd rather die facing it.

"Go I said!" Patti yelled firing the gun at the beast.

"Run where, Pat?!" he yelled back "We're in the middle of nowhere!"

The beast had pulled the Sheriff all the way out of the car now and holding him by the throat with one clawed hand it reached down and ripped into the man's guts with the other and repeatedly reached in and pulled his intestines out in handfuls slowly. It held that same horrible grin on its grizzled face the whole time. Patti watched, trying not to puke and unloaded the gun into it. It still stood unfazed by the bullets and continued to mutilate the twitching corpse of the Sheriff until the body fell limp. Then it dropped the body to the ground and jumped up onto the roof of the car with one leap, blood dripping from its claws and arms. Patti and Cassidy both looked at it horrified.

"You should have saved your bullets for us, Pat." Cassidy said under his breath.

It threw its head back and howled again then it leapt, slashing out at Cassidy cutting him deep across the face and throat. He fell to his knees bleeding profusely. Patti quickly tried to reload the gun and fired into it but it didn't stop it or even slow it down. It only pissed it off. It turned its attention on him next. It quickly walked over and slashed through his throat as well.

Patti fell to the ground on his knees just as Cassidy had. The beast reached down and picked him up by the shirt. It lifted Patti into the air and then threw him ten yards like a bag of sand. He hit the ground and his legs broke, most of his ribs broke and his neck broke. He wasn't dead, but he couldn't move and he was in miserable pain.

Cassidy could move, but he stayed very still. Maybe it would think he was dead. He was bleeding very heavy from the mortal wounds he received from its lashes to his throat and face. If he laid here too much longer he would be dead. He could see it hovering over Patti's body from where he lay bleeding. It was surreal to watch. He blinked over and over to get the blood out of his eyes. He saw it turn convinced Pat was dead and watched it walk back his way.

Suddenly, a light filled the sky. Cassidy could make out the sounds of chopper blades. There was a bright light shining down on it from the air. "Was it from outer space?" Cassidy thought trying to make himself laugh. It didn't seem to be very fond of the helicopter. It roared and growled at it, just the way it had done to the squad car. Suddenly there were men in big orange and white suits and crash helmets surrounding it. How did these people, whoever they were, know it was here? What was going on? No one knew Cassidy was watching this. Who would believe him? Then he heard gunfire. The beast was roaring and howling, and then it fell to the ground. He wasn't sure what they hit it with, but they took it down quickly. Where had they been thirty minutes ago? He watched as they shackled its arms and legs. Then they lowered a net from the helicopter and pulled the beast onto it. It seemed to be completely sedated or dead. These people seemed to know a lot about it. Once it was loaded onto the net one of the men signaled the chopper, and it lifted the creature away. With the beast gone Cassidy decided it was safe to pass out now.

~~~~~~~~~~~*~~~~~~~~~~~

Unlikely Brothers

Cassidy awoke 22 hours later in his girlfriend's bed. She was bustling around getting ready for work. She was beautiful, a gypsy girl with long wavy dark hair and sparkling green eyes. Most people would see her with Cassidy and wonder why she was with him. He was such trouble and she was so bright. Why did she put herself through it? She worked at the town bookstore, this little town was lucky to have one of anything, and she was running late for work. He started to stir and stretch, he rubbed his face into the pillow. Then it suddenly occurred to him where he was. He jolted himself awake and sat up in the bed. Becca walked back through the room and over to the closet. She seemed irritated with him. Nothing new.

"So," she said kind of huffy. She had a decidedly Latin accent. "You finally decided to get up?"

Cassidy looked over at her as she was flipping through her clothes. He was still a little hazy and stunned. He wondered how the Hell he got here.

"What's with that bandage around your neck?" Were you fighting again?"

He reached up to his neck and felt a gauze bandage; it was taped all the way around his throat. It took him a minute to answer her.

"Are you still drunk? Answer me." She said as she finally found the sweater she wanted and threw it on.

"How did I get here?" he asked her.

"Oh, so you were drunk." She began sarcastically, unable to humor his perceived lack of memory; "You don't remember the two nice officers bringing you here at two o'clock yesterday morning? And why did they bring you to me? I told you I was through with you and this," she paused for the right words, "bullshit of yours." She stood across the room with her arms crossed waiting for a response.

"I don't know. I guess 'cause this address is still on my license. Wait." He squinted and put his hand on his head. Did she say officers? This was too much to absorb. "Yesterday morning?"

"Yes, in the middle of the night. You're lucky they didn't keep you in jail." She huffed into the living room and began looking for her shoes. She was finally getting sick of the constant drama being with Cassidy always seemed to bring her. Like every other girl on the planet she had dreams of her own, and she one day wanted a family. She was smart enough to realize she wouldn't find that with Cassidy, and that hurt because she really did love him. But she felt she was wasting her time, and it was embarrassing. When they first met, he was exciting and so sexy. Now he was just a big violent pain in her ass that she always had to explain, especially to her brother. She had been keeping Cassidy a secret from her younger brother Carlo the whole time, because she knew Cass was not the kind of man he would want for her. He was trouble and she didn't want to drag Carlo into it. She had hoped she could offer him something better and he would change. She wanted to save him. She loved him. She was probably the only person on the planet that could say that and mean it. Even now.

He crawled out of the bed and wrapped the bed sheet around himself and looked around for his pants. He couldn't find them. Did they bring him home naked? He gave up looking for now and followed into the living room. "What officers, Becca?" he grunted, his head still spinning, "There are only two cops in this shit-hole town and you know them."

"Yes, thanks to you I do. I don't know, Cassidy. I was half awake. I didn't ask them for their credentials. They were in uniforms of some sort and you were drunk. They carried you in here and put you in the bed. Now I'm late for work. Please be out of here when I get home." She slid her shoes on, grabbed her keys and slammed the door. The sound of the door slamming sounded like a cannon going off in his ears. He reached up and held his head for a minute. He nearly fell down. Everything was so loud this morning. Why were his ears so sensitive? He walked over to the mirror above the fireplace to take a look at his wounds. His face must be hideous. The gaping wound over his left eye was really bleeding. Could any of this shit have really happened? And who dressed his wounds? He looked into the mirror and saw the same thing he saw every morning.

Razor stubble. He had expected to see big scars with stitches in them, or gaping wounds. He expected to look a little like Frankenstein, but nothing? Where were the wounds? The scars? He would have needed stitches at the very least if he hadn't bled to death. He didn't understand. Nothing was making any sense. He took off the neck bandage and found the same thing underneath. Nothing! He got closer to the mirror. His throat had been slashed open! He knew it! He felt it! He was there!

"What?!!" he shouted, "This can't be right!" He kept feeling his neck for a wound but found nothing. Not even a scratch. This was all too much to believe. What the Hell happened? Who put this bandage on him? It damn sure wasn't Becca. And who brought him here? He decided to get cleaned up and go out to the jailhouse to retrace the events. He needed answers. He had to find out if this was all just a bad hangover. But he knew in his heart he hadn't been that drunk. He had drunk ten times that before, and he still didn't dream shit like this. It was way too real.

~~~~~~~~~~*~~~~~~~~~~

After a shower, Cassidy called a cab and went back to the tavern to pick up his car. He drove a fully restored clean black Mustang, a '67. He didn't worry about leaving it anywhere because everyone in this town knew it was his and no one would touch it for fear of an ass whipping. He got in and headed for the station. On the way there he was compelled to get out and survey the spot where it all took place. Even though he had been a little drunk and it was very dark, he knew he was in the right place because he found the rubber burns on the pavement where the Sheriff had slammed on the brakes. But he didn't find anything else. Not one clue or shred of evidence that anything other than a car slamming on its brakes had happened here. There was no blood. No broken glass. No bullet casings. Nothing. He got back in the car and headed on to the jailhouse.

When he got there it was the same as the road and his wounds. No clues that anything was wrong. The cruiser was nowhere to be found and the front door was open. To anyone else it would've just looked like they were out on a call or something. Cassidy went in and took off his shades. "Ah," he grinned, "My home away from home." He walked around and peeked into the Sheriff's office. No one was there. "Hello!" he shouted just to be sure, but no one was there. It looked deserted and it was kind of creepy. He walked over to the Coke machine and bought a Coke. He decided he would hang around for a few hours and wait for someone to get there, or the phone to ring or something. He sat down in the lobby and got comfortable. He picked a seat with a clear view of the front door and he waited.

After a little while he began to doze off. Then, suddenly, something hit the ground with a clang. It startled him and he stood up. It sounded like it came from the back of the jailhouse. That's where the cells were. When he first came in he never thought of checking out the cells because he was looking for Patti. He guessed if anyone were in there they would have answered him when he first came in and hollered. He hesitated before just rushing back there. He was still very edgy and he certainly didn't want a replay of what had happened the other night. What if that beast was back there? He thought maybe he should arm himself with something first. He looked around and finally found a bully stick in the corner. That won't do he thought, knowing it would be no defense against that creature. He sat it down and walked over to Pat's desk. A couple of the drawers were locked. "Damn it!" he bitched under his breath. There had to be something he thought. This was a fuckin' jailhouse! He wandered into the Sheriff's office. "Ahh," he smiled, "Just what Daddy needed." He had found the shotgun case. He quickly grabbed a letter opener off the man's desk and jimmied the lock. He grabbed the sawed-off shotgun, checked that it was loaded, and then headed for the cell room.

He approached every corner carefully. He could hear something grumbling and moaning. He finally got to the entrance to the cells and whipped around the corner cocking the gun.

"Whoa, whoa, whoa, whoa . . . Whoa!" a very startled man yelled and threw his hands up. Cassidy immediately lowered the shotgun. "How fuckin' long have you been here?"

"You tell me." A cranky voice answered back. It was Patti. He was locked up in one of his own jail cells wearing nothing but his boxer shorts and a brace on one leg, a vest brace on his chest, and a neck brace around his neck. There was another leg brace lying on the floor. Cassidy figured that must have been the noise he heard earlier.

"Just what the hell are you doing here? And where the Hell did you get that damn shotgun?" Patti wanted to know.

"I'll tell you that if you tell me why the fuck you're locked in one of your own cages wearing nothing but hospital braces." Cassidy smarted off shaking the bars of the cell with his free hand. Patti took a minute to look around and assess the situation, thought about how strange it did look then answered as he ruffled his hair.

"That is a good question." He started to stand up. "What the Hell?" He started to pull at the brace on his leg. "Go get the keys and open this cage up." He told Cassidy, pointing to the desk behind him.

"Maybe I will, maybe I won't." Cassidy smiled. He was enjoying watching Patti try to stand up on that leg brace, trapped in one of his own cages. "It's kinda fun being on the other side of the cage for a change."

"Yeah, well you'd see less of it if you weren't such an asshole. Now would you get me the God damn keys please?" He snapped.

"I don't know. Maybe I'll just take them outside and toss them in the floorboard of my car." Cassidy growled.

Patti pulled and tugged at the leg brace trying to find a way out of it. His leg felt fine. So did the rest of him but his head sure did ring. "Ha, Ha, Ha. Would you, please?!" He yelled. Why was he wearing these damn things anyway? Must be somebody's idea of a joke, he thought. Though he couldn't imagine whom.

Cassidy reached over on the table and grabbed the keys that were lying out on the watchman's desk. Then he tossed them into the cage deliberately hitting Patti in the head with them.

"Damn it!!" Patti yelled. Cassidy thought it was very funny as he stood there and watched with his shotgun cocked. Suddenly the keys came flying back at him. "You have to open it from your side, dickhead!"

"Damn you, "Cassidy cussed as he unlocked the cage. "Hurry up. We have to talk. Now."

"About what?" Patti snapped intolerantly. He continued to struggle with the body braces, finally managing to get the last one off of his neck. Cassidy looked shocked. Maybe he *was* drunker than he thought. But, no, wait a minute explain *this* situation. Patti looked like one of Jerry's kids. Or was he just going crazy? Maybe he was a little punch drunk from fighting so much. "About what?" he yelled. "Are you kidding?"

Patti scratched his head and walked out of the jail cell in his underwear like it was any other day. Cassidy followed close behind him holding on tight to the shotgun. He poked Patti in the ass with it, "Hey, mother fucker," he huffed. Patti whirled around and took the gun away from him. "Give me that." He snapped.

"Hey!" Cassidy threw his hands up and tried again. "Don't you remember what happened the other night?"

Patti stood at his desk in a daze for a moment. The question suddenly hit him. He must have been in shock or drugged or something. How could he have forgotten that? He finally looked up at Cassidy in a very serious way.

"The Sheriff's dead." He was almost asking Cassidy rather than stating it. Like he needed the reassurance.

Cassidy smirked at him and shrugged his shoulders. "Yeah." He said solemnly, "And why aren't we?"

This sudden realization and flood of memory caused Patti to have to sit down for a minute. Cassidy pulled a chair up next to him. "Do you know how long we've been out of it, Patti?" Cassidy asked him in a very serious tone.

Patti looked up, afraid to ask, he shook his head 'No'. Cassidy held up two fingers.

"Almost two days, my friend." He waited a minute for Pat to absorb it then he added, "Do you know where I woke up?"

Again Pat could only shake his head, 'No'.

"At my girlfriend's house. She told me two officers brought me home drunk and unconscious at two in the morning."

This got Patti's attention. "Two officers?"

"That's what *I* said. And haven't you wondered why neither one of us have any marks on us? Look at your neck. We were attacked by some kind of mutant animal and were left for dead. It slashed out our throats and we're bull shittin' today. Doesn't that seem fucked up to you? And who dressed our wounds? And where the Hell is the squad car?" Cassidy then offered him a ride home. He stood up and offered Patti a hand up. "Come on. I can't look at you in those fuckin' underpants anymore. You look like fuckin' Sponge Bob." Patti couldn't speak, he was still stunned by all this but he decided to trust Cassidy. Once more these two men on opposite sides of the law were going to have to help each other. Patti looked at him trying to take in everything he just said. "What do you mean, 'where's the squad car?'"

"Come on. Tell me where you live. We'll go over it again in the car." Cassidy urged him up and drove him home so they could regroup. It was the start of a very strange kinship. And it was about to get even stranger.

~~~~~~~~~~*~~~~~~~~~~

ONE MONTH LATER . . .

Luke Williams wasn't always the big hunter type. He really didn't like killing anything. Even fish. But he loved the comradery he got from going deer hunting with his cousins and friends. Every year they took one of these hunting trips together. They had done it for as long as he could remember. When they were all kids, it was Luke's dad Jerry and his Uncle Ted that always took them. Now it was a tradition, and *they* in turn always took the two neighbor boys they had grown up with. Growing up they all had lived in the same cul-de-sac, so they were all pretty close.

They would draw straws to decide where to go each year, and each year it was somewhere new. They tried to never go to the same place twice. It was a kind of code with them. That way, they figured, they could visit anywhere in the U.S. they hadn't been before and kind of up the adventure level a notch each time. This year it was the Big Belt Mountains in Montana. They would make it a road trip, a two-day travel adventure. They would camp out along the way there and on the way back. It would be fun, he thought.

So the trip began. It seemed to go as any of the many other trips had, fighting, joking and laughing, and lots of horseplay. It was the way it would end that would change the course of this tradition forever. And change the life of Luke Williams unsympathetically.

~~~~~~~~~~*~~~~~~~~~~

For the last couple of days Cassidy had slept on Patti's couch. There was something uncharacteristically wrong with both of them. There had been ever since the bizarre accident that had fated them as friends. Cassidy's temper would flare without warning, and he was far more aggressive than usual. Not much off his normal pace of things but upped a notch. Which moved him from potentially hazardous to lethal. He had become particularly more aggressive and intolerant with Becca. The occasional slap to the face he would sometimes administer to her had become two and three uncontrolled backhands. And for a man of his strength and size, the force of those blows could render her unconscious. He decided to put the distance between them she had been begging him for. At least for a few days, until his libido got the better of him. He had become more aggressive in that area as well, and Becca had told him it was over more than once.

For Patti Leason, the change was different. Oh, he too had become more easily provoked. And that was a leap for the usually easy going, calm tempered, level headed Deputy Sheriff he used to be. But the biggest change in him was intent. It was as though he suddenly had forgiveness for certain crimes. Like letting petty thieves get by with a fine, and ignoring most of the calls that came in for domestic violence. Placing bets on backyard fighting matches and drag racing speeders in the cruiser, which had oddly re-appeared at the police station without a scratch on it. It was as if he suddenly became an outlaw, thus his sudden tolerance of Cassidy. They both needed guidance and purpose desperately. They needed someone to call them down. And they were about to get just that.

But Patti and Cassidy weren't the only ones going through some strange days. It had been two months since the attack that nearly killed Tad Thayer and his friend Liam McConnell. For two months they had become stronger, faster, quicker witted, and their physical and intuitive senses had become a Hell of a lot keener. They had been sleeping and eating a lot more as well, like their metabolisms were in uncontrolled overdrive. They tried to keep up the pace of their work and they had almost completed the video work they had started earlier that year. But being smart men they had realized their attack in the woods was far from over. The monster was in them now. They knew it. They had already become it. And though they had gained very supernatural and beneficial powers, they also had inherited its curse. They knew the first time it happened a month ago, when they were stricken, and helplessly watched each other stretch into the very same beast that had mauled them. They blacked out losing track of almost 12 hours and then woke up naked and covered in blood. Oh, yes. They knew. But apart from Cassidy and Patti, they tried to gain as much control and dignity as they could and accepted their fate for now. They would simply look after each other and fight each battle as it came. And in time they would learn to utilize this new infliction, until they could find a cure, if there was one.

~~~~~~~~~~*~~~~~~~~~~

The Omega

The drive to the Big Belt Mountains had been a seemingly long one. The guys all seemed to be getting along pretty well, there was just something different about this trip and Luke couldn't quite put his finger on it. He had a terrible feeling and just couldn't help feeling it. He didn't know why, but ever since they had decided on the Big Belt, he had had this foreboding sense that there wouldn't ever be another one of these trips.

So they arrived, and though they didn't really have designated hunting or camping sites in this section of the woods, the guys managed to find a really good location pretty close to a small lake. So they would have a good water source. A good water source was also a good place to find deer. It was a win/win. They got camp set up and being that it was still pretty early in the day, a couple of the guys, Sam & John, Luke's cousin and neighbor, decided to go ahead and scope out the area. Luke was all too happy to stay behind. He was still a little road weary, and as before he really wasn't there to kill anything, just hang out with the guys.

It wasn't long before Sam and John came back. They had picked up some firewood along the way and before long a nice roaring fire was blazing and they were all getting seated around it to have a little bite to eat and tell bullshit stories. It was exciting and everyone's adrenalin was pumped. Tomorrow they would hunt, and though they couldn't have known it, tomorrow night, they would be hunted.

~~~~~~~~~~~*~~~~~~~~~~~

Tad and Liam could already feel it under their skin. They could feel their blood getting hotter. Even after just one experience they were in

---

43

tune to the biology of their new D.N.A., and they knew it would be less than twenty-four hours now until the beast appeared. They would confine themselves to the cabin until then. They had wondered what had happened to the one that made them. Had the Gortex Nazis killed it? They couldn't be sure, and so they would be on the lookout for it to make another appearance. Only this time they would defeat it.

Their keener senses had become fine-tuned over the last sixty days. Every month the curse brewed in their blood they got stronger and sharper and gained more control over it and its symptoms. They wondered how long this disease had reigned all over the Earth. Were they Gods? Or were they lepers, contagious and festering? They weren't sure. But they were sure they would eventually be able to manipulate it enough to be aware of their actions. Then they would find a way to either live in peace with it raging inside them or they would extinguish its fire forever. Only time would tell.

~~~~~~~~~~~*~~~~~~~~~~~

These new feelings had emerged inside of Cassidy and Patti as well. They knew something was definitely wrong, and up until now they had just given in to their new behavior. But clearly their nightmare wasn't over. Though they had only spoken about the night they were attacked once since it happened, they, like Tad and Liam, knew what was wrong. They just didn't want to say it out loud. Maybe it would go away. Maybe all their personality changes were just a result of shock from the trauma they had sustained. But there was no denying their physical changes, and the fevers boiling them in their own skins. If you had asked Cassidy he would have told you he could feel his bones stretching under his hide. They knew what had attacked them. They knew that night, and they knew how it worked. The fullest moon was tomorrow night. It had been waxing all week long. They could feel it too. All they could do was wait.

~~~~~~~~~~~*~~~~~~~~~~~

On the peek of the mountain, the people in the research facility were busy too. They also knew what was going to happen. But no one else knew what they knew. And no one else could guess what they were doing. The drivers that had taken Tad and Liam home and the teams of Gortex covered poachers were all gearing up for the coming events. The team of doctors and scientists all working on privately funded government experiments were busy in their lab coats, working in their government laboratories on serums and weapons. And the man who treated and released Tad & Liam, and sedated, bandaged and braced Cassidy and Patti, was busy making plans. Secret plans, that he and his team would be executing very soon. With none to the wiser if all went on as planned.

Even the wolf pack that Tad and Liam were studying knew that something was going to happen. They had become fond of the researchers and spent a lot of time outside the cabin. It wasn't uncommon for them to eat raw meat right off the deck that the guys would put out for them, and spend a few hours after basking in the sun before moving on home to their own dens. But when the moon was waxing they were nowhere to be found. They didn't want to be around when the other wolves were present. They would only emerge the day after the full moon, and stay only until it rose again. This had become the way of things here on the mountain.

~~~~~~~~~~~*~~~~~~~~~~~

Cassidy, ironically enough, always wore a silver pentagram around his neck on a silver chain. Becca had given it to him when they first started dating. Over the past couple of days it had begun to make his skin itch and tonight it was burning. He didn't care though he liked it. It made him feel powerful. He would leave it on. He laid on the couch not really wanting to go anywhere and scratched at the irritation around his throat. Pat was supposed to be bringing something to eat after he left the station. I'm starving, he thought. How fuckin' long was he going to be?

Finally Patti came through the door with two large grocery bags. He tossed them on the table. "Get off your ass and go out on the porch and fire up the grill." He bossed at Cassidy. Cassidy sat up on the couch and looked over at the bags. He grunted, "You mean we got to cook it? I'm fuckin' hungry now." He snarled.

"Shut up, you asshole and fire it up." Patti bitched back at him as he began taking the grill utensils out of the cabinet. This was pretty much what their dialogue had become over the past month. Cassidy got up and strolled over to the table and looked down into the bags. Meat. They were full to the top with steaks, both of them.

"Holy shit, Pat." Cassidy said as he reached in and pulled out possibly the biggest T-bone steak he had ever seen, "How hungry are you?"

Pat was busy putting the beer and cokes into the fridge. He pointed to the terrace again. "Go. Fire. Now."

Cassidy dropped the steak back into the bag and headed through the sliding doors that lead to the second floor terrace. He uncovered the grill and then he stood there in his pentagram and cut-off denim shorts, spraying the coals with lighter fluid. He pulled a matchbook out of his pocket and tossed a lit match onto the grill. After it was hot, Patti came out and tossed 5 or 6 huge pieces of meat onto the fire. He tossed Cassidy a beer and they both sat down and watched it cook. Once the food was barely cooked to rare, they both tore into it like starving people. They didn't even look up at each other until they had eaten every bite. Then they both passed out cold in the lawn chairs. They would sleep for the next twelve hours, and when they woke up, everything would change for them.

~~~~~~~~~~~*~~~~~~~~~~~

Tad, being a biologist, decided that the fever that burned in them was their body's reaction to a foreign intolerance. A fever was the body's way of fighting off infection, and so he figured that was why they were constantly burning up. And the closer it got to the full moon, and the closer they got to transforming, the higher their temperatures shot up. It was this constant pain and agonizing heat that, in turn, fueled the uncontrolled rage that coursed through them when they changed. The science of this phenomenon was fascinating, he had to admit, and he had been keeping a journal of the events ever since they were returned home after their attack. There had to be a connection somewhere that would make enough sense he could work with the disease, and find a cure for it, or at least a way to temper it.

He and Liam lay on opposite couches, fatigued and hazy. This seemed to be the way of things before the shift. They had already stuffed themselves on nearly raw red meat and now they would sleep for the next twelve hours or so until they were stricken with the beastly transformation again. There was simply nothing they could do to fight it. Neither of them had the strength to speak, but they didn't need to. Their intuitive senses had grown so that they could communicate telepathically. They each knew what the other was thinking and feeling. Another fascinating side effect of the affliction.

~~~~~~~~~~~*~~~~~~~~~~~

The six guys sat around the campfire and sang. They made fun of each other and told stories that no one believed. This was why Luke loved these outings. His cousins and best friends always found a way to boost each other's spirits no matter what had come their way. They decided shortly after they ate to go ahead and bed down for the night. They wanted to get an early start in the morning. All was quiet and peaceful, as so many of these trips had been. But Luke still couldn't shake that horrible, creepy feeling he'd had for the whole trip. What was it about this place, he thought? He closed his eyes and fell asleep. It would be the last time in his life he would sleep without nightmares.

The next morning, the campers got up bright and early, ate a quick breakfast, loaded their guns, put on their fatigues and headed into the forest. They were excited and ready to hunt. They trekked deep into the forest. They reached a highpoint where they could look out over the valley and see their campsite and the lake. It was a breath-taking view. The forest was heavy with tall pine trees and the air was clean and crisp. They also spotted a cabin. A fairly large cabin that they hadn't noticed when they arrived. It was nestled among the trees about a block and a half from where they had set up camp. Luke pointed it out to the others.

"Hey," he said as he pointed to it, "Did any of you guys notice that cabin before?"

"No." Sam answered, "I hope we aren't to close to their property line or anything. I wouldn't want to be shot at." He grabbed the binoculars out of his pack to get a better look, and see if he could tell if anyone was living there.

"I hope we didn't make too much noise last night." Luke added.

"Ahh," Sam said, "I think if we had they would have come over and told us to leave. We're set up close to them, but not so close we would be a problem. There's a Jeep down there. I guess it's occupied." He put the binocs back in his pack and tossed it back over his shoulder. "Let's just enjoy our trip, and if they ask us to leave we'll move on. O.K?" he patted Luke on the shoulder. Sam knew what a worrier he was.

"O.K." Luke smiled reassured. He wouldn't be as nervous if he hadn't had this sick feeling all week. He looked back over his shoulder and looked at the cabin one more time before turning and following the others up the trail. He'd feel a whole lot better once this trip was over, he thought to himself.

The trek was a washout. Not one deer. Not one duck or quail or even a rabbit. It was like the whole damn forest was spooked. They had never experienced this kind of disappointment on a hunting trip ever before. They marched back down the trail to the campsite. They would have to pack up tomorrow morning and go home empty handed. Luke wanted to leave tonight. This whole damn thing had unnerved him. It was too weird. Where was all the wildlife? They didn't even spot any predators. He mentioned going home to his cousins. It was getting late and he wanted to leave before the sun went all the way down. He would just feel better once they were on their way home.

"Hey, Tommy," he tugged on his older cousins jacket, "You want to go ahead and leave tonight? I'll drive."

Tommy smiled at him. "Why?" he grinned, "Are you spooked or somethin'?"

"Well yeah, aren't you?" he said, "This is very weird, don't you think? I mean, if something spooked the wildlife where was it? We didn't even see any trace of a cougar or bear or wolves. Isn't that weird to you?"

"Well yeah," Tommy shrugged, "I guess that is a little strange. But I don't think it's anything to worry about. And the guys aren't gonna want to load everything up and drive all night. At the very least we can do a little fishing and camp out one more night. So it's not a totally wasted trip. Ya know?"

Luke agreed, reluctantly, and went to grab his pole. Fishing he didn't mind. But he would rather load up and go on home.

~~~~~~~~~~~*~~~~~~~~~~~

Back at Patti's apartment things were getting heavy. The guys had only been up a couple of hours. Their bodies ached, their ears were ringing and the heat in their bodies was boiling. Patti grabbed the keys to the patrol car. This was it, he knew it and he was frenzied. They knew what was going to happen. If they hadn't fully believed it before, they believed it now. He yelled at Cassidy.

"Come on," he shook the keys at him, "We've got to get away from town." He yanked the door open and headed down the hall. Cassidy followed him still scratching at the medallion around his neck. His throat was red from him digging at it for two days. They jumped in the cruiser and headed for the mountains. It wasn't too far from town, but far enough, Patti thought. He just hoped they would get there in time.

~~~~~~~~~~*~~~~~~~~~~

Tad and Liam were holding their guts in pain. It was a wrenching twisting pain that made them growl and yell out loud. Tad sat up on his knees and ripped his shirt off. He wouldn't need it in a few minutes. Liam struggled to his feet and ran to the back door. He and Tad tried to get as far away from the cabin and the main road leading up to it as they could when this happened. He pulled his t-shirt off, threw his glasses down and ran outside, and up into the woods. He had nothing to fear at night in these woods anymore, because he and Tad were what was to be feared.

~~~~~~~~~~*~~~~~~~~~~

Patti turned on the lights of the squad car and put the pedal to the floor. Cassidy was in the seat next to him, holding his stomach, gritting his teeth in pain. He reached out and grabbed the dashboard. His fingers were stretching. It was all Pat could do to ignore the pain in his own body and try to drive. They hit the main highway that led them to the heart of the mountains and Patti laid down the lead. They weren't far now. Luckily Pat had put a bigger engine in the squad car. He hoped he would survive what was happening to him. He looked over at Cassidy. He was trembling all over holding onto his gut. He looked back at Patti, spit was flying out of his mouth and his eyes weren't the same. They were big and yellow with red around the centers, and the pupils glowed from the inside, reflecting the light. Just like the beast that had attacked them. Patti's guts were burning he held onto his stomach and clenched his teeth. He tried to talk to Cass.

"How are you doing, man?" He could feel his own physiology changing too. He wondered how crazy he must look. Cassidy, shaking stuttered out, "How.tth,the f,f,fuck . . . ddo you th,thin,think I am,m,mm, D,Duke b,b,boy?"

Patti had learned to like Cassidy's wit and sarcasm, but tonight he just wanted to beat the shit out of him. He tried to focus on the road, but his vision was changing. He had to pull over. He skidded to a halt just off the side of the road. They weren't very far from the heart of the mountains now, and they were already far enough up in the woods that he felt they were safely away from everyone.

They both threw their doors open and fell out onto the road. Cassidy lay at the edge of the woods. He rolled on the ground howling, his body stretching and metamorphing into the shape of a wolf. His vision had altered and he could no longer talk. He could see everything in a clear light but it all looked like a black and white movie to him. From his point on the ground he could see Patti twisting and writhing on the other side of the cruiser. He stretched out his arms in front of him, some of the pain was subsiding now and he tried to focus his new eyes on his hands. There were long crooked hairy fingers with razor sharp and shiny long black nails where his hands used to be. He shook his head and tried to stand up. He kept rising up and up. He had gained more than one full foot of height. He staggered in his new body trying to gain his footing. His blood still boiled and his bones ached from stretching. He was bloodthirsty and he couldn't shake the feeling. He didn't really want to, though, he wanted to embrace it.

Patti was starting to stretch out now. His new wolf body almost complete. Cassidy staggered over to his side of the car and roared at him. With what little strength he had, Patti kicked at him with his new wolf feet. Cassidy's face started to express the man within, as he tilted his head and grinned that same sadistic way he always did when he was up to no good. He threw his head back swiftly and howled long and clear. Sending a warning to anything in his path.

The campers were just about to call it a night when they heard the howl. It was a raspy shrill bone-chilling sound. They all got quiet and looked at each other long and hard. Luke started to worry. Maybe that was why there wasn't any wildlife in this forest, he thought. Whatever that was didn't sound very friendly.

"What the Hell was that," Tommy said, suddenly thinking Luke may have been right to want to head home early.

"Let's load the guns." John suggested and they all got up and cocked their rifles. They turned their backs to the fire and tried to make out any shapes in the darkness. Then they heard it again. This time it seemed to come from higher up in the mountainside, farther to the North. It sounded like packs of wolves communicating, but different than any of the wolves they had ever encountered.

Patti finally got up and lurched after Cassidy. Cassidy seemed to take to his new form a lot quicker than Patti was. Patti was dazed and angry. He tried to get a grip on his new physiology and focused his new eyes on the road. He wanted to kill something. Maybe Cassidy. He felt strong and powerful, and his blood ran so hot in his veins he just wanted to rip something apart. He could see Cassidy running way out ahead of him. He tried to yell at him. He couldn't. All that came out were grunts and growls. He threw his head back and howled. Cassidy stopped and turned to look at him. He dropped his front feet to the ground and ran, full speed back in Patti's direction. Patti stood in the middle of the road and roared at him. Cassidy hit him with all his strength knocking them both to the ground hard and causing them to skid backwards. Patti immediately got up and started swinging at him. This is what Cassidy wanted. He wanted to make him angrier, he wanted to fight or kill something, and he wanted Patti to feel that too. They fought each other in the road for a few minutes, till Cassidy felt Patti was good and pissed off, then he turned and dropped to his hands and ran full speed back into the woods. Patti chased after him. They had never felt so free. And they were headed straight for the campsite.

~~~~~~~~~~~*~~~~~~~~~~~

Farther up on the mountain Tad and Liam stood in their wolf-skins and faced each other. They had heard the howls and growling of the others and had smelled the campsite. They had purposely avoided the campers, but the wolf howls were unexpected. Tad had returned the first howl. Could it be the one that changed them? They looked at each other and snarled, they too wanted to rip into something. They chose not to hurt the campers. But this other wolf-man was fair game. They collectively decided to face it. They turned to head back down the mountain but before they could, bright lights suddenly surrounded them. Behind those lights were the Gortex poachers. Tad and Liam were ready to fight.

They stood and roared at the men. The men stood their ground and cocked their guns. Tad lunged forward and the men immediately shot him. They hit him, PLAM! PLAM! PLAM! quickly with one of their strange weapons. He growled and staggered about finally falling to the ground. Liam was next, he snarled and bared his teeth. He turned his head and looked around him, he was surrounded. He swung out at one of the poachers. He missed him. Then he heard a familiar voice. "Don't toy with him!" the man said, "Take him down. NOW!" It was the man that had saved them when they were attacked. He was sure of it. He recognized the accent. Liam swung around toward the voice and tried to get a look at him, but the lights were too bright that surrounded him. Had they killed Tad? Then they shot him too. PLAM! PLAM! PLAM! the bullets stung his hide, he swaggered and fell to the ground. He was still slightly coherent as he felt them put shackles around his wrists. Right before he passed out, he could vaguely make out the man's voice again.

"Aren't they magnificent? What a prize these two are!" he shouted, "Now don't fool around, and don't underestimate that one." He pointed to Tad, "I want him just as he is." He leaned down and checked the beast's eyes. "They seem to be out. Take two more vials of blood then leave them here. We need to see to the new arrivals. But make sure they are sedated. I don't want them to wake before morning." The poachers did as he said, then all of the men loaded up into their trucks and headed for the campsite.

~~~~~~~~~~*~~~~~~~~~~

Territorial Bleeding

The guys were really fearful now. They had heard the howls of the unseen predator that came for them, and then they heard strange gunshots. They shook as they stood guard around the campfire. Luke was all but crying. He wouldn't have been so afraid if he hadn't had that feeling of dread for the whole trip. Everything was deathly quiet. Even the crickets had stopped chirping. Only the crackling of the fire could be heard over their terrified breathing.

The bushes to the front of the trail began to rustle. Luke could feel his ears prick up. Deep growls echoed against the trees and rocks that surrounded them all. A large looming shadow began to take form in front of them. The large black beast rose and stood about thirty feet from them. It had a wolf's appearance, but stood like a man. It grunted and sniffed the air. The guys were speechless. They trembled and began to sweat profusely. John raised his gun with shaking hands. He swallowed hard. They all hoped it would just turn and run the other way. Luke could feel his skin go cold. He knew it. He just knew this would end very badly. He just knew it. This had to be what had crept around with him the whole trip. At the same time, how could he have known? Werewolves? He would have never guessed *this* was what he had feared.

Cassidy snarled in his wolf-skin. He never felt so alive! He could smell everything! He could hear everything! He could feel his muscles rippling beneath his new skin. He could smell the gunpowder and the metal casings inside of the guns. The moonlight reflected off of his retinas and lit the way for him to see, like little flashlights in a black and white movie. He could smell their sweat. He liked their fear. It made him feel powerful. He reveled in it.

Then, from the bushes and trees beside them, they heard more growling. Luke was afraid to take his eyes off the one in front of them, but he had to look. "Oh, God." he whispered, "There are two of them." His sense of impending doom was doubled. He already felt defeated, as did his comrades. How would they beat two of these gigantic beasts?

The new beast turned to the first one and grunted. It stood and looked over the campsite, sniffing the air. Then it turned to the other beast and roared. The first beast roared back and began to move in closer. John cocked his rifle. The beast's ears pricked up and they looked at John's gun.

Cassidy was ready to rip them apart. He didn't care who they were, what they wanted, or if they were a threat. He intended to unleash his fury on them. Patti was torn; he didn't really want to hurt anyone. He raged inside as Cassidy did, but it wasn't in his human nature to destroy life. He wasn't as brutal as Cassidy, and he fought against himself to hurt these people. He would much rather hurt Cassidy.

Cassidy didn't wait any longer. He didn't care what Patti did or didn't do. He lunged forward and before the man could fire a shot, ripped the gun from John's arm ripping most of the man's flesh along with it. The other men yelled, and began firing at Cassidy. He ripped through them like they were made of paper mache'. Their bullets did nothing to him. He could feel the heat from the shots but the bullets only tore his flesh a little. The men's screams rattled Patti's eardrums. He reached up and put his clawed hands to his long ears and tried to shake the sound of them from his mind. He had to stop the stinging. He jumped forward and swung hard at one of the men, knocking him to the ground. Patti threw his head up and howled. The man, still on the ground took aim and shot Patti in the chest, BLAM! BLAM! Patti staggered back, for a brief moment dazed by the shots to his chest. Stunned but realizing he was unharmed, he leaned down over the man and knocked the gun out of his hands. Then picked him up over his head and threw him full force against a tree, breaking the poor man's back and killing him instantly. Patti hadn't realized his new strength. He hadn't meant to kill the man.

Cassidy was tearing through the other four men, swinging his claws and shredding their flesh. Pulling them apart one at a time. It didn't take him very long either. He ripped the throat out of the last one. Then he saw Luke. He approached the young man slowly. He was within inches of Luke's face. Luke looked into the face of his would-be assassin. He could see every detail against the light from the fire. The sound of his family and friends dying around him echoed in his head. He had dropped his gun earlier and knew it wouldn't help him anyway. The beast grinned at him as it looked down at his face. Luke noticed something shining around its neck. It was a silver pentagram. The beast threw its head back and let out another long howl. Luke took the opportunity to try and kill it. His hunting knife was still around his waist. He pulled it out and stabbed the beast in the side. Cassidy yelped loudly and staggered backwards. Luke, still holding on tight to his knife, held it high in the air. Where was the other one? He thought for a moment. He didn't want to take his eyes off the first one. Cassidy smiled through the flesh of his alter ego, sadistically, as Cassidy always did. The other men were dead now so Luke had both beasts' full attention. The other one walked over to stand next to its friend. Luke only shifted his attention for a split second, and then swiftly, Cassidy lashed out with his long clawed fingers and cut through Luke's flesh. Spilling his blood instantly. It happened so quickly Luke never even felt it. He dropped to his knees, stunned. He could feel his pulse in the wounds on his throat and chest. They were deep, mortally deep. He knew this was his end. The last thing he saw before slumping to the ground was the two beasts fighting each other against the campfire. Why?

Cassidy and Patti fought like huge dogs over the bodies of their first kill. Patti wanted to kill Cassidy over all of this. He hadn't wanted to hurt anybody and none of this would be happening if Cassidy hadn't started a fight at the pub last month in the first place. They growled and swung and bit. Over the roars of their own dogfight they hadn't heard the poachers sneaking up behind them. Suddenly shots were fired, PLAM! PLAM! PLAM! Then Cassidy staggered backwards and fell to the ground. Patti, still standing in front of the fire, stood still as a rock and snarled and looked from side to side, as the Gortex covered men approached him. He was confused. What had they shot Cassidy with? Who were they?

They got within six feet of him, then they shot him too, PLAM! PLAM! PLAM! Whatever it was they shot him with made him feel hazy almost immediately. He blacked out and fell to the ground a couple feet away from Cassidy. Cassidy wasn't all the way out. He couldn't move, but he could feel them putting cuffs on his wrists, and he could hear them all talking. His eyes were still open but he couldn't focus very well. He was very heavily drugged.

A man approached him. Cassidy could only make out a blur with glasses, but he clearly heard an accent. "Shoot this one again. He's still conscious." The man ordered the Gortex covered men to shoot him again. These were the same suited men Cassidy remembered from his attack. PLAM! It was only seconds before he passed out completely. The man with the accent reached down and checked Cassidy's eyes. "He's out this time." He stood and started to assess the damages the werewolves had done. He ordered the poachers to check all the bodies for signs of life.

"Sir!" one of the men yelled from a few feet away. "This one is badly wounded, but he's not quite dead yet. What should we do?"

The man walked over to where Luke was lying. He reached down with one hand and looked into Luke's pupils. Then he checked his pulse on the wrist. "He's unconscious. But not dead." He looked to the poacher, "I should like to save this one. Bring me my medical kit, and make sure there are no other survivors. Hurry! He doesn't have too much longer. He's lost a lot of blood." The poacher immediately followed orders, and went to retrieve the medical kit. The man turned back to Luke. "Yes," he smiled "This should be a very interesting experiment."

The poacher quickly returned with the medical bag and the man cleaned Luke's wounds and gave him an injection to slow his heart rate. Once he felt confident the boy would be fine he turned his attention to the werewolves. He approached Cassidy first. The Gortex soldiers had shackled both manimals and were standing guard over them both with their guns. "I want two vials of blood." The man bossed another order. "From both of the beasts. And make sure you implant tracking devices on both of them, and the boy." He pointed in Luke's direction. Two technicians immediately did as he said, and began drawing blood from the creatures. The man then approached the head poacher, he wore a Gortex suit like the others, but he also wore a red sash around the bicep of one arm, to indicate authority. It was impossible to recognize the poachers with their helmets on. He asked for further instruction from the man in charge.

"Sir," he started, "What should we do with the bodies?"

The man looked over the devastation of the scene, then he answered, "Leave them. Let them wake up to the horror of what they have done. We'll come back later and clean up."

"And the boy?"

"Leave him too. Let us see what impact this has on him. But place the werewolves in the tall thatch."

The head poacher saluted the man, and then retreated to the darkness of the forest. The others finished up and followed. The man and his accomplices returned in their trucks to the research center on the mountain. They would return later to remove any trace of the incident, but for now they would leave the scene almost as they had found it.

~~~~~~~~~~*~~~~~~~~~~

THE NEXT MORNING . . .

Wolves. There were five of them. Luke sat in silence and watched the animals watch him from the campsite. They were beautiful. It was peaceful. They seemed to be smiling at him. The warm sun was shining on Luke's skin and a calm breeze blew over him. He stood. When he did the animals leaped up and crouched in a playful gesture. He smiled at them. All at once they began to snarl and growl, then, without warning they bolted and ran full speed into the woods. Luke could feel himself try to speak but nothing came out, 'Wait", he mouthed the word silently, and reached out for them. When he did he noticed dried blood on his hand. He turned it over. He decided to wash it in the lake. When he turned about he was face to face with a dark haired man with dark eyes. He was naked except for the dried blood all over his body, and the silver pentagram around his neck. The man looked sinister and reached out and grabbed Luke's shoulder. "Welcome, Brother", the man smiled. Luke tried to scream, and break free of the man's grip, but he couldn't. Everything turned black except for the blood-soaked smiling madman holding him tight by the shoulders. He twisted and writhed, trying to get away, and then finally! He awoke with a jolt.

"AHHH!" he was yelling, and pulling on his own shirt. He slowed down and took a moment to re-orient himself with reality. It was a nightmare, he thought. It was all just a nightmare. The whole thing! He looked around himself. He was lying out in the open in the bushes. He must have let his paranoia get the better of him. It was all so real. He dusted himself off and started to stand up. Then he noticed there really was dried blood on his hands. His heart started to pound. He was afraid to look up. He raised his head slowly and surveyed the campsite. He felt weak. His knees buckled and gave out underneath him. Tears flowed uncontrollably from his eyes. There, in front of him, were his cousins, Sam, Tommy & Casey, and his childhood friends John and Chris, all torn to ribbons. Lying lifeless and disheveled in the morning sun. He sobbed and screamed from the pit of his soul, on his knees in the forest. "NOOOO!" he screamed, "NO, NO, NO, NO!" He shook his head and put his face in his hands. "This can't be real!" He was angry, he had never known such pain, he cried out, "Why did this happen?!"

He would remain there in this state for another two hours until he could gain enough composure to go look for help. He finally stopped shaking and stood up. He remembered having his throat cut open. He reached up but didn't feel anything that would indicate a wound. Obviously it hadn't been that bad, he couldn't worry about that right now anyway. He looked for his backpack, and he loaded and cocked one of the rifles. He remembered the cabin they had seen the day before. It wasn't too far maybe he could get some help. He said a prayer for his fallen comrades and turned to go toward the cabin. As he headed toward the lake he remembered how he had felt the day they chose this place to hunt, if he had only talked them into leaving sooner. He would never get over these events. They would haunt him forever. In his grief-stricken state, he never even noticed Pat and Cassidy lying blood covered and naked, a few feet away in the tall thatch.

~~~~~~~~~~~*~~~~~~~~~~~

Tad and Liam had woken much earlier that same morning. They staggered back to the cabin naked and disoriented. They had been drugged. Whoever those poachers were, they had prevented the guys from doing any damage. Tad showered and took something for the tremendous headache pounding in his head. Liam went immediately to his room, crawled into bed and passed out again. They would talk about what happened later.

It was just after lunch when someone pounded on the cabin door. Tad had been making notes in his journal about their latest encounter as werewolves, he scooted away from the table and went to the door. When he opened it he found a young man, barely able to stand, looking like he was in shock in front of him. Tad immediately felt a strong familiarity about the boy. He asked him, "Are you alright?"

Luke wanted to speak but he didn't know where to start. He was emotionally exhausted. He hung his head and started to cry and leaned on the doorframe for support. Tad didn't know what to make of this. He offered a hand out to the poor guy. Luke looked up at him, and all he could say was, "Help", he sobbed "Please".

Tad grabbed his other arm and placed it over his shoulder to help him inside. The poor fellow looked like he was going to pass out. His legs got weaker as they approached the couch. Tad helped him to sit down and then he went back to the front door and pulled the boys' pack inside and closed the door behind him, and then went and got the boy some water.

"Hey," he said to the boy, "Here." He handed him the water and sat down next to him. "What's happened? What's your name?"

Luke could barely find the strength to speak. "Luke." He sputtered, "My name's Luke Williams."

Tad's senses pulled at him harder. He knew what the young man was to become. He decided to go get Liam up to help. "You wait here. Drink that water. I'll be right back. You're O.K. here." He reassured the boy and went to Liam's room.

"Liam." He shoved his friend's shoulder to wake him, "Liam. Get up. We have a situation."

Liam started to wake up. He turned over and rubbed his eyes. "What's the problem?"

"Come look." Tad said as he left the room. Liam pulled himself together, threw on a robe and joined Tad in the living room. The boy cried and shook as he told them about what happened. He didn't care if they didn't believe him he just wanted some help, any kind of help, even if they sent him to the nut house. At least he would be safe. He would never feel safe again. As he told his story Tad and Liam exchanged serious glances. They both knew what had happened. They also knew they hadn't done it.

Tad offered the boy a place to stay. They had one more bedroom in the cabin that wasn't being used. He could stay with them for now. Tad went into the kitchen and got the boy an animal tranquilizer. That was all he had to help the young man sleep. He couldn't have been more than 23 or 24. He was definitely in shock. They helped get him settled and once they were certain he was knocked out, they decided they would check out the campsite.

While Tad and Liam were calming Luke and getting him taken care of, Patti and Cassidy were just waking up. Patti ached all over and scratched and stretched. Cassidy felt wide open. He stood, completely naked and yelled at the top of his lungs. He looked out across the bodies of the campers he had slaughtered the night before and yelled up to the heavens, "Aaagghhhh!!!"

"Shut up! Damn it, Cassidy! SHUT UP!" Patti yelled back at him. Cassidy turned to look at his partner in crime, the Sheriff Deputy.

"What?" he turned to talk to him, "Don't you feel more alive than ever before?"

"Quite frankly, NO." Patti answered him, disgusted. "I feel a lot closer to dead. Look what we've done, Cassidy." He pointed to the campsite, sick with himself. "We killed those people, you and me. Well mostly YOU!" he shouted and pointed at Cassidy in disgust with both of them. He stood up and reached for one of the backpacks lying on the ground. He opened it and searched for some pants or something to cover himself with. Cassidy just stood there naked, reveling in his new super power. Cold to what he had done.

"They shot at us didn't they?" Cassidy tried to make excuses. Patti ignored him. He found a pair of brown fatigues and put them on. Then he tossed a pair of jeans to Cassidy. "Put these on." He said with disdain. He was sick with both of them. He had done what he didn't really want to do. And he couldn't stomach Cassidy's lack of remorse. He looked out over the campsite and suddenly he felt sick. He put his hands on his knees and puked.

Cassidy put the pants on and looked over at Patti. "Get a hold of yourself, man." He said grinning at Patti's humanity.

Patti wiped his mouth and gave him a dirty look. "I'm sorry I'm not as loathsome as you. You really are a bastard, Cassidy, you know that?"

Cassidy just smiled. "What are we, Pat? Are we Gods?" He asked him casually.

Patti stood up and sneered at him. "I'm quite certain you're just a devil."

Cassidy flexed his arms and looked up to the sky and started shouting again, "WHAT ARE WE?!!!"

Just then a voice came from behind them. "I can tell you." The two startled men turned and saw Tad and Liam. They hadn't even heard the two men walking up. Tad approached them slowly.

Cassidy got cocky immediately. "Oh really? Who the fuck are you two?"

Patti just watched and tried to remember if he had seen the two men before. They seemed familiar. Tad got closer to the blood covered Cassidy. He could feel the kismet. He looked him directly in the eyes. "We're your new brothers."

Cassidy looked back at Patti, shocked and confused. He wanted to know what they knew. Could one of them be the one that turned them? Who were they really and what they were doing here? Tad stared them both in the eyes for a moment. Then he took a few steps forward and looked over the campsite. Liam stood back; he wasn't interested in getting too close. They all exchanged glances for a minute or two, then Tad decided to introduce himself. "I'm Tad Thayer, and this is Liam McConnell. We're research biologists. We've leased a cabin and this land to research timber wolves." He stood with his arms crossed and waited for one of them to say something. Patti decided to go next. This was all very strange.

"I'm Patti Leason, Deputy Sheriff in the nearby town. This is Cassidy Caine." He looked over at Cassidy trying to think of the best words then decided on the obvious. "He's the town criminal. I know all this looks bad, and I really can't explain it, but what did you mean by what you said a few minutes ago?"

"I meant I know you're werewolves." Tad answered him with a solemn knowledge that made his blood run cold. How could he know that? Tad read his mind and answered his next question before he asked it.

"I know because we are too. We have been living in these woods for several months, and we've witnessed plenty of strange things. One of them was being attacked ourselves."

"Were you the one who made us?" Patti couldn't believe he was really having this conversation with other grown men. It was so unreal, he felt like he was seven years old and playing a game.

Tad just solemnly shook his head. He stepped forward and got face to face with Cassidy. He had already felt the challenge that was about to present itself, and he was prepared to stand his ground. They were all going to need each other, and Tad knew it. So would that boy back in the cabin. They were his family now. Tad knew that Cassidy was probably responsible for that as well. He had him figured out instantly. Tad also knew that just as with all pack animals, it was imperative that an alpha is chosen immediately, and he was going to be sure it wouldn't be Cassidy.

Cassidy had already felt the challenge too. He was provoking it. Without saying a word between them, it was on. Tad looked Cassidy straight in the eyes, "You've got quite a mess to clean up."

Cassidy smiled. "Do I? Whatever do you mean?" he was forever the smart ass.

"I mean just what I said." Tad warned him, "You are going to clean up your mess, all of it. Right now. We'll help you."

It wasn't often that someone took Cassidy by surprise. It also wasn't often that Cassidy met someone who could best him. Tad knew what had to be done. He knew Cassidy would be trouble the minute he met him. It was time to defend his territory and his right to be the leader. If he didn't, their already volatile state could get even more out of control and they all could agree that Cassidy was far too vengeful to lead. So Tad began to roll up his sleeves.

Patti decided now would be a good time to get acquainted with Liam and stay the Hell away from the explosion that was about to happen. He walked over to him and shook his hand. "I really don't understand what's happening to me. I hope we can all find a way to help each other."

Liam shook his hand in return. "I don't have a problem with helping you both, but your friend should key down a little. Is he always this combative?"

"You have no idea." Patti sighed. "He's a complete bastard."

He and Liam were both willing to back down from the leader vantage point and let Tad have it. Cassidy could cause them too much trouble, and they couldn't afford any more. That's what Tad was making clear right now.

Cassidy made Tad familiar with his smile. He grinned in delight at the idea of a fistfight after a bloodbath. He was fueled with his new sensibilities, and more full of himself than usual. He put his fists up and glared at the arrogance of this whole idea. Who was this guy to play leader? You don't know me, he thought.

Once the fighting commenced it was like watching a bare knuckles version of The Ultimate Fighting Challenge. Both men were equally matched in size, strength and fighting ability. Patti was amazed by Tad. He had never seen anyone match Cassidy blow for blow and keep standing. They both had superhuman strength and endurance now, but Tad was just a bit tougher and just a bit more determined to win this match than Cassidy. Cassidy was used to fighting it out to the end, but for no apparent reason. Tad had a very good reason behind winning this match. He knew they would all need each other now, and they would need a leader with a level head. Tad wasn't about to subject any of their well being, including his own, on this asshole playing dictator. He had to make things clear from the get-go, and he had to do it in a way this bastard would understand.

They fought hard and furious and as soon as Tad saw his moment, he took it. Cassidy threw a quick right hook and Tad dodged it, then grabbed Cassidy's arm and quickly twisted it around behind him, then threw him with full force to the ground, wrapping his arm behind his back and pushing his knee into the back of Cassidy's neck hard. Pinning him to the ground and firmly holding him there. Cassidy kicked and squirmed and cursed at Tad, trying to break free of the tremendous chokehold he had on him. He couldn't pull loose. Tad held him there forcefully and let him cuss and wear himself out.

Patti was astonished, and in light of things, relieved. It was nice to have someone else deal with Cassidy in a way he understood. He respected the way Tad handled Cassidy like he was scolding a rowdy child. Very matter-of-fact, very shut-up and settle it. He decided to trust Tad from that moment on.

After Cassidy hostily gave yield, they all took care of cleaning up any other details they found to be pertinent. Like figuring out the best way to deal with the situation and what to tell Luke's family. Patti decided to file it as bear attack and called the coroner. They would simply pronounce Luke missing. After that was decided and handled, they decided to go share the details with Luke and preparedly introduce him to Cassidy and Patti, and explain what was going to happen to him.

~~~~~~~~~~~*~~~~~~~~~~~

Brother Wolf & Sister Moon

It had been three months since the events that drastically altered Luke's life forever. He remembered waking up in the cabin and having to come face to face with his would be killer, the same killer that had slain his cousins and friends and robbed him of his future. Cassidy did far more damage by leaving him alive. He had meant to kill him, but Luke had lived and this harsh new reality wasn't really living at all. He had to face the stark reality of his new situation. He was a werewolf. He was a living breathing fairy tale monster. He couldn't go home, but he did have this place. He would not forget Tad's kindness and guidance throughout this journey. It had been a fiery one.

The forest was beautiful this time of year. The weather was breezy and cool and the leaves on the trees were all shades of yellow and red and orange and purple. There were deer afoot at every turn and at night you could catch glimpses of big hoot owls swooping out of the trees to feast on rodents. The sound of crisp drying leaves crunching underfoot made Luke homesick for his family. He had always loved Halloween. No need for a costume this year, he thought if my friends could see me now. He had been spending his time at the cabin learning about the local wildlife from Tad and Liam, and helping them with their on-going research. He really respected them. He had had to learn to tolerate Cassidy. He feared him more than anything else, and Patti he could give or take. Tad repeatedly reminded him they were all brothers now and they would all have to re-learn reality. But to Luke nothing was more different than the moon and he would never see it the same way again. It was totally new to him now.

It was October now and the little town just outside the woods they all shared was gearing up for the annual festival activities. Every year the town played host to an event called The Full Moon Festival. It consisted of all varieties of medieval and post-Salem witch hunt types of activities. There were Maypoles and Unicorns and lectures on unnatural beasts, fortune-tellers, belly dancers, ghost hunters and mediums and fantasy events of all kinds. Backed with live entertainment like jugglers and acrobats and loaded with lots of unique souvenirs. It usually pulled in a lot of tourists and provided the town with funding as well as fun and adventure from all over the planet. It was basically a convention held outdoors during the week of the waxing moon in October. Befitting of Halloween and all fall weather type occasions. In light of this year's creature sightings, it should be a real buzz. Luke was particularly looking forward to it.

About once a month Tad and Liam and Luke took a trip into town over to the local Farmer's Market for supplies. It was on the other side of the mountain valley they called home. Luke always went along to help Tad and Liam load the supplies. That, and he liked to admire the shopkeeper's daughter, Chloe. She was a pretty freckle-faced Irish girl about seventeen years old. With fiery curly red hair and bright green smiling Irish eyes. He would always come up with some lame question to ask her, and she would always play along and smile at him and lead him through the store on some wild goose chase for products they didn't really care about at all. But today would be different because today he had finally decided to ask her out.

They arrived at the store and Luke immediately began looking around for her. He tried to be subtle but he was actually *very* obvious, at least to Tad and Liam. They just smiled and pretended not to notice. They went on about their shopping and let Luke have a little peace. It seemed to be the only thing to distract him from the nightmare his life had become, and the nightmares he had every night. Why not let him have it?

He finally spotted her tagging birdseed. As he approached she looked up and smiled. She thought he was so cute. "Hey." He kind of snickered. She made him feel all fluttery inside. He acted like a doofus around her. They talked for a little bit then Luke decided to ask her. "You . . . wouldn't want to go to the festival with me would you?"

She smiled so big and so hard he thought for a moment she might cry, "Yes!" she squealed out, then she quickly covered her mouth and looked around for her stepfather and uncle. They owned and ran the store and they were less than friendly, especially to her. She lowered her voice, "Yes. I would love to go with yu."

"Great." Luke smiled back at her, "Should I ask your dad for permission?"

Her smile faded quickly, "Step dad, and no. I'd better do tha askin'. Yu could come with me though."

They walked over to the counter and Chloe motioned to her Uncle Darby. He approached the counter with the usual glare in his eyes. He was a very sour and hateful man. He was tall and round and had Chloe's complexion and hair color. She lowered her eyes and began to stutter a little. Luke could feel the tension radiating between them. He could sense her fear very strongly, and the cold vibe from her Uncle made Luke instantly dislike him. Darby became very impatient. "What?!" he huffed loudly.

"Um, um Uncle Darby this is Luke," she kept her head down and fidgeted with her apron. Roughly twisting it back and forth in her hands. Darby gave a sour glance over at Luke and then back to her. She spit out a little more, "Yu know. He always comes in with Dr. Thayer and Mr. McConnell?"

"Spit it out, Chloe. I've got stock ta shelve and a truck ta unload." He grunted out very hatefully and unkind.

She stuttered worse, "Um, um," Her lip quivered like she was going to cry. She was behaving very submissively and frightened. Luke decided to rescue her. He stuck his hand out towards Mr. O'Bannon. "Hello. Um, Mr. O'Bannon." His handshake gesture was returned with an unyielding glare. Chloe looked over at Luke, delighted by this show of chivalry. She reached over and held onto his hand.

Luke put his hand down. "Mr. O'Bannon I'd like to take your niece to the festival this week. Would that be alright with you?"

"No. Git back to work, Chloe." He grunted without flinching and turned to go back to the stockroom. Chloe's smile had completely faded. Tad was watching from behind the hand tools display. He felt Luke's anger and disappointment. He decided he would try. He approached the counter.

"Darby?" he shouted getting Darby's attention. The man turned around and halfway smiled at Tad. He and Jared Duggan, Chloe's step dad, were always friendly and put-on towards the customers. Especially the one's like Tad and Liam whom spent a lot of money there. "Can I help yu there, Thadeas?" He chuckled a little in his Irish brogue. It made Chloe sick the way they sucked up to people.

"Well, you can help my brother out." He smiled back. Chloe thought Tad was charming.

"Pardin'?" Darby asked, raising his eyebrows. Tad threw his arm around Luke. "My younger brother, Luke. He would like to take your Chloe out. I promise to chaperone myself."

Darby looked very irritated with this turn of events. He didn't want Chloe having any fun, but even more he didn't want to lose Tad's business. He leered over at Luke whom was grinning like a cat, then to Chloe who looked like she was begging. "Well," he grunted, "I suppose that would be alright. But be home by ten o'clock!" he shouted.

"I'll drive her home myself." Tad added, "We'll come by here and pick her up at dusk on Friday, alright?"

"All right." Darby grumbled and shook Tad's outstretched hand. Then he turned and returned to the stockroom. Tad smiled over at Chloe and Luke and winked at them before returning to his shopping. Chloe smiled back and whispered 'Thank Yu'.

"Whew!" Luke smiled at her. Then he leaned in and kissed her cheek. "I'll see you Friday, O.K.?"

Chloe nodded at him as she blushed. She had never been this close to a guy she liked before. She liked the way he made her feel. She felt safe with him. She decided at that moment she would let him be her first.

~~~~~~~~~~*~~~~~~~~~~

Cassidy didn't do very much of anything anymore that wasn't devious in some way. He spent most of his free time stalking Becca. She had made it perfectly clear she no longer wanted his company. Well, it was perfectly clear to everyone except for Cassidy. The rest of the time he followed around with Patti, helping him break up fistfights or drag races or domestic disputes. Actually the way they handled the situations were more like, joining in on the fistfights, instigating drag races in the cruiser, and kicking the living shit out of abusive bastards, that Patti had decided were undeserving of the jail cell. Patti had become somewhat of an outlaw, an anti-hero of sorts. The changes in him had turned him into a vigilante, and he was re-writing the law as he went along. It had earned him a new level of respect from the local townsfolk. But then again, fear can be an effective control device. It had also made him ironically tolerant of Cassidy who encompassed many of the same non-values as the people they were fighting. Their reasoning was somewhat, to say the least, as altered as they were.

He and Cassidy were involved in one of these situations when Tad called Pat on his cell phone. They were in a brawl in the middle of town. A crowd had gathered and was cheering them on. Patti leaned up against a light pole to answer the phone, while Cassidy continued to fight the three shoplifters they were beating some justice into. Patti tried to catch his breath, "Uh-huh, Hello?"

"Pat?" Tad asked a little confused, "What are you doing? You sound winded."

"Me and the rogue male are just taking care of a couple of shoplifters resisting arrest." One of the criminals flew through the air and landed on the cruiser. The mob roared like it was the Friday night fights. Cassidy jumped on top of him and beat the snot out of him on the hood of the car. Patti lowered the phone, "Hey! Get his ass off my car!" Then his attention returned to Tad's call, "What's up?"

"When you get done there, why don't you come out to the cabin, we've got a little situation brewing out here with some bikers. I think they'll need a full intervention."

"You got it. See you in few." Patti shut his phone and tossed it to the sidewalk then ran full force into one of the thieves, knocking his ass to the ground before he could jump on Cassidy. Cassidy finished fighting the other two and waited for Patti in the car, leaving the men lying were they had landed. He lit a cigarette and watched the abrasions on his knuckles heal right before his eyes. It wasn't long before Patti jumped into the car and cranked it up. The new engine roared under the hood. Patti had made a few modifications to it after it had mysteriously re-appeared at the station. He leaned forward and rubbed at a scratch on the windshield, "Awe, shit!" he bitched. "You put a scratch on the glass!" Cassidy calmly flicked his cigarette out the window and looked over at Patti, "Fuck you." He smiled. The crowd cheered and applauded them as they took off, like they were Bo and Luke Duke.

Patti headed for the cabin. It didn't take long for them to arrive. The squad car could really burn the road up now. They turned down the long driveway, but they didn't have to go too very far before they saw the bikes. Evidentially the same bikers Cassidy had gotten into a brawl with the night they were attacked by the werewolf had returned and were making themselves comfortable by the lake near the cabin now.

Tad and Liam and Luke walked out and met them at the car. Cassidy crawled out of the window and started checking out the motorcycles like he was shopping. He read the name on the saddlebags. The Regulators. It was the same biker gang he fought with before at The Tavern. Patti got out and asked Tad and Liam what was going on.

"Well, the bikes were here when we got back from the Feed 'N Seed." Liam told him. "We crept up the hill and checked out the situation without them hearing us, and basically they're all setting up camp beside the lake. They've been raising Hell and taking potshots at the wildlife. Tad wants to kill them. He found blood and paw prints around the deck at the cabin. He thinks they've wounded one of the wolves."

Cassidy walked over and joined them. "Well since we're all home, let's go introduce ourselves." He began to grin wide and hard. It was like he never got enough chaos. He soaked up destruction and violence like a sponge. Tad was busy strapping the .44 to the new leg holster he bought earlier. He stood and put his hand on Cassidy's chest.

"I'll lead." He said firmly.

"What ever you say Ma'am." Cassidy grinned and backed off letting Tad pass by him. They all approached the bikers cautiously. They were stealthy and quiet and when they wanted to, they worked well as a team. Even Cassidy trusted Tad's lead and intuition. He didn't like it, but he trusted it. They decided to let the bikers know they were there. Cassidy recognized them. They were the same bikers all right. He spotted Roy. He stood and began walking towards them where they could see him coming. He stretched his arms out and smiled like he was greeting old friends. Tad and Patti approached beside him keeping their pistols in plain view. Liam and Luke stood back a little and waited for further signals from Tad.

"Well, well!" Roy smiled and stood up, "If it ain't Rocky Balboa. How you doin', smart ass?"

Cassidy grinned big like he was facing an archenemy he enjoyed the company of. "I'm doin' just fine, Roy. But it looks like you're nearin' the end of your good ole' boy days."

Cassidy continued to smile, as Roy got closer to him. There were probably ten or twelve bikers and only five of them. But not one of them was worried about the outcome of this situation.

"Really? Is 'sat so?" He slurred, "You threatenin' me, Muth'r Fuck'r?" The other bikers stood and were getting closer to the guys. Tad let Cassidy do what he did best for a few minutes. Antagonize. Cassidy leaned around Roy and waved at Cowboy.

"I see you and your girlfriend are still together." Cassidy giggled. "She's put on a little weight."

"Keep it up, Jackass. There ain't no Sheriff out here to spoil it this time, and I might just have to finish you."

"Ooooo!" Cassidy laughed and widened his eyes.

Patti walked over beside Cassidy and took the safety off his revolver and flipped it side to side in Roy's face. "That's where you'd be wrong, partner."

Roy lowered his shit-eating grin and took a step or two back as Pat put the gun in the back of his pants and pulled his badge out of the front pocket of his jeans. He let the light catch it and flashed it against the sun a couple of times where they all could see it. Then Tad spoke up. He was firm and clear.

"This is private property. I want you all off of it now! Or I will enforce my right to protect it."

Roy turned back to Cassidy, "Well ain't you just King Shit." He glanced over at Tad and the others. "Maybe we'll leave, maybe we won't. We just wanna do a little drinkin' and shoot at a few useless animals. But we could always shoot at you fuckr's instead."

"That would be a really big mistake, Roy." Cassidy snarled taking offense. "Either way you wouldn't breathe long enough to be sorry."

Roy threw his head back and laughed, followed in laughter by his comrades. They all had guns too, and they weren't the type of men to be easily intimidated. Patti and Tad and Cassidy laughed along with them for a minute and exchanged glances. They knew the joke was on Roy. Tad decided to get serious. He pulled his gun and fired it in the air twice, BLAM! BLAM! The laughter silenced. "Maybe you think I'm joking. I assure you I am not. I said get off this property right now!"

Patti clipped his badge to his shirt collar and pulled his gun back out and cocked it. He held it in the air and shouted, "You would be wise to do what he says, gentlemen. I don't want to catch any of you out here again, or at that festival this weekend. And if I find one injured or dead animal, I assure you, you will not like the price you'll have to pay!"

Roy thought about it a minute and his grin faded quickly into a scowl. He decided, for now, they would oblige. But they would be back and exact a little revenge later. They didn't like being ordered around. He motioned to the others to round up their gear and hit the road. He gave Cassidy and Tad a dirty look or two as he headed towards the bikes. The guys exchanged glances too; they knew what Roy had on his mind. They knew these guys wouldn't just drop it so easily, and they knew how to handle it. The full moon was only nine days away. Cassidy couldn't wait. He was going to miss Roy.

~~~~~~~~~~*~~~~~~~~~~~

At home Chloe got treated every bit as disrespectfully as she did at work by her Uncle and stepfather and all of their friends. Only it was worse at home because there were no customers around to impress. She was forced to wait on them and serve them dinner and clean up after them and their friends. She had to tolerate being constantly told she was worthless and miserable. Jared Duggan would man handle her and treat her roughly. He had always disliked her. He had married her mother when Chloe was ten years old, and when her mother died of cancer, God rest her, Jared was ten times the bastard he had ever been before. He only wanted the store. It was her mother's. She had worked hard her whole life for it, and she was who had made it what it was.

Jared had treated her shamefully as well, and her brother Darby was no better. Jared was his best friend. He had set them up, in turn setting himself up after her death as Jared's business partner. Chloe had been robbed of a childhood, of her mother, and of her inheritance. She wasn't sure how much longer she could endure it without snapping. She did vow to herself she would not be robbed of anything else.

They were having a get together with their friends tonight and Chloe was to prepare the food and serve it to them. Just as Darby had set his sister up with Jared, they had plans on passing Chloe off to one of their middle-aged redneck beer-chugging friends, and he would be present tonight to get a look at her. Chloe had not been informed of this yet, but it may be enough to cause her to crack. She blocked all of them out with dreams of Luke whisking her away from it all and rescuing her. She couldn't wait for Friday night. She couldn't wait for them to be alone. She wanted to kiss him and feel him close to her. She was in love with him he was her hero.

Jared entered the room while she was doing the dishes. He hollered at her two or three times, but she hadn't heard him, she was caught up in the happy place in her mind. He grabbed her roughly around the wrist and twisted. She came too and cried out. "Owe! Jared stop it that hurts!"

"Don't you tell me what to do, you little Bitch!" He let go of her and shoved her backwards, "I'll do with you what I please! Quit fucking with those damn dishes and get the food out here. Everybody's here and ready to eat."

"Fine. I'll be right out." She said clenching her teeth. She hated him and Darby.

"Well hurry up. There's somebody here I want you to meet." He snapped at her. He threw a beer can across the room into the garbage can, got another one out of the fridge, popped it open and returned to the dining room.

She held her wrist and cringed at the idea of another redneck she had to tolerate slapping her on the ass. She took the hot wings out of the oven and carried them on a tray to the dining room table. As soon as she got there she was introduced to her "future husband".

"Chloe!" Jared snapped, "Turn around here and meet Jim Rickford." She took a deep breath and turned around. Just like every other one of Jared's friends this guy was in his mid-forties, unshaven, dirty and vulgar. He made her feel nasty the way he looked at her. Dirty old men, she thought. He was wearing a red flannel button-up shirt and hiking boots with jeans. He looked like a dirty lumberjack. She wondered what made him so special that she got such an introduction. He was smacking his gum and staring at her. Jared grinned and grunted and hugged his shoulders. "What do think, Jim? She'd make a fine little wife, huh?" Both men grinned and snickered at their dirty thoughts.

Chloe thought she would be sick. Had he actually traded her to this pervert? She couldn't hold her tongue. "What?!" she shouted. Jared got hateful with her.

"That's right, red. This is your future husband. If he'll have you."

"Oh I'll have her." Jim grinned. It disgusted her. How much lower would they go? She almost fainted. She fell against the table and spilled a drink. Jared snagged her up by the arm hard. "Snap out of it, dumbass you're embarrassing me."

Jim grabbed him by the arm. "Hey now. Don't be talking to my little woman like that." Both men started laughing, and walked into the living room. "I think you'll make a fine pair." Jared yelled out. Chloe thought she was going to throw up. She needed air. She went onto the front porch and sat on the stairs and put her head down. Shortly afterwards Darby came outside. "What's the matter with yu? Yu're offending our guests. Git off your ars and finish the table."

"Uncle Darby, Jared's betrothin' me to that Jim guy, didn't you hear him?"

"Yes, yes. What of it? Yu think yu're too good fer a hard-working man like Jim Rickford? Yu should be Thankful."

"Thankful?!" Chloe shouted and stood up next to her low-life Uncle. "He's forty-five years old! I'm only seventeen! I haven't finished High Schul yet!"

"Well yu're not goin' ta. We're pulling yu out of schul in the spring for the wedding. What does a little dumb ars like yu need with a diploma? Now git yur ungrateful ars back in thar and play nice."

"But Uncle Darby, I like Luke. Yu know the boy from the store this afternuun?"

"Well don't yu go gittin attached to that boy. Yu're only gittin to go because I don't want ta lose his brother as a customer. And dun't be lettin' him put his hands or anything else on yu. We promised Jim a pure bride. So yu'd better come home with yur cherry intact! Now get yur ars in the house."

Chloe wasn't shocked by much of anything he said to her anymore. She hung her head like a beat dog. "How can yu treat me like this? Didn't yu evr love me or Mama at all?"

He looked for a moment like he might bear some kind of compassion, but it faded quickly and he immediately returned to normal. "Yu shut up about yur Mama! Now git in there an' cook!" He grabbed her by the arm and dragged her back into the house. She returned to the kitchen. At least she could be alone in there for a while. She felt like Cinderella. She was angry and sad and frightened all at once. She decided she had to run away. Maybe Luke would help her. She couldn't wait for Friday night. Only a couple days more. Her dreams would have to save her until then.

~~~~~~~~~~*~~~~~~~~~~

Who Do You Love?

TWO DAYS LATER & ONE TOWN OVER

It was around six o'clock in the evening when Jessica picked up her friend from the apartment they shared. She was excited about their little road trip and even more excited about the event they were going to attend. She couldn't wait to get going. "Hurry up, Hannah!" she yelled from behind the car. She was standing there with the trunk open flagging her hands. She checked her watch as Hannah, a pretty blonde haired girl wearing low-rise jeans and a black baby-tee ran towards her huffing two large duffle bags. Jessica stood back as Hannah heaved them both into the trunk on top of the other suitcase she had loaded earlier. Jess peered into the trunk and then back at her friend.

"Jeez, Hannah. It's only for a week ya know?"

"Yeah, I know," Hannah panted, winded from wrestling the duffle bags to the car, "But I want to look my very best in case there's any hot guys at this thing." She smiled slyly and nudged her best friend in the ribs a little.

Jessica slammed the trunk shut and giggled at her, "Yeah, that's just what you need. One more boyfriend." Jessica shook her head and got into the driver's seat. Hannah plopped into the other side and buckled up.

"I told you Hannah," Jessica said as she fastened her seatbelt, "This is an occult convention. It's just gonna be packed with nerds like me who love and study this type of thing. Oh, and freaks who think they are that kind of thing. It's really not your kind of thing at all. I just thought you'd enjoy a road trip." She put the car into gear and backed out of the parking

---

74

lot. Hannah just smiled at her and flipped through the CD's. She knew there was a man in her taste budget everywhere she went.

She smiled over at her best friend, "Even you might get lucky there, Velma." She laughed and pinched Jessica's cheek. She often teased her friend and called her Velma after the character on Scooby-Doo. Hannah thought they were just alike. Mainly because they were both into studying monsters and witchcraft and stuff but they didn't really look alike. Jessica had long dark brown hair and big pretty green eyes. She hoped to write her own book on the paranormal one day, and like Velma, she would love a little fieldwork.

"Just how long has it been since you had a boyfriend?" Hannah asked her. She couldn't remember the last time Jessica had her head out of a book long enough to notice the opposite sex. Ever since they started collage two years ago Jessica had been totally career driven. While Hannah, on the other hand, had found the time for several boyfriends and many parties. So she was determined to find her friend a boyfriend at this thing. Surely she could find someone to interest Jessica at one of these events. It was her element. In Hanna's opinion no one needed to be all business all the time.

"I'll bet you ten bucks this thing turns out to be a week of hot, randy sex for you." Hannah laughed.

"Thanks a lot." Jessica smiled, "But you know how I feel about that. I want someone to want me for my mind."

Hannah couldn't help herself from laughing out loud. "Are you kidding me?!" she giggled, "You have got to lighten up!"

They continued to laugh all the way to the event. It was only about one hour from where they lived, nestled in the valley town at the foothills of The Big Belt Mountains. The ride out there was relaxing and peaceful. The weather was great. Jessica loved this kind of weather. She loved this time of year. She liked to inhale the air deeply. You could almost smell Halloween in the leaves that fell to the ground. Her excitement grew as they approached the city limits. She just couldn't wait to jump right in.

~~~~~~~~~~*~~~~~~~~~~

Tad and Luke had picked up Chloe at the Feed 'N Seed Store right on time and took off for the festival. It should be interesting, Tad thought. Maybe he could pick up a book or two on Lycanthropy. See what the old-world had to say about his infliction. Liam had decided to meet them there a little later. He was going to ride with Cassidy and Patti. He hoped they wouldn't get Liam into any trouble. Don't misunderstand, Liam could hold his own in a fight. He did, after all, have the same instincts and super powers the others did. But it wasn't his forte' and he didn't like confrontation.

Once there, Luke and Chloe took off. They promised Tad they'd meet him back at the entrance by nine-thirty. Tad sauntered over to the drink counter and bought a cup of wine. Liam and the others shortly joined him and Liam seemed unscathed. The ride over must have been uneventful. He stood near the entrance with them watching the goings on. There were quite a few freaky-deakies attending opening night. This was the first time Tad had ever been to anything like this. It was definitely entertaining. It was also the first time all of them had been out in any kind of social situation together. They were truly acting like brothers tonight. As the months had passed they had had to be a close-knit group. They were all they had.

Hannah and Jessica quickly checked in to the hotel and headed out for the festival. It was supposed to begin at dusk and last through the full moon the following Friday. Seven days total. Jessica had been looking forward to it for weeks. It was the first time she had attended one of these Full Moon Festivals, though she had wanted to go ever since she heard about them for the first time two years ago. She had gotten the passes to it from one of her professors at school. He and his wife always went every year but couldn't go this year due to another engagement. He was more than happy to give them to Jessica his A+ student.

Once they got inside it was hard to decide where to go first. It was all outdoors with tents and stages and bonfires. It was quite a collection of types. People dressed in robes standing in circles chanting, gypsies telling fortunes, vampires eyeing them from dark shadows. Hannah seemed to find the whole thing very amusing.

"Can you believe these people?" she smirked, "I mean, where do they go when the lights go on?"

"Keep your voice down Hannah, please. Don't offend any of them." Jessica said under her breath. "I told you what to expect before we got here, and most of these people are more than just in character. They're in that character's head. I mean they really believe that they are supernatural. So keep it down."

"O.K. alright," Hannah giggled, "Like we're actually going to meet a real werewolf or something. I'll chill, but you better have fun too or I'll have to feed you to those ghouls over there." Hannah pointed to a group of green-faced monster-like creatures in a tent to their left. Jessica covered her face and giggled hard, clutching Hannah's arm. She had to admit that much of it was over the top. But it was also a whole lot of fun. She promised Hannah she would enjoy herself the whole trip.

"I'm gonna go get refreshments. Do creeps drink alcohol?" Hannah asked.

"Yeah. I'm sure you can find some wine or something," she paused for a second surveying the lay of the land then pointed to a beverage booth, "There." She pointed straight ahead. "I'll wait for you here. I want to look over this program. Just bring me one of whatever you get, O.K.?"

"Got it." Hannah smiled, "Be right back."

Jessica flipped through her program. She stopped at the calendar of events, pulled a pen out of her pocket and started marking the ones she wanted to attend. She was totally unaware of the fact that she was being watched.

Jessica had caught Tad's attention from the moment she walked through the gateway. She was beautiful, he thought. He was so captivated by her he hadn't noticed Liam was talking to him. "Tad!" Liam shouted and snapped his fingers in front of his face. Tad shook out of it.

"What?" he asked. He looked dazed.

"Me and the guys are going to wander around and check this thing out for a minute. You want to come with?"

"Nah, I think I'll go talk to this girl." Tad smiled. Liam looked at the girl she was striking. Cassidy had noticed her too. He began to grin wide at Tad. "Good luck." He sneered.

"Just go on," Tad smiled back, "I'll catch up to you turds in an hour or two. Do me a favor and check up on Luke too. But don't embarrass him, Cassidy."

Cassidy just grinned at him as he lit up a cigarette and turned to follow the others. He didn't make any promises because he never made a promise he couldn't keep. Tad returned his attention to the dark haired beauty. He approached her and tapped her on the shoulder.

Jessica almost jumped out of her skin. She whipped around half expecting to see one of those vampire men behind her. But what she found instead was one of the most handsome men she had ever seen.

He was blonde headed and very tall and well built. His eyes were green like hers and they sparkled against the dim light in a very strange way. It was as if they cast light from the inside out. She dismissed it though, deciding they were light reflecting contacts or something. God she hoped he wasn't some nut-job.

"Oh my God you startled me." She smiled relieved at what she had found when she turned around. He was so good-looking. She could feel herself blush. This was quite possibly the best looking man she had ever seen in her entire life. And seemingly normal considering where they were.

"I'm sorry." He smiled and almost purred. "I'm Tad." He reached out to shake her hand. She couldn't quit smiling at him.

"I'm Jessica." She answered. He thought she was just beautiful. Her smile melted him and she seemed very kind. He was glad he decided to talk to her. He hadn't thought about the opposite sex in a very good while. Ever since the attack he had been pre-occupied with his new physiology. Although, his carnal needs were stronger than they used to be, he just hadn't wanted to deal with that infliction on top of everything else. But now that he was feeling more acquainted with his new skin, he decided it was time to move on with his life and the rest of his primal urges. True to his nature, however, he would move cautiously and start with a girlfriend he could trust.

Meanwhile, Hannah was hitting it off with the cute bartender at the beverage counter. His name was Carlo. He was Latin, with dark curly hair and this great gypsy type of accent that made Hannah all giggly around him. They had been flirting and teasing each other for about twenty minutes. Hannah had forgotten all about Jessica's drink when suddenly it occurred to her. She glanced over at the entryway, and she immediately noticed Jessica was pre-occupied herself. Great! Hannah thought to herself. That's just what she needed. She only hoped he was as good as he looked! She decided to stay where she was and flirt with Carlo some more. Jess knew where she was if she needed her. She would leave her alone with her new friend for now.

Meanwhile, the guys were making their rounds. They were spying on Luke and Chloe when Cassidy spotted Becca at the old books counter. He stood back and just watched her for a moment. Cassidy was a predator in every sense of the word. He liked the taste of blood. He had killer instincts. He loved the killing and hunting and chasing. He was wild and untamed. And he knew how to lie just the right way to seduce any woman he wanted. But he didn't want just any woman, only Becca. Like an animal he wanted to be petted, and he wanted it to be from her. For Becca, it was over, and had been for a long time. For Cassidy it would never be over. She belonged to him. That's just the way he felt about it. True to his predatory nature, he was territorial, and his scent was all over her. He would never see it any other way, and he would protect what was his at all costs. Loyalty may have been the only positive trait he gained from his lupine half-brothers.

He let Liam and Pat go on and torment Luke. He stood still and watched Becca from a few yards away. He stood in the shadows so she wouldn't know he was there. She looked beautiful. She was dressed as a belly dancer minding the booth her boss had rented for the festival. He wanted her to sell some of their occult books and to promote the shop a little. Every time a man glanced in her direction Cassidy flared up. He would just have to kill the next mother fucker that touched her. He decided he would make his presence known and deter anybody else from trying. He didn't care if she liked it or not.

She was facing the back of the booth when he approached it. She turned around and saw him standing right behind her. He had let himself in and he had startled her. "Damn it, Cassidy!" she shouted. He had caused her to drop the books she was holding. She bent down to pick them up. He crouched down to help her. He hadn't said anything to her yet. She didn't like it when he did that. She didn't know what it meant for her. She looked him in the eyes. "What do you want?" she whispered.

"I want you." He said it without that creepy grin. He said it quietly. He said it like he meant it. It didn't make any difference to her though. They were over. She couldn't trust him anymore, no matter how charming he could be. She kept her eyes locked onto his as they stood up. He took the books and set them down. He held her face in his hands and leaned in and kissed her gently on the lips. She didn't move. She closed her eyes. She tingled all over. It felt the way it used to but only for a moment. What was he trying to do to her? Her heart was not a toy. She pulled away from him quickly.

"Get out." She said firmly and held the curtain back for him to leave. She didn't know what had happened to him. But there was something not right. She could feel it. It was a spooky, eerie feeling, and what was with his eyes? They seemed so different and strange. It all went back to that night those strange policemen brought him home in the middle of the night. He had gradually become weirder and weirder. At any rate, she didn't want to be a part of it. No matter how much she missed the old him. The man she fell in love with was gone. That's the way she coped with the loss of this relationship. She simply told herself that the Cassidy she had loved so much was dead, and this other person wearing his skin wasn't really him. Just some fragment of the man she had known and loved and wanted to save.

He made himself comfortable against the counter. "I want to talk to you. I *need* to talk to you. I have to tell you something." He said. He knew what to say and how to say it, to get what he wanted. "If you won't talk to me now, I'll just come to the store tomorrow."

"Fine then." She snapped, "Just get out of here. I don't have time for these games of yours Cassidy." It hurt her and made her angry with him whenever he would do this to her. She wanted him to just let her go, but she knew he wouldn't.

He decided he would leave her alone for now. He walked out of the booth and wandered back into the shadows. He could smell her on his shirt. He held it up to his face and inhaled it deeply. Slowly that sadistic smile crept back across his face. He would get to her tomorrow. He knew that. It was time to tell her.

~~~~~~~~~~~*~~~~~~~~~~~

Tad and Jessica were hitting it off great. They had walked around and talked for a couple of hours now. Jessica hadn't looked at one thing she had set out to yet, she was instead captivated by this great guy she had picked up. He had told her about the cabin and his research on timber wolves. She had told him about Hannah and collage and the book on the paranormal she hoped to write.

"I guess I just need to do a little more field work first. Like you." She smiled.

If only you knew, he thought. But he held his tongue, and smiled back at her. He suddenly sensed Cassidy. Within about a minute or two he saw him approaching. He leaned in and told Jessica to wait there. He really liked this girl. They had a lot in common. He wasn't really ready to have Cassidy that close to her yet. He walked over and met him halfway. While he talked to Cassidy, Hannah snuck up behind Jessica.

"Surprise!!" she yelled. Jessica screeched and spun around. Her scream caused Tad and Cassidy to turn and look at her. She waved at Tad. "I'm fine." She yelled then she turned to look at Hannah. She was still laughing at her.

"That's embarrassing! Why did you do that?" Jessica laughed and smacked her friend playfully.

"So?" Hannah smiled, waiting for details, "What do you think?"

Jessica just sighed and smiled big. "Oh, Hannah! He's terrific. I didn't look at the first thing here tonight I was so wrapped up in conversation."

"Well?" Hannah was still waiting for any juicy details. She put her hands out in front of her like she was groping for information. "How old is he? What's his name? Who's his hunky friend?" She gestured toward Cassidy.

Jessica smiled big and sighed, "Twenty-nine. *Dr.*," Jessica paused on the word for a moment for added emphasis, "Thadeas Thayer, Tad for short. And, I have no idea who his friend is, I haven't been introduced."

"Twenty-nine, huh?" Hannah grinned at her slyly. Teasing her a little. "An older man. How nice for you. "She grabbed her friend's wrists, "And he's *gorgeous*!"

Jessica blushed and laughed with her best buddy, "I know!!"

They were shortly rejoined by Tad. Jessica introduced Hannah who immediately wanted to know about Cassidy. "Where did your friend go?"

"He went to get our other friends. I guess we're leaving for tonight." He held Jessica's hands in his, "Maybe we'll see each other tomorrow? I'd love to join you for that lecture on werewolves." He smiled big. His good looks hiding the secret he held beneath his flesh.

Her disappointment quickly altered to titillation. "You're on." She smiled. "Walk us out?"

"Of course. I wouldn't dream of letting you ladies go to your car alone. Not at this hour anyway, and certainly not in this crowd." He smiled again.

They headed for the gateway. There was only one way in and out of the festival and it was through that gateway. When they got there they got to stop and meet Tad's friends whom were already waiting for them there. Tad introduced everyone. He explained the reason they had to leave so early was to get Chloe home. She explained how she didn't want the night to end. Then they met Cassidy. He gave Jessica the creeps immediately.

There was just something malevolent about him. Jessica had always had a keen sense about people and she didn't like the darkness that emanated around him. She didn't want to look him in the eyes. Of course no amount of darkness could deter Hannah. She practically bit him she was so giddy. Jess decided she would talk to her about it in the car.

So they said their goodnights and as soon as she cranked the car Jessica immediately went into her strange feelings about Cassidy. "Hannah, did you get a weird feeling from that Cassidy?"

"The dark haired guy? Not yet, but I'd like to." Hannah smiled. "God! He was gorgeous! He really lit me up!"

"I agree he's gorgeous, but that's not what I meant." Jessica decided to say it more directly this time. "I mean there's something wicked and dark about him. Didn't he creep you out?"

"I don't know *what* you're talking about." Hannah always trusted Jessica's judgment. She was rarely wrong about people. "But don't worry. I'm not going after him. I really had a great time with Carlo. He's what I'm after. So don't worry O.K.?" She smiled reassuringly at Jess.

Jessica nodded and hugged her. She got through to her Thank goodness!

~~~~~~~~~~~*~~~~~~~~~~~

Chloe didn't want to go home. She had a taste of love and freedom and she wanted more. She and Luke had found an out of the way place beside a tree to kiss and hold each other. She was so smitten. They held hands and watched the bands play and made out in the back seats at a lecture. She definitely was hungry for more and she wanted it all right now. She had explained a little bit about how she was mistreated to Luke, but she hadn't gone into full detail because she didn't want to scare him off. He was really wonderful. She was so disappointed when Patti and Liam had found them and told them it was time to go, she thought she would cry. But she didn't, instead she held onto the hope that this was just the beginning.

They got her home and Tad and Luke both walked her to the front door. Of coarse, Darby was very friendly to Tad. He agreed to let Luke take her to the movies one day later in the week, although he didn't really like the idea at all. He wouldn't say 'No' to Tad, however. Luke hoped they could get past that. He liked Chloe a lot. She led him away from his nightmares.

Back in the Mustang, Liam, Patti and Cassidy were heading for the River Bridge. It crossed the river that divided the mountain from the valley. It wasn't a particularly long bridge, but it was tall, and vagrants and bums and hitchhikers frequently gathered underneath its arches near the water. Tonight the guys decided to check out a hunch Patti had had earlier that day.

They cut the lights off and coasted to a stop. They didn't want the sound of the engine to give away their arrival. They all hopped out and trekked down the little trail toward the water. Then they saw what they had hoped to see. Ten or twelve motorcycles lined up by the base of the bridge structure. Patti's hunch was right. The Regulators were camping out here to wait for the right moment to sneak back out to the cabin.

Now the surprise would be on them. When the moon reached its peak fullness, they would be back, all five of them to finish this. There would be no mercy. Not even from Tad. He had found the injured wolf, it was near death and its entire left hip had been shattered by a gunshot. Tad took it to a veterinarian whom had to do surgery on it. It would take weeks to heal and rehabilitate it for re-release into the wild, if it could be. Luckily it hadn't bled to death before Tad had found it. He was ready to even the score on the wolves' behalf. The Regulators would pay in blood.

~~~~~~~~~~~*~~~~~~~~~~~

The Real Me

The next day Cassidy arrived at the bookstore, just like he had promised he would. He waited till around four in the afternoon to give it time to slow down before closing. He pulled up out front and shut off the car. Becca heard him pull up. The sound of his car was unmistakable. She looked out the front window just to be sure. 'Black Diamond' was printed on the front license plate of the sleek black car. She immediately got very nervous. Her curiosity was peaked though. When he walked through the door she got the butterflies in her stomach feeling. Not from excitement, from stress. She thought her heart would pound right through her chest. It was an anxiety attack.

He walked in and took off his glasses. His eyes still seemed strange to her. He looked good though. Maybe being around Pat had rubbed off on his character a little. She hoped he hadn't rubbed off on Pat. "So what is it?" She asked him right off the bat. He looked around the room. They were alone. He was about to speak when the door flew open and three teenage boys walked in.

Becca recognized them and greeted them with a big smile. "Hi boys. Here to do a little homework?"

They waved and smiled back at her. "You know it, Becca."

"Well let me know if you need anything, O.K.?" she told them. Cassidy laughed a little and watched them pick a table in the back of the room, where they could talk shit but still have a clear view of Becca. He knew their game. They weren't there to study, just to get horny over his girl. He turned around to her and pointed at them. "What's this shit?" he laughed.

"Oh, they're just some boys from the High School. They come over here a couple of times a week after school to do their homework and study. That's all."

"They come here because you give 'em wood." Cassidy said it loud enough for them to over hear.

"Cassidy! They'll hear you. Besides that isn't true. They're good boys." She defended them. But Cassidy didn't have time for this bullshit. He wanted to lock the store up and be alone with his girl for a minute. He strolled over to their table. There were a couple of tables in the store for people to sit at and read. They always chose the one in back. Cassidy pulled up another chair and sat in it backwards. The boys started to get a little tense.

"Don't you boys have the internet at one of your houses?"

They were a little afraid of Cassidy. He didn't look like he was too friendly, and they knew he knew why they were in there. One of them spoke up. "Uh, yeah. Mike does." He pointed to the boy across from him.

"Cassidy!" Becca yelled at him from the counter, "Leave them alone. It's O.K. boys, he won't hurt you."

He let her finish then he turned back to them smiling and said, "Yeah I will. Go home and look at women on your computers. Don't let me catch you in here looking at mine again. Got me?"

"Got it." The boy said and they quickly got their books and hauled ass out the front door. Becca was apologizing to them on the way out. "I'm so sorry, boys. He doesn't mean it. Don't let him scare you."

But they hit the door quick. She turned to Cassidy with hostility in her face. "Why did you do that? They are just boys."

He ignored her and locked the front door. Then he got her by the hand and pulled her around the counter. He wouldn't let go of her hand. "I need to talk to you."

"About what?" she huffed. She was loosing her patience. But before he could answer the power went out. "Oh great!" she snapped and went back to the front counter and pulled a flashlight out from under it. There was still enough daylight coming through the front windows to light the front half of the room. "We blew another fuse."

"Where's the box?" Cassidy asked her.

"It's in the stock room." She answered. She was already headed in that direction. It was in the very back of the room. She pulled the keys from a long chain around her neck and started to unlock the stock room door. Cassidy had decided to come with her. She unlocked it and before she entered the room she turned around. When she turned he was right in her face. She jumped. "You know," she started, "You don't have to come with me. This happens all the time. I can handle it."

"I wouldn't dream of letting you go in there alone." He smiled and took the flashlight from her. He was definitely up to something, she just wasn't sure what. That was what bothered her the most. He was acting very strangely and it was creeping her out. They walked in and Becca was able to open the fuse box and replace the fuse in under a minute. She had started keeping the new fuses on the shelf next to the box. It was an old building and things were buzzing out on it all the time lately. As soon as the power came back on, she pulled the light cord to the light that was dangling above them. The room was packed full with books. Shelves on all four sides lined the walls, and books, new and old, filled them to the very top. There were so many, some of them were lying on the floor.

Cassidy turned around and started to look at the ones behind him. They were dusty. He wiped the dust off the spines of a few. Most of them were on werewolves and witchcraft. Perfect, he thought. He sat the flashlight on a nearby shelf then turned back around and leaned up against the shelves with his arms crossed in front of him. Becca stood a few feet away from him. They stared at each other for a minute or two without saying a word. Then she asked him. "What is it, Cassidy? Why did you come here today and what did you want last night? I can't do this anymore."

He reached out and pulled her up close to him. He could feel her heart pounding. He could sense her fear. He smelled her hair and breathed it in deeply. He wrapped one arm around her waist and put the other to her face. He stared into her eyes without saying anything. Then he kissed her, passionately, gently, and softly. She returned this kiss. She wanted to cry. It was like having someone you thought was dead come back and be exactly the way you remembered them. The way they were in your dreams. She kissed him back, he held her close to him and wrapped his arms tighter around her. He shut his eyes and tilted his head back against the dusty books that explained him. She couldn't stop kissing him. God! How she had missed him! The old him. Her fear had turned to passion as she kissed his face and neck. He smiled and growled in his throat a little as she gnawed on his neck and whispered, "I've missed you," softly into his ear.

Suddenly, she stopped. The pendant she had given him when they met was hot. She pulled away a little. She looked at the pendant and chain, and she touched it. She pulled it away from his neck and she could make out what looked like burn marks beneath where it lay on him. "Cassidy?" she asked him, a little concern in her voice. "What's wrong with your neck?" He loosened his arms from around her. It had felt good to have her so close. He lowered his head and touched the pendant.

She was getting a little fearful again. She backed away from him slowly. "Cassidy? You feel so hot, are you all right? What are those marks on your skin?"

He lifted his head to look at her, when he did, the light reflected off his eyes. She scooted back some more. Fear was clearly on her face and in her voice again. "What's wrong with you? Your eyes?" Her voice was quivering and tears were streaking her face. It was as if she had awoken from that dream. He was dead to her all over again. She braced herself for what he might say.

But he didn't say anything. He reached backwards, behind his head and pulled a book off the shelf without turning around. He blew the dust off of it and handed it to her. She reluctantly reached out and took it. She took a minute before looking down at it. Then, with her tears falling onto its cover, she read it out loud. "Of Wolf and Man." She let the book fall from her hand to the floor. She put her other hand over her mouth. She stood in stunned silence crying and shaking her head at him. "It can't be true. This is myth. Fairy tale! Tell me you're lying to me!" she was screaming now. "This isn't funny, Cassidy! Say something!!" she demanded.

"It happened two nights before the those strange policemen brought me home. I wasn't drunk. I was sedated. I can't explain it all."

"Well why not?!!" she cried harder, grief stricken and upset at what she was hearing. He must be crazy, she thought.

"Because I don't know it all yet!" He growled, angry at his own lack of knowledge. His eyes flashed brighter. It was becoming clearer that the symptoms of this affliction could be brought on by moments of heightened emotion. Anger, pain, arousal, fear, excitement, all of these things invoked the curse, and brought it on sooner. Cassidy had already begun to figure this out. He could already change at will. But he still wasn't sure what myths pertaining to it held true. He knew silver would damage them, and probably kill them if they got enough of it, just like in the storybooks. That's why his skin burned under his medallion. The nearer the full moon, the more it burned. It was his arousal tonight that had set it off and made his eyes lighten, and his anger was raising the fever that accompanied it.

"Why does your necklace burn you?" she sniffled. She needed reasons. Rational reasons.

"It's silver. It burns me because I'm allergic to it." He answered her as calmly as he could.

"Well, since when?!" she was raising her voice again. She was almost hysterical. He just stood and stared at her. He wanted her to understand. But he was getting angry. Then came the inevitable. She took a long breath then asked him, "Have you killed anybody?"

He took a long moment to find the right words. He wanted to answer her in way that would end all other questions. He answered her with a very serious face and he looked her deep in the eyes, "More than once."

Becca didn't know what to say or what to do. This couldn't really be happening. Could she believe him? She knew she couldn't trust him. She would never trust him again. She pointed to the door. "Go. I want no more to do with you!" She lowered her head. "Go, I said!" she yelled at him. "You are cursed! Unholy! How dare you want to make me a part of that! You call that Love? I want no part of your curse! Get out!"

He tried to stay calm. Not let his anger take over. He knew she was afraid, but her words hurt him. "It's not a curse, Becca. It's an affliction, a disease. Like rabies."

"Well this . . . *sickness* is poisoning your mind! I knew there was something terribly wrong with you. But this . . . you've gone mad, Cassidy! And you've broken my heart. Now you are Damned! A killer! Dead to me!"

He became angry at her rejection of him. She should take him as he was! This was an accident! Didn't she understand? He hadn't asked for this! How dare she turn away from him! No one would love her as he did. No one. He would see to that! He intended on killing anyone who tried to be with her. She would have to take him, or die alone. He was so angry and hurt he couldn't speak. He stepped forward and slapped her hard across the face. She fell to the floor holding her cheek. She wisely decided to stay down. He stood over her for a few seconds clenching his fists. Filled with pain and rage. Then he turned and left her crying in the floor. She waited for the sound of his car to start before she got up. Then she ran into the front room and locked the door.

She stood with her back to the door, shaking and crying. Trying to rationalize what she had just learned. She picked up the phone and shakily dialed her brother's number.

~~~~~~~~~~~*~~~~~~~~~~~

On the mountain, in the research facility, the man M was overlooking some photos. He was the same man that had sutured Tad and Liam's wounds after the attack and helped them recover. Though the boys had not learned it, his name was M. No one was sure if that was the initial of his first name, or his last name or middle initial. Or if it was just some form of code but that's what he insisted on being called, that and only that. So they only called him M. And he was the head over all of the metaphysical research being done by the facility. M must have stood for Mastermind, because the research he was conducting was unlike any other. He was joined in his office by another man, a professor of mythology. He threw down a few journals on the table then he took a seat across from M.

"These are my findings so far. But I really need to get a closer look at them. Sedated . . . of course."

"Of course." M responded. Both men were very serious. "I would like your findings on their living habits. Their ability to reproduce blood-born offspring and track the way they kill. What can you get for me?"

The Professor raised his eyebrows and leaned back in his seat. "That's a very tall order. But I'll see what I can do." He leaned forward again and asked, "Can we study their blood a little closer?"

M just nodded. "Join me in the lab. I think you will be amazed at what we have discovered."

~~~~~~~~~~~*~~~~~~~~~~~

The next day, Jess and Hannah got to the festival early. It was only around one in the afternoon. Early for this type of thing, but some of the daytime events included lectures that really peaked Jessica's interest. It was, in fact, what she had originally come here for. Tad had agreed to meet her at two o'clock for the lecture and discussion on werewolves. A professor of mythology that Jessica held in very high regard was leading it, and she was thrilled at the opportunity to meet him in person. Not to mention thrilled to be around Tad again! Hannah was still getting quite a kick out of the whole thing, but she was learning to appreciate the event alot too. After all, she had met Carlo the first night they were there, and he was going to take her on a picnic by the town's garden pond today. She couldn't be happier. She was feeling so light-hearted and silly that she pinched a gnome right on the ass as they passed by him.

"Hannah!" Jessica giggled, "You might piss him off."

But she hadn't pissed him off at all. He ran up behind her and pinched her back. She yelped out, "Whoa!" They both turned around to find him standing there grinning at them. He smiled and said, "Hey baby, once you go gnome, you never go home!" He put his arms out and winked at them. Jessica started to giggle. Hannah politely sent him on his way, "Thanks, but I've already got a pet."

"It's all good, baby. But if you change your mind, you know where to find me!" he smiled and skipped away.

Hannah turned to Jessica, who was still laughing at the whole thing, and smiled, "Well there's a lesson learned. Remind me not to do that again."

"I told you." Jessica grinned.

Hannah walked Jessica to the lecture tent then ran off to meet up with Carlo. Jessica went on inside and found a seat a couple of rows from the front. She was early so she started to read the pamphlets offered on the Professor at the entrance. She was deep in thought reading about his many books on the subject of mythical beasts, and so she didn't notice Tad until he was right in front her. She put the leaflet down and stood to greet him. He leaned in and kissed her on the cheek. Wow! He smelled good!

"Have you been here long?" he asked her.

"No, not at all. I just got here too." She smiled. They sat down and she showed him a picture of Professor Saunders on the back of the pamphlet, and she gave him a brief run-down of the subject matter the Professor was an expert of. She explained how she had been fascinated with the subject of super powerful beasts and shape-shifting her whole life. Now she was in collage learning to do what Professor Saunders travels the world to do. She was sort of an unofficial expert, Tad thought. He guessed he picked the right girl.

"So." She began, "Do you know anything about werewolves?"

He couldn't believe what she just asked him. He smiled and took a minute to answer. "Not as much as I hope to learn today."

"You know," she kind of blushed, "I'm really glad I met you. I know this sounds corny, but . . . I really feel a great chemistry between us, you seem so familiar to me. And I'm not just saying that. I get a good vibe from you, ya know?"

"I don't think it sounds corny at all. I like you too." He smiled and leaned over and kissed her. His charm and wicked good looks melted her. She had forgotten how nice it was to have a man kiss her and pay attention to her. She got all fluttery inside and she felt so light she could have floated away. Had it really been that long, she thought? He had her now. Boy, did he have her now! She was hooked.

Before anything further could happen, Professor Saunders walked in. He didn't really notice them at first. He went straight to his lecture board to prepare. He sat his books down on the table and immediately started to draw and write on the freestanding chalkboard they had provided for him. Tad and Jessica just sat and watched him quietly. They didn't want to disrupt this ritual. Finally he turned around and noticed them. "Oh!" he shouted, clutching his chest. "You startled me!" he shouted at them. He wasn't angry just shocked. Jessica thought it was because they startled him. But it was more than that. He was frightened by Tad. It was as if he knew what he was underneath.

Jessica ran up to the table and apologized for the jolt. "I'm sorry, Professor. I thought you saw us there."

He took a breath not taking his eyes off of Tad, who at this point had joined Jessica at the table. "Are you alright?" Tad asked him. The gentleman seemed to be about fifty-ish, and looked a little like Sean Connery with a short beard.

"Oh. Oh, I'm fine. Yes. You just took me by surprise. I get a little caught up in my preparations sometimes. It's good to meet you both." He reached out to shake Tad's hand, he still seemed a little frightened. Was it possible he can tell what I am, Tad wondered? In all his years working on this subject, maybe he had seen enough to know it at a glance. Tad shook his hand.

The Professor turned his attention slowly to Jessica, "It's good to meet you, thank you for attending." He reached out and kissed her hand. "Now I just need a minute more to prepare, Um . . . for the lecture." He seemed distracted now. Tad and Jessica obliged and went back to their seats. Jessica leaned in and whispered to Tad, "Does he seem a little strange to you?"

Tad leaned in and whispered back, "Not at all."

~~~~~~~~~~~~*~~~~~~~~~~~~

Meanwhile, Carlo and Hannah were just arriving at the park. They walked around the walkway and found a nice place to lie out a blanket in front of the pond. It was chilly out, but sunny. So as long as she wore her sweater, Hannah was comfortable. Carlo seemed a little distracted.

"What is it, Carlo?" Hannah asked, "You seem distracted."

"Oh," he began with his flavorful accent, "It's my sister. She called me to come and get her from work yesterday evening. She was very upset. Frightened. Something happened and she won't tell me what it is."

"Is she alright?"

"She seems to be. She was just very freaked out, and her face was bruised. Someone hit her and if I find him, he'll be very sorry." He stopped and shook his head for a second. "I'm sorry," he smiled and held Hannah by the hands, "I'll not ruin our lunch with this. She'll be fine, I'm sure of it."

"That's O.K., I think it's sweet that you're worried about her. She's very lucky to have a brother that cares so much about her." Hannah would do anything to make sure he kept talking. She loved his accent, it was like an aphrodisiac to her. Plus she was finding out a lot about the rest of his family and his character this way.

"We are very close. She practically raised me. It was just us against the world when we were kids. And now, well she's just so secretive. I think it has something to do with this guy she's been hiding from me."

"Why would she keep her boyfriend secret from you?"

"I don't know. She must know I wouldn't approve of him, or she feels like she's protecting me for some reason. I just don't know. But if I find out who it is, and he has anything to do with last night, I'll kill him."

Hannah held his hands, and then she leaned in and kissed him. He suddenly forgot his troubles and rose up on his knees to move in closer to her, and they kissed in the sunlight with the sound of the fountain in the pond trickling behind them. Hannah was in Heaven! This was the most romantic moment of her life! All Carlo's passion had been re-directed towards romancing her. And she was so glad she had come to this thing! She would have to Thank Jessica later!

Pheromones

After a bite to eat and a kiss and a promise, Tad had returned Jessica to her friend, and went back to the cabin to meet the guys. He was starting to fall for her. He had only known her for two days but she was a lot like him. Her dedication to her work and school, over playtime was all too familiar to him, and he felt they both deserved a break. He was going to hook up with her again tomorrow and bring her out to the cabin for dinner. He would need to make arrangements for the guys to take Luke and go out somewhere for a few hours. When he arrived at the cabin all of them were there. The moon was waxing and they were all feeling its effects. The closer it got the more they reacted to it.

Patti had shirked his patrol duties to lay around on Tad's couch, Luke paced around in his room with romantic thoughts of Chloe, and Liam scrolled through the internet researching their condition, while Cassidy paced in anger and frustration over his meeting with Becca. When Tad walked through the door he was immediately bombarded with requests, information and opinions from all corners. All he really wanted to do was have a glass of rum and lay down for the night.

He threw his hands up. "Whoa. What is the matter with all of you?"

Cassidy had to go first. He just wanted to vent really, and the others had already heard enough about it. They tended to agree with Becca anyway. She made the right choice. Then Liam had to show him the website he found about werewolves. Luke had to brag about how Chloe had called him and told him she wanted to get him alone and Pat just bitched about how tired and hungry he was. Tad couldn't listen to anymore he grabbed the rum out of the kitchen cabinet, grabbed a glass and retreated to his bedroom and locked the door without another word

---

to anybody. He would talk to them about Jessica tomorrow. They were way too high strung tonight.

Jessica couldn't stop swooning over Tad. He was fantastic! And she was really excited about going out to the cabin tomorrow. She told Hannah all about it. Hannah was just as excited over Carlo, but Hannah was always out to get a new guy. Jessica hadn't had a boyfriend since twelfth grade, and that was four years ago.

"So how does he kiss?" Hannah asked her while she did her toenails. She was sitting in the middle of her hotel bed with jammies on and cotton between her toes painting them. Jessica had drifted off into a daze. "Jess?" Hannah hollered at her to wake her up out of her Tad trance.

"What?" She smiled at Hannah from her position on her bed. She too was wearing her jammies, but she was lying backwards on the bed on her stomach hugging a pillow. "I didn't hear you."

"Uh, yeah, I got that. I said, how does he kiss?" Hannah repeated.

"Oh, Hannah. I just don't know where to begin. He asked me to come out to his cabin tomorrow for dinner. He's going to pick me up, so I guess I'll leave you with the car."

"No. Uh-uh. Bad idea." Hannah was such a buzz-kill.

Jessica sat up for this one, "Why not?"

"Uh, well, for one thing, you've only known him for two days, and he could be some kind of freak trying to get you out in the woods all alone. You might just need the car to escape. Didn't you think about that?"

"No." Jessica laughed, "He's not a maniac, Hannah"

"Well how do you know for sure? After all, you did meet him at that freak fair going on down the road."

Jessica considered her point for a moment, agreed it was a valid one, and then dismissed it on account of her gut feeling about Tad. "No, Hannah, I really feel like he's alright. Besides, he invited me to bring you along as well."

Hannah gave her a look as if to say 'Oh really?', "Well. I think I'll pass. He was just being cordial, I'm sure. I'm quite certain his intentions are to get you alone. In his *bed*!" Hannah said the last word in a funny way that made Jessica laugh and throw a pillow at her.

"Hey!" Hannah yelled after she blocked the pillow, "My nails. Anyway, I think it's time Carlo and I got to investigate, I mean, know each other better." She smiled, as if to imply something dirty, and then she added, "I'm going over to his place to meet his sister and watch some movies. So please, go, with my blessing. And get laid for crying out loud!" She threw a pillow back at her friend nearly knocking her off the bed. They laughed and threw pillows the rest of the night. They were both so very excited. This trip had become more fun then they could have asked for. And Jessica had all but forgotten about her research for now.

~~~~~~~~~~~*~~~~~~~~~

THE NEXT AFTERNOON . . .

Pheromones. According to the Cambridge International Dictionary of English, pheromone is described as: noun; a chemical substance which an animal releases that influences the behavior of another creature of the same type, for example by attracting it sexually.

This was essentially what was happening to the guys. Women were fawning over them everywhere they went. True enough they were all very attractive men to begin with, but it was the pheromones they were putting off that Tad had decided was making them so accessible. And it was especially higher when the moon was waxing, and so the effect got stronger the fuller the moon got. It was like this was a perk of the infliction for them. It was their 'time of the month'. A feature Patti was absorbing quite gratefully.

Tad had picked Jessica up at the festival around three P.M., giving her time to take in a few events with her best friend before he had arrived. He decided to take her out to dinner instead and then back over to the cabin. Giving the guys time to vacate for the evening. Jessica had expressed an interest in viewing the footage of the wolf pack he tended to. So he planned on an evening by the fire.

Cassidy and Liam and Luke and Patti decided to hang around the festival together and give Tad his requested "Evening alone with his new girl". It was also a way for them to do something more constructive than loll around waiting for the moon to rise. They wandered around and spotted an opportunity for a little mischief at one of the lecture tents. Professor Saunders was giving the second of five of his werewolf lectures. The guys wandered in and picked some seats in the back of the tent. The Professor looked down over his glasses at them as he spoke and switched through the slides on his projector. The tent was packed, far more so than some of the other speakers' tents. This must be a very popular subject, they collectively thought. The girls in the row in front of them kept giggling and turning around to look at them. They smiled and flirted with the men playfully. Pheromones. And the moon in it's waxing phase was putting a lunar supercharge on it. There were also girls in seats to the left and right of them winking and smiling in their direction.

Liam leaned to his right and whispered to the others, "Man, I have never gotten this much female attention before in my *life*." Patti leaned back to his left over Cassidy to answer him, "Yeah, I know it man. I've gotten more action in the past three months than I have in my entire life! What did Tad say it was?"

Cassidy answered them, while chewing on a toothpick, and winking back at the three girls in front of them, "Pheromones."

"Oh, well, I guess you'd know all about it wouldn't you stud muffin?" Liam quipped causing them all to chuckle out loud a little and disrupt the lecture for a second. They joked but it was true. Cassidy always got attention from women. He was every woman's type, and he was aware of it. He had to retort, just the same, "Flash 'em your boobs and maybe you'll get a free lap dance, Liam."

The giggling resumed, "Cute." Liam smiled; even he could be charmed by Cassidy's lighter side. "This is crazy though. What are we? Would they want us if they knew?"

"Most of the women at *this* festival would, I'm sure." Cassidy purred as he leaned back in his seat and crossed his arms in front of him. One of the girls reached behind her seat and dropped a piece of paper in front of him. He leaned down and picked it up. She turned and watched him read it out of her peripheral vision.

Patti leaned over to read it. "What does it say?"

Cassidy grinned wide, "I want you. Call me."

"It does not." Liam scoffed, "Does it?"

Cassidy flashed it in his direction. The girl winked and turned back around. As soon as she did Cassidy handed it down to Liam. "Here." He said, "She likes brunettes. Try not to turn her off."

The Professor could not keep from being distracted by them. Not because they were being disruptive, but because he knew what they were. And more than that he knew *who* they were. He had prepared for such an encounter earlier. He observed how the women in the tent were distracted by their presence. They truly had that animal appeal most men would pay good money for. He was amazed and fascinated by them. And Cassidy was of particular interest to him.

Liam had finally taken notice of what the discussion was about, and he was tuning out the women and the guys to listen to what the Professor was saying. It was as if he was speaking to them directly. He was talking about the strong pull that werewolves had on the opposite sex. He went on to say that even in their transfigured state, historically most females found them sexually appealing. Liam leaned over Luke to talk to Patti again. "Hey! Did you hear what he just said?"

Patti had been listening too, "Yeah, I did. How fucked up is that?"

Luke had been quiet the whole time and finally decided to say something, "Do you guys get how he talks about werewolves as if they really exist?"

All three of the others turned from their respective viewpoints and just stared at him for a second, and then they all burst into chuckling again, "Have you noticed how gay you are?" Cassidy grinned.

Luke ignored him, "No. I mean the way he speaks to the attendants. He really believes."

Cassidy sat up in his seat and looked Luke square in the face, "Do you need me to slap you?"

"You know what I mean." He said, ignoring Cassidy. And they did know what he meant. It was very odd the way the Professor spoke about werewolves and all mythical beasts. He spoke as if he had first hand experience with them. Luke had been listening to him the whole time, fascinated by his conviction and understanding of mythical things. "I mean I think he knows what we are. And do you see the way he keeps looking over at us?"

Cassidy held his position in his folding chair. He was sitting straight up on the edge of it facing Luke and Liam. The girl in front of him could not resist the chance to touch him. She was compelled to reach out and stroke his bicep. "I know what we are too." Cassidy purred with the old smile whisking slowly across his face. He reached over with his left hand and grabbed the girl's hand gently and kissed it causing her to blush and giggle uncontrollably and loudly with her friends. Then he finished his thought never losing eye contact with his brethren, "We are Gods."

Patti exchanged looks with the others. It gave them all cold chills. It was this side of Cassidy that intrigued them, even Tad. Cassidy encouraged their fantasies and reminded them that they were superhuman. It sounded great but it wasn't enough for them to ever trust him as leader, because they also knew he was rash and chaotic and cruel. Tad kept them grounded and realistic, and they could trust him to make the right decisions for them as a group. Cassidy only did what felt good for him at that moment. But he was a terrific war general, and he knew how to keep their attention.

Before they could respond to Cassidy's latest remark, a voice came from behind them. It was a man's voice. He had a strange southern colonial type of accent, old world, with a powerful draw on the annunciations of his words. "You are no God, beast. You only think you are." They all turned around in their seats towards him. When they turned they saw an older gentleman, probably in his mid forties. He had a well-groomed goatee that followed his jaw-line almost all the way to his ears. His hair was straight and shoulder-length, and it was a reddish brown almost auburn color. His clothes were covered in dust, he looked like he had been set up on a shelf collecting dust for a long time. He was smoking a big fat cigar, and he bore a strange metal choker collar around his neck with little lights on it that blinked occasionally, causing him to squint. He sat in his chair slowly dragging his stogie. He didn't move too fast and he seemed familiar with them all.

The old bastard, Cassidy thought, mind your own business. The man definitely got his attention, "Oh really? Is that so? How the fuck would you know what I am?"

He took a long slow drag off his cigar, and then he answered him, "Because I made you, beast." They all exchanged glances. It was he. The one who made them, the werewolf that had attacked them! That's why he felt familiar! It was his curse in their veins. The man just let them think on it for a minute or two and then he chimed in, "That's right. Discuss it amongst yourselves." He was a strange man, but very decadent and cool, and he had no fear of them. They could definitely feel the familiarity among them.

Cassidy stood and put a finger in his face, "Just who are you, and where did you come from?"

The man took his time when answering, "They call me The Founder, and you should want to ask me *when* I came from, beast."

Cassidy came right back with, "Who are *they*? What the fuck do you mean *when*? And what's with this *beast* shit?"

"Well, that's what you are, isn't it?" He answered the last question first, choosing to ignore the other two.

"And you're a mother fucker." Cassidy sarcastically responded. The others just watched in shock. They all had so many questions but didn't know what to say. Cassidy was rarely at a loss for words.

The man smiled and kind of chuckled at him. He found Cassidy amusing. "Charming demeanor. I can see why the blonde one is leader." He flicked his cigar and stood up. He was tall and solid, like them only rougher around the edges. Road worn. "It was good to meet you all . . . in person this time." Without offering them another explanation, he turned his back to them and walked off and out of the tent. The women turned and watched him too. The Founder saluted the Professor on his way out.

The guys didn't say anything out loud for a few seconds, then, of course, Cassidy had to be the first. "Well, what the fuck was that?" He was standing in the isle and talking very loud. Everyone, especially the Professor was looking at him. He realized it and flipped the whole group a bird. Then he slapped Luke on the arm, "Let's go."

~~~~~~~~~~~*~~~~~~~~~~~

Tad and Jessica were just arriving at the cabin. When they walked inside Jessica was awestruck by its size. There were fourteen-foot ceilings with exposed beams. A loft type office wedged in one corner of the A-Frame, and a huge great room with the biggest stone fireplace she had ever seen. It was like an enormous ski-lodge. It was very posh for a cabin.

"Wow," she said gawking around the room. "When you said cabin . . . I was picturing . . . logs. Not casa de Thadeas."

"I know," he smiled, "Pretty luxurious, huh? When I first saw it I thought it was a bit much for our needs. But now, I've gotten quite comfortable. I guess we're a little spoiled to it."

"I guess so." She smiled as she unbuttoned her coat.

He took her coat for her and hung it on the coat tree by the door. Even though it was chilly outside, he had no need for a coat. His blood was keeping him plenty warm. It was these subtle nuances of their condition that the guys had already become accustomed to and no longer noticed, but were quite apparent to other people.

"Aren't you a little cold?" she asked and rubbed her arms as if trying to warm herself. He touched her back and led her to the sofa. "Sorry," he said, "I guess my body has gotten used to the climate in here." He excused his hot natured-ness and went over to the fireplace to light it.

While he worked on the fire, Jessica got up and strolled around the room. She looked at the pictures of him and Liam with various types of wild animals that were sitting out on the end tables.

"How long have you and Liam been friends?" she asked. She wanted to know more details about him and his past. Women like details. It gives them a lot of insight on the man behind the good looks and flair.

"Well, we met in collage. We shared a dorm. We were in a lot of the same classes, had mutual friends, you know. We just hit it off. Like long lost brothers. Then, after collage we ended up working together for the same environmental firm. The rest is history."

Jessica nodded showing her understanding of the bonds of friendship. She had known Hannah far longer in perspective, but she knew what he meant by long lost brothers. Hannah and Jess had always been close as sisters.

"And Luke and the others?" she asked. Not yet satisfied with the tidbits of info she had on him.

"New acquaintances." He answered as he stoked the fire.

"Oh, they seem nice." She offered a compliment. It was really a hidden way of asking a question. She figured he would comment on their character, and he did.

"Well, Patti is a nice guy and Luke. Cassidy has his moments." He left it at that. It was what she expected him to say. Finally the fire was roaring. She walked over and joined him beside it. "Here." He said as he reached past her to grab a large white furry blanket. He spread it out in front of the fire for them. She kicked her shoes off and sat right in the center of it. "There, are you more comfortable now?" he asked her.

"Oh, yeah. This is great. You're quite the gentleman." She smiled up at him. He kneeled down and got eye level with her. He was drawing her in. She felt compelled to pounce on him, but she decided to keep it to herself for now. He had all this strong animal magnetism. It was almost intoxicating. She hadn't been this turned on by a guy ever, in her life. She couldn't explain it. He leaned in and kissed her quickly on the lips, and then he rose and headed for the kitchen.

"You want some wine?" he called back to her. She was still in a trance over the little kiss she just received, "Uh, yeah. Please . . . thank you!" she called back to him.

It didn't take him long to return. He lowered the lights a little and he brought a tray of wine and cheeses with crackers. They laughed and talked and snacked for about an hour. Then it turned romantic. It had been leading to that all night, but Tad didn't want to move too fast and intimidate her. But Jessica was ready. She had never been *this* ready in her life. He moved their tray to the side and they fell into a kiss, a fast, hard, passionate kiss. Jessica was tingling all over. She had only slept with two other guys in her lifetime, and they were amateurs. Boys. This was a man, a very experienced, very intriguing, very sexy man. She hoped she wouldn't disappoint him.

He was more than ready for her too. He was horny out of his mind really. It had been awhile for him. He hadn't realized just how long until now. He didn't want to move too fast for her and scare her. He got the impression she was fairly innocent. Not completely, but not in her friend Hannah's league of expertise, he was sure. And he liked that about her. He didn't want a woman everyone else had been with.

She brought his hand up to her breasts and looked him deep in the eyes. She kissed him over and over again all over his mouth, and then his neck. She let him unbutton her shirt. She pulled and tugged at his t-shirt finally pulling away long enough to pull it off him. He was muscular and strong. She kissed him hard again, then leaned back and quickly finished unbuttoning her own shirt and pulling it and her bra off and threw them to the floor. She felt like she was practically raping him! She was so turned on. She couldn't help herself.

They were acting like two starving people. They fell back onto the blanket and Tad rolled over on top of her. She couldn't get close enough to him. She wanted him hard and fast. She wanted him now. They finally got their clothes off and engaged. It was the most unbound pleasure she had ever known. His power, his muscles the smell of his cologne, it was all driving her wild! She was moaning loudly and enjoying him. She was so stricken with pleasure that she would have let him do anything. Her inhibitions were gone. He pulled her up onto his lap. She scratched his back and yelped as he thrust deeper into her. It felt good; it hurt a little but she liked it! She threw her head back and smiled as he chewed on her neck. The fire roared beside them and cast a sexy silhouette against the wall. She was illuminated with fire and lust and orgasm. She had no idea sex could be this good. She also had no idea she was making love with a werewolf. She couldn't have known. The sex was great. But the danger was even greater.

~~~~~~~~~~*~~~~~~~~~~

The Benefactor

After the ordeal with The Founder in the werewolf tent and knowing they couldn't run out to the cabin and tell Tad about it yet, they all decided to go back over to Patti's apartment and have a few drinks to discuss the situation. There were just so many questions, and no real answers. Well, no logical answers, anyway. They talked for a while about it, but as the evening progressed, so did their aggravation with the whole thing. They eventually grew tired of the subject and the drunker they got the more tired they got and finally they all passed out.

The next morning, after several attempts to wake Cassidy up, Patti, Liam and Luke resigned to leave him alone and go on over to the cabin. After all, Cassidy had his own car and he knew where they'd be if he wanted to join them later. They couldn't wait any longer to discuss this matter with Tad.

Shortly after the guys left, Cassidy awoke. He staggered into the bathroom and splashed cold water on his face. He felt like a haggard old pirate. The rum he had drunk the night before was really kicking his ass this morning. He stared into the mirror for a minute. He began to scratch the stubble on his face and neck. He reached up to scratch his head and when he felt around behind his left ear, he felt something strange. He cocked his head to the side and looked in the mirror as best as he could, but it was in an odd location, sort of low on his neck. So he picked up a hand mirror and angled it so as to get a rear view of his ear. He noticed a knot. Knowing his new physiology, he knew he was immune now to disease and injury, and it felt like something was in there, under his skin. He walked back into the living room and grabbed his leather jacket and started rifling through the pockets. He finally found what he was after, his pocketknife. He threw the coat down on the couch and returned to the bathroom. Knowing he couldn't do himself any real harm he began to poke at the object in his neck. It was lodged there just below his left ear. When he touched it with the knife it caused him to flinch with pain, but he continued anyway. He pressed the blade in further finally slicing into his own flesh. When he did, he didn't have to dig too far to find his blade touching hard plastic or metal of some kind. He snarled and growled and yelled out loud from the pain he was inflicting upon himself. But he knew he'd be fine in an hour or two, so he pressed on, shoving the blade down and behind the object. He whittled the knife back and forth, gritting his teeth to fight the pain, and then finally popped the device out of his hide. It fell into the sink. He tossed the knife in the sink with it and held his hand to his neck for a minute, waiting for the bleeding to stop. He picked up the object with his other hand and held it close to his face to examine it.

"What the fuck?" he said to himself. It appeared to be some sort of monitor or tracking device. It only took him a moment to decide to grab his keys and head out to the cabin to join the others and let them in on this new tidbit of information. He didn't even bother to put on a shirt. He grabbed his coat on the way out instead and headed for the Mustang. The more he thought about it the more angry he got. He could feel his fever kick in and he could feel his retinas burning as they always did before the shift. But he wasn't changing yet. He was just furious.

~~~~~~~~~~*~~~~~~~~~~

The night before had left Jessica a little weak legged, but she'd survive. Tad had taken her home a few hours after they made love at her request. She didn't want Hannah to worry about her and she couldn't wait to tell her all about it. Besides, she would see him again. In fact she was to join Tad at the cabin later tonight as well. This time he had asked that she stay all night with him. She had agreed and now had to tell Hannah what her plans were. She just knew her good friend would give her all kinds of Hell over this one, but she woke her anyway and braced herself. She knew this would just make her day, and she hadn't been able to tell her when she got to the hotel last night because Hannah got there even later and Jess had fallen asleep. Jessica had totally forgotten what she had come to the festival for. She was so enamored with this great new guy of hers, that she hadn't written down the first note about the paranormal, and there were only a few more days left of it. She wondered what would become of her Tad when she returned to the collage. Would he come visit her? It wasn't too very far from him. Maybe they could take turns coming and going. Oh well, she thought. We'll figure it out. She shook her friend awake. Hannah removed her eye mask to find Jessica beaming from ear to ear. She didn't even have to ask. She knew why. She returned the smile and sat up for the juicy details she always loved to hear.

~~~~~~~~~~*~~~~~~~~~~

As soon as the guys got to the cabin they raced inside and began hollering excitedly and all at once over The Founder. Tad was overwhelmed but fascinated. He sat down with his coffee and took in every detail. This was just the information he had hoped to find at that festival.

They had been mulling over the details for about an hour when Cassidy burst into the cabin. This was to no surprise of his comrades as they had heard him approaching from the moment he turned off the main road. Their new D.N.A. enabling them with the heightened senses that come so naturally to their lupine namesakes. They had smelled the blood on him too, but it was as familiar as their own, so they knew it was his. His neck in fact was bleeding and his hands were covered in it too. He slapped a bloody gadget that looked much like a hearing aid, down on the table.

"Look at this!" he shouted wildly. He was livid. The ride out there had given him time to brew on it and he was hot. His jaws clenched as he spoke and his eyes were shimmering, reflecting light like prisms, another side effect of the affliction that plagued them. "Look!" he yelled again, pointing at it.

"What is that?" Luke asked, as he leaned across the table and peered at it, then he added with a disgusted look on his face, "And where the Hell did you get it?"

Cassidy gritted his teeth. He turned his head and pulled back his hair, still sticky with his own blood, revealing a wound the size of a quarter in his neck just below his left ear.

"It was in my neck!!" he shouted, "That's where I got it!" He yelled and seethed with anger. They could see he had cut it out himself because the flesh around the wound looked a little like hamburger meat. It was looking better than when he first did it, however, as it had already begun to heal. There wouldn't even be a scar there in another hour. Werewolves have that ability as well. No scarring or illness or open wounds or aging or infections. It was another perk to the infliction. That and immortality, but that was questionable as a perk. Some would find that a curse as well.

Tad walked over to the table to survey the situation. He looked at Cassidy's neck. Then he picked up the device.

"What do you think it is, Tad?" Liam asked. He approached to get a better look at it himself. Patti decided to check it out too. Tad examined it a moment then looked at Cassidy, and in an even and serious tone he said, "It looks like a tracking device."

Cassidy and Tad locked eyes. Cassidy nodded, saying nothing. His nostrils flared. He stood bracing himself against the table trying to control his rage. Something he always had a hard time with.

"A tracking device? But who?" asked Patti, "And how? When? He damn sure wasn't born with it."

Liam looked at Tad. They each knew what the other was thinking. All of them were able to communicate with each other in a sort of telepathic way now. They had been able to do this ever since they were attacked. It was yet another ability known only to them. The others didn't know about what Tad and Liam knew yet, but they sensed there was something amiss.

"What?" Patti asked them.

"The F.A.P.R.," answered Liam, turning his gaze toward Patti. Tad walked over to middle of the room and let Liam have the floor for a minute.

"The what, who?" Patti asked again.

"The F.A.P.R.," Liam repeated, then he filled in a few blanks for them, "It stands for, Federal Agency of Paranormal Research. They have a facility located at the top of the mountain to the West of us. My guess is we all have one of those." He pointed to the device in Tad's hand. This fresh thought caused Luke to reach up and touch his own neck.

"What?!" Patti shouted, outraged, "Who the Hell are these people? I didn't know anything about it, and I'm the fuckin' Deputy Sheriff in this back ass fuckin' town! How did you two know about them when I didn't?" he finished his rant with his hands on his hips. Now *his* nostrils were flared.

"They rescued us." Liam began, "The night we were attacked."

"Yeah," Tad added, "Right after they let it happen."

A grim reality suddenly set in among them, and in their collective thought they all realized . . . they were being studied! The Founder, their wounds being dressed, the mysterious blackouts from time to time, they had been set up and now they were being researched and used, but for what purpose?

"Mother Fuckers!!" Cassidy yelled, no longer able to keep his anger in check. He slammed his fists into the table so hard it cracked and gave a little in the middle. "Don't they know what they're fucking with?!"

"Yes, Cass!" Tad's voice was raised now. He could feel a confrontation coming on. Cassidy would take any opportunity to vent and swell his anger. Violence was all he understood. "Yes they do. They know very well what they're fucking with!" He held the tracking device in the air for a minute to remind them all, and then hurled it across the room. He approached Cassidy, keeping eye contact with him the whole time. The others moved back and kept quiet. They rarely interfered and never challenged Tad's judgment where Cassidy was concerned. They were used to these battles for control between Tad and Cassidy. Keeping Cassidy in line usually required kicking his ass, hard.

"The question is," Tad continued, "Do we know what we're fucking with?"

"I'm not a God damn guinea pig, Thadeas, and I'm *not* just going to sit like a dog because you say so! I'll handle this myself!" Cassidy snarled.

Tad tossed a chair out of the way as he crossed the room and got nose to nose with Cassidy. "You will damn well do just that until we all figure out how to handle this situation collectively."

"I didn't sign up for this fucking experiment, and I'm not taking any of your bullshit, Tad!" Cassidy snapped, "I'll handle this my way!"

"You will do what is best for all of us, Cass!" he pointed to a chair, "Now sit the Hell down so we can figure this out!"

"Fuck you!" Cassidy hissed. Tad put his finger in Cassidy's face and snarled through his teeth, "You may not have signed up, mother fucker, but your fate is the same as us all now. You will *not* jeopardize the rest of us with your uncontrolled anger and stupidity. You will mind your place!!"

Cassidy was hotter than Hell, but he was mindful of Tad's unpredictability and strength. He snarled back at him though with ferocity, reminding Tad what *he* was dealing with, "I'm not your dog. I have no *place* in this . . . *pack.*"

"Oh you have a place, my brother," Tad growled back, "Right below mine."

This pissed Cassidy off to no end. But he didn't want to push any harder with Tad. Though he was an avid fighter and enjoyed the challenge, he couldn't forget that Tad shared his abilities now, and he was the one person Cassidy hadn't beat yet. In his heart of hearts he knew Tad was probably right, but it didn't stop him from pushing buttons; his anger was his Achilles heel. He just couldn't stop himself.

"Oh really?" he started, sarcastically as usual, "How did we determine that?" He paced around the room and began lashing out at the rest of them, "Don't the rest of you bastards have anything to say?"

He turned and looked at Luke. "What about you, Luke?" He got a little closer, taking his spite out on his subordinate. Luke seldom said anything. Being the youngest and newest of the guys, he kept his quiet. He was still in shock a little by his new reality, but he knew his place, and he, like the others, agreed with Tad being in charge. Especially when it came to Cassidy. "What about me?" Luke answered him. He feared Cassidy but he didn't back down from him.

Cassidy began his speech; "Well I made you, right?" He sort of smiled diabolically, "I mean it was an accident that you lived, but . . ." he paused, "I did make you."

"That's enough Cassidy." Patti spoke up, sick of it. This was serious and they didn't have time for Cassidy's little boy games. "Knock it off."

Cassidy threw his hand up at Patti, "Shah! Please, Patti."

"What's your point, Cass?" Luke was getting sick of it too, he wished Tad would just kick his ass already, so they could move on.

"Well doesn't that make you mine? Shouldn't you be following *my* fucking orders?!" He started shouting again. Luke didn't like it when Cassidy got revved up like this, it made him nervous, but he answered him, "Hell no! You're a nut! You'll get us all killed."

"Well aren't we half gone already?!" Cassidy yelled.

Tad had finally had enough, "Alright, Cassidy just knock it off! Everybody's done with your little speech. If you want to fight about it, then let's fight about it. Get it out of your system so we can get back to business!" He held the screen door open, "You want to go for it again? Then come on, Brother!"

Cassidy smiled big, "Let's go, wolf man."

They hit the yard swinging. Patti, Liam and Luke went outside to watch. Every blow between them was like a cannon going off. They were big and they swung hard. The kind of blows they were laying out could have killed a regular man, but their new D.N.A. made them virtually bulletproof, unless, of course, those bullets were silver. Their muscles were like steel and they were all extremely agile, swift and powerful. This could have gone on for hours because of their charged adrenal glands alone, but fortunately, Tad knew how to win at this game with Cassidy. He swung a quick left hook hitting Cassidy square on the nose, knocking him to the ground hard. Where after he quickly kneeled down placing his knee in Cassidy's chest, pinning him to the ground with all his weight and strength. "Call it!!" he yelled, Cassidy just huffed at him. "Call it!!" Tad roared at him again.

"Alright!!" Cassidy growled reluctantly. One day he'd get the bastard, he thought, he was still mad as Hell. "Alright!!" Tad's knee was sliding across his windpipe. He could barely breathe, let alone talk. He had both hands around Tad's leg trying to push him off. Tad waited a minute before getting up to make sure he truly yielded. Then he got to his feet and offered Cassidy a hand up. He took it and started dusting himself off. He rubbed at his neck and chest and snarled at Tad, "You're so holier than thou. You're just as stricken as the rest of us when the moon is full. How long do you think you can hold *your* place, Tad?"

Tad turned and looked at Cassidy and the others for minute then he answered, "As long as I'm tougher than any of you mother fuckers." Then he turned and went inside, followed by Pat, Liam and Luke. He was rubbing his jaw. Cassidy really was a formidable bastard, Tad thought. Cassidy waited outside for a minute to collect himself. He spit, mostly blood, then he too followed inside. Sometimes he just needed to fight out his frustration, and Tad understood that. The five men, now bonded by fate, would have to work together. Just like a pack. They all needed each other now more than ever. Even Cassidy. But could he be trusted?

~~~~~~~~~~~*~~~~~~~~~~~

At the F.A.P.R., the man M was leading the Professor down a long corridor to an elevator. They entered the elevator and rode it down what seemed like a hundred floors. Armed guards accompanied them with laser type weapons. When the elevator stopped, the Professor looked up at the floor indicator, it read Level 10. The doors shot open and they all stepped out. They walked down another long corridor. Only this one had large glass windows on both sides of them. There was some sort of laboratory on their left, and to the right, behind glass and then behind thick four inch bars, was The Founder.

The men entered the room containing him. He was pacing when they arrived. The sound of the elevator had woken him. He approached the bars. "Well, well. Professor Saunders, sir. How are you?" he greeted them in true Southern style, his dialect reflecting another place in time. The Professor avoided direct eye contact with him, but returned the courtesy. "Why fine William, fine."

"Can the niceties." The man M announced loudly. "We're here to work."

The Professor was very nervous. He didn't like to be in these confined quarters with The Founder. He had been with them when he was unleashed and he feared the beast's capabilities and intelligence. He had never seen where they kept him confined, or how. He leaned in and asked M, "Are you quite certain he can't get out of there?"

M looked over at The Founder, and then answered. "I'm positive. Those bars are a specially engineered composite metal made up of steel, lead . . ." he paused to wink at The Founder, "and silver. So I am quite positive we are protected." He slapped the Professor hard on the back. "So relax and let's get to work." He was busy setting up the microscope and other lab essentials to his liking.

The Founder spoke up. "Yes, besides Jack, it's not me you two should be worried about." He smiled and lit up a cigar. He sat on one of the chairs provided for him. The inside of the enclosure was actually quite elaborate. He had fine comforts inside that suited his needs. Tufted pillows and chairs, a dining set, an enclosed bath and bedroom. It was very posh, for a cage, but it was a cage none-the-less.

What he had said worried the Professor further. He was a very nervous man by nature anyway. "What do you mean?"

"Well," the creature began, "It's the beasts outside this confinement you should worry about. You underestimate the newcomers. The pugilist, Cassidy . . ." he smiled, "He's a nasty one. Real trouble. He'll kill you all slow, I'm sure."

The Professor flashed a frightened glance back at M. "Maybe he's right. I mean, what have we done to protect ourselves from them?"

M smiled at The Founder, who was smiling back at him sarcastically, then he turned to the worried professor, "Do not listen to him, Jack. We have taken all the right precautions. No need to worry yourself about Cassidy, or the others. We are perfectly safe here."

"Sure we are, in here, but what about out there?" The Professor was getting a little panicky at the thought of his favorite fairy tale monster coming to kill him slowly or any other way. He knew, as an expert and fan of the werewolf what they were capable of, especially after all this first-hand experience. "What about me? Out there . . . at that festival. I'm not armed with any super weapons like your soldiers here." He pointed to the armed gunmen facing the enclosure.

M humored his friend's fears and reassuringly patted him on the back. "Jack, trust me. I won't let them find out about you."

They looked over at The Founder. "Well," the Professor started, "What's to keep him from telling them?"

The Founder grinned back at them and drew on his stogie. "We have a deal, he & I. Your secret is safe here. Isn't that right, William?" M asked him.

"Oh yes. I won't let them poison themselves on your blood, Jack. But, M." he stood and took a long slow drag off his cigar, "I hope I'm there when they rip your throat out."

"You just keep dreaming William, and keep doing as you are told. Before your usefulness runs out. You will be going to visit them again tonight."

The Founder resettled himself in his chair. He was laughing from his gut. He couldn't care less about M's threats. He prayed everyday that they would end his eternal torment and kill him, but he knew they wouldn't because of the legacy. With his end would come the end of the pack M so reverently coveted. He watched from his easy chair as the man M prepared the restraining collar for him to wear. The collar would prevent him from changing or escaping. It was specially designed to inhibit his ability to manipulate the curse, as he normally had the power to do so. He had, after all, been turned into a werewolf a long, long time ago.

He watched them prepare the sleeping potion he would soon be injected with so that they could safely apply the collar. Then, when he awoke or when they woke him with stimulants, he would be briefed as to his duty around the pack tonight, and be told what to say and do. He smiled as he watched. He knew their days were numbered. He knew nature could not be contained for long, especially not human nature. And the nature of the beast within the men they toyed with would rise to the occasion, most certainly.

The Founder watched M load two darts with the tranquilizer potion. The darts were then loaded into one of the poacher's weapons. The Founder tossed his cigar to the floor then he sat up and pulled his shirt open over his chest. He waited for the guard to take aim and fire. PLIMP! PLIMP! He leaned back into his chair and smiled sadistically as the drug took effect. The last thing he saw before he closed his eyes and lost consciousness, were photographs of Cassidy, Liam, Luke, Patti & Tad, looking back at him from the lab's wallboard. They were being underestimated. The end was near for them all.

~~~~~~~~~~*~~~~~~~~~~

Fell On Black Days

After a brief meeting and deciding they had to arm themselves or prepare in some way, the guys decided to take a trip over to the Feed 'N Seed. They had all discussed the existence of the armed poachers that struck them with tranquilizing darts, and they all shared their recollections from the nights they were attacked, all but Luke whom was very uncomfortable with the conversation. He choked back emotion as they discussed how the poachers hit them with darts the night Cassidy & Patti first changed, and how Liam distinctly remembered hearing the sound of the doctor's voice around them.

These men whoever they really were, had staged and set up these incidents, and The Founder was connected too. The guys had to be prepared for anything, as obviously these men had weapons that would definitely challenge their sub-natural ones. Cassidy and Liam both recollected about how easily they had sedated and netted The Founder on the nights they were attacked. They got in the Mustang and the Cruiser and headed for the Farmer's market.

Once they were there they spread out and started looking around for anything to arm themselves with. It was clear their wolf-skins were no defense, because the poachers were better prepared with highly sophisticated weapons. As they stood in the isles and searched for things, the silence was suddenly broken by the sound of a girl screeching, and some bickering. Luke knew it was Chloe. All of the guys picked their heads up and listened turning their finely tuned ears toward the sound. It was coming from outside the docking bay doors.

Tad and Cassidy locked eyes. Tad nodded and Cassidy smiled and headed for the docking bay. Luke started to follow but Tad put his hand up against his chest and shook his head at him. It was better to send Cassidy in for this situation. He knew how to handle it. Luke trusted Tad and stood down. He couldn't help but be distracted by Chloe's screams though.

Cassidy walked through the hanging plastic sheets that hung in front of the load in ramp and stealthily walked outside. He could see Chloe being held by the arm roughly by her stepfather. He was cussing her and she was crying and yelling back at him, trying to pull his hands off her arm.

"You're hurtin' me Jared! Let go!" she tugged and pulled. He just kept spitting obscene words at her. "You little bitch. I'll teach you to try to run away from me!" Just as he reared back to backhand her in the face, Cassidy made his presence known. He stepped out where they could see him.

"Having a little trouble with your teen, there Jared?" he smiled as he lit a cigarette. Chloe looked relieved but unsure. She didn't know Cassidy that well.

Jared quickly lowered his arm. He damn sure didn't want his customers to see him beating his kid. He was still holding on tightly to her arm. It was swollen and red and blue from the pressure he was using to detain her. A forced smile rolled across Jared's face. He quickly began to kiss ass.

"Well, you know how it is. They think they know everything." He stuttered nervously as Cassidy approached them slowly, he knew of Cassidy's reputation. "It's nothing really. Don't you worry yourself about it, Cassidy. You just go on back inside and do your shoppin'"

Cassidy got close enough and reached out and grabbed Chloe's other arm, pulling her away from Duggan slowly, keeping constant eye contact with the man. Jared reluctantly loosened his grip. He resented Cassidy's interference here. This wasn't any of his business. He tried to be curt but cordial.

"This really isn't a matter of concern for you, you know?" Jared said, losing his smile. Chloe stood closer to Cassidy. She didn't know him that well, she had only just met him, but she felt better standing next to him.

"You're right. But I thought you should know everybody in your store could hear this little . . . disagreement of yours. You might want to re-think abusing your stepdaughter at work." Cassidy snarled. He wasn't ordinarily chivalrous, but he had his moments. It was more out of hatred for men like Jared Duggan, than chivalry, really. But he helped her, none-the-less.

"Chloe get back to work!" Jared shouted at her. She quickly ran back inside. Then Jared, choosing his words carefully, looked at Cassidy. "Thank you for the information. I'll be inside if you decide to buy somethin'" Then he turned and huffed back inside too. He was angry as Hell but he wouldn't dare take on a man like Cassidy. And he couldn't afford for his customers to witness such an entanglement either.

After they went inside Cassidy stood there, reveling in himself and smoking his cigarette. Suddenly he had a diabolical thought. He smiled the way he always did, and he walked over to the car Jared had gotten out of. He put the cig in his mouth and squatted down to the back of the car and reached out and grabbed the license plate with both hands. Then with one powerful tug, he yanked the plate right off the car. He pulled it with such force that the entire car body rocked on its chassis. Before he went back inside he went around to the front of the store and tossed the tag into the backseat of the Mustang. He had a few plans he wanted to set into motion later.

Back inside, Chloe had cleaned up her make-up and wandered back into the store. As soon as Luke saw her he ran up to her. Jared was watching them from the counter. He scowled at the romance in front of him.

The guys had found a few things they thought would be helpful in a gunfight. They had machete's and razor wire and hatchets. Things they thought might cut through the Gortex suits the poachers always wore. They also had to pick things they could handle in their wolf-skins, because that was usually when they saw them. It was an unusual purchase for them. Not the types of things O'Bannon & Duggan ordinarily sold to them, but they rang it up without any questions asked.

When they got to the parking lot, Tad advised them he had to go meet Jessica and that she would be staying all night this time. So it would be another stay over at Patti's house. This would work out perfectly for Cassidy. He could set his diabolical plans in motion. Liam and Patti wanted another chance to go to the festival and find The Founder anyway.

Tad got cleaned up before he headed out to the festival to meet Jessica. Before they left the cabin the guys stood beside the cars and made arrangements. Liam agreed to take Luke and go on to the festival with Tad and hang around there until Pat and Cassidy showed up. They wanted to get a head start looking for The Founder. Cassidy took his car but told Patti he would follow him on out to the station for a minute. There was something he had wanted to check out. So they exchanged cars and went off in separate directions.

~~~~~~~~~~~*~~~~~~~~~~~

Meanwhile, at the festival, Jessica and Hannah were just getting there. They grabbed something to munch on and rode a couple of rides and then Jess bought a book on werewolves from a dark haired gypsy girl. Hannah began flipping through it while they sat in another lecture tent. Hannah had agreed to join Jessica for this one while they each waited on their respective dates to arrive. Carlo had to work late and Tad had said he'd be late. So they attended a lecture on ghosts. Hannah must have found this lecture pretty interesting. She didn't give it her usual critique. Jessica decided to use her little voice recorder to record it. She had to make notes for the thesis she was writing for extra credit. It was the first day since they arrived she was able to get any work done.

A dusty older man smoking a cigar decided to sit right behind them. He was sure to blow smoke in their direction, hoping to get their attention. It worked; Hannah flipped around in her seat and shot the man a hateful look. "Do you mind?" she huffed at him, "I'm quite certain I don't want to look like you later in life. So please blow your poisonous gas away from me."

He smiled at her and politely put the cigar out in his hand. "I do apologize, young lady, for the inconvenience. Pardon me."

"Whatever." She snapped and turned back around. He chuckled at her a little. He wasn't the least bit offended by her attitude. He found her to be quite entertaining. Jessica leaned over and gave her friend a nudge. "Would you lighten up? You're gonna get us killed if you don't filter your mouth." Jessica placed a glance behind her and smiled at the man trying to apologize for her friend's rude behavior. He nodded at her as if he understood.

Tad showed up right before the lecture ended. "How did you find us?" Jessica smiled and kissed him when he sat down next to her.

"I followed your perfume." He smiled back and returned the kiss. She thought it was a sweet romantic thing to say, she didn't know it was true. He leaned in and said hello to Hannah. The Founder watched all this intently and as yet, unnoticed by Tad. Tad wouldn't have recognized him yet anyway, as this was his first encounter with the one that made him.

"Just let me record the last couple minutes of this lecture and we can go, alright?" Jessica asked him.

"Sure." He smiled. Suddenly he felt a strange pull on his senses. The same sense he used to detect the guys when they were near. He looked at the tent door for Liam or Luke. Then he turned around and saw The Founder. Their eyes locked and instantly Tad knew who he was. The Founder sat up in his seat and reached out to shake his hand. "How do you do Thadeas. It's been a while."

Tad shook his hand but never lost eye contact. He didn't want to alarm the girls, and he didn't want this man near them. He wasn't sure how to feel about him yet. He excused them both to the girls. His pulse was racing. It was like coming back from the dead and being introduced to your murderer. Tad was freaked.

"Jess," he looked at her, "I'm gonna step right outside and have a word with my friend here. Do you mind?"

Jessica looked back at The Founder, who was standing up now, then back at Tad. "Oh, you know him? Sure. I'll join you right after the lecture."

"Good." He kissed her hand then stood and walked outside letting The Founder lead. Hannah leaned over to Jess after they left. "You mean he knows that old loon?"

"I guess so." Jessica got one of her weird feelings, she would tell Tad about it later.

Once outside the tent the two men faced off. Tad went first. "How did you find us?"

"Let's just say," The Founder answered him slowly in his Southern way and re-lit his cigar, "I didn't follow your perfume."

"Funny. Just how much of this are you in on?"

"Most of it. None of it voluntarily." He pulled his shirt collar down to reveal the collar. "I'm nothing more than a trained poodle."

"Who are you?" Tad asked the basics this time. He was beginning to get the feeling this man was not entirely an enemy.

"They call me The Founder. My real name is Colonel William Jack. I was a soldier of the Confederacy. Call me what you like. I was turned a long time ago, much of my life was over then."

Tad looked down for minute. He had pity on the old soldier. He was a very cool and dignified man, at one time an ambassador for freedom.

He tried to show respect. "Why me? Why Liam and the others? You could have finished us."

"I had my orders, sir. I am a man of war. Even as a beast." Col. Jack didn't offer answers to what he was not explicitly asked. As much as he might have wanted to tell Tad everything, he held back.

Tad couldn't believe what he was hearing. He had so much to ask, so much to say, and not enough time to figure it out. He tried to ask the most pertinent questions he could think of. "What do they want with us?"

The Founder smiled, "You are guinea pigs, son, a government experiment. Test animals for future wars. My time is limited. I grow tired of being hand fed my meat and my women. I'm tired of siring wolfmen."

"How many have you been a part of?" Tad was in shock, but it made sense now. The tracking devices, the Gortex, the tranquilizers, the entire set-up even the location.

"That doesn't matter. You are the one's that have shined for them. They are proud of their little pack. And it's not over yet. There is more."

"More? What do you mean?"

The Founder finished his cigar and ignored the last question. "It's time for me to go. I'm sorry I couldn't tell you more. Next time we meet, well, I hope we are free. Good night, son. And good luck."

"Wait!" Tad shouted as The Founder turned and walked away. "Wait . . . William!" He didn't turn around as Tad called to him. He kept walking toward the trees. For some reason Tad didn't follow him. Somehow he knew they would meet again.

~~~~~~~~~~~*~~~~~~~~~~~

At the police station, Patti and Cassidy were busy collecting guns and high-powered rifles from the gun case. Cassidy helped Patti pull the guns and ammo and carry it all to the cruiser. He ran over and grabbed the license tag out of his car and ran back in. Finally Patti placed an interest in what he was doing. "What the fuck are you doing?" He asked him.

Cassidy just sat down at Patti's computer and sat the tag down on the desk. Patti walked over and picked it up. "What the Hell is this?" He waved it at Cassidy. Cassidy reached up and took it away from him and kept on pecking at the computer. Patti walked around to the other side of the desk so he could get a look at what he was doing. Finally Cassidy asked for help. "How the fuck do you look up a tag number?"

"I don't know. That depends on whether or not you tell me what the fuck you're doing, shithead." Patti retorted.

"Fine!" Cassidy snapped and whirled around in his seat to look at him. "I'm looking this tag number up so I can hunt down the bastard it belongs to. O.K.?"

Patti looked him in the eyes and held it for a minute. Then he finally answered, "O.K." Then he leaned over Cassidy and typed in the number on the appropriate page and pulled it up. "Jared Duggan?" he looked over at Cassidy. That familiar smile whipped across his face as he took in the directions and address on the screen. Patti didn't want to know. He shook his head and threw his hands up. Whatever it was he wanted no part of it and he didn't ask any more questions about it. He knew it probably had something to do with their little altercation today, and that was enough. He held the front door open for Cassidy. "Come on asshole, we've got to get to that festival."

"Just what the fuck are we supposed to do with these guns anyway?" Cassidy asked on his way out the door.

"What do you mean?" was Patti's response.

"I mean, how the Hell are we supposed to fire weapons in our wolf hides?"

"Oh that." Patti teased, "We won't." He smiled widely at Cassidy and got in the car. Cass just shook his head and hopped in the Mustang.

~~~~~~~~~~~*~~~~~~~~~~~

By the time they got to the festival, The Founder had gone. But Tad waited for them to arrive so he could tell them about it before he left with Jessica. Liam and Luke had found Tad right after the fact. There was still a lot to do and only three nights left before the full moon, and the full moon was being saved for The Regulators. Tad would have to explain to Jessica why he couldn't see her again after tonight. He would wait till tomorrow of course, and he hoped she would understand. He would have to tell her something other than the truth, however, because the truth might be too much for her. He did want to see her again. After the moon.

Tad said his 'see ya laters' to his comrades and took his girl home with him. Jess said 'tootles' to Hannah who was on her way over to Carlo's booth, and the guys stood around deciding what to do next.

"Well, I'm goin' back over to the apartment since we missed our guy. You guys commin' with me?" Patti asked them.

"Sure." Liam shrugged, "Maybe we ought to pick up a couple of these women before we go."

"That might happen." Patti agreed. "Cassidy, you and Luke want to join us?"

"You know I don't want to take anything home with me. Besides, if Luke here agrees with me, I'd like to take him for a ride and get to know him better. I'm sure his little girlfriend would appreciate that, huh?" Cassidy smiled and grabbed Luke around the shoulders.

"I guess." Luke said reluctantly. He couldn't really figure out what Cassidy had in mind and he really wasn't that jazzed about hanging out with him alone. But he was right about Chloe not wanting him hitting on other girls.

"Maybe we can go pick her up?" Cassidy threw another promise in that made Luke feel more comfortable about it. Patti and Liam just looked at each other, both of them not really sure this was a good idea. Patti pulled Cassidy aside, "What the fuck are you doing?" he asked him.

"What? I can't bond with the boy? I made him." Cassidy grinned.

"Less than twelve hours ago you tried to fight him. Now you want to go joyriding with him?"

Cassidy shrugged, "Sure."

"Whatever." Patti let go of his arm and threw his hands up, "What the fuck *ever*!"

Cassidy smiled pleased with himself for aggravating Patti once again. Then he looked over at Luke, "Well?"

"Let's go, I guess." Luke answered. They waved at the guys as they headed for the gateway to leave. Patti and Liam just stood and watched them leave. "Tad isn't going to like this." Liam said as he shook his head. Patti nodded in agreeance, "I know." He sighed. Then they turned and entered the belly-dancing tent. Liam made one last glance toward the gateway before he went inside the tent. He hoped the boy would be all right.

They hopped in the Mustang and Cassidy fired it up. Luke already felt uncomfortable. He didn't know what to say to Cassidy, and he feared him. He was beginning to feel like this was a big mistake. He decided to make small talk.

"I really love this car." Luke said. Cassidy lit up a cigarette and unrolled the window a little.

"Yeah? It's a '67. My favorite." Cassidy returned the small talk.

"What's under the hood?"

"A supercharged 302. Fuel injected. Can't beat it." Cassidy smiled over at him and revved the engine a couple of times then he punched it and flew out across the road, causing traffic to screech to a halt. Luke pressed back into his seat and braced himself. The car shot like a bullet down the highway. Luke was freaked out and excited at the same time. Cassidy flew by the seat of his pants and Luke could see the charge in living life that way. Cassidy wasn't afraid of anything, Luke really did admire that but he was also mean and that wasn't the way Luke was brought up to be.

They raced down the road and out into the boonies. It was fun but Luke's nerves were still on edge. He didn't trust Cassidy, and really wasn't interested in being friendly with the murderer of his kin. To make it worse, Cassidy had this haphazard way of driving that made Luke nauseas. He had one hand on the wheel and the other in the back floorboard, feeling around in the dark for something, and the embers from his cigarette were flying into Luke's face from the open window. Finally he pulled back into his seat with a bottle of Bacardi rum in his hand. "Here." He shoved it at Luke then started flipping around the radio stations. He finally decided to throw in a CD, classic Van Halen, and turned it up, then he grabbed the rum bottle and stuck it between his legs and twisted the cap off. He kicked the bottle back and chugged. Luke had never seen anyone drink liquor like that before. They had been drinking beer the night before at Patti's and Cassidy had drunk rum, but he didn't kick it back that hard. This was perfect, Luke thought, he was in the middle of nowhere flying down a dark highway in a bullet with a rummed madman at the wheel. Luke felt like the song playing was written for him, 'Runnin' with the Devil', how poetic, he thought. Luke was so tense he was turning white. Cassidy shoved the bottle back at him. "Here. You hit it it'll loosen you up."

He took the bottle, if for no other reason then to free up Cassidy's other hand so he could put it back on the wheel. He did, and then he took his left hand and flicked his cigarette, then let *it* hang out the window. Cassidy glanced over at him, "Drink."

"I really don't like rum." Luke offered an excuse.

"I really don't care. Drink it. You look like you've got rigor mortis."

Luke reluctantly kicked back the bottle and sipped it. He squinched his eyes at the powerful burn. It was like drinking rubbing alcohol. "Oh my God!" he yelled and coughed. Cassidy laughed at him.

"Hit it again, it gets better."

So Luke threw it back again. It was still bad, but after about the fifth time, it *was* better, or at least, he could no longer taste it. He was buzzed enough that he just didn't care. Cassidy was flying, his foot to the floor. They were topping 140. But Luke was not as concerned since he was getting drunk. He looked over at Cassidy, "How fast are we going?"

Cassidy looked at the gauge then over at Luke, "You don't want to know."

"Aren't you afraid we'll wreck?" Luke slurred.

"Why? It won't kill us. We're immortal now."

Luke thought about it for a minute then he said, "Yeah, but it'll hurt like Hell."

Cassidy laughed at him and started to slow down some. They were entering a residential neighborhood. He slowed even more and turned down another street with fewer houses on it. He turned down the stereo, turned the engine and lights off and coasted to a stop across the street from a little white, run-down looking house on their left. Luke was curious. He sat up in his seat and asked Cassidy what they were doing.

"Wait. Have another drink." Cassidy handed him the bottle. After about three minutes they heard yelling. There were about four cars in front of the house and they could hear a lot of male voices laughing and yelling loudly.

"I want to teach you something." Cassidy whispered, "Do you know whose house this is?"

Luke looked at the house and then nodded his head.

"Your girlfriend lives here." Cassidy smiled. Luke looked over at him with a question mark on his face.

"I know." He said.

"Did she tell you she was abused?" Cassidy purred. He knew exactly what he was doing. He chose his words carefully. He had wanted the opportunity to make Luke a little more like him, and a little less like Tad.

"She said," Luke stopped to think for a minute, the rum playing games with his memory and thought process. Cassidy had fed him just enough to mold him. "She told me they weren't very good to her. She said Jared slaps her sometimes. She wants to run away."

"She wants you to save her, Luke boy. That's why she told you that." Cassidy grinned slyly from the shadows of his car. It was black like him. He turned up the bottle.

Luke's heart was involved and his temper was flaring a little. The thought of Chloe in that hovel being mistreated was peaking his anger, and Cassidy knew it.

"You know," Cassidy began again, "When I caught them this afternoon, Jared was going to hit her. He stopped when he saw me, but he had his hand reared back ready to hit her. She was crying, Luke. It was terrible." Cassidy smiled like a Cheshire cat, "Did you see the bruises on her arm?"

Luke was seething with anger. His breathing was shallow, his fever was rising, and his retinas were burning. He slammed a fist into the dash and turned to look at Cassidy. "Yes I saw them!" he shouted. His eyes were changed. They were yellow in the iris and fire red around the outside, and his pupils glowed white from within. The curse was peeking in him. It was three days until the full moon, but Cassidy had figured out that with the right trigger the curse could be fired up at will. Cassidy was going to test what he already knew could be done. He smiled his favorite way and continued to fuel the fire he had started.

~~~~~~~~~~*~~~~~~~~~~

Bloodshed Is For Brothers

The night had been long and lustful for Tad and Jessica. The pair had pleasured each other on every surface in the cabin, and finally made it into Tad's bed. Jessica lay sleeping next to him. He looked over at her and wondered how he would tell her about himself. He had to tell her goodbye tomorrow because of the events that were to follow the full moon. He didn't want her within range of any of that violence. And he would eventually have to reveal his alter ego to her if he wanted to keep on seeing her. He needed to keep seeing her. He couldn't keep himself isolated from life and screw around like Patti and Liam. He needed someone he could trust, but how? If she did believe him, would she still want him? He had a lot of thinking to do between now and morning. It would be a long night for him. He had to choose his words carefully. He wouldn't sleep.

~~~~~~~~~~*~~~~~~~~~~

Patti and Liam had hooked up at the belly dancer tent. After partying their asses off, and even joining in on a dance or two, the guys had picked up five of the women in the tent to take home with them. Three of them were dancers and the other two were ardent admirers. Patti and Liam fans, who knew? They were really taking full advantage of this pheromone thing. Why not? It was one of the few perks to this lupine disease. They loaded up the cruiser, threw on the lights and drove back to the apartment . . . drunk.

~~~~~~~~~~*~~~~~~~~~~

Meanwhile, back in the Mustang parked on Redbush Drive, Cassidy was conducting his little experiment. Three days until the fullest moon, would it be full enough tonight to light up some chaos? Cassidy lived for this shit. It's what he did best. He continued to enrage Luke with stories of neglect and abuse coming from within the walls of Chloe's little run-down house. Finally he talked Luke into getting out of the car and sneaking around the house with him so he could see for himself. This, Cassidy figured, should be enough to bring on the beast in him.

They got out of the car and snuck across the road and over to the side of the house that was the darkest. They slowly stood as tall as they could and peered into the available window that looked into the kitchen across the sink. There little Chloe was, scrubbing the dishes like Cinderella. They could look past her into the next room, the dining room, and then past that into the family room. Only there wasn't much family about this house. There were Jared, Darby and about three or four other greasy bastards, whooping it up in the family room. Beer cans flying to the floor that Jared would scream at Chloe about picking up. They were watching a game on T.V. and laughing and jumping out of their seats wildly, and slamming their bottles and cans to the floor. Every time causing the poor browbeaten girl to flinch.

Luke watched and as he watched he seethed with anger. Cassidy was right. He hadn't been lying like Luke had thought he might be. Unfortunately he was right. They continued to watch unnoticed by Chloe. Then Darby yelled at her from the living room. "Git in here yu worthless li'l wretch, an' pick up these God damn beer bottles!! It's the last time I'm askin' yu nicely!!"

Luke's nostrils flared and he went to head for the front door. He was going to pull Chloe out of this shit-hole right now! He couldn't stand it any longer. Cassidy stopped him and put a finger to his lips, "Shhh, just wait." He whispered, "Wait for the right moment, boy." Luke stared him in the eyes. Their pupils shined and flashed. He would listen to Cassidy, maybe they were finally bonding. They turned back to the window in time to see Chloe on the floor picking up bottles and cans and to see Jim Rickford, her pronounced and forced fiancé', reach out and grab a handful of her ass. She stood up and whirled around, dropping the bottles and shouted, "Don' touch me!!" to his face only to have Jared stand up and backhand her hard across the cheek, knocking her to the ground. "You little BITCH!! You're his in a few months and he can do to you what he damn well wants!! So show some respect!!" Then, while she was still down he stuck his foot out and kicked her in the side with the heel of his boot.

Cassidy had to forcibly retain Luke; he was shaking and growling, deeply. Gutturally. It was happening! Just a little longer. "Wait, Luke. Wait for it." Cassidy coached. The excitement and adrenal rush of it was lighting up his own eyes, emotion *was* the trigger. He smiled behind Luke, you know the way, and held him by the arms. Chloe wasn't getting up. Jim Rickford just sat back in his chair and laughed. All of them laughed and pelted her with cans. Darby finally got up and grabbing her by the arm, yanked her to her feet. "Finish this mess before yu git werse, yu little twat!!"

She staggered, holding her side and crying to the sink. They had made her carry the cans and bottles with her. She dropped them in the garbage and leaned on the sink clutching her side crying, and coughing, and gasping. Luke and Cassidy ducked down and back into the shadows so they could see her but she couldn't see them. Luke didn't want her to see him like this, but he didn't want her mistreated even more. His body began to shake and tremble as the transformation process had begun. He growled and stretched and tried to do it quietly. Cassidy cheered him on, "Come on Luke, boy! Come on! We can do it! We can finish them and save the girl! Just like the storybooks!" His voice was quaking and getting raspy. He was pushing himself to shift. He welcomed it. It empowered him. He thought about his last meeting with Becca and he used the pain in his heart to fuel his rage. He growled and shook as his body too began to stretch. He smiled and stared up to the sky as the fever flooded his body.

Just then Chloe took a quick glance behind her to the family room and creeped over to the dining room that led to the front porch. Then, pulling all of her strength she ran for the front door, yanking it quickly open and running out off the porch, down the stairs and into the street. She held her side in pain as she ran and she didn't look back as Jared came out the door behind her. She ran up the street and past the Mustang into the night. He screamed at her and slammed a beer can to the ground in anger. "You little Bitch!! Don't you dare come back or I'll beat you where no one will know you!!" Cassidy held onto Luke in the bushes as they watched these events through their new eyes. This was it! Their moment! As soon as Chloe was out of sight Cassidy let him loose, they were both in the final stages of the shift.

Jared stood on the stoop and cursed under his breath, he was about to go back inside when he heard it, a deep growling sound coming from beside the house. He started to walk slowly towards it. Then he saw the eyes flashing at him from the darkness. He could feel his skin go pale. Chills ran up his spine. The eyes were bright and the growling was deep, indicating to him that this was one big animal in the bushes. He backed up slowly and hauled ass for the front door. He ran inside and slammed the door shut causing the other men to rise to their feet. He was out of breath and stuttering.

"Good Lord, man, what is it?" Darby asked him. But before Jared could answer the growling was on the porch and through the windows the men could see the shapes of two very large animals on the porch. "What the Hell?" Jim Rickford whispered. Jared shakily and slowly turned around and backed back into the room with his buddies. They stood in the dining room and watched, fear stricken as the shapes went from a four-legged position to a standing one and wiggled the doorknob. Through the frosted glass on the front door they could see the shadows of two wolf-like heads atop two hairy man-like bodies. They could see the wide toothy grins and drooling mouths. The animals were toying with them. Cassidy was heightening the suspense by taking his time, a tactic he had learned from his own experience with The Founder. The men trembled with fear, afraid to talk. Then they watched in horror as the door opened a crack and slowly creaked open to reveal the creatures standing on the other side. Cassidy and Luke jumped through the doorway in their wolf-skins and walked on wolfy legs toward the petrified men.

Darby yelled out at them. "What do yu want?!! Git out!!" Then, as if on cue, Hell broke loose. The men parted and fell into different rooms. Jim Rickford and his two buddies rolled into the family room, while Darby and Jared headed for the kitchen. Cassidy went for the rednecks in the front room and let Luke have at O'Bannon and Duggan. He snapped at them with big wolfy jaws as they ran past him into the kitchen. Jim and his pals tried to surround Cassidy. Then one of them spotted the shotgun in the corner of the room. Cassidy just stood reveling in the power of himself and *let* them grab it. He knew it was there before they did. He had smelled the gunpowder when they first came into the room. He was playing with them.

In the kitchen, Luke had already gone for Jared. The men were backed against the sink. When Luke came at them, they went in opposite directions. Luke followed Jared. He was infuriated. He hated the man. Jared cursed and cussed at him. "You ugly beast!! Come on, I'll fight ya!!" He put his fists up at the creature. "Come on!!"

Just then the shotgun went off, KABLAM!! Luke and his prey all flinched at the sound and turned to look in Cassidy's direction. One of the men had grabbed the gun and fired it, grazing Cassidy's shoulder. The beast smiled and walked over and took the rifle away from the man, and holding it by the barrel, began pummeling him to death with it. Cassidy swung and swung and bashed at the man across the face and head. Back and forth like he was swinging a bat. The man's skull crunched and cracked as he was struck blow after blow, till he fell into a bloody heap onto the floor. The other two men began smashing furniture over Cassidy's back and head trying to stop him. Cassidy threw down the rifle. He turned and quickly grabbed the man to his right by the throat and began to squeeze as he lifted him off the floor. The man choked and grasped at Cassidy's claws trying to free himself from the animal's grip. But within seconds his throat was crushed and Cassidy threw his limp body to the ground next to his bloody beaten cohort. Then he whipped around to face Jim Rickford. The man shook all over and reached for one of the old swords hanging on the wall behind him. Cassidy let him yank it off the wall and swing at him. Once, then twice, the blades tip sliced Cassidy's chest. He flinched then reached out and with lightning speed and deadly accuracy; he snapped Jim's wrist causing him to release the sword. With his free hand, Rickford reached out and grabbed the pendant dangling around the beast's neck. It snapped off and fell to the floor as Cassidy picked him up over his head then quickly back down snapping his back across the coffee table, killing him instantly.

Back in the kitchen Luke had Jared pinned. He finally got close enough to lunge at him, ripping and slashing at the bastard as he moved. His claws were like scalpels. Luke slashed him open across his chest and stomach, just enough to cause him excruciating pain and suffering while he bled to death. All he saw was red. All he thought of was Chloe suffering. He wanted Jared and Darby to suffer too. He had lost his humanity. As Jared slumped to the floor and gurgled and choked on his own blood, Luke leaned over him and with one more slash to the stomach, ripped Jared's beer gut open and spilled his guts all over the floor. Blood washed over his clawed wolf feet as Luke watched Jared die through hollow yellow eyes.

Suddenly, Darby smashed into him with a steel chair from behind. Luke stood straight as if to stretch his back out, then turned slowly to face him. As Luke drew closer to him, he backed up and up till he found himself against the wall. Luke got close to Darby's face and let the man feel his own doom. He stared into Darby's widened eyes and he snarled. He growled and he put his wolfy claws around the man's neck and began to raise him up off the floor. Darby was trembling with fear. He couldn't take his eyes off of the beast's face. But as they shared a stare, Luke suddenly became aware of what he was doing. The rage was lifting as he looked into the frightened man's eyes. His humanity was returning. Luke's face softened, his ears lowered and his lip uncurled. He started to loosen the grip he had around the man's throat. What he didn't see, however, was that Darby was reaching out to his right, trying to grab a butcher knife off the counter next to them while Luke was distracted.

Just as Darby got a good grip on the handle, just as he had it raised to stab Luke in the head, Cassidy came out of nowhere and grabbed the man's wrist and slammed it to the wall. Luke turned to see the knife in Darby's hand, and suddenly found his rage again. He turned to look the man in the face once more, and squeezed hard on his throat, angry and snarling and drooling. Darby shook and choked as Cassidy applied fast pressure to his wrist, breaking all of the bones in it. He could hear the bones in his own body crushing. He loosened his grip. The knife fell. But before it hit the floor Luke had swiftly, in one fluid movement, released his grip on Darby's neck and lunged forward with his mouth wide and crunched down, wrapping his mouth all the way around the bastard's neck slicing and tearing and snapping through it. He kept squeezing down with his jaws, sawing and cutting quickly through ligaments and the man's jugular. Warm blood tricked down Luke's throat and sprayed out of his mouth. He kept biting and crushing as he pictured Chloe being kicked and beaten and pelted with beer bottles, till finally his teeth met, and the head of Darby O'Bannon rolled over his face and off his shoulder and hit the floor with a PLUMP! The whole thing seemed to be in slow motion to Luke. It had seemed to happen slowly and taken forever, but in fact he had moved with such speed that it had actually only taken seconds. So fast in fact that the man's head hit the floor only a split second behind the butcher knife.

Luke stepped back on blood soaked haunches and let Darby's body fall. Blood poured out of Darby's headless corpse all over the floor.

Luke looked over at Cassidy. Cassidy had helped him. He looked into the eyes of his new brother. Cassidy grinned that sadistic grin through his wolf-skin, and then he shook his head from side to side hard, like an animal would do. Blood went flying from his fur and splattered all over the walls of the kitchen. It all still seemed to be in slow motion to Luke and in technacolor. It was horrific. Even from behind his inner-lit eyesight, the colors were vivid and nightmarish. He threw his head back and howled long and hard joined by Cassidy, then he watched as Cassidy reached down and picked up Darby's head and threw it like a baseball through the front room window and out into the yard.

They exchanged another glance then Luke followed Cassidy outside the house. Neighbor dogs were barking at them as they walked on animal feet towards the Mustang. They began to shake the blood off themselves in the street. There weren't many houses on this street, but they were close enough that Luke was certain someone had to have heard the attack, or at least the gunshot. A few lights had come on in some windows. His heightened awareness was bringing him back to himself. He tried to shake off the wolfiness. Cassidy had come back almost fully and had opened the driver's side door and gotten in. He reached over and opened the other door so Luke could get in too.

They took a few more minutes to become themselves then Cassidy cranked the car. Luke supposed Cassidy didn't worry about anything at all. He didn't seem the least bit affected by what had just happened. He wasn't in a hurry trying to leave the scene or anything. He just sat there lighting a cigarette and unrolling the window, naked and blood covered. Luke's eyes were still lit and his heart was pounding through his chest. He was panting and breathless. He couldn't believe what he had just done. What would Chloe do now? What would Patti do? Someone was bound to call in more police to investigate. They didn't say anything to each other for a few minutes. Cassidy finished his cigarette, then reached down and picked up his rum bottle. He chugged it down then handed it to Luke, and then reached into the glove box and started to feel around for something. Luke chugged it too. He wanted to get the taste of Darby's blood out of his mouth. Cassidy finally pulled back into his seat. He had a joint in his hand and he began to light it. He hit it then handed it over to Luke. This was something else Luke rarely did, but he took it and hit it. He needed something to deaden himself for a while. His head and body were reeling.

Cassidy exhaled then put the car into gear and made a big loop in the road and punched it, squealing the tires and flying up the road and back out onto the highway again. He began to smile as he drove. His mission accomplished. He felt positively invincible. The wind rushed through his hair as they barreled down the road. This was his reality and he liked it. Luke decided not to worry anymore tonight. He unrolled his window and leaned back in the seat and smoked the rest of Cassidy's joint and drank his rum. He looked up at the moon through his car window, no longer worried about whether Cassidy would wreck the car, or getting caught after what they did, or if Chloe would be O.K. now. He knew she would. He was a little concerned over Tad kicking his ass, but maybe he would understand, it was for Chloe. He looked over at Cassidy smoking a cigarette and tried to reason how he should feel about the man now. He was an evil bastard, but Luke couldn't help but admire him. No matter how dark he was.

~~~~~~~~~~*~~~~~~~~~~

The next morning, Tad awoke to Jessica biting his neck and stroking him. So after another screaming, scratching romp in the sack, they made their way to the shower for yet another encounter. Tad had lost count through the night just how many times, and *ways*, they had enraptured each other. He was already getting spoiled to this. It was going to be very hard to say goodbye to her later.

He finally made his way back into his pants and decided to go to the kitchen to make some breakfast for them. As he walked out of the bedroom he was surprised to find The Founder sitting in his great room, smoking.

Tad pulled the door shut behind him and whispered, "What the fuck are you doing here?"

"I hope you don't mind, I let myself in."

"Yah, well, you've got lousy timing. But make yourself more comfortable, please." Tad answered sarcastically as he approached the adjacent sofa.

"Sorry, lad." The Founder smiled, "I don't mean to intrude. That's quite a little Hellcat you've got yourself there. I could hear her screaming all the way up the driveway. You must be quite a stud. It's a good thing you are all the way up here in the mountains."

Tad's nostrils flared, but at the same time he *was* feeling a little proud of his own sexual prowess. He tried not to overreact so he calmly asked, "What is it that you want, William?"

The Founder stood and began to stroll around the room. Tad could see the restraining collar around his neck peeking up out of his shirt. "I thought you should know . . . something happened last night. Something that will affect your plans for the moon."

"Oh?" Tad was curious, "What?"

"Your boys did a little damage. Damage that will require a lot of cleaning up." He drew on his stogie, slowly. He always took his time with everything. Time was all he had, and he had *plenty* of it. "You might want to think about getting that girl out of here pretty soon."

"What do you mean?" Tad got closer to him. He actually liked the old bastard despite what he had cost him. "Which boys?" He stared into The Founder's eyes to retrieve more answers. "Cassidy."

Tad shook his head and ran his hands over his hair. He turned back around to look at The Founder. "Why did you come here? You know I'll find out about Cassidy. What do you really want?"

The Founder smiled at him, "You really are the most clever, Thadeas." He paused, "I want to warn you."

"Warn me about what? Don't they know you're here? Didn't they send you down here this morning?"

"They did." He walked over and got as close to Tad as he could so they could make eye contact. What he had to say he didn't want the Agency to hear. It only took a moment for Tad to understand. In his mind he heard The Founder say, 'Your girl'. He looked very concerned and he backed up a little. He kept eye contact with The Founder and nodded. The old man was trying to help him.

"I'm sorry I can't stay longer. I must go. Tell your she-wolf in there I said, 'ado'. Until next time, my boy." The Founder saluted Thadeas as he headed out the side doorway.

Tad stood in the same spot and pondered what the man had told him for a minute. What did they want with Jessica? He'd be damned if they'd get their hands on her. He turned around and went into the bedroom after her. He'd deal with Cassidy later. Right now he had to get Jessica out of the cabin.

~~~~~~~~~~*~~~~~~~~~~

The Blood Spilleth Over

Carlo was a good brother. He loved his sister very much. When they were kids she had taken care of him, and protected him. Now he was big enough to take care of her. She was frightened, and he wasn't sure why. She was keeping a lot of secrets from him here lately, and all he could figure was that it had something to do with this man she was hiding from him. She was protecting him, but from what, from who? He had to figure it out. He had to help her.

He had to work the festival every night of the event and some days too. He was representing the new pub he had purchased. While it was being renovated, he was at the festival. So in between, he was trying to find time for Becca and his new girlfriend Hannah. He liked Hannah, she was funny and he liked her loyalty to her friend Jessica. It said a lot about her character. She had also been really hitting it off well with his sister. He was going to see if maybe Hannah could get something out of Becca. Maybe she would confide in another woman. He hoped it would work.

Hannah had agreed to help him out at the festival tonight. It ought to be fun. She was very motivated and supportive of his owning his own business. She might just be the one. She was just what he needed, right when he needed it the most. It had been a hard year.

He dropped Becca off at work and picked Hannah up early at the Hotel. He wasn't looking forward to her leaving in two days, but they had already made arrangements to see each other after the festival. His new pub, The Golden Earring, was located halfway between them, off the main highway. Great location, and it wouldn't be a problem for them to see each other all the time. That was a good thing.

He smiled at her as she approached the car. "You look beautiful this morning." His compliment gained him a smile and a great French kiss.

"Where is Jessica? Is she coming with us?" he asked with Hannah's arms still around his neck.

"No," Hannah kind of frowned, "She's still at Tad's. She said he had something to tell her, so she'll meet us at the festival later."

"Alright, then. You ready?" he smiled.

"I am!" Hannah beamed. She was very excited over Carlo, and she was looking forward to working with him today. It would be fun. Besides, she didn't have anything else planned. She had come to this thing to hit on guys, and she found the best one available on the first night there, so she was content. She had decided to see him exclusively for a while after the festival too. That was something relatively new for her. She was a party girl. Maybe, she thought, it was time to grow out of that. Carlo and Becca were terrific people.

~~~~~~~~~~~*~~~~~~~~~~~

Back at the cabin, Tad had decided to break it to Jessica that he wouldn't be able to see her again after today, at least for a few days. He planned on calling her after this whole thing blew over, but he didn't want her around where something could happen to her. He was falling for her, hard. It was more than just the sex. The sex between them was white hot, but it was so much more than that. It was everything about her. Her demeanor was perfect for him, she was even tempered and well educated, she was beautiful and articulate, she had the same work ethic he did, she wasn't loose and she had this whole inside scoop on the supernatural. She knew more about werewolves than he did and he *was* one! Which brings us to the task before him. He had to decide if it was really fair to keep her and have these feelings for her knowing what he was bringing her into. If what he was feeling was love, then how could he involve her in this half-life, full of murder and moonlight and intrigue? It may have sounded romantic, but it was really very indecent. It may be forever, and that was a long time to share a curse.

He decided to take her out of the cabin for breakfast. He had told her he needed to talk to her about something, and he had pondered as to whether he should tell her the truth yet all night. He had decided it was too much too soon. So he had come up with a reasonable excuse that wasn't completely lying either. What a way to start a relationship, he thought.

They sat down for breakfast and she immediately wanted to know what was up. "So what's up?" she asked him point blank. She could feel the strong chemistry between them so she wasn't *completely* worried about what he had to say, she really didn't think he was going to give her the brush off, but she *was* still worried. She could tell something was troubling him. He reached across the table and held her hands in his and kissed them. Then he began with, "How do you feel about me?"

She decided to be honest. She had nothing but honesty to give him so here goes, she thought, "Well. The truth is . . ." she paused. This was a lot tougher than she had thought it would be. She decided to just spit it out, "I think I'm in love with you."

He smiled at her, and he leaned across the table and kissed her. That was what he had hoped to hear. He admired her honesty. He hated himself for not being able to give her that in return, at least not today. He started differently, but got to the same subject. "I have some *very* strong feelings for you too. I want us to keep seeing each other. Is that O.K. with you?"

She was still smiling, only not as wide as she had been. He hadn't used the 'L' word. Was that bad? She didn't have very much experience in this arena. Not very *good* experience anyway. "Um," she looked down and composed herself. She pulled her hands into her lap. She was afraid she might cry. She was very fragile when it came to Tad. She very much wanted to keep him. "Yes. I think that would be great." She decided she would take what she could get out of him. Maybe he would fall in love with her over time.

He sensed she was upset. He got up and moved over to her side of the booth. She scooted over for him and he held her face in his hands. "I'm falling hard for you too." He whispered. Her spirits refilled themselves. She felt her heart pounding. She cried anyway. "I was so worried you were going to tell me to go."

He held her hands, "I'm not going to be able to see you again until after the festival." He just spit it out before any confusion set in. "Liam and I, we have a chance to do some full moon field work over the next couple of days, and we're going to be camped out in the mountains. I'm sorry."

"Oh." She was trying to understand. She wanted to trust him but she still felt he wasn't telling her everything, and this meant she would be back at school when his field trip was over. She tried to hide her immense disappointment. "Oh, well O.K., I still have some field work of my own to do at the festival before it ends. I'll be fine."

"I promise. As soon as the full moon is over, I'll come up and get you. I promise you." He kissed her, he knew she was still worried, "Trust me, please. Alright?"

She nodded and smiled sweetly at him, "Alright." What choice did she have, really? This relationship was so new. She had to believe in his promises.

They ate breakfast, and then Tad returned Jessica to where he had found her only five nights ago, at the gateway to the Full Moon Festival. He walked her inside and kissed her goodbye. Then, as hard as it was, he turned and left. He had to get out to Patti's and rally the guys. He had to clean up whatever mess they had gotten into.

~~~~~~~~~~*~~~~~~~~~~

SOMEWHERE NEAR THE LAKE . . .

Cassidy got up and got out of the car and wandered down to the lake to bathe. He dove in and shook his hair around in the water to wash it out. He stretched his arms out and flexed them a couple of times to get his blood flowing, and he breathed the air in deeply. He truly felt alive. He shook his head hard from side to side to get the water out and after he felt he was clean he got out and walked back up to the Mustang. He reached in and got the keys out of the ignition and opened the trunk. He had most of his clothes in there from where Becca had kicked him out the last time. He threw on a pair of jeans and a T-shirt, grabbed a couple of things for Luke and slammed the trunk lid down hard.

The sound of the trunk slamming jolted Luke awake in the passenger side. He reached up and grabbed his head. It was ringing and he was light headed. Cassidy tossed the clean clothes onto the hood then jumped in the driver's seat and grabbed his cigs off the dash. He lit one and exhaled in Luke's direction, then offered a comment, "You look like Hell."

Luke scooted up in his seat. His whole body ached. His hair was sticky with dried blood and it was all over his face too. He was naked and his ass was sticking to the leather seats. He looked over at Cassidy, who was surprisingly clean. "Don't we live there? Where are we at?"

"The lake. Go get a bath." He pointed out the front window to the lake in front of them. Luke looked at the water then back at Cassidy, "What happened last night, Cassidy? I don't feel right. Why did we do that?"

"You're still drunk. Go get a bath. You're fuckin' up my car." Cassidy offered no explanations, reasons or excuses. He just gave orders. Luke took another minute to shake off the alcohol then he staggered out of the car and down to the lake and got in the water. It was cold. "Oh, shit!!!" he shouted as he walked in, shivering violently. Cassidy laughed at him and then started to groom himself in the rear view mirror. He noticed his medallion was missing. "Damn it!" he shouted, "That fuckin' redneck broke my pendant. Damn it! Damn it! Damn it!"

He finished bitching about his necklace then he got out of the car and grabbed his leather cleaner and some rags out of the backseat and began washing down the Mustang's interior. Luke finally made his way back up to the car, shivering cold. "Here." Cassidy tossed him the clothes off the hood, "Put these on till you get home."

Luke got dressed and waited for Cassidy to finish cleaning up the car. He leaned against the hood. "Why did you take me there last night, Cassidy?"

Cassidy finished up the car and tossed the leather cleaner back in the backseat and tossed the blood-covered rags in the bushes. He drew on his cigarette and smiled at Luke. "Why? Didn't you enjoy yourself?"

"I don't think that's the way I would put it. I'm not sure it was the right thing to do."

Cassidy walked around the car and flicked his cigarette down. "Get in the car." He said, and he didn't say anything else about it all the way to the cabin. Luke decided to not push it. He just couldn't wait to get home.

~~~~~~~~~~*~~~~~~~~~~

When Tad got to Patti's he decided to just go on in. Pat never locked the door anymore. He had no need to. There wasn't much worse than them that could get in. Tad opened the door and walked in. It stank like beer and incense and it was completely dark. All the shades and curtains were drawn. He walked over and pulled one of the blinds. When he turned around, there was Liam, sprawled out on the floor covered in half-naked harem girls. It looked like the Taj Mahal.

Tad laughed a little then walked over and squatted down and shook him. "Liam." He whispered, and shook him again, trying not to wake the women, "Liam!" he shouted a little louder this time. Liam woke up and blinked his eyes up at Tad. Though his vision had been altered from the curse, he still needed his glasses as a human. He reached over and put them on. He wouldn't have needed them to know Tad though.

"What arc you doing here? Where's Jessica?" Liam asked him. He pulled himself up and out from underneath the legs and arms of sweet smelling women. He still had their scent all over him. He liked it. It was a good feeling. He smiled at Tad, proud of himself. Tad helped him up.

"I took her back where I found her for now."

Liam was still smiling at him, waiting for a comment or slap on the back from his friend. Tad quickly realized it and smiled. "Three women?" he nodded at Liam, "You're a real stud."

Liam stood nodding and grinning, "I know." After another minute of congratulations, Tad explained to him that they needed to get out to the cabin and regroup for the moon. Without waking the women, Liam grabbed his clothes and Tad woke Patti up. There were two women in the bed with Patti. Tad just shook his head. He'd want to hear about this later, for sure. He knew he wouldn't have to ask. Then he asked them where Luke was.

Pat and Liam exchanged glances. Tad knew instantly. "Awe, Hell." He shook his head at them, "You didn't let him go off with Cassidy?"

Liam and Patti both just shrugged and Liam offered an excuse, "Well, he didn't want to pick up women with us and Cassidy said he wanted to get to know him . . . I mean . . . well, we knew it was a bad idea, but . . ."

"Never mind." Tad threw his hands up and shook his head some more, "Let's go."

When they got outside Tad told them what The Founder had told him. When Patti heard that Cassidy had done something, a bell went off. "Shit!" Patti yelled out. "Shit! Shit! Shit!" he yanked his sunglasses off and leaned up next to the squad car.

"What now?" Tad wanted to know. He was afraid to ask. He still couldn't believe Liam would let that boy go anywhere with Cassidy alone.

"It's Cassidy. I think I have an idea where they went last night." Patti just remembered the tag. "I need to go check on something. I'll meet you out at the cabin in about an hour."

"All right. But don't be too long. We have to figure this shit out." Tad turned to Liam, "You go on with Patti. I'll see you guys at the cabin."

Liam nodded and got in the squad car. On the way, Patti told Liam what he thought Cassidy was up to.

~~~~~~~~~~~*~~~~~~~~~~~

Becca was finding it hard to keep her mind on her work. After the revelation that was landed on her by Cassidy she found it hard to hold on to any of her beliefs. This reality of sub-reality that was most definitely real, was making her unsure of everything else. It made things both more believable and less believable. She was so confused. She was glad he hadn't been back. But she feared he would be. He had never left her alone for too very long.

She stepped outside the shop and began to sweep the front walk. There was an old Indian man wearing flip-flops sitting in a folding chair outside the door of the shop next door to hers. His name was Mr. Whitehorse. He owned the weapons shop next door, and specialized in all sorts of ancient and modern weapons and relics. His shop was stocked full of everything from Indian arrowheads and bows and knives, to weapons made to ward off and fight supernatural beasts. Some of them were antiques and some were items he had fashioned himself. His store was quite popular among the avid deer and rabbit hunters of the area, as well as hunters from other parts of the country. He really knew his shit.

He sat outside and sipped on his hot tea and smiled at Becca as she walked outside. He was a very sweet old man, and he worried about Becca. She was there quite late most nights by herself. What he knew of Cassidy he didn't like and he had been noticing the changes in him. He said 'Good morning' to her.

She smiled back at him. She loved the old man. He was a lot of company to her most days, and he would sometimes close his shop for lunch and join her in the bookstore for a story and a bite to eat. "Oh," she smiled, "Good morning Mr. Whitehorse, how are you doing today?"

"Oh, just fine, and you?"

"I'll make it I guess."

He smiled and saluted her with his mug in agreeance and took a sip of his tea.

While she was sweeping, a man strolled through the door. Becca turned and said 'Bye' to Mr. Whitehorse who returned a wave then she turned and entered the bookstore behind the customer. He was great looking, kind of sexy and charming. He had sandy blonde hair and a big smile with sultry teal colored bedroom eyes. He approached her and asked her where he could find books on horses.

She fell back into her usual friendly demeanor and tried to put Cassidy out of her mind for a little while. "They are in the back." She pointed to her right and to the back of the room. "Here, I'll show you."

"Thanks." He smiled big at her and she noticed his great dimples, the kind that ran all the way down his face. She smiled back at him and led him to the shelves where the books on animals were at, "Here you go. If what you can't find what you're looking for, let me know and maybe I can order it for you."

"Oh, I think I've found more than I was looking for already." He grinned even bigger. He was flirting with her. It made her smile. It felt good to have someone flirt with her. "O.K." she said and she walked back over to the front counter and began dusting. She couldn't help but smile back at him. He *was* a real cutie. For a moment, she was able to let Cassidy go.

~~~~~~~~~~*~~~~~~~~~~

By the time Tad got back to the cabin, Cassidy had already dropped Luke off and left. He walked inside to find Luke wet and barefoot at the table eating cereal. Luke looked up at him from his bowl, he was ashamed of himself and he didn't quite know what to say. He pushed the bowl away from himself and leaned on the table as Tad sat down across from him, and lowered his head. He wasn't sure how, but he knew Tad must know something. The vibe he was putting out was clearly an angry one.

"So," Tad began, "What happened last night?"

Luke felt like he had been caught stealing the car. He decided to just tell him, "Cassidy." This was harder than he thought, he was leery of Tad when he was angry. After all, he knew whom he was dealing with. Tad had been good to him, Luke felt like he had really let him down. "He took me over to Chloe's house."

"And." Tad snapped at him. He had never had to be gruff with Luke before. He didn't like having to do it now. He knew what was really in Luke's heart and he knew Cassidy could be a strong influence over him, but he could *not* have dissention, especially not now. He was going to have to nip this hard. He hated to, but it was necessary for their well-being. His leadership had to remain uncontested if they were to survive. He wanted Luke to say what he had done out loud. He knew this would have an impact on him.

"We killed her uncle, her step dad, and their friends." Luke felt like he was going to be sick. He couldn't believe he was saying it. He didn't like to say it. He hated himself for going a long with it, and he was afraid of what would happen to them all because of it.

"How?" Tad asked him firmly and matter-of-factly. "Tell me, Luke. How did you do it?"

Luke didn't like Tad being angry and disappointed with him. Tad had been like a surrogate father to him. He could kill Cassidy for leaving him to deal with this, and for getting him into this kind of trouble in the first place! He remembered why he hated him. He felt like he was no better than Cassidy now.

"We . . . shifted and we . . . we . . ." he was having a hard time telling Tad this. "We . . . I . . . tore Darby O'Bannon's head off. And I . . . I ripped . . ." Luke was starting to tear up. He couldn't believe he had done anything this awful. He choked it out while Tad sat still leering at him from across the table. "I ripped Jared's guts out," he was shaking and held his hands up and looked at Tad, "With these . . ." he cried, "I ripped that man's insides out, and watched him die."

Tad didn't alter his expression. By this point he had shared in similar acts of brutality, but none so uncalculated and thoughtless. This clearly had Cassidy written all over it. Tad would have known that anyway without Luke's confession. He felt he had made his point with the boy.

"I will deal with Cassidy when I catch up to him. I expect this sort of thing out of him. But you, Luke, you have so much more sense than this. I expect so much more from you. Even without myself or Liam or Patti present I expect you to make the right decisions. Do you know what trouble this is going to cause us all? I know you feel for Chloe, but it wasn't your place to exact that kind of justice."

"I know! I know!" Luke yelled and put his hands over his face. Tad leaned in and pulled them down away from his face, so he could look him in the eyes, then he said calmly, "We are what we are. We may not have had a choice in that. But we do have a choice in what we do with it."

Luke stopped crying and nodded at him. He felt ashamed of himself and sick. Tad had made his point loud and clear. Luke would not trust

Cassidy again. Tad stood up and walked into the great room. 'Where did Cassidy run off to?"

"I don't know. I think he went to see Becca." Luke answered from the table.

Tad stopped and turned to look at Luke. "Perfect." He said, and then he called Pat.

~~~~~~~~~~*~~~~~~~~~~

Patti and Liam made their way over to Chloe's house. They parked in front and Patti grabbed a couple of evidence bags and his wallet before they got out and started to walk around. Patti was certain what he'd find. Cassidy had become more aggressive over the past couple of months, and more full of himself. He was, in every sense of the word, a killer. He had acquired a taste for it, and he would not pull his punches.

It wasn't long before they found Luke and Cassidy's clothes and shoes on the right side of the house. They exchanged glances, without saying a word they knew what had happened here. Conspicuously, they carried the clothes and shoes to the squad car. Then they decided to go inside and assess the damage.

Patti knocked on the door first, just in case they were wrong in assuming the outcome of things. No one answered, so he reached out for the doorknob. Before he could touch it, it fell open. They walked in, and what they found would have made ordinary men sick. It was just what Patti had feared. This would be hard to cover up. He hoped none of the neighbors had noticed anything yet.

Liam grabbed Patti's arm. "Wait. What about Chloe?" he asked him concerned. Patti looked around the room and shook his head.

"We'll check out the rest of the house, but I don't think that was in Cassidy's plan, and we both know Luke wouldn't hurt her."

"Yeah, I think you're right. I'll go search the bedrooms." Liam offered to do the looking and let Patti do the assessing. After all, he was the expert here. Patti went to the kitchen first. It was hot in the house and the smell of blood was thick in the air. He saw the bodies of Jared Duggan and whom he assumed was Darby O'Bannon lying in the kitchen. Darby's head was missing, but the body type matched. Patti turned his nose up at the smell in the kitchen, his unoppressed olfactory sense working against him. He squinted and turned to leave. He didn't want to step into the kitchen and get blood all over his shoes and track it around the house. The entire kitchen floor was covered in it. Flies had already begun accumulating around the bodies. It was disgusting.

He turned and strolled into the living room and checked the other bodies. He didn't recognize these men. He looked at the way they were killed. One of them had his head bashed in, very unwerewolf-like, but very Cassidy. This was definitely his type of violence. He was about to leave the room when he noticed something shining under the T.V. stand. He grabbed an evidence bag out of his shirt pocket and reached through it to pick up the object. When he pulled it up into the air he recognized it immediately. Liam returned to the room as he stood looking at it. It was a silver pentagram medallion on a chain. Proof positive. Pat put the chain and pendant into the bag and put it in his pocket. Then he turned to Liam.

"Anything?" He asked him. Liam shook his head, and then he asked a question, "Where do you think she is?"

"Probably with a neighbor, or a friend. I don't think she's been here all night. But I bet Cass would know."

"What are we gonna do, Pat? This is bad. I mean real bad."

"Yeah, I know. You should see the kitchen." Patti sighed and looked around the room one more time, deciding what to do. Then the cell phone rang. They both jumped. Patti answered it. "Hello?"

It was Tad. "Hey. Find me Cassidy. Bring him to me now."

Patti had heard him sound like this before. He knew. "I'm on it. Is Luke there?"

"He is." Tad answered as he looked over at his humble ward.

"Man, you would not believe what he's done here. Tell him to call Chloe if he knows where she is and get her to come out to the cabin. Don't let her come home yet. We have a big mess to clean up here."

"He's already talked to her. She left him a message last night and he called her when he got home. He's supposed to pick her up at a friend's house. I'll send him right now to get her."

"I'm gonna do what I can to secure things here, then I'll try to find Cass. Any ideas?"

"Try the bookstore." Tad suggested then he hung up, and sent the boy after Chloe. "Go get Chloe, and bring her here now. Keep her away from her house. We'll let Patti tell her."

Before Pat and Liam could reach the sidewalk, three black unmarked cars rolled up in front of the house and screeched to a halt. Uniformed men wearing wires in their ears jumped out and pulled their guns, pointing them at the guys. "Hold it!!" One of them yelled at Pat and Liam. "Don't you fuckin' move!!" They were surrounded. Patti and Liam threw their hands up in the air quickly and stood there stunned.

"Oh, shit." Pat said under his breath. "This is real trouble."

"Who the fuck are they?" Liam whispered back.

"Feds." Patti told him, "We're in deep shit. Follow my lead."

One of the men in black approached them slowly, "Just keep your hands high, gentlemen." He said firmly.

"I'm a police officer." Patti told them, "I have my credentials in my pocket. I'm not wearing my uniform, but I have my I.D., and I came here in the cruiser." He nodded in the direction of the police car. "I'm responding to a call."

The man looked at the car. He lowered his gun and turned and lifted off his shades to get a better look at the cruiser. He turned back to the guys. "What the fuck is that?" He was referring to the shaker hood and blower mounted above the hood on the squad car.

"Can I please lower my hands? Then I will be happy to explain my car to you."

The man looked him in the eyes and walked up to him. "Just hold perfectly still, and keep your hands up." He said firmly, still untrusting of the two of them, he held his gun on Pat and never lost eye contact as he reached into Pat's back pocket and pulled out his wallet. He backed away and flipped through it finding his badge. Then he lowered his gun and uncocked it. "O.K., you check out. Put your hands down. Who are you?" He looked at Liam.

Patti reached into Liam's back pocket and tossed his wallet at the officer. "He's an animal biologist. A friend. I asked him to come with me and confirm a possible animal attack. A neighbor reported seeing a large animal over here last night."

The man flipped though Liam's wallet, then he asked him, "What's your name and birth date?" Liam answered him quickly, "Liam McConnell. My birth date is June 10th, 1972."

The officer stared at him for a minute then tossed his wallet back to him. "O.K. put 'em down." He turned and made a motion to the other officers to lower their guns. Then he turned back to Patti, "O.K. then, what happened here? We had a report from a hysterical woman claiming that her boys found a man's head in this yard early this morning. She also claimed she called us because the local police were not responding. Can you explain that to me please?"

Another officer searching the front yard called out to the one in charge. "Sir! Over here."

They all joined him in the left side yard to find the brutally severed head of Darby O'Bannon staring up at them from the grass. The agents were all over the house and yard now and Patti and Liam were trying to remain as calm as possible. Patti was doing better than Liam, he was freaking inside. An agent from inside the house came running out and hung his head over the porch rails to puke. The lead investigator looked at Liam. "What do you think, McConnell? Does this look like the work of an animal to you?"

Liam tried to compose himself and reminded himself not to stutter as he squatted down and tried to look like the expert Patti claimed him to be. He was a biologist but he was not a forensics analyst, he did his best to cover. "It's hard to tell for certain without properly testing it, but yes, it does look like it was chewed by an animal. The way the flesh is torn around the neck is indicative of cutting by a predator's incisors, a large predator. It will need further testing to determine the species of animal that could have done this."

Patti stared at him impressed with his cool demeanor and the way he pulled that off. It seemed to impress the lead investigator as well. Liam seemed to be what he claimed to be. He radioed for a forensics team to arrive, and then turned to finally introduce himself to Deputy Leason.

"I'm sorry for the rude greeting. You can't take any chances on a call like this you know. I'm Agent Hannigan." He reached out and shook Patti's hand and then Liam's. Then he asked another invasive question. He couldn't help it. It was in his formal training. "Where's your Sheriff, Deputy? It is customary in a small town like this for him to be present at any major investigation."

Patti had never reported the Sheriff missing after the attack. So many unusual things were happening that Patti had decided to just handle things himself and cover for Sheriff Milligan. The man had no family that would miss him, just Patti. So he kept it to himself and covered where he needed to. He didn't need them replacing the Sheriff with someone new. Not under the circumstances. So he continued to cover. "He's on vacation, sir. He's due back in about two weeks. Just left two days ago.

First vacation the man's had in twenty years. His new girlfriend convinced him he needed it."

"Really?" Agent Hannigan asked, "How nice for him. What's the population of this town, son?"

Patti knew where his questioning was headed. He was nosing around to see if they needed to send in an Agent to cover for the Sheriff until the investigation was over. It was all procedure. This guy was clearly a by the book kind of guy.

"It's about 140 sir. Very small." He didn't want to lie about some small technicality like that. It would ruin his credibility with the man if he checked it out. And he probably would.

"O.K." he pointed to the cruiser, "Now you want to explain that to me?"

"Well, sir, the local boys around here don't have a lot more to do with their time than either get drunk or super build their cars. Some of them are built like rockets. The interceptor wasn't keeping up. So I had it modified. Just the sight of it is a deterrent to speeders."

"Really? Well it isn't regulation, you know. Your superiors might frown on it. But I guess if it helps you keep crime at bay, in a small town like this, I'll overlook it."

"Well Agent, it looks like you've got everything under control here. I have a report to fill out and another call to see about. If you're done with us we'd like to go." Patti asked.

"Well," Agent Hannigan surveyed the yard a moment. A van full of C.S.I. equipment and officials pulled up and began unloading. He decided that was O.K. for now. "Go ahead, but stay within range of your office in case we need anything further. We still need you to be on call for this investigation."

"Oh, yes, sir. Of course." Patti nodded and shook his hand one more time. Liam too. Pat turned and handed the agent a card with his cell phone number on it, then they turned and tried not to run back to the car. Once they got to the cruiser, they jumped in and both took a deep breath or two and got the Hell out of there. "I am going to fuck Cassidy *up*!" Patti growled under his breath. This was a close one, and they still weren't in the clear yet. Once Hannigan got inside and saw the men Cassidy had murdered, it would be clear that those men were not attacked by an animal. They hauled ass for the cabin.

~~~~~~~~~~~*~~~~~~~~~~~

Smash It Up

M was holding a meeting. The Professor was present and the General guard, and about a half dozen other delegates for the mission. He began his speech in the boardroom. There was a large map on the wall behind him of the little town with marker tacks stuck to it of varying colors, indicating where different attacks had occurred. M placed a new one in the map over Chloe O'Bannon's house.

"Well!" M shouted, getting everyone's attention as he pushed the tack into place, "It seems our beasts have found a new ability! This is very exciting for us, because it confirms what we had hypothesized about early on in this project. The Founder has not made it easy for us to determine this substantial gift, but our new boys did." He smiled proudly as he paced at the end of the table. One of his superiors interrupted his triumphant speech. "Just how are we to control them?"

"We have managed to control The Founder quite well. I'm sure it will only take a few minor adjustments to control our pack boys in the same fashion. The restraining collar has been quite effective. It releases a heavy dose of a serum we have specially devised at close intervals, to keep the wolf at bay, as it were."

The man spoke out again, not comfortable with M's flippant answer, "Yes, but that is one tired old man. We are talking about five strong young men. A *pack* of werewolves no less. I find it hard to reasonably assume that they can be contained and controlled so easily. Therefore how are we to assume that, if used on a mission, these man-beasts would not turn on the hand that rules them?"

"Well, I will just have to get a little more creative in my efforts." M smiled, "And prove it to you."

Another gentleman spoke up. It was the General Guard. "To assume you can control an animal is one thing. But these are more than that. These are wild, untamed animals with a man's psychology. I have seen what they are capable of in the field. All of our missions have surprised me at how tactful and calculated they can be, and how powerful. It is very clear, as we have learned from The Founder, that they know what they are doing. We have had to go to extreme measures to protect ourselves. Even the Gortex has been compromised a few times."

M seemed irritated with the Generals counter attitude. He stood firmly in one spot and tried again to reassure them. "Gentlemen, I have been working on one more angle no one else has considered. I do believe that the way to ultimately control these beasts has presented itself in the form of a woman."

The room was filled with intrigue and whispering. This had definitely refreshed their interest in M's efforts. And it was lucky for him too; because his superiors were growing very concerned over all the murders and uncontrolled occurrences these werewolves were bringing to the surface. It had all seemed to be getting out of their control, and that M's plan had unbalanced. They were about to pull out funding and acknowledgment.

The man M continued to explain his ideas for the she-wolf. After about an hour's worth of deliberating, M got the go ahead he was hoping for. It was a close call. He almost lost his counter-balance. Afterwards they discussed how to go about helping their little pack clean up Cassidy's mess. It would not be easy for the guys without their help. One of the neighbors had already reported the disturbance to the F.B.I., it would take The Research Facility stepping in now. Their government ties would allow them to step in and override the F.B.I.'s investigation.

~~~~~~~~~~*~~~~~~~~~~

Cassidy had returned to Patti's apartment to get cleaned up. He wanted a real shower and a nap before going back out to the cabin. He figured it would be a bitch session with Tad when he got there, so he wanted to refresh himself with some peace and quiet, and maybe some food before he went back out there. He got there and walked in. There were women everywhere. "What the fuck?" he whispered as he strolled around the room looking at the half naked harem in Pat's living room. "This won't do." He squatted down and shook one of them. "Hey!" he huffed, "Hey bitch get up!"

The girl rolled over and turned her back to him, "Let me have one more hour." She whispered. Cassidy kind of rolled his eyes then tried again.

"Hey!" he shouted again, this time rousing the other two women. One of them yawned and stretched and pulled a blanket up over herself, and then she looked over at Cassidy. "Oh. Hey." She smiled at him, "Who are you?"

"Get up." He huffed at her, "Now. And take your whore friends with you. I don't want to be bothered."

"You sure?" she smiled up at him, laughing at his rudeness. She didn't care what he thought of her, and she was too dingy to be afraid.

"Oh, I'm quite sure." He grunted. Then he heard giggling coming from Patti's room. He stood up and wandered in. The girls in Patti's bed were already up and getting dressed when he pushed the door open. "I don't believe this shit." He shook his head. The girls jumped a little at his presence, then they smiled. One of them offered him a favor. He had lost his patience. He threw the door all the way open causing it to hit the wall. "Get, the Fuck, out!" He yelled at all of them, "Now!!" The girls gave him a disgruntled look and hurriedly picked up the rest of their clothes.

Cassidy turned and headed for the kitchen. He filled a pan with cold water and carried it back into the living room and trickled it all over the women on the floor. They all shrieked and stumbled trying to get up and cover themselves at the same time. He emptied the pan on them then threw it across the room hard to let them know he wasn't going to be friendly about it. One of the girls from the bedroom got a little mouthy as she entered the room and began picking up her shoes. "Who the fuck are you anyway? Where's Pat?"

Cassidy turned around and gave her a hateful look as he reached out and grabbed her by the arm. "Get your shit and get the fuck out!" he growled at her as he escorted her to the front door and shoved her out of it. Her friend from the bedroom hurried her ass out the door behind her, and the others still half naked and shivering from the ice cold water quickly grabbed what they could of their clothes as he drug another woman out the door. One of them ran out in the blanket she was covering herself with. He slammed the door shut hard behind them. The mouthy one was still cussing him from the hallway while he threw them out. She flipped him a bird as the door slammed.

As soon as they had gone he retreated to the shower. He couldn't care less about hooking up with cheap sluts like those. It might be fine for Pat and Liam who don't have anything else, but for Cassidy there were no women but Becca. He didn't want to try. He could have had all of those girls and any others he wanted, but he didn't. He just wanted to get cleaned up, and take a nap, and maybe ride by the bookstore before he went back to the cabin.

~~~~~~~~~~*~~~~~~~~~~

Luke cleaned himself up a little better, then following Tad's orders he took the Jeep and went to retrieve Chloe. The directions she gave him were really simple and even though he didn't know the area real well, he didn't have any trouble finding the place. He had no sooner shut the car door behind him than Chloe came bounding down the driveway to him and jumped up and threw her arms around his neck, planting a huge kiss on his mouth. She was excited and free, only she didn't yet know just how free. Her friend followed her to the car. Luke found it hard to look her in the eyes, and he couldn't hide the solemn look that poured over his face. He was riddled with guilt and disgust with himself. He felt like some kind of cheat.

She pulled away from him and suddenly her face got very serious. "What is it?" she asked very worried, "What's wrong?"

"Something," he started, and then he remembered that Tad had wanted Patti to tell her. He shook his head and looked at the ground, "Just come with me. I'm taking you to my place. We'll talk when we get there."

"Yu're worrying me. Tell me now. Did yu meet someone else?" she was looking a little angry with him now, the thought just crossing her mind.

"No!" he suddenly shouted, snapping out of his stupor, "God, no! You're perfect for me. There is no one else."

"What is it then?" she asked again relieved. Then she told him about her great escape. The one he already knew about. He tried to look surprised. He was no actor. "I ran away from home last night. Do yu think I can stay with yu? Just for li'l while?"

"Uh, I don't know how Tad would feel about that. It's his house." He answered weekly, swerving from the direction of the conversation, "Let's go and you can ask him." He herded her towards her side of the Jeep and opened the door for her.

"If not, Kitty says I can stay here." Kitty handed her her jacket as she got into the car, "Oh, by the way, Luke this is my friend Kitty." Luke turned and shook her hand and pushed out a smile. The girl smiled back and shook his hand. "Hi." She smiled, then she waved at Chloe, "Call me, Chloe, O.K.?"

"I will." Chloe said as Luke shut the door and walked around to his side and got in. She unrolled the window, "Thanks for everythin', all the help. I'll call yu later." She hollered out the window to her friend as they pulled out and drove away.

It was a long ride back. Luke tried not to say anything. He offered to buy her some lunch. Maybe he would feel a little better himself if he had some real food in him. They turned around and headed back toward town.

~~~~~~~~~~*~~~~~~~~~~

Patti and Liam got to the cabin and hysterically told Tad about what happened. They still hadn't located Cassidy. They hadn't tried looking, after the incident with the State Police, Patti's nerves were too shot to do anything else. Besides, they knew he'd turn up sooner or later. They all sat around the table and ran over the details. There really wasn't any way at all it could be linked to any of them. Pat and Liam had retrieved the only evidence available at the crime scene just minutes before they had gotten busted. If they had been even five minutes later in arriving at the O'Bannon house, the F.B.I. would have all the evidence they needed to catch up with Cassidy and Luke.

The three of them hurriedly unloaded the police cruiser of the evidence and cleaned out the trunk. They put Cassidy and Luke's clothes in the wash and hosed off their boots and left them to dry on the deck. The only thing left was the pendant. Patti pulled it out of his pocket and washed it off in the kitchen sink. Thoroughly removing any trace of D.N.A. that might still be on it. If it weren't for Luke, Patti would just as soon let Cassidy hang for this. But they were a tribe now, a pack, and there had to be unity. They had to help each other. They were all they had, and each of them wondered if Cassidy knew that.

~~~~~~~~~~~*~~~~~~~~~~~

Cassidy had gotten cleaned up and decided to skip the nap. He was too keyed up from leftover violence to sleep now. And he was excited about the violence that was yet to come. He knew it would be another fistfight with Tad and he didn't care. And under the moon tomorrow night there would be more bloodshed. The guys didn't really sleep as much before a change anymore. Their metabolisms had finally adjusted to the fluctuations in their blood sugar. In fact, now it was quite the opposite, they were usually hyperaware and high strung. He cranked up the Mustang and headed for the bookstore. He got there in time to see cutie-pie leaving with a book in his hand, flirting with Becca. He could feel himself fill up with rage and jealousy. He seethed from behind the wheel of his hot rod and just watched as Becca followed the man out the door and waved at him with a big smile on her face. She used to look at him that way. Cassidy slammed his fists on the steering wheel still unnoticed by his girl, but not unnoticed by the old Indian seated outside the weapons shop. Cassidy waited until the man had gone and watched Becca kiss Mr. Whitehorse on the cheek. Then after she re-entered the bookstore he peeled out and took his anger out on the road. He would store this up and save it for later. He headed for the cabin, ready for that fistfight now.

~~~~~~~~~~~*~~~~~~~~~~~

M had arranged for a trip to the O'Bannon house. His high guardsman flanked him as well as four other heavily armed foot soldiers plus he had all the authority he needed to put a stop to this investigation. He approached Agent Hannigan and began by flashing his credentials at him. Then within minutes, the Feds were called off and loading up the task vans and C.S.I. equipment, with no further questioning. Agent Hannigan had to submit, he was heavily outranked. That would be the last of the interference from the F.B.I. or the State Police on this case.

After they had dispersed, M made a call on his transmitter, and a new crew arrived. The change unnoticed by the neighbors, the clean-up effort had begun. It would take them all night, but by morning, no one would be the wiser to the carnage that had occurred there the night before. On paper, M would make it look like they were all killed in a hunting accident.

~~~~~~~~~~*~~~~~~~~~~~

As soon as Cassidy pulled into the driveway and stepped out of the car he was greeted on the porch by Tad. Cassidy didn't give him time to bitch he immediately started swinging. The fight ensued into the house. Tables were crashing, lamps were breaking and Tad and Cassidy were beating the Hell out of each other. Normally Patti and Liam didn't interfere, but this was serious, they didn't have time for this macho shit. They tried to pull them off each other. Patti grabbed Cass in the same fashion he had so many times before, and Liam grabbed Tad. They were finally able to pull them apart. Nobody was saying anything for a few minutes; they were all so pissed off and worried.

After a few minutes of panting and saying nothing they finally calmed down enough to speak. "What the fuck, Cass?" Patti started. Cassidy leaned up against a long sofa table next to the front window and licked his wounds, his mouth was cut from Tad's ring, and he smiled, "What do you mean?" He knew exactly what this was about. It was just typical Cassidy bullshit, and Patti knew it.

"Do you have any idea how much trouble you've caused us all?!" Pat tried again. He just wanted for Cassidy to take the situation seriously. Cassidy sat up on the sofa table and grinned at him. Patti was livid. He was building up a rant far worse than Tad could have this time. Cassidy snickered at him, "What? So I can't kill a couple of rednecks every now and then without everybody getting all bent out of shape?"

Patti looked over at Tad, who just shook his head and looked down, then back to Cassidy. "They were people, Cassidy!" He scolded him.

Cassidy dropped his smile and shook his head at Pat, "They weren't people."

Patti threw his hands up in the air, and turned a couple of circles. He tried to compose himself and reason with Cass one more time. He wanted him to have some sense of responsibility over this, some remorse, something. He needed him to realize how serious this was for them all.

"Cassidy, do you realize they have called in the State Police? The F.B.I.? There was a U.S. Marshall standing in Chloe's living room spot-checking the crime scene this afternoon. I could barely explain my squad car, let alone my lack of a Sheriff. Thank God I got there first. Your clothes were still in the yard, damn you! Do you have any idea what we are up against here?!" His voice was starting to elevate again. Cassidy had never seen him like this before. He thought it was funny, he started to chuckle at him.

"What are you all so worked up about? Are you worried that they'll find us? You picked up our clothes. There is no other evidence that would lead them to us." Cassidy rationalized calmly.

Patti put his hands on his hips and sighed and stood there shaking his head for a minute, then he reached into his shirt pocket and pulled out the once bloody medallion, and slapped it into Cassidy's hand. "Not any more."

Cassidy jumped off the table and smiled excitedly, "Hey! You found it!" He smiled wide as he lifted the silver chain out of his hand. He examined it further then scowled a little, "Awe!! He broke it! Damn redneck!"

Patti's eyes got wider and he raised his hands high into the air and shook his head in disbelief at Cassidy's lack of remorse. He looked over at Tad as if to say 'What now?' and turned and fell down on the couch, totally out of ideas. He supposed Cassidy was right. Most of the crime scene looked like an animal attack, and there wasn't any other evidence, but that wouldn't stop them from invading the jailhouse and making trouble for Patti later on.

Tad approached Cassidy with his arms crossed in front of him, "Cassidy!" he said firmly, "What you have done is awful. You have orphaned that girl, and brutally murdered five people. Those State Police aren't just going to magically go away tomorrow, you know. And we still have the Regulators to deal with."

Cassidy just stared him in the eyes as he lit a cigarette and listened to him with that filthy grin on his face. Tad turned to the others. "That's another thing," he made sure he had all of their attention, "The Founder was here this morning. He warned me about The Agency's plans." He looked back at Cassidy, "And he already knew about what you had done."

Cassidy looked confused, "How would he know about that?" he said, finally taking it a bit seriously.

"I imagine The Agency is following us. We all still have our tracking devices, except for you. And as far as I can tell they have been covering up for us this whole time, and drugging us in the beginning. No telling what else." Tad responded.

Now Patti looked confused, he twisted around on the couch and sat up, "But why?"

"Protecting their investment, I guess. The Founder told me to be careful." He wanted them to be careful about what else they said, after all, their attack had been a set-up, he was sure of that now. And they had rented the land and the cabin from the very same government that was conducting this "research". He'd rather not help them out any further. He looked over at Liam. "We need to do a little minor surgery." He tapped on his neck.

Liam nodded in agreement and went to check the field bag. He was a zoologist and usually had all the necessary devices for conducting such minor surgery. They would wait for Luke to arrive with Chloe tonight and handle the situation at hand, and then tomorrow they would pop a few pain pills and let Liam remove the tracking devices.

An hour later Luke arrived with Chloe. When he walked in the guys were finishing cleaning up the mess from the fight, all but Cassidy, anyway. "What happened in here?" he asked Liam.

"Guess." Liam answered. Tad approached and took Chloe's coat. It made her notice that Luke and the others weren't even wearing sweaters. There was no fire in the fireplace and they were all wearing t-shirts. It was weird. The cabin was freezing. She began to rub her arms to warm up. It reminded Tad to act normal and he began to start a fire for her.

"How are you, Chloe?" Patti asked her. She found all the attention a little unnerving. She glanced over her shoulder at Cassidy sitting on the sofa table smoking. She remembered what he had done for her before. Luke had been acting weird all day, and it was making her uneasy.

"Good. Thank yu." She answered him.

"Why don't you come over here and sit down on the couch, I want to talk to you about something." Patti led her by the hand to the couch. She looked over at Luke, he nodded at her to let her know it was O.K., she was really nervous now. Was she in trouble? Had Jared turned her in to the police for running away? Luke stood beside the couch and crossed his arms. Patti tried to find a delicate way of telling her. He sat across from her and petted her hands.

"Chloe, honey." He began, "I have some terrible news for you."

She looked over at Luke and he hung his head. Patti continued, "I had the boy bring you out here, because I didn't want you to go home yet, and I thought it might be a little easier to hear with him here. It's about your guardians."

She immediately could feel her heart racing and the color leave her face. "What happened? Just tell me. Please." She asked him. Luke kneeled down next to her, readying himself to console her.

Patti continued, "Honey they're dead."

She sat there in shock for a moment. Not crying. Not moving. Then she stood up. Patti and Luke stood as well. Tad watched on from the fireplace. "Seriously?" She asked Patti.

"Yes. Are you alright?" He answered. Then a smile started to slip across her face. Patti looked over at Luke with a puzzled look. He was used to people freaking out over news like this, but he wasn't prepared for them to be happy. She smiled, she couldn't stop it and she couldn't say anything. She sat back down.

He asked her again, "Are . . . you alright?" She started to laugh a little. She was so relieved. This was the most terrific news she had ever had! Morbid as it was, it had freed her. Cassidy was the only one that seemed to understand. He began to chuckle.

Luke kneeled back down, "Chloe did you hear him? They're dead. Aren't you upset?"

She looked at him still laughing, "No. Do yu have any idea how unbelievably cruel they were ta me?" She stood up ready to stand on her soapbox. "Well do yu?"

The guys just stood and listened. They didn't know what to say. Was she in shock or did she mean it? They knew she was mistreated, but only Cassidy and Luke had gotten to see how badly, and Luke felt like she should still be remorseful. Cassidy smirked with pride from his spot on the sofa table and smoked as she began to rant.

"They beat me, almost daily. I was forced to live like fucking Cinderella in me own house!" She was beginning to shout now, filled with rage and revelry and emancipation. "They took my birthright and buried my mother in a cheap pine box! They stole that store, that my mother had built and bled for all by herself and put their names on it!!" She turned to Patti and Tad, "They were going to pull me out of schul and force me to marry that hobo looking, greasy fucking redneck Jim Rickford! I hope he was there too, the letching pervert!!" She was snarling and red with anger, her honest Irish temper flaring, "I'm glad they're dead!!"

"Chloe!" Luke shouted at her. Patti grabbed his arm and looked him in the eyes and shook his head, calming him down.

"How did they die?" She asked Patti. He wasn't sure he wanted to tell her. He hesitated, and that gave Cassidy time to step in. "They had their heads ripped off by a wild animal." Cassidy smiled delighted with himself.

"Cassidy!" Tad yelled at him, but Cass just kept smiling.

"Gud!" Chloe shouted in her native accent, "Gud, I say! I thank the heavens for the beast that was sent to free me! I will forever be in its debt!"

"Chloe!" Luke shouted again, "You don't know what you're saying!"

"Shut up!" Cassidy growled at him, and he stood up and smiled at her. The others were speechless. "I like her." Cassidy grinned at her. She smiled at him meekly and suddenly became aware of how crazy she must have sounded. She slowly sat down.

"Well," Patti started after a minute or two of quiet, "I have to tell you not to go near your house until the investigation is over. The county will provide a nice hotel room for you to stay in and transportation to work or school as needed until you can return to the house. You're still under 18, and the law requires me to appoint you with a guardian, but I'm willing to overlook that as long as you behave. I'll also help you acquire a lawyer to figure out any paper work or deeds of trust that you will receive as the primary heir, and help with any necessary arrangements for the funerals of your uncle and stepfather, all right?"

Chloe nodded and tried to resist the urge to laugh or spout more obscenities. She figured she had freaked them out enough tonight. Patti looked over at Luke, "Is she going to stay here with you tonight, or do you want me to follow you to town and get her a room?"

Luke didn't know what to say. To tell the truth of it he didn't know what to feel. He was a little put off by her cold anger towards these people. However, they had been so awfully cruel to her. He just wasn't sure how to feel or what to say. He decided it would be better to take her on to the hotel. He looked to Tad and he could tell Tad would prefer that too. He held her hand so she wouldn't feel unwelcome and he told Patti, "Let's go on into town."

Chloe looked up at Luke from her seat on the couch. She felt bad for showing out so badly and embarrassing him like that. Now she was a little embarrassed herself. She stood up and looked at all of them while Luke got her coat. "I am really sorry. I didn't mean to sound so," she paused a minute, "So cold. It's really quite a shock."

"It's O.K., Chloe." Tad walked over and hugged her, "We understand. More than you know." This made her feel much better. She said 'Bye' to the others and followed Patti and Luke out the door. Luke would get over it as soon as they got her checked in, because she would give herself to him that night. It was better than she had hoped it would be. Her life belonged to her now.

'M' Is For Madman

Hannah decided to spend the rest of the evening with Jessica since she was a little down about Tad. But Jessica didn't want her best friend to miss the last night at the festival with Carlo on her account, so she told her she'd hook up with her the next day before the ride back home, and she excused herself. Jessica wandered over to the werewolf tent and sat in the empty chairs lost in thought over Tad. This is where they had snuck their first kiss, and after tomorrow it would be torn down and put away until next year. She hoped the same thing wouldn't happen to her heart. While she sat there, not taking notes or working on her thesis, The Founder stalked in and sat behind her. He was so quiet and stealthy she hadn't even heard him. "Why so glum, sugar?" he purred. She jumped clutching her chest and rose out of her seat and was staring at him wildly.

"Where did you come from?" she asked him stepping backwards a few steps. She was getting that creepy, eerie feeling again. A lot like the one she got whenever Cassidy was nearby. It was all around him. Her 'Spidey-sense' was going wild.

"Don't fret young lady." He smiled and removed his hat moving slowly and unthreateningly. "I only wanted to talk. I saw you here alone, and thought I would join you. Why so sad?"

Jessica didn't want to be rude. He seemed friendly enough. Maybe this place was just making her jumpy. Then she remembered him. He was talking to Tad the last time they were in this tent together. Hannah had been rude to him. Of course! She sat back down. "I'm sorry." She said, "I didn't mean to be rude. You just startled me that's all. I think we've met before. You know my boyfriend, Tad Thayer?"

Of course he had known this the whole time, but he played along. "Oh, of course." He said, "I thought you seemed familiar. You're friend was offended by my smoke."

"Oh, I'm so sorry about that. She's very outspoken." She extended her hand, "I'm Jessica."

He reached out and keeping eye contact with her, he kissed her hand. "Charmed, young lady. Tad is a lucky man. I'm William."

"Nice to meet you William." She smiled and decided to pry a little, "So, how do you know Tad?"

"Well, we go back a ways. I guess you could say we share an interest in wolves. Kindred spirits, as it were."

"Ahh," she nodded, content with his answer, "He is amazing with them."

"Yes, fascinating creatures. I've always found them near to my heart. You didn't answer my question before. Why so sad?"

"Oh, it's Tad." She sighed, "I wanted to spend more time with him, but he had some research to do this weekend and I won't get to be with him before I leave for home tomorrow. I just hope he wasn't giving me the brush off."

"You know, he is more crazy about you than you know." The Founder reassured her.

"Really? I hope so, because I've really fallen for him." Jessica smiled, glad to hear it from someone who knew him.

"M, hmm. There is so much more to him than you know. Trust in him for what he tells you. And be wary when he is not around."

"Thank you, I think." She smiled at him a little confused by his words, then she asked, "You know, you have a very unusual accent. Where are you from?"

"A long, time ago, Miss Jessica." He stood up and put his hat back on, "A long, long time ago." Then he made his way back out of the tent and into the darkness. Jessica sat there puzzled for a moment, and then she reminded herself she *was* at a "freak fair", as Hannah put it. He was probably just a nice old man that Tad couldn't be mean to. She didn't let it freak her out she just sat and pondered until it got dark. She had started to doze off when she noticed the Professor Saunders walking in. He approached her. She stretched and yawned and prepared to stand up, she decided it was time to go back to the hotel and lay down.

"Professor Saunders," she yawned, "I'm sorry. I didn't mean to stay so long. I'll go."

"Don't rush off on my account." He answered, and as she stood she noticed two other men in dark suits she hadn't noticed before. They almost blended in with the darkness of the night. She began to feel uneasy, but before she could excuse herself or call for help, they grabbed her and held her while Professor Saunders covered her mouth with a chloroform rag. She instantly fell limp. Knocked out cold. They laid her inside a heavy trunk and quickly rushed her out of the tent and into a nearby car. The Professor nervously looked all around all the way to the car, afraid of Tad catching him. As much as he loved these mythical monsters, he feared them even more, and he lived in fear of them coming for him one day. He got into the car and it sped away toward the research facility. He sighed with relief that no one saw him do it.

The Founder watched from the trees. He had seen it happen, but they hadn't seen him. He smiled and smoked his stogie. "Well, well, well." He said to himself. "How *very* interesting."

~~~~~~~~~~~*~~~~~~~~~~~

Night had fallen and it was time for Carlo to pick up Becca from work. Hannah helped him close up the beverage booth and lock it down for the night. Then she accompanied him to the car. She really felt bad for Jessica she hoped she would be all right in the hotel room by herself tonight. They were closer than sisters, and she knew how bummed Jessica had been tonight.

They arrived at the bookstore and Hannah waited in the car while Carlo hopped out and told Becca he was there. "O.K.'" Becca said, "Just let me turn everything off and lock up, and I'll be right out, alright?"

"Sure," he said and he stepped outside. He took a minute to speak to Mr. Whitehorse on his way back to the car, "Good evening, Mr. Whitehorse, how are you?"

The old Indian was locking up his own shop and then turned to Carlo giving him a firm and friendly handshake, "Fine, just fine, Carlo. It is good to see you. How have you been? Your sister seems a little troubled lately."

"Yes, sir." Carlo began, "I love her very much, but she won't confide in me. I wish she would let me help her. I think it's this man she's seeing that troubles her. I think he has frightened her. Do you know anything about it?"

The man smiled knowingly and without saying too much, as he didn't want to cause trouble for her, he answered, "It is not the man she is afraid of. Give her time. Let her tell you, and when she does . . . believe her." Mr. Whitehorse patted Carlo on the shoulder, "She is a lovely woman, and strong, but she needs your strength to help her this time." Then he dismissed himself, "It was nice to see you again. Perhaps you will need to come visit my store soon, huh?" he smiled and shook Carlo's hand again then turned, leaving him puzzled, to wait for his sister.

Becca came out and locked the door. "O.K., let's go." She said.

"What is in his tea?" he asked her.

"Whose? Mr. Whitehorse?" she asked smiling, "Nothing, I suppose. Why?"

"No reason," he laughed, "He just says the most bizarre things sometimes. Let's go."

~~~~~~~~~~*~~~~~~~~~~

Cassidy finally felt like going back to the apartment. He left the cabin and headed down the dark highway back towards town. About a mile or two down the road he had to suddenly swerve to avoid hitting a deer that galloped out in front of the car. He came to a complete stop then got out to look at his car. He had slid hard into the gravel and rocks on the shoulder and he wanted to make sure he didn't have a flat tire. Once outside the car, he suddenly felt like he wasn't alone. He stood putting his new keener senses to work for him. He could hear branches snapping and cracking. He smelled the air. He couldn't pick up anything familiar or different. The air was clear and calm. He suddenly caught motion out of his peripheral vision, but he couldn't focus in on it.

He decided to get back in the car. He walked around and opened the driver's side door but before he could get in he was hit, PLIMP! PLIMP! Two darts came out of the darkness and hit him square in the neck. He tried to turn around and see who shot him, but the drugs were strong and had already started taking effect. PLIMP! Another dart, this one hitting him in the chest. "Aghh!" he yelled out. He held onto the frame of the car as he was falling backwards trying to keep himself up, but it was no good. The drugs took full effect and he fell onto the road, out cold.

Poachers, dressed totally in what looked like black ninja suits, and armed to the teeth emerged from the forest and gathered Cassidy's limp body off the road and loaded him into the back of a large black Suburban. They shackled his hands and feet and shut the door. M monitored him from the backseat.

Checking his pulse and pupils. "Very Good." M said to his poachers, "Now, move that car off the road and lock it up, then bring me the keys. We'll need it when we free him later."

~~~~~~~~~~~*~~~~~~~~~~~

When Jessica awoke, she found herself restrained to a hospital gurney. She was still a little woozy from the chloroform, but she was coming around fast. The back of the gurney was slightly elevated, and she was able to look around the room. It looked like some kind of lab room at a hospital. She remembered what had happened. Professor Saunders! She couldn't believe it! What was he doing? Where had he brought her? She was beginning to get very frightened. Across the large room from her was a curtain, just like you see in hospitals, designed to give the neighboring patient privacy. It looked as though there was someone else on a gurney behind it, but it was hard to tell as the curtain was pulled all the way around it. She could just see the wheels of the gurney below it.

"Hello?" She decided to try to talk to whoever was behind it. Maybe they had been abducted too. "Hello, can you here me? Is someone there?"

No one answered, but she felt certain there was someone over there. She was beginning to panic. Her heart was racing. She tried to pull her hands out of the restraints, but they were on very tight and it was only making her wrists hurt to try. Then she heard someone approaching the door. A man walked in with two nurses. At least she thought they were nurses, they were dressed as such. The man who looked to be in charge sat down on the side of the bed, and placed his hands in his lap.

"Who are you people?" she asked with a shaky voice, "What do you want with me? Where is Professor Saunders?"

"He will be in to see you shortly." The man spoke with a strong European accent. She couldn't place the dialect. "You can call me M."

"I really don't care who you are, just let me go, please." Jessica pleaded with him. He smiled at her and shook his head.

"I'm afraid I can't do that, young lady. "He spoke to her in a very condescending way, as if she were insane, or a child. "You see, you have the privilege of playing a very important role in what we do here, undoubtedly one that will make me an icon in the record books of science. You should be honored to be a part of it."

"No thanks. I could give a shit less about your science experiments, or you! Now let me go!" She shouted at him and tugged and pulled on her restraints. He flashed a smile at her and got up and joined one of the nurses in preparing syringes she supposed were for her. Oh, God, she thought, were they going to kill her? He continued to tell her about the nature of his experiments.

"You see," he spoke as he worked with the needles, "We have been conducting research on some of the local . . . 'wildlife' in this area. Your boyfriend is already a major part of our studies here."

"Tad?" she asked, "You know Tad?" Surely he didn't know about any of this. He couldn't be a part of what these people were about. She just couldn't believe that.

"Oh my, yes." The man smiled, "We know him very well. He was a very pivotal part of this research." He began to tell her the whole gruesome story, of the true existence of werewolves and about the government's involvement with them, of how the poachers 'rescued' the boys, after they let The Founder attack them. Of how they chose the pack carefully, hand picking the group selectively, and of how they had been studying them ever since. How they would be used as peace dogs, assassins for war, once they could find a way to control them better, and that's where she came in.

This could not be true! This wasn't happening! She was in shock. How could Tad not have told her? She felt like a fool. She knew he was too good to be true. He should have known he could trust her. She had so many questions. This didn't seem real. She couldn't believe they were real. "Do they know about you? Do they know about this? Does Tad know what you're doing to me?" she asked.

M laughed a little, "Oh my, no. Thayer would have my head for this, I'm sure. But by the time he finds out, it will be too late, and I will be safely hidden."

"What *are* you doing to me?" her lip quivered.

"Tonight, my dear," he began, "You will receive a blood transfusion. It will be the first time we have attempted anything like this before.

Quite groundbreaking. Until now, our werewolves have been made the old-fashioned way, by blood exposure and trauma. I hope it doesn't kill you." He smiled, like some evil snake. Jessica's heart was racing.

M pulled a silver cart over to her bed and the nurse began trying to prep her arm, but Jessica was jerking around and screaming so much she couldn't do it. "Help me!! Somebody! Please!!" she yelled.

"It won't do you any good to yell, young woman. No one can hear you where you are. You are inside my research facility way up high on the mountain top." He made a gesture with his hands in the air to indicate distance. She began to feel hopeless.

"No!!" she yelled and cried and continued to struggle. The man left the room and signaled for more nurses to help restrain her. Two male nurses joined them in the room and held her down by the shoulders and wrists. She began to cry as they held her tighter.

"It will hurt less if you hold still, my dear." The man grinned, and then he took the end of the needle and inserted it into her arm. It had a long tube attached to it, and the tube attached to the transfusion device. "Hold this still." He said to his head nurse, and then he turned and walked over to the curtain.

"Meet your blood-donor." He said, and then he whipped back the curtain.

When he pulled it back, Jessica gasped. Lying on the other bed across the room was Cassidy. He was restrained, not only by the wrists and ankles, but around the neck as well. And his harnesses were made of metal. He appeared to be knocked out cold. She hoped he was anyway. Now it all made sense. That creepy vibe she got off him. The way their eyes looked. She had been afraid of him before, but now, she was too terrified to speak. Although, he might be able to help her if he was awake. As creeped out by him as she was, she still feared these "scientists" more.

She decided to try to wake him. "Cassidy!!" she yelled, "Cassidy, wake up!!"

"I see you know him." The man said, "It's no good. He can't hear you. I doubt he would help you if he could."

"Does he know about this?" she whimpered.

"Good Heavens, no!" M chuckled, "He'd kill us all!" He laughed maniacally. "He is probably the finest specimen of the unadulterated werewolf we have ever studied. He is positively brutal. Lethal.

Fascinating!" he smiled and slapped Cassidy on the stomach. "Isn't he beautiful?"

"He's a freak, and you're a sadistic bastard!" Jessica cried, "He'll kill you."

"Maybe one day, but not tonight." M began to pull Cassidy's gurney across the room to hers. "He is quite heavily sedated, and tightly restrained." M did a light examination on Cassidy, checking his heart rate and pupils to make sure he was, in fact, out. "Yes. *Heavily* sedated."

Jessica kicked with her feet and tried again, "Cassidy, damn you, wake up!!" she turned to M, "Please. Stop this, you're crazy." She cried.

M ignored her and continued to put the other end of the needle into Cassidy's arm, attached the tubing to the machine and then turned on the pump. Jessica watched in horror as the blood flowed up the tube and through the other side, down the tubing and entered her flesh. She felt it the minute it was in her veins. It was searing hot! She began screaming. His blood was boiling! "Why does his blood burn?!" she screamed.

M began taking notes. He turned to his assistant, "Interesting in deed. Call in The Professor." He turned back to Jessica, "Lie still and it won't hurt as much."

She couldn't stop screaming. She could feel it flowing through every vein in her body. When it reached her heart she though it would explode. It felt like it was swelling. She began to gasp for air. The Professor entered the room. He watched her convulse.

"Maybe we should have sedated her first." He turned to M, "It is too much for her. His white cells are attacking her organs, she might stroke when it reaches her brain."

"Calm yourself, Saunders. It is all to be expected. It is part of the process. It has simply been accelerated."

"There is no way to know what this will do to her! You're taking too many chances!" The Professor yelled at M. "You can't just abduct people at random and do this to them."

"This is hardly random, Saunders. She is Thayer's girlfriend. His mate. She is perfect for this experiment. It is positively poetic. Besides, I checked her blood type when she arrived it is the same as Cassidy's. She is simply rejecting his blood's influence. The convulsing will stop in a moment or two."

"She's in pain, M!" The Professor was regretting his involvement, "Can't you do something?"

"Of course I can," M smiled, "I just don't want to yet. Look away if it disturbs you so."

Jessica finally stopped convulsing and fell limp into the gurney. She was unconscious. The Professor was worried. What if she died? They'd come for him for sure. M turned off the transfusion pump and disconnected it from her arm. His nurses were checking her vital signs. The head nurse looked at M. "Her heart rate is elevated, but she is otherwise normal." She said.

"Good," M smiled, "Thank you. Please take her to a recovery room right away. Alert me of *any* changes."

Professor Saunders grabbed M by the arm, "They will hunt us down for this! What do you think will happen when Thayer finds out?"

M pulled loose from his grip, "Exactly what I hope will happen. Time will pass and I will have made scientific history! But before that happens we will use her as bait to control Tad and the pack, and make *military* history!"

"Aren't you afraid he'll kill us for this?"

"He will have to catch us first. He is already too late to change this. The only one who can end this now is William."

"Where is he? Does he know?" Saunders wrung his hands; "You know he favors them now."

"He has temporarily slipped away from us. We will retrieve him in due time. He can't go very far with the restraining collar on. Now come, let's return this one to the wild." M gestured toward Cassidy, "We will take another supply of his blood first."

Professor Saunders was fearful now more than ever. He didn't really want to be anywhere near Cassidy when he woke up, and he didn't like the idea of The Founder out running loose. And he liked even less this whole 'experiment'. He just wanted more accurate information for his latest book. He hadn't wanted to be party to Jessica's kidnapping and blood tampering. He still had one more night to be at that festival, and he would be right out in the open. He just wanted to get it over with.

After taking more blood from Cassidy, M had him placed in the Suburban and rode along to make sure he was returned the way he wanted. They placed him behind the wheel of the Mustang and M injected him with a stimulant to revive him. It would take a few hours to kick in, giving them plenty of time to vacate before he came two. In any ordinary person, M would have worried about overdosing him, but in the werewolf this wasn't even possible. As the poachers shut the car door they noticed another vehicle slowly approaching. They hopped into the Suburban followed by M, and quickly disappeared down the road.

~~~~~~~~~~~*~~~~~~~~~~~

The Killing Moon

The next morning Patti got up, got into uniform and decided to make an appearance out at the O'Bannon house. He thought he would just check in since he hadn't heard from Agent Hannigan. It was kind of strange that he hadn't even so much as touched base with him since they met the day before. When he pulled up out front of the house he was surprised to find no one there. He parked the car and got out and yanked his sunglasses off.

"What the Hell?" he whispered out loud, and he wandered up to the front porch. He peered through the front windows into the house. He couldn't believe what he was seeing. Nothing! There was nothing there! No trace of the murders. No blood. No damage to the house. No bodies. No State Police. No police tape. This was way too weird. He immediately headed back to the squad car and called Tad.

~~~~~~~~~~~*~~~~~~~~~~~

Hannah arrived back at the hotel room around 10:00 A.M., Carlo was with her. "Jess!" she yelled out as she walked into the room. No one answered so she stepped into the bathroom and checked out the shower, "Jessica." She wasn't there. Hannah stepped back into the front room and searched through the drawers. "That's funny," she said as she searched around for a trace that her friend had been there.

"What is it?" Carlo asked her, "Is she not here?"

"No," Hannah sighed, confused, "And it doesn't look like she's even been here all night. Look, her bed is still made."

"Well, maybe Tad met up with her a little later and took her out to his place. Do you have his number?"

Hannah looked at Carlo, her fingernails in her mouth and shook her head no, "No. I never thought about getting it from her."

"Is there anywhere else she might be? Anyone else you think she might be with?"

"No." she shook her head again and dropped her hands to her sides, "No, I mean. You're it."

"Well," Carlo walked over and hugged her, "I'm sure she's just fine. Maybe she just got up a little early and headed on down to the festival."

"But her bed is made." Hannah countered, hugging him back.

"Well maybe she made it herself before she left." He reassured her.

"Phhh!" Hannah puffed, "You really don't know us very well do you?"

He smiled and kissed her, "You want to wait here for her for a little while? Maybe she'll be right back. We can . . . make her bed for her again."

Hannah looked into his eyes and smiled. She knew exactly where he was headed with this. She kissed him and then laughing threw him back on the bed.

~~~~~~~~~~~*~~~~~~~~~~~

Cassidy was so hung over when he came two he could barely even walk. He got out of the car and stretched his legs for a minute and tried to get his bearings back. What the fuck had happened to him last night? It was another one of those weird black outs they all had been having. He remembered being hit with darts, he never did get a look at his captors, but he knew whom they were. He swore if he ever got the chance he would kill whoever was responsible for this shit. Since he wasn't far from the cabin, he decided he would just turn around and go back there. Tad would probably be interested in knowing this anyway. So he shook his head hard a few times to reorient himself and then he got back in the car and headed that way.

~~~~~~~~~~~*~~~~~~~~~~~

Luke rolled over and woke Chloe with a kiss. He almost hated to wake her she looked so peaceful sleeping. She was so beautiful. He couldn't believe the magic of the night before, and he really didn't want this feeling to end. But Patti had just called from the lobby and was waiting on him. Tad had wanted Pat to pick him up early. They had to re-group at the cabin and talk about the O'Bannon house and remove the tracking devices before tonight.

"How did you sleep?" he asked her with a smile.

She stretched and smiled hard. Very content for the first time in her life since she was a child. "I feel fantastic. Is that weird?" She felt so safe with Luke around, and now that her bastard stepfather and uncle were gone, she had her whole life to start over. She wanted Luke to be a part of it.

"Not at all. You have a lot ahead of you." He stroked her hair.

"Yes." She lay there and looked into his unusual eyes, "And I want yu to always be there with me."

"I'm here. Don't worry." Luke reassured her. But inside he knew as long as he was what he was, that really wasn't an option for him. He decided to break this line of talk until later. "That was Pat on the phone. Tad needs me to help with a research trek this afternoon, and he sent him to get me. I have to go."

She sat up and wrapped the blankets around her. "When will yu be back?"

"Not until tomorrow. Will you be O.K.?" He reached up and touched her cheek. She looked disappointed.

"Well, sure. But . . . I don't want ta be alone right now. Can't yu get out of it?"

"Not this time. I'm sorry." He felt bad about leaving her, but this couldn't wait. The moon would be at it's fullest tonight, and he still wasn't as skilled as Cassidy about controlling the shift, and he had promised Tad he would help with The Regulators. "I'd better get a shower." He added and he kissed her before he got out of the bed. Then he remembered something Pat had told him, "Hey, why don't you get Kitty to come and stay with you tonight? Patti said just to order anything you want and charge it to the room. It might be fun."

She considered this option for a minute, and then decided it was a good idea and began to dial her friend's number.

~~~~~~~~~~~*~~~~~~~~~~~

The man M had called a conference. He wanted to make sure the higher-ups knew about his plans. At this stage in the game they could pull out funding for any reason, and withholding current data would be good enough for them right now. M was still on the proving ground.

Before heading to the boardroom he stopped in and checked on Jessica. He wanted to see if the moon's pull was having any early effects on her. She was still unconscious. This worried him a little, but as long as her vital signs were normal, he felt confidant she would pull through.

He left her and went on to the meeting. All the regulars were present as well as the men from the day before. He went straight to the head of the table and began.

"As you all know from our meeting the other day, I had a new plan for securing our interest in these . . . manimals. Your concerns were that, once built, we would have no way to control the actions of the pack. Well! As outlined in the briefing, I have pulled in the she-wolf. She is, thus far, resting nicely, and I expect her to be one hundred percent by the time the moon is full in the sky tonight." He paced back and forth making sure he spoke strongly and confidently as to convince his backers this *was* a good idea. He continued, "At this time it is not certain what her abilities will be, but I am positive, beyond a shadow of a doubt, that she will aid us in leading this pack. Any questions so far?"

One of the men spoke up, "Just what will be this girl's role here? How is just her presence our insurance of a successful mission?"

The man M smiled, "By controlling the Alpha female, we shall manipulate the entire pack. Thayer, the leader, will not do anything to jeopardize his mate's well being, and I also feel confident in time, they will bring us full-blooded offspring to continue our work on a whole new level."

The man spoke again, "Yes, but you speak of them entirely in terms of them as animals. These are still humans at the core, am I right? What is their true genus after all, M?"

M looked agitated. Why couldn't they just let him run this? Why so many ridiculous questions?! He had no choice but to answer, "They are a totally independent species now, gentlemen! I am excited to bring you the news that I was given the go-ahead to name the genus myself. It is quite an honor."

M pulled down a chart from a wall mount that outlined the werewolf as an individual animal. Then he stood proudly and announced the proper scientific name as defined by him, "Meet Canis Lupus Sapiens." He turned and smiled at the subdued whispering and excitement at the table around him. "It means, quite simply, wolf-man."

"It's brilliant, M. truly." His superior shouted, and hand clapping ensued. M was relieved and proud of himself. He continued to explain what future plans for the creatures he had, and went into better detail over the biology of them. He also explained what he hoped the outcome of his experiment with Jessica was and then he took them all down to meet her. Even though she was still unconscious, he wanted them to be able to actually see her.

After about two hours worth of conference and examples, they gave M the thumbs up. Funding and support would continue for the next six months. At which time M promised to have gained full control of the pack.

~~~~~~~~~~*~~~~~~~~~~

WHEN THE MOON ROSE . . .

Once at the cabin, all of the guys, minus Cassidy, took turns letting Liam remove the tracking devices from their necks. They didn't want any interference from the F.A.P.R. tonight. They discussed how Patti found nothing out at the O'Bannon house. What had happened? It was very strange, but not overly puzzling. They all knew that the F.A.P.R. had plenty to do with it. It just confirmed Tad's theory that the facility had been covering up for them the whole time. And it solidified their involvement with everything that had happened. Lastly, Tad helped remove the tracker from Liam's neck and then they sat around the front porch and waited for the moon to rise.

The guys could feel the lunar pull on their bodies all day, but it continually got stronger as the day progressed. After gorging themselves to near capacity on red meat, they sat on the front porch of the cabin, drinking a few beers and saying nothing to each other as they all watched the sun go down. But as soon as it sank beneath the skyline of the tall pine trees, the shift began.

As if all at once, the men rose from their places on the porch stricken with the curse that infused them, and fell out into the yard. Cassidy smiled and rose slowly out of his seat, tearing his shirt off and stretching his arms out behind his back. He loved the shift. He had become accustomed to the pain involved and he looked forward to the feeling of power and strength at the end of it. He felt like a superhero, invincible and animated. They all had grown accustomed to it. It didn't take as long to shift if they didn't fight against it, and so it didn't hurt as much either.

Tracers of light flooded their eyes as their eyesight changed to night vision. Their bones and muscles cracked and stretched, causing the bulk of the pain. But their tissues healed so rapidly they could hardly remember it happening. Their blood sugar spiked and their blood boiled as the metabolism of their bodies was quickly altered, and they howled and roared as their adrenalin levels jumped through the roof. Finally the shift was complete, and they stood as a pack, black claws gleaming, with long fur, long ears and tufted tails, and an overwhelming desire to slaughter something. This time in true pack formation in a calculated assault on their old enemies, The Regulators.

Tad lurched out front and looked each of the others in the eyes. They could no longer speak with their mouths, but telepathically they were always connected. He threw his head back and howled a battle cry, long and hard, joined in unison by his mates. All of them were psyched up for this, even Luke, who was fast becoming a lethal killer. Every part of them was on fire and their senses were so heightened, they could smell The Regulator's mix of campfire, sweat and motor oil from five miles away.

Cassidy breathed in the air and smiled in his wolf-skin. He was going to enjoy this! Finally Tad gave the motion to follow him and they all leaped into the darkness hand over foot through the rustic evergreens. The Regulators would be over tonight.

~~~~~~~~~~*~~~~~~~~~~

Five miles away, under the bridge trestle, Roy perked up his ears. He had heard the howls coming from way off in the distance. His comrades were drinking and laughing and cleaning their guns and knives, totally unaware of the gravity of their situation. The radios on their bikes, cranked. Roy stood up to get a better listen. He slapped Cowboy on the arm, "Hey!" he whispered, "D'you hear that?"

Cowboy listened intently for a minute, then answered, "Hear what?"

"It sounded like wolves howlin', only creepier." He glanced down at his friend, "You didn't hear it?"

"Why Hell no." Cowboy grunted, "Ov'r 'is noise. 'You kiddin'?"

"Well I don't like it. Where's my gun?" Roy walked over to his bike and searched around in his saddlebags for his revolver. Finally finding it, he made sure it was loaded and then tucked it into the belt of his pants.

"You scared?" Cowboy teased.

"Hell, no!" Roy barked, "Jus' careful."

But truly, if Roy were careful, he never would have shot at the wolf pack. The Regulators had sealed their own fate with that last act of cruelty. Now the playing field was about to be wiped clean.

~~~~~~~~~~*~~~~~~~~~~

Within about a half an hour, Tad's pack of werewolves had reached the bridge. They stood at the railing and leaned over it to glance down at their prey. They used a combination of senses to determine the biker's numbers and assess the natural obstacles in the path leading to the water.

Roy had dozed off with his gun in his arms. He woke for an instant as his head began to slip off the rock he was leaned against, and when he did, he just caught a glimpse of something strange looking down from the top of the bridge. He jumped to his feet, his heart pounding through his chest at what he thought he saw, and he began to shout at his buddies. Some of who had already passed out. "Git up!!" he shouted, and he kicked at Cowboy, "Git up I said! Now!"

Cassidy noticed the commotion and signaled the others to get back out of sight. He let Tad know he wanted Roy. Tad nodded his big wolfy head in acknowledgement of the gesture.

Roy cocked his gun and balancing it shakily against his forearm, pointed it up at the bridge. The other bikers were beginning to think he had had too much to drink. By the time they looked up there, the werewolves were gone. One of them asked him, "What the Hell is it, Roy? Are you drunk or somethin'?" They all chimed in with the giggling.

"Don't none of yall assholes see 'em? They's there." He pointed up to the bridge again.

"Hell, Roy, they ain't nothin' up there, you just had way too much booze tonight. Now shut up soes we can all git some sleep." Cowboy argued.

"They's there, I tell ya. I seen 'em." Roy griped.

"Saw what?" One of them asked him again.

He finally decided to tell them. He knew they would really think he was nuts now, but he was scared. "They looked like . . . werewolves."

It only took seconds before the whole lot of them burst into laughter. Cowboy stood up and slapped his friend on the back, "Ahh Hell, Roy. You must be on Quaaludes or somethin'. Go back to sleep." The laughter resumed. Then, without a sound something grabbed Cowboy around the head and twisted it so hard it came clean off his shoulders. The bikers stood in awed silence and looked past Cowboy's falling body to the monstrosities standing behind it.

They looked on in horrified silence at the large wolf-like beast holding Cowboy's head in its long grasping claws, the stunned look of confusion still glued to the disembodied head of their comrade. Tad cocked his head sideways and back slowly, cracking his neck, readying himself for the next kill. Letting the remaining Regulators soak up a good dose of fear before they died. For an instant, it seemed to be in slow motion as Tad let go of the head, letting it drop with a squish to the ground, and then suddenly, threw his head back swiftly and howled. As if on cue Patti, Luke, Cassidy and Liam ran past him into the group of fear-struck bikers without hesitation. Tad looked Roy in the face, made eye contact with him, and then moved past him with lightening speed.

Unnoticed by the bikers or the wolf pack, The Founder wandered up on the bank by the edge of the woods and leaned up against a tree with his stogie to watch the goings-on. The collar he wore flashed and blinked in the darkness. He grimaced as it injected him with serum and he blew out smoke rings as he watched the carnage before him. He certainly wasn't a virgin to this kind of thing, but this was the first time he had watched it from this perspective. Not since the battlefield had he witnessed this much ruthless brutality and bloodshed. But at least in combat the weapons were fair.

Some of the bikers decided to try to shoot at the beasts. It was no good. Their bullets bounced off the werewolves hides like rubber. One of them pulled out a large chain and swung it at Cassidy, but Cassidy was much faster. He had heard the sound of the chain whipping through the air behind him and flipped around in time to catch it before it hit him. He yanked it so hard he pulled the terrified biker's hand off at the wrist. Then he beat the man mercilessly with his own weapon until he was dead.

Blood was everywhere. It was spraying through the air like a fine mist and it was pouring over the ground and splashing over the manimals' feet.

One of them swung a lead pipe at Tad. But Tad caught the man's arm and bent it backwards, breaking it halfway up his arm, and then swiftly Tad placed his clawed hands together and plunged them straight into the man's chest and pulled his ribcage apart, opening it like a bible. The man was alive long enough to feel his own lungs spill out all over the ground.

The brutality was so furied and so heated it only took them minutes to wipe out the entire gang. As Patti and Liam were fighting the last couple of bikers, Cassidy noticed Roy making his way across the rocks on the riverbank in an attempt to get away. Unnoticed by his brethren, Cassidy snuck up and around the parked motorcycles and came out in front of old Roy and faced him in the water. Roy stopped in his tracks, petrified. He was trembling and shaking so hard he couldn't even speak. He began to cry as he slowly looked up into Cassidy's glowing eyes and then fell to his knees in the shallow water. Giving up. He had never known any kind of terror like this before.

Cassidy let him tremble and cry for a minute or two, and then he reached down and wrapped his long clawed fingers around Roy's leather vest and pulled him up, his feet dangling. He wanted Roy to know who he was. Roy was afraid to look in its face, but he did. And when he did he noticed the bit of silver dangling from around the beast's neck. His mind raced as he tried to place it. Then it suddenly became clear to him where he had seen that necklace before. Images of the barroom brawl flashed into his mind, and then the lake. He remembered! It was that smart ass from the bar! His eyes got wider with the realization that you never really know whom you're fucking with and now he couldn't quit staring in the beast's face. Cassidy waited long enough for it to sink in to Roy's mind and then he slowly began to nod and smile as he lowered Roy back into the water and then let go of him.

Is he going to kill me? Roy thought. He didn't want to move. He couldn't quit staring up at the huge gruesome beast in front of him. Cassidy kept eye contact with him for a long time, then, satisfied with himself, he turned and slowly lurched away from the man. Leaving him frightened and grateful in the water. That image would forever burn in Roy's mind. The images of the death of his comrades and the sounds of their screams would eventually be blocked from his memories, but the face of that unnatural beast would be frozen in his mind till the day he died, and he was so Thankful to God that it hadn't been this day. He slowly began to move forward in the water, not looking back at them, afraid that at any minute that maniac would return to kill him. He followed the moonlight on the water until he was out of sight. Thanking God all the way to safety. But he would never really feel safe again.

It was finally silent on the riverbank. Cassidy shook the water off his feet and joined his brethren as they overlooked the field of battle before them. Then they smelled the smoke. Cherry tobacco. They all looked at each other, and then, in unison they all turned and looked up at the edge of the forest to find what they already knew was there, The Founder.

Lankily Tad strolled up the hill toward him. He panted and snarled at The Founder. The Founder just took his time and smiled and took another drag from his cigar, and then he said, "Thought I'd invite myself to your little bar-b-que here. Hope you don't mind."

Tad growled and slowly turned his head and surveyed the mutilated corpses of the bikers flooding the water with a red shimmer then he turned back to The Founder. They kept eye contact with each other so they could communicate more clearly. The Founder kept his grin and glanced at the other two wolf-men approaching, Liam and Patti. Luke and Cassidy followed closely and The Founder waited until he had all of their attention before he spoke again. They all stood around him growling low and guttural, and swaying slowly to steady their tall massive bodies.

"I guess you all want to know what I'm doing here." He stood straight and tossed his stogie down and finished speaking. "I'm going to tell you all something you should know. Especially you." He said as he pointed at Tad. Being a wolf-man himself, he could tell who was who. He strolled past the wolfy apparitions leering over him and sat down on a nearby stump to light another cigar. Cowboy's head was staring up at him from the ground. He regarded it a minute and then he put the cigar in his mouth and picked up the head, and flung it over his shoulder and into the river. Then he dusted off his hands and continued, "It's about your lady friend."

The boys all exchanged glances and then Tad moved forward and leaned down in The Founder's face and roared, his eyes wide and wild. The Founder continued, not flinching or budging an inch, even with Tad's hot bloody breath upon him. He took a deep slow drag off his cigar and blew it out in Tad's direction, finally finishing what he came there to tell them, "They've abducted your woman, my friend. They have plans for us all."

Tad threw his head up and back and roared into the moonlight. He wasted no more time with The Founder; he turned and began to try to shake off his wolf-skin. He breathed in deeply and shook his head from side to side and tried not to think angry thoughts as his form slowly began to return to normal. The Founder and the others watched on as Tad shed his wolf-hide in a matter of minutes and started rummaging through the biker's duffle bags and packs trying to find a pair of pants. Once he did he threw them on, and then found one of the bikes with the keys still in it, and jumped on barefooted. The Founder walked up to him as he cranked the motorcycle and placed a hand on his shoulder, "Start at the werewolf tent at the Festival. Talk to Saunders, he knows more than he's lettin' on." Tad wasted no more time, he nodded without saying a word and after one last glance at Liam, he let out on the throttle, kicking up dirt behind him and wielded the bike up the embankment and then on toward town.

Liam motioned for the others to follow Tad, so they all lurched past The Founder towards the road. Colonel Jack stopped Cassidy as he was leaving by standing in front of him and placing a hand on his furry chest. He took the cigar out of his mouth and smiled up at Cassidy, he had seen what had happened between him and Roy, "What was that, my boy?" he pointed toward the trestle with his cigar between his fingers, "You aren't going soft on me now, are you?"

Cassidy snarled and roared loudly in The Founder's face. The Founder began to laugh out loud and shook his head, "You kiss your mama with that mouth?" he chuckled and took a calm drag off his cigar. Cassidy snarled and grunted at him as he lanked away.

"You gotta love that boy." William smiled and sat down to finish his smoke while he watched the moonlight dance off the bodies in the water.

~~~~~~~~~~~*~~~~~~~~~~~

What Big Eyes You've Got

The park was closed. Tad dropped the motorcycle to the ground after he dismounted it and proceeded to yank the park gates open. He pulled with all of his supernatural strength against the locked iron gates, finally wrenching them loose enough for him to walk through. Then he made his way to the werewolf tent. He could make out the Professor's silhouette against the lamplight burning behind the canvas as he was loading all of his lecture gear into a large trunk. Out of tracking watch for the time being, Tad wanted to put the fear of God into the man. Uninterrupted.

He snuck into the tent without the Professor noticing, swiftly and stealthily. He stood still behind him, waiting for him to pick up on his presence. Professor Saunders could feel the hairs on the back of his neck prick up and he suddenly had this creeped-out feeling something was there. He whipped around quickly and found Tad Thayer standing about two feet away, and he didn't look very friendly. He had a serious expression of anger on his face, and blood covered his entire chest, his face and was tangled through his hair. Professor Jack Saunders knew why he was there.

Tad stood glaring at him for a couple of minutes. He wanted him terrified. His breathing was deep and fast. He snarled at the man, and the Professor swallowed hard and began to shake.

"Where's my girl?" Thayer was growling the words at Saunders through his teeth. The Professor was trembling to the point his whole body was visibly shaking. How did he know? He could barely speak, but he had to. He had to find the right words to keep the large angry creature from killing him. He had to make himself needed and absolve himself of any responsibility, but how much did Thayer know, already? He noticed that

Tad was in human form, and it was a clear full moon night. His eyes were wide and wild and the pupils were still large and dilated, refracting the glow of the lamplight from within. The Professor's theory had held true. His findings were correct. They *could* change at will after a reasonable amount of time, and even reverse the shift with the moon at it's fullest! The Founder would never really confirm nor deny this ability. Now they knew for sure.

Tad grew angrier by the very sight of the man. "I said where is she?"

"I . . . I d,d,don't know." The Professor cowered and yelled out loud as Tad lunged forward, drawing even closer. "I mean it!" Saunders yelled, cowering even more, "I . . . I told him not to do it! I t,t,told him you would come for us all! He wouldn't listen! It's not my f,fault, Please! I swear!" Saunders lied through his teeth and lowered his head and put his hands out in front of himself. If the end was coming, he didn't want to watch.

Before the man could utter another lie, he felt the presence of more creatures. He slowly lifted his sweaty head to find, standing behind Tad, four tall, snarling, drooling, and blood-covered wolf-like apparitions. It was his greatest fear. They had finally come for him. They were horrendous, ominous beasts with tall muscled bodies equipped with built-in weapons and the skills to use them efficiently. They had large gaping jaws full of chiseled teeth and eyes that knew him. Worse than that, behind those eyes were minds, fully functioning, hostile, intelligent minds. Minds with memories. Minds that knew what was happening to them, the minds of men. Men in the hides of one of nature's most prominent predators. He had no way to escape. No fancy handguns or weapons of his own. No way to get away.

But what he thought would happen, didn't. Instead Tad reared back and swung, hitting him. WHAM! WHAM! WHAM! Three hard swift blows to the face. The blows came so hard and fast, all the man saw were lights flashing before his eyes. He stumbled backwards and fell down. He hadn't been in a fistfight in thirty years, and he wasn't a big fighter in his prime. He could tell the punches had loosened his jaw. In fact, it was broken. His glasses had flown to the ground and the manimals were all blurry now. He was still shaking and couldn't talk. He was damn near crying and not sure if they were done with him.

Tad's strength was unbelievable, and he hadn't delivered the blows with all of his force. If he had, the Professor's head would have twisted on his shoulders. Jack Saunders knew that.

Tad hovered over him for a minute or two then growled down at him. "You tell them I'm coming for her. You tell them that." Then he signaled to the pack and they all turned and left. It wasn't until Cassidy left he truly felt he had survived. He could tell which beast was he by the silver pentagram medallion dangling around his furry throat. After they left, and all was quiet, Professor Saunders shakily picked himself up and pulled his phone out of his pocket, and then hit speed dial 1. On the other end of the line, after about three rings, a familiar voice answered, "Hello. Hello?" M could hardly make out the muffled ramblings on the other end of the line, "Saunders? Saunders is that you?"

From his end of the line, The Professor could barely utter out the words, "Help me." M immediately traced the panic device in his phone and sent a car to get him.

~~~~~~~~~~*~~~~~~~~~~

By the time the pack returned to the cabin, the moon's influence was beginning to fade. Tad hopped off the bike and joined the others in the front yard. They were approaching the porch and noticed The Founder seated on it smoking his usual brand, with his feet propped up on the banister. They began to shake and growl in the front yard, shaking off the effects of the shift. They were still sticky and nasty and blood-covered.

The Founder grinned wide at them, "My, my, my! Why I've had nightmares that look better than you all." Ah, he,he,he! He laughed at them.

"Can it, you old bastard." Cassidy growled, his voice still low and throaty as he morphed and shifted back. He returned to normal and searched for the remains of his pants in the front yard.

"Did you all find Saunders?" William asked them still smiling.

Tad nodded, "He won't forget our little talk. But I need you to tell us how to get inside that facility. I'm going to get my girl back."

The Founder stood up slowly, shaking his head, "There is no need."

"Why not?" Tad asked him patiently awaiting an answer. Still agitated.

"Because I'm going home now, and I'll see to it she gets returned to you . . . forth with. Besides, that would be just what they wanted. You would walk right into the cage they have designed for you." He tapped the restraining collar with his fingers, still holding his cigar between them.

Then he slapped a hand on Tad's shoulder as he sauntered off the porch and into the yard. "Good evening gentlemen." He waved a hand in the air without looking back, and headed down the dark gravel driveway.

They all watched him until he was out of sight. They were not sure how to take any of this. Cassidy looked at Tad and said, "Tell me we aren't going to listen to old Foghorn Leghorn?" But Tad decided to trust The Founder. Aside from the original attacks on them, he had been a constant resource for information and Tad believed he would not let him down here. He went inside without answering Cassidy, and had a long hot shower and a Brandy.

~~~~~~~~~~~*~~~~~~~~~~~

Once inside the safe confines of the F.A.P.R., Jack Saunders received an exam by M. He signaled with his hand gestures that he needed a pen and paper. He was in excruciating pain. He could not move his jaw at all now since the swelling had taken over. The rest of his face was just as swollen and bruised. A nurse brought him what he had requested, and he immediately began to write, HOW BAD IS IT? He showed it to M. M replied shaking his head, "Not good, my old friend. Not good at all. It is definitely broken, but it could have been much worse. How did this happen?"

Jack wrote: THAYER, HE HIT ME. HE SAID TO TELL YOU, HE'S COMING FOR JESSICA, AND HE'S COMING FOR US. HE WAS IN HUMAN FORM WHEN HE DID THIS TO ME!!

M read it out loud then responded with interest, "Really? In the moonlight? How amazing! Remarkable creatures! And the others?" M asked, "Were they as men as well?"

Jack shook his head slowly to indicate 'no'.

"Fantastic! They can manipulate the curse already! Such willful spirits they are! And they worked together as a pack?" M asked as he worked on Jack's wounds.

Jack nodded 'yes'.

"I'll give her back, in due time. Slightly improved, I hope. So far, the moon has had no effect on her. I might have wasted my time." M smiled, "Maybe I should try once more before I release her."

Jack was filled with fear and worry. He quickly wrote out: PLEASE DON'T! JUST LET HIM HAVE HER! THEY WILL KILL US ALL!!

But M just dismissed this dread, "Not to worry my fearful friend. Everything will be fine." He patted The Professor on the shoulder and loaded a syringe with a reddish tincture from an injection bottle. "Hold still, please Jack. This should help you rest and aid your healing while we adjust your jaw." He reassured him and then injected him with the serum. After which he explained, "This is something new. You have been the first human to try it. It was made from The Founder's white cells."

Jack suddenly panicked. How could he treat him like this?! He was no guinea pig! The man was mad! Utterly mad! M could see that Jack was over anxious and freaking out. He explained further. "Relax, Jack, it won't hurt you. It should accelerate the healing process in your body without any long term . . ." he paused for the punch-line, "Side-effects. Its benefits are only temporary, however. So allow yourself to rest, no matter how good you may feel, uh-huh?" Then M and his nurses set The Professor's jaw, and left the room so he could rest.

Within an hour, the serum had begun to take effect. Jack opened his eyes and sat up in the bed. He hadn't felt this good in years! M was right! It did help and he felt great! This was fantastic! His jaw was still painful and stiff, but it was getting looser by the minute. He felt like he was healing all over. Every ache, every pain, gone! This stuff was incredible! It could save millions of people from their illnesses, their pains, everything! Jack felt like he could actually take Thayer now! Amazing! M was a genius! But how had he done it? This research was important! If this was the result it was extremely important! Jack couldn't imagine what could be wrong with a drug like this one, aside from the obvious; it had come from werewolf venom. Why wasn't M selling this discovery to the higher-ups? He felt like doing back flips! All the benefits of lycanthropy without the curses! But M had warned him not to get overly excited and to rest, so he decided to heed the warnings. He lay back down, but wanted to dance *so* badly.

~~~~~~~~~~*~~~~~~~~~~

Hannah and Carlo had fallen asleep and spent the greater part of the day waiting for Jessica to return to the hotel room, and now it was night. Late at night. And Hannah was very worried. Carlo was concerned for Hannah. He had left earlier to pick up Becca from work and take her home, and pick up something for them to eat. Hannah refused to leave until she found Jessica. So he returned as quickly as he could to her. "Anything?" he asked her as he walked through the door.

Hannah had been crying, worried for her friend. She knew she shouldn't have let her wander off alone. "Maybe we should call the police." Hannah said, hopeless. "I just don't know what to do. Should I go looking for her, should I stay here? Should I go and see Tad? I just don't know." She started to cry again. Carlo held her for a minute, and then offered an idea.

"How about, we eat something, and I'll call the police station in the morning. We will stay here tonight in case she calls or comes back, O.K.?"

Hannah nodded and kissed his cheek, "You are so fantastic." She whispered, looking into his eyes, "How was I lucky enough to find you?"

He smiled and kissed her gently, "Beautiful women always seem to find me." He teased, making her laugh.

~~~~~~~~~~*~~~~~~~~~~

The Founder was greeted by M when he returned to the Research Facility. He immediately began to rant at the beast and had his guards shackle him. The Founder didn't resist, he really had nowhere else to go. This was the only home he had known for many years. Besides, the serum the collar injected him with was still strong in his veins. He couldn't shift now if he needed to. He stared down at M, with revolt.

"So!" M raved, "You have decided their cause is now your cause. Is that it? Are you not pampered enough, that you must escape and be willful?"

"I don't care what else you do to me, but you return that girl to whence she came." The Founder stated slowly and eloquently as usual. "You had no right to tamper with her, and you have sealed your own doom."

"Is that so?!" M snapped, appalled at this beast for giving him orders. "I will do as I please! To you or to her, and neither Thayer nor you, nor the entire pack can do anything about it!"

"I'm only going to warn you once. Return that girl tonight. You have unleashed a creation you cannot possibly control. Hell hath no fury, remember?"

M thought long and hard about The Founder's words, and then he signaled the guards to take him down to his quarters. She hadn't really come around yet, and M had been hoping for something, anything that would indicate the experiment took. One thing was for certain; he damn sure wasn't going to let The Founder tell *him* what to do. He would return that girl when and if *he* was ready to.

~~~~~~~~~~*~~~~~~~~~~

Once downstairs The Founder was ready to get comfortable in his easy chair. It was becoming clear that M was not going to return Jessica anytime soon. It had already been too long. The guards were very careful with The Founder; M took rigid precautions where these creatures were concerned. The suits they wore were encrusted with chain male breast coats and they had Gortex gorge's that came up and over that, covering their necks and chests. One of the guardsmen held his gun on The Founder while the other one took off the shackles and pushed him in the direction of the open gate. He walked on inside and sat down. The first guardsman put the shackles in their place and then left the room, returning to the elevator down the hall, and waited. The other locked the gate, and as he began to hook the keys back to his belt, the drill alarm sounded, causing him to drop them without realizing it. He bolted from the room, greeted at the door by his partner and then they both ran to the elevators. They were late for drills.

The Founder looked down at the keys, "Well, well, well!" he smiled and reached through the bars to retrieve them. He dangled them in the air and looked at them, and then he thrust them into his pocket. He would wait for the right moment, and then he would use them to get the girl back to Tad.

~~~~~~~~~~*~~~~~~~~~~

The moon was beginning to wane. The festival was over and so were The Regulators. Justice had come swift and brutal for them. They died by the sword they had lived by. They had been feared by people and had a reputation of being killers, rapists and devil worshippers. Some of it was true, some of it was exaggeration, but in the end they got a dose of the medicine they administered to others. Fate has a poetic way of leveling the playing field.

For whatever reason, Cassidy had spared Roy, maybe because he felt a kindred spirit with the old biker. They shared a favored character. Maybe it was because he made Cassidy laugh, he wasn't ordinarily merciful. But that was Cassidy's true nature, unpredictability. Roy, being the only survivor, would spend the rest of his life as a minister and would be an advocate for anyone plagued by the supernatural. He lived in fear of an animal totem coming for him every day for the rest of his life, and hid within the walls of the church.

But the guys were not done. They still had a mission to dissolve the research facility, and now that old business had been dealt with, it was on to the new. It was barely daybreak when they reconvened at the cabin and began to deliberate over the coming moon's plans. They needed The Founder, and they needed a cure. They also needed to get Jessica back safely.

They were seated around the table eating and discussing what to do next, when they all sensed of The Founder. All at the same time they looked up from their plates, locked eyes, then as if on cue, jumped up from the table and headed outside. Once in the front yard they spotted him coming up the driveway with a limp girl in his arms. It was Jessica. Tad immediately ran down the driveway to meet him followed fast by the others.

Tad felt her pulse and stroked her head, then looked up at The Founder. "She's alive, boy, but barely. Here, you'd better take her inside."

Tad transferred her from The Founder's arms to his own and quickly hustled her inside and laid her on the couch. He patted her hands a couple of times to try to wake her and he patted her face. Then he turned to Liam, "Liam, go get a wet rag. Please."

Patti's phone was ringing, he stepped back outside to answer it. The others circled the couch and looked upon Jessica. Tad looked to The Founder, "What happened?"

The Founder shook his head, "I don't rightly know, son. I wish I did. They had her strapped to a table when I found her. I just brought her to you."

Patti ran back inside and interrupted, "Tad!" They all turned to look at him. "That was Hannah, Jess's friend. She just reported her missing. How do you want me to handle this?"

Tad looked at Jessica, and then at The Founder whom was lighting up a cigar while looking back at him. Then he told Patti, "Call her back and tell her you are going to come out here and check first, and then you will come out there to fill out a report."

"Gotcha." Patti said as he headed back outside to make the phone call.

Cassidy stared down at her from the back of the couch. He was oddly quiet. He for some reason felt somehow connected to her. He hadn't paid much attention to her before. What was it? He just couldn't put his finger on it. Then Tad decided to move her.

"I'm going to put her in my room for now. When we talk to Hannah we are going to make it like she's been here with me the whole time. O.K.?" He looked at them all, they all nodded. Then Tad noticed Cassidy's quiet interest, "What's with you?" he asked him while holding Jessica in his arms.

It broke Cassidy's confused look, "Nothing. Why?"

"Well for one thing, you haven't said a single word for about ten minutes." Tad added.

"So?" Cassidy smirked and slid off the couch. "I think I'll go into town for a little while. Can we catch up later?"

"Sure." Tad said, confused. He'd never seen Cassidy act the least bit normal. It was strange. Tad turned to The Founder, he lifted an eyebrow at Tad and shrugged.

~~~~~~~~~~~*~~~~~~~~~~~

M was infuriated when he discovered that not only was The Founder gone again, but that his savior experiment, Jessica was gone as well. There really wasn't anything he could do about it at this point. He would have to wait for The Founder to return. M was angry enough to kill him over this. But he knew better, he knew he couldn't kill William without it withdrawing the curse in his pack. For now he would have to find some other way to get even. M huffed back to his laboratory to figure some things out.

The She

I am the she; there are none like to me,
& never again shall there be . . .

She was in a car on a long dark highway somewhere. There was a full moon and the wind was blowing through her hair from the open window. Jessica smiled, the wind was nice. She came to a T-junction in the road and suddenly a sleek black Mustang came barreling up the road beside her. She slammed on the brakes! The cars screeched to a halt just barely missing each other. Her car spun around in the road till it was almost facing the other direction. She was frightened.

The driver jumped out of his car. Oh my God! He looks angry, she thought. She couldn't really tell what he looked like in the darkness, but he seemed familiar to her. His face was all shadowy except for his intense eyes, and his black hair kept flying into his face. She was alone out there on that wide-open highway. The full moon was casting the only light available and a mist had risen across the acres and acres of open grassy fields surrounding them.

She frantically searched through her seats and purse for something to make a weapon out of. He approached her car and yanked the door open, without saying a word he reached in and grabbed her by the arm, pulling her out of the car. He had such a strong sexual pull. His influence was intoxicating and she couldn't shake the feeling that they were connected somehow already, even though she didn't really know him and his face was still shadowy.

He dragged her firmly over to his car, and flung her across the hood. She lie there on the hood, no longer frightened, but highly aroused. He tore his black t-shirt off and then proceeded to crawl upon her and kiss her. He threw her skirt up and wrapped her legs around his waist. He kissed her passionately, with handfuls of her hair in his fists. It was quiet except for the sounds of their passion as they attacked one another, and there seemed to be a rhythmic pulse to the air, thumping like African drums against the backdrop of the night. What was she doing? She couldn't tell him no. She *wouldn't* tell him no.

They engaged feverishly, making love on the hood of his custom black beauty, all the while she was unable to make out his face. But his eyes burned with a familiar glow from within. While in the throws of the most powerful climax she could ever imagine, he finally rose up enough for her to finally see his face, as if he was ready for her to see him, and smiling he said, "Thank you . . . my sister."

Jessica gasped for air! She suddenly knew why he was so familiar! It was Cassidy! She began to scream and pound him in the chest trying to get him off of her. She was sick. He stood and only smiled at her in a sort of psychotic way. She screamed and screamed and then . . . !

She woke up. She was still screaming. She sat up in the bed. It was a nightmare, a horrible, sexy, sick bad dream! She was panting and shaking all over. She was still aroused and freaked out all at the same time. Then she looked around the room, where was she? She knew this place. It was Tad's bedroom. But how . . . ?

Before she could think about anything else, Tad, followed by Liam and Luke, came bursting into the room and kneeled next to her on the bed. Tad put his hands on her shoulders and looked her in the eyes. "Jessica. Jessica it's O.K., you're safe now. I'm here."

She just stared back at him stunned for a minute. She was so disoriented. Had she dreamt the other stuff too? She was certain Professor Saunders had abducted her, but then, how did she get here?

Tad petted her and kissed her forehead, "It's O.K., Jess. Can you say something for me?"

She was still a little woozy and shaky, partly from the dream, and partly from the sedation, and partly from the confusion. It took her a minute to re-orient herself. "How long have I been here?" she asked

Tad. He looked over his shoulder at his brothers and then back to her. "A couple of hours." He answered.

She looked even more confused. "Then it was real?" she looked back to Tad.

"What was real, baby?" he asked patiently. He didn't want to overload her with what he knew already. He thought it best to let her mind unfold it on her own.

"Professor Saunders, he . . ." she started to remember, "He kidnapped me." She looked to Tad again, "He kidnapped me! He did! And then I woke up and there was this other man and he . . ." she stopped suddenly remembering Cassidy and the transfusion. She looked at her left arm, in the bend of it and it was bruised and sore. Then she began to recall what the man had told her. Suddenly a flood of thought came over her. What had they done? Oh my God! She remembered! She touched the bruise on her arm. She could still feel his blood in her veins. He was so heavily sedated that once the transfusion began the juice in his blood knocked her out too. That was a blessing though because the pain was intense. Oh God, what does that make him to me? Blood brother? The dream began to make a little more sense now.

She had been captive in thought for a few minutes. Tad didn't want to break her train of thought, but he decided to try to talk to her again. "Honey? What is it?"

She looked at him. She looked him in the eyes and she remembered what the man had told her about them all. She suddenly scooted up and pulled back and away from him, pulling herself up next to the headboard of the bed. She looked at the others then back to Tad. She pointed a finger in his face, "You!" She was getting angry. He didn't move, he didn't know what was happening but he could sense her fear. "You never told me. Why didn't you tell me? I know you haven't known me that long, but it's like we've known each other forever. You should have trusted me!" Then she reached out and swiftly slapped him hard across the face. He hadn't seen that coming. It made Liam and Luke jump too. Tad jumped to his feet and backed out the door as she jumped off the bed and came at him. She swung again, and again, slapping him harder and harder in the face. She was swinging at him as he was trying to grab her hands. She was hitting him hard enough to cause his head to turn. She was quick. Very quick. Unnaturally quick.

"Stop it!" Tad yelled at her, "Jess! Stop it! What's wrong with you?"

"What's wrong with me?" she yelled as she backed him up till he fell on the couch, no longer fearful. He fell back and she immediately threw herself on top of him and continued to slap and hit him, "What's wrong with you? Huh? I'm like you now! That's what's wrong with me! Why didn't you tell me?!!" She had no fear of him. She wasn't afraid of any of them. Patti came through the front door and saw her swinging at Tad. He immediately ran over and pulled her off him, giving Tad time to get up. Luke and Liam were afraid to move.

"What the Hell is going on here?" Patti demanded. "Hey, hey, hey!" he yelled. Jessica started to cry. Tad sat up on the couch, confused but unscathed.

"What are you talking about, Jess?" he asked her, rubbing his stinging face.

Patti let go of her wrists and helped her over to the adjacent sofa to sit down. She just cried for a few minutes. Luke and Liam sat down next to her. Liam had brought her some tissue. She wiped her eyes and looked over at Tad. "Why didn't you tell me what you were?"

Tad sat quietly for a moment and focused on her eyes, trying to decide if she meant what he thought she meant. Finally he answered, "Would you have believed me?"

She looked at Liam, sitting next to her. She looked past his glasses at his eyes. They were the same, reflecting light from the inside. Luke and Patti's too. "You're werewolves. I'm in love with the supernatural, and . . ." she paused, "I'm in love with you. I would have *tried* to believe you."

"I'm sorry, Jess. But you have to understand how unreal all of this seems. Even to me. What was I supposed to say?" Tad answered.

"Do you love me?" she asked him.

He looked only at her, "Yes." He answered.

She smiled, "Then you should have trusted me. Why did you send me away?"

"I'm cursed Jessica. I won't grow any older. You will. I'm surrounded by darkness. I'll absorb your light." He stood and walked slowly toward her. His brothers stood by quietly and watched. "I'm a killer. My friends are killers. I had to separate the man from the beast." He kneeled down in front of her, "And what kind of man would I be if I drug the woman I love into Hell with me?" he stared into her eyes; she began to cry and touched his face. "I had to make a decision I didn't want to make." He finished and waited for her to understand. "To protect you."

She lowered her head and began to cry harder. "Well." She sobbed, "Now I can make it for you." She held his hands and prepared to tell him what had happened to her at the research facility. "This man, I mentioned earlier."

"Yes," Tad followed.

"He performed an experiment on me."

Tad looked over at Liam. His blood went cold at the sound of it. Patti came closer and sat down on the coffee table beside Tad. They waited patiently for the rest of the story. She finished, "He gave me a transfusion."

"What? Like a blood transfusion?" Patti asked.

She nodded, "Yes." She paused again and looked into Tad's eyes, "And Cassidy was the donor."

The men all stood and looked upon one another, in shock. Tad was angry, angrier than he had ever been before. His blood went from cold to boiling. That was why he was looking at Jess funny, Tad thought. He looked at Jessica, "Does he know?" If she had said yes, Tad would have tracked him down and killed him.

"No." she answered, "He was out cold. I tried to wake him for help, but they had him very heavily sedated. They were afraid of him. I imagine they abducted him too."

Tad was oddly relieved. He knew Cassidy was a bastard, but he had faith that he would not betray the pack. "We have to tell him." Tad said, then he told Jessica about Hannah calling, and they discussed what they should tell her, and what they should *not* tell her. Patti had not made the second call back to the hotel yet. He was waiting for enough time to pass. Then he would call Hannah back to tell her that he found Jessica out at Tad's.

~~~~~~~~~~~*~~~~~~~~~~~

Cassidy pulled up across the street from the bookstore. He parked in a way Becca would not notice his car. He thought he would wait for her to come to work and just watch her for a while. The Founder was with him. He had followed Cassidy out to the car and gotten in it before he left the cabin. Cassidy had told him to get out, and when he didn't he decided to just bring him along.

"So. What are we doin'?" The Founder asked him. He just loved to annoy the boy. He was actually The Founder's favorite among them all.

Cassidy made him laugh. He lit up a cigar and waited patiently for the sarcasm.

"I'm keeping a close watch on my girl. Is that O.K. with you?" Cassidy rudely responded while he flipped through his CD's, finally settling on The Who.

"Fine by me. Is it fine by her?" The Founder pried. Cassidy stopped what he was doing and just looked over at the grinning bastard.

"It doesn't have to be fine with her. It's for her own good. She's very vulnerable right now. She doesn't need anyone fucking with her."

"Or maybe *you* don't want anyone hitting on your piece of ass?" The Founder cocked an eyebrow up and smiled over at Cassidy.

"Shut up you old fucker." Cassidy crudely snarled at him.

The Founder chuckled out loud and drew on his stogie and blew his smoke out the window, "Just an observation, my boy, just and observation." He said and he put the cigar back in his mouth.

"Yeah, well why don't you keep your bullshit to yourself from now on where I'm concerned, and can that 'boy' shit while you're at it. In fact, why don't you go back to calling me 'beast'? I feel like I'm out with my Dad." Cassidy growled at him and turned the radio up. The Founder chuckled like Santa Clause at him. He loved to get him going.

'The Real Me' was playing in the car as Becca approached the bookstore with her brother. Carlo had brought her to work after he and Hannah heard back from the Sheriff Deputy that he had found Jessica. He kissed his sister on the cheek and turned to leave after he made sure she was safe.

"Who's that?" The Founder poked, trying to get Cassidy riled up.

"That's her brother, you bitch."

William laughed louder, "Are you sure? You look a little pissed."

Cassidy looked over at him, "You shouldn't use words like 'piss', it doesn't match that tantalizing Southern charm of yours. And, yes. I'm sure it's her brother. His name is Carlo. I've only seen pictures of him, but that's him."

"You never met him in person?" The Founder was curious now.

"No." is all Cassidy would say about it.

They sat quietly for a few minutes then The Founder spoke up again. "I like this song. I never really got behind a lot of the loud music in my time, but this I like. It suits you."

"You aren't going to ask me out are you?" Cassidy smirked.

The Founder laughed at him, "Do you want me too?" he continued to chuckle and chew on his stogie. The car was filled with the smell of cherry tobacco.

"Well I'm glad you're having such a good time. Now get out."

William chuckled and looked over at Cass, ignoring the last comment, "Do you do a whole lot of this." He waved his stogie around in a circle then placed it back in his mouth, referring to Cassidy's stalking.

Before Cassidy could answer, along came Chris. The new guy Becca had met a few days before in the bookstore. It caught Cassidy's attention. "Welly-well. Cutie Pie is back."

"Old boyfriend of yours?" The Founder asked. But Cassidy was too preoccupied with Chris's presence to quip back. He clenched the steering wheel until his knuckles turned white, waiting for the man to emerge from the bookstore. Finally he did, followed out the door by Becca. She was smiling at that fool. Cassidy grimaced and ground his teeth. Chris reached out and kissed Becca's hand. "Pussy." Cassidy growled and lit up another cigarette, tossing the rest of the pack hard against the console. He watched as Becca gave him a little piece of paper. It was probably her phone number. Cassidy was beside himself with rage! He resisted the urge to get out of the car and deliver a little introduction of his own on the dude. Then he saw Mr. Whitehorse approach his shop front. Becca leaned over to hug and kiss the old man, and then introduced him to Chris. She always did love that old man, Cassidy thought to himself.

After Chris left, Becca stood outside for a minute and talked to Mr. Whitehorse. Cassidy watched her from his car. He missed coming to the bookstore to see her. He would pull up and she would meet him at the door sometimes and embrace him. Cassidy's heart was breaking. He watched her walk back inside. He was sick with himself, he was sick of the world, and he most definitely was sick of the old bastard that had hitched a ride with him this morning. He looked over at The Founder, whom was already looking over at him, still smoking and grinning.

Cassidy stared at him for a moment then he revved the engine and put the car into gear, "Let's go pick a fight." He said to the old veteran. The Founder nodded in compliance then Cassidy let out on the clutch and burned up the road.

Mr. Whitehorse watched from the sidewalk. He would say nothing to Becca about this and worry her, but he would have to let Carlo know somehow. He didn't want anything to happen to the poor girl. He worried over her like a father would a daughter.

~~~~~~~~~~*~~~~~~~~~~

Jack Saunders awoke the next morning able to move his jaw again. That serum was miraculous! A lot of its effects had worn off, however and he didn't feel as spry as he had a few hours before. But at least his jaw had healed. He walked over to the mirror and examined his face. Much of the bruising was gone as well. "How incredible!" He whispered. Amazed at the effectiveness of it. He wondered what the effects of long-term use would be.

He gathered his things and walked out of the room and down to M's office. He had to thank him for the serum. But when he entered M's office, he discovered the man angry and ranting.

"M!" Saunders shouted at him, "M what's wrong?"

M stopped raving like a nut and looked at his friend, "It's that beast! That big meddling beast!!"

"M, I just wanted to thank you for the treatment. Look at my jaw. Isn't this amazing?"

M sauntered over to Saunders and examined his jaw briefly. Momentarily distracted by another of his experiments gone right. "Fantastic, Saunders! Truly amazing."

"And look," Jack added, showing M his eyes. "No 'side-effects'."

"Well at least I have that going for me." M grunted.

"What happened? Why are you so upset?" Jack asked.

"The Founder. He has escaped yet again."

Saunders interrupted, "Wait, I thought you knew he was loose."

"He returned. Last night." M continued, "And he escaped again this morning. Only this time he took Jessica with him."

"What?!" Saunders yelled. "How? When?"

"I don't know exactly!" M snapped, his patience worn to a frazzle completely. "All I know is that he is gone! And my funding is going to cease if I don't locate him or that girl quickly! I've spent all morning in the lab trying to put together some preliminary results for my superiors."

He threw a stack of file folders down on the desk and plopped down in the chair behind it. He lowered his head into his hands and sighed long and hard. Jack said nothing. He could tell M was very upset, and he had no desire to be outside the safety of the research facility. He decided he would stay and help M figure out how to safely retrieve The Founder for now.

~~~~~~~~~~*~~~~~~~~~~

Peace Dogs

After Carlo had dropped Becca off at work, he and Hannah returned to the hotel room to pack up the girls' things. They were to go out to Tad's cabin and talk to Jessica. Hannah couldn't help but have this weird feeling, though. Even though she had talked to Jess on the phone, she still could tell there was something not quite right. Maybe it was the tone in her voice, or something she wasn't trying to say, or maybe it was just intuition. Either way, Hannah and Jess had been like sisters far too long for Hannah not to know when her friend needed her. She would take her aside when they got out there and get some answers.

~~~~~~~~~~~*~~~~~~~~~~~

Cassidy had no luck finding anyone to beat up. It was too early in the day for anyone asshole enough to deserve a good beating to be out and about, and the bars weren't open yet either. Besides that, The Founder had been bitching about being hungry for an hour, so Cassidy decided to treat him to a hamburger before they returned to the cabin, to get him to shut up.

The minute they arrived at the cabin and walked in Tad and Patti greeted them at the door, and Tad was clearly upset about something. He put a hand on Cassidy's chest, "Hey, I need to tell you something right now."

The Founder was still slurping on a giant milkshake. It was very distracting and unbecoming on him. Tad had to ask, "What's this?" he pointed at The Founder.

"Chocolate milkshake." The Founder purred, "And it's fantastic! I haven't had a burger and fries with a milkshake in years. "Then he glanced inside the door at Jessica, "I see your lady friend has recovered. I'll just go over and say 'Hello'. Excuse me gentlemen." He grinned at Tad and Patti, and then he sauntered over to the couch and sat down next to Jessica.

"Burger and fries?" Patti halfway smiled at Cassidy, it just didn't fit The Founder's mysterious persona, nor was it like Cassidy to be hospitable. "I've never even seen him eat."

"Oh, he eats." Cassidy bitched, "I had to buy the bastard three fucking hamburgers, loaded, two large fries, and that is his *second* fucking milkshake." Cassidy pointed over at him, "I spent over twenty dollars on his ass. Bitchy old bastard."

Tad interrupted, "Screw all that. Listen, you need to know something, right now, and it's a real mind-fuck."

"Oh wow." Cassidy sneered, "I haven't had one of those in weeks." He condescended.

Tad rolled his eyes, "Can I tell you?"

"Go ahead." Cassidy grunted, "Surprise me." His day had already been a bad one.

Tad glanced back over his shoulder at Jessica and the others on the couches. They were all engulfed in some off-the-wall story that The Founder was telling them. He turned back to Cassidy, "It's about Jessica." Tad decided to go outside and tell him, "Come on." He grabbed Cassidy by the shirt and pulled him out onto the front porch. Patti followed.

Once they were outside, Tad continued, "The other night, before the full moon, you said something weird happened?" he asked Cassidy, "You woke up in your car? Hung-over?"

"Yeah, somebody shot me with darts and knocked me out. But I didn't get a look at who did it. I think we pretty much know who did it, right? But I don't know why. It was like they shot me and left me there to wake up again." Cassidy answered.

"Well," Tad found it hard to find the right words, "I think we know why now." He sighed then continued, "They used you as a blood-donor."

"What?" Cassidy smirked, "How do you know that?"

"Because Jessica saw it. They used you as a blood-donor . . ." he paused, "for her." Tad made sure their eyes connected when he told him. He wanted him to know the full implications of what that meant.

"Your girlfriend?!" Cassidy was shocked, he put his hands on his hips, "Do we know why? Why don't I remember anything about it?"

"They evidently had you so heavily sedated it knocked her out for two days. I imagine *that's* why." Tad grunted. He was still very upset with the idea of *any* part of Cassidy being inside *his* girlfriend. Let alone the possibilities of what she could become. As unnatural as their curse already was, this was even more so.

"I did have a mother fucker of a headache when I got up. Well," Cassidy smirked, "That's one way I haven't been inside a woman before."

Tad reared back and punched him in the face. Cassidy's smile returned but before he could return the punch, Patti jumped in between them. "Hey, hey, hey, hey *HEY*!" he yelled at them both. Tad was bowed up ready to swing again. He didn't need Cassidy's crude humor right now, and he was feeling very territorial over Jessica. In turn, Cassidy was pent up with rage over Becca. It was a very combustible situation.

"Knock it off!" Patti yelled, "Let's go back inside and figure out what we're going to do!" He tried to insinuate himself between them and break the tension. Their eyes were locked, and this time it was Tad picking the fight. "Tad!" Patti yelled at him, trying to break the stare, "Tad!" Patti shoved at him. Tad shoved him back hard and walked past him without breaking eye contact with Cassidy, and went back inside.

Patti looked over at Cassidy who was lighting up a cigarette now. "You have no tact what so ever, do you? No timing, no sense of grace?"

"Who needs tact?" Cassidy grinned at him, "I've got you." Then he went inside as well.

"What next?" Patti shook his head and whispered. "Vampires?"

~~~~~~~~~~~*~~~~~~~~~~~

M decided he would load up the Suburbans and wait at the end of Tad's driveway, near the main road for The Founder at dark. They would wait and retrieve him as he wandered out. It was the only way M knew to get to the rest of them. He would start with The Founder, and then gather the rest of them up one at a time if he had to. He had a month to prove to his superiors that his new plan of action with Jessica would work, and he wasn't going to let that old bastard fuck it up for him. "This is only a minor set-back," he convinced himself, "Soon to be rectified."

~~~~~~~~~~~~*~~~~~~~~~~~~

Jessica took a hot shower and had a bite to eat before Hannah arrived. She was actually feeling really well. The bruises that were on her arm when she awoke were all but gone now, and she wasn't feeling nauseas anymore. Evidently some part of the transfusion took, because she was certainly feeling strange. Her hearing and sense of smell were greatly improved. She could barely handle the smell of the shampoo she had used, it was so strong that it was overwhelming. She and Cassidy didn't really know what to say to each other, but they would occasionally lock eyes, and when they did it was like she had known him forever. It was strange and creepy. She wondered if this was how the pack communicated all the time. They were all connected now.

She really liked The Founder. She knew that through Cassidy, some part of him must be flowing through her now too. But it was more than that. Maybe it was because he rescued her, or maybe it was just because his life was so fascinating. He was from the time of the Civil War. That in itself was amazing, she could hardly believe it was true. His old world charm and accent made all her previous encounters with him before she knew him make sense now. He wasn't an old man when he was turned, he was only forty-two, and he was really very attractive. Or was that the pheromones? Tad had explained some about their nature to her earlier that morning. He let her read the journal he had been keeping. They all had a long discussion about what they had discovered about this intriguing ailment. She finished eating and then joined the others in the great room to wait for Hannah. It was strange. In light of what was happening, she was oddly at peace, calmly unafraid of anything. But Hannah, what was she going to say to her?

In the great room, The Founder was enlightening the others with all he knew. He was aware of the fact that he probably wouldn't get another chance to tell them anything after tonight. He knew that M would come for him, and this time he would make no mistakes in tying him down. Jessica found a spot across from him next to Tad, and curled up to listen.

"These madmen keep me here to build others, like you. To study and examine, and to build super-human mercenaries for their wars and causes. Unfair weapons strategy, I say! But I come from a different time, and my time was over long ago. The Civil War was far from civil, but the weapons you could see and predict, and you could count on their honesty." They were all entranced with The Founder's story and the vital information he was forthcoming with. They were quiet and listening to him, and they waited patiently as he lit another cigar and sipped his Brandy for him to continue.

He began again, looking at his favorite brand of cigar, and watching it burn, "I've grown so tired of this half-life. I've been a killer for so long. I'm through siring wolf-men. You are the last I would do for them, and I'm sorry for that." He sighed and drew on his stogie, "I would end it if I could. But they won't kill me, and I can't kill myself. No matter the cause, I would not die if the wounds were self-inflicted, so I am told, and my death seems to be the only way to free all of you of this curse. It's more of the hocus pocus part of this ancient nightmare that I don't totally understand. Rules of the supernatural, as it were. That is why their scientific techniques cannot fully unlock its code. It is protected by the unknown and disbelief."

He turned to look at Cassidy, "Beware boy. You are the heir apparent to this lunar legacy. They covet your brutality over all the others. You are the most like me."

Cassidy said nothing for a minute or two, then he fell back into his usual grit, "Well that's good to know. I only hope I'm as decrepit as you in two hundred years."

The Founder laughed out loud at the comment. Patti shushed Cassidy, "Shut up Cassidy." Cassidy flipped him a bird.

"Oh it's alright," The Founder chuckled as he rose from his seat, "I think he's cute."

Then Liam rose and spoke, "I think we all need to hit the road before Jess's friend arrives. Give them time to talk. What do you guys say? You want to go into town for some drinks? You too William." Liam smiled and slapped The Founder on the arm.

"Why certainly," he accepted, "A drink sounds terrific! Besides, I like riding in that fast car of Cassidy's."

"Oh, Hell no." Cassidy grunted, "You're not riding with me again."

The Founder chuckled at him and returned the cigar to his mouth. Then Patti patted him on the back, "That's alright William, I've got a fast car too. You can ride with me."

"Oh, yes? Well now, much obliged, much obliged. I'd be honored to share a carriage with you." The Founder smiled.

"Oh please." Cassidy snarled, "Are you kidding me? Is this family night? Should we go bowling?"

"Afraid I can take the Mustang, Cass?" Patti teased.

Cassidy grinned back at him, "Never."

So they loaded up the two cars, Liam and Cassidy in the Mustang, and Patti and Luke and The Founder in the squad car, leaving Tad behind with Jessica, as they headed for the main road to drag race. They drove right by the government Suburbans hidden in the woods just across the driveway without noticing they were being watched.

Once on the main highway, they lined the cars up nose to nose and revved them up. The Mustang's powerful motor roared and shook the road. Likewise the blower poking out of the shaker hood Patti had installed on the cruiser, wiggled with every punch to the gas, and the breather flaps opened and closed as the engine rumbled.

Cassidy drew on his cigarette as he looked to his left past The Founder sitting shotgun in the police car, into Patti's eyes just on the other side and punched on the gas. They grinned at each other, they loved this shit, and then Cassidy suddenly flicked his cigarette to the road, laid both hands on the wheel and popped the clutch. Liam grasped the dash as both cars suddenly lurched forward in a fury of burning rubber and smoke, and barreled down the highway. They were neck in neck, each topping 60 MPH in a matter of seconds. The Founder grinned like a boy as the G-force held him back in his seat. The cars roared down the road, Cassidy shifted gears and threw it in to high launching the Mustang way out front. Another car was coming down the road the opposite way, causing Patti to throw the squad car into Cassidy's lane just in time to miss hitting it.

Liam jumped up and sat on the door of the Mustang and hollered back at the squad car as they plundered down the highway. This was more fun than he had ever had in his life.

~~~~~~~~~~~*~~~~~~~~~~~

Carlo and Hannah followed Tad's instructions out to the cabin and arrived just before dark. Jessica ran out the door and hugged Hannah long and hard, and tried not to cry. Hannah wasn't as lucky, she was already crying. She had been so worried that something horrible had happened to her friend, that she had been beside herself all weekend.

Tad walked around and shook Carlo's hand. The men had not been formally introduced, though they had seen plenty of each other over the last week at the festival. They all went inside and sat down to talk.

"Wow!" Carlo said astonished at the size and luxury of the cabin, "This is really nice, man."

"Yeah," Tad sighed, "I've really gotten spoiled to it. I'm going to try to buy it when my lease runs out. I really love it out here."

Hannah was impressed as well, "Oh my God, Jess!" she held her friend's hands in hers, afraid to let go of her for the moment, "You really did well for yourself. No wonder you hid out here all weekend."

"Yeah, well. I just was so glad Tad asked me over I guess I didn't think about calling. I'm really sorry Hannah. I guess the time got away from me. I didn't mean to worry you." Jessica didn't like lying to her best friend. She had never kept any kind of secrets from her before, even though she and Tad had decided it was best for now for her not to know, it was still very hard for Jess to be dishonest with her best friend.

But Hannah wasn't totally convinced, she could sense that there was something else going on. It wasn't what she thought it might be, and she would have never guessed what it really was, but it was something. She could feel it, Jessica seemed different to her somehow. Her eyes seemed strange. She decided to pry a little, "Jess, are you alright? Your eyes look a little week."

"Oh," Jessica sighed, "I guess I haven't gotten much sleep over the past two days."

Hannah smiled really big and slapped her arm, "You little slut! I've been worried sick for two days and you've been out here at 'Shay Tad's' shacking up! You're turning into me!" She joked making Jessica laugh and hugged her friend tightly once more. "I love you, girlie." She whispered and they both cried a little more. Hannah decided to just be Thankful her friend was alive for now. They joined the boys on the couch and Tad lit a fire. He could tell Carlo and Hannah were getting cold. He also noticed that Jessica wasn't, as he watched her from the fireplace, and he was getting sick over it. Tad couldn't stand the idea of Cassidy's blood coursing through her. He hoped it didn't turn her into an asshole.

~~~~~~~~~~*~~~~~~~~~~

Back in town the guys had decided to go to Cassidy's favorite place, The Tavern. Of course the owner, Webber, was none too happy about it, and he was even less than pleased that the Sheriff Deputy was out partying it up with him. Who would he call if things got raucous? Where was the Sheriff? He approached the table.

"Well, Deputy Leason, what brings you out here? And with such a bastard as this one." He pointed to Cassidy with his thumb.

"Keep pointing that thumb at me Webber and I'll break it." Cassidy growled.

Webber whipped around and put his hands on his hips, "Now listen you, you . . . miscreant." Cassidy raised his eyebrows and looked at his buddies, not taking Webber seriously at all. "You just mind your manners in here tonight, or I'll shoot you."

"Did you hear that, Patti?" Cassidy smiled, "He'll shoot me."

Patti took a sip of beer from the large frosty mug the waitress had just brought him and answered, "Yeah I heard him," he looked up at Webber, "Go ahead and shoot him now, Webber. It'll save time."

Cassidy chuckled and laughed from across the table. They all kind of chuckled. Of course they knew it wouldn't hurt any of them to get shot, and Patti was having too much fun to be bothered with it.

Webber turned to look at Patti, "Where is your Sheriff?"

"He's on vacation. Screwing hookers. You won't be able to reach him for a long while." Patti answered cockily. They all snickered some more.

"Look here." Webber huffed, "You look like you're already three sheets to the wind and you just got here. Now, I don't know what's going on here, but all I want is a peaceful night in my bar. Got it?" he turned back to Cassidy, "No fighting!" He snapped at him then he stomped away.

"I say," The Founder began, "That little man seems a little to prissy to be a barkeep." He smiled as he drank from his mug.

Cassidy grinned at The Founder, "Is he your type?"

"No, but he sure seems to like you." The Founder grinned back.

"Ha, Ha!" Cassidy snarled, and then he signaled the waitress to come back. She walked over to the table and smiled at all of them. She was eyeing The Founder and smiled even bigger at him. He winked at her. "What'll it be ornery?" she teased Cassidy. She knew him. Everybody at The Tavern knew him. The men at The Tavern didn't like him so much, but the women sure did.

"Rum. Bring me the whole damn bottle and a tumbler." He said bossily.

"O.K., anything else for you gentlemen?" she asked them all. The others shook their heads and drank their beers. The Founder spoke up, "I'll take two more of these," he waived his beer mug at her and added, "And your room key." He tipped his head at her and raised his eyebrows. She smiled really wide and said, "Well. I thought this one was trouble." She pointed at Cassidy, "but I see better now. I'll be right back with your bottle." She turned and kept her gaze on The Founder as she walked away for a minute.

Cassidy and the others looked over at The Founder strangely. They had never seen him this frisky before. He sure was pulling out all the stops today. Cassidy had to comment, "You freak. Who do you think is paying for all this?"

The Founder looked back at him and lit up a stogie, "Why, you are."

"Old bastard." Cassidy growled.

Liam looked over his shoulder at the waitress again. She was still looking at The Founder. Liam looked in his eyes, he didn't have to say anything, he just smiled and The Founder picked up on his thoughts.

"What can I say, I'm irresistible to women." He smiled.

"Isn't she a little old for you?" Patti asked. Her name was Bronte' and she had worked at The Tavern for years. She was a very attractive older woman, probably in her late forties.

"Sonny," The Founder started, "I'm older than this entire State. So as far as I'm concerned, any woman still above ground is a young woman."

They all laughed and Cassidy had to add to it with his usual grit and humor, "You are an *old* bastard. I wonder if she knows she's robbing the grave."

"You just keep your mouth shut there boy, before I have to *smack* it." The Founder retorted, "Besides, what does age matter when you are faced with a beautiful woman?"

The bantering and drinking continued for a while. They were all bonding and having a good time, but there was just one thing missing, the thing that Cassidy loved most in the world. Chaos. He had been looking for a fight all day to vent his anger over Becca, and it had been hard to find. So he decided he might as well start one here.

He got out of his chair and walked around the table to Patti and pulled him up out of his seat. Pat looked confused at him, he knew he was up to something. Before he could ask him what the fuck he was doing, that ornery smile pulled across Cassidy's face and then Patti knew all he could do was brace himself. WHAM! Cassidy punched Patti right in the mouth, knocking him back down in his chair and back into Luke. The Founder was to the left of Patti; he scooted his drinks back out of the way slowly and kept on smoking. By now the entire bar was at attention.

Patti looked up at Cassidy dazed for a second, and watched him standing there with his grin on and his fists clenched, waiting. Then he too began to smile and he quickly pushed himself up and out of the chair and tackled Cassidy around the waist. Both of them fell on top of the table behind them and rolled onto the ground. They were laughing and beating the shit out of each other. No anger just good, old-fashioned male horseplay.

Liam and Luke watched the whole thing with The Founder and laughed as the whole bar began to erupt. Cassidy and Patti stopped fighting each other and turned to fight new adversaries. Once the brawl had commenced, Luke and Liam jumped up and leapt across the table to join in. Webber was freaking out. He ran out of his office with his hands on his head. "Oh my God! Not again! Damn you Cassidy!!" he was yelling over the roar of the crowd. "Damn you! Damn you!"

Most of the women in the room had adjourned to the back of the bar, where it was safer. Bronte' was trying to get out of the way when she was knocked off balance and landed in The Founder's lap. He was still sitting right where he had been, unfazed by the chaos around him, sipping his beer. He caught her and chivalrously helped her to her feet amidst the madness.

"Come, my lady. Lest we away from all this childish nonsense and violence." He held her hand and kissed it. She smiled at him, "Thank you, sir." She smiled, playing along gracefully.

Before he could follow her out, Cassidy tapped him on the shoulder, "Hey Pops!"

The Founder turned around and Cassidy popped him in the mouth, breaking his cigar in half while it was still on his lips. The Founder cracked his neck and let go of Bronte's hand. Then he slowly pulled the broken cigar out of his mouth and looked at it a minute. Cassidy stood smiling wildly at him with his dukes up. "Why you unconscionable little brat. You broke my cigar. This is war, sir."

Cassidy just gave him the 'come on', gesture with his hands and kept smiling. He couldn't wait to get a few in on the old dog. He enjoyed punching him in the mouth. Bronte' moved out of the way, and watched as Cassidy and William swung at the same time. Nazareth blared from the juke box in the background, "Now you're messin' with a . . . a Son-of-a-Bitch!" It was fevered, and the boys felt truly alive.

Webber was hysterical. The whole place was lit up! The bouncers were fighting, the customers were fighting, and friends were fighting! The only police officer he could call for help was out there fighting as well! He ran back into his office, hid under his desk and loaded his gun. He threatened Cassidy with it all the time, but he wasn't the kind of man to really use it. He just wanted to hold on to it in case he needed it. He was definitely not a fighter.

The fever began to smolder out in the place after about twenty minutes, and everyone was picking themselves up off the floor. Cassidy and the others staggered outside to get some fresh air. Cassidy was still wired, he jumped onto the hood of Patti's car and stretched his arms up and growled and yelled into the sky. He felt great!! Fighting really unleashed his demons. He always loved the passion and the fury of a good fistfight. No teeth and claws, no moon, just honest fall in the dirt, blow-for-blow, fist fighting!

Patti stumbled over to the squad car and shoved him, "Get off my car, you mother fucker!!" he yelled loudly and shoved him again. Cassidy ignored him and closed his eyes and breathed the air in deeply.

The Founder leaned up against the back of the Mustang with Luke and Liam. He lit up another cigar, and regarded it for a minute. Liam lay back across the trunk. He had never had this much fun before! He wondered how he had managed to miss so much free rage in his lifetime. His glasses were broken but he could care less.

They were soon joined by Cassidy and Patti, who crawled up onto the back of the cruiser parked next to them. Cassidy pulled his cigs out of his pocket, they were all broken so Patti laughed at him. He threw the pack down and rummaged through the Mustang for more. Then Bronte' walked out to the cars and met them. "Well," she began, "I guess I have the rest of the night off. Would you like to spend it with me?" She smiled slyly at The Founder.

He stood and bent an arm out for her. "Why that is the single best offer I've had in *many* years." He turned to look at the boys, "Well gentlemen,

I'll be off." Cassidy found his cigarettes, opened them and lit one as he approached The Founder. Liam and Patti sat up to listen, and Luke shook his hand. The Founder saluted them. "Thank you boys for an evening I've not experienced in over 100 years. It felt great to choose my own woman and fight like a man once more. There is nothing like racing, fighting and being rewarded with love from a beautiful woman, to make a man feel like a real man. Ado'" Then he turned and followed Bronte' to her car. They knew exactly what he meant. The night was still young and so were they. Forever.

~~~~~~~~~~*~~~~~~~~~~

Legacy Of Brutality

LATER THAT NIGHT . . .

The guys were fueled up and still looking for trouble, but aside from another fistfight at a local gas station with a truckload of rednecks, there just wasn't any more to be found. Luke decided he wanted Patti to drop him off at the Hotel to be with Chloe. He hadn't seen her since before they fought The Regulators, and he was sure she was feeling abandoned. Afterwards, Cassidy went his own way and Liam and Patti went on back to Pat's apartment. Each of them thought of The Founder as they fell back into their beds. Even though he was the exact cause of all their infliction, they all had pity for him and they liked him.

~~~~~~~~~~~*~~~~~~~~~~~

Cassidy had driven around for a while, not sure what to do with himself. He was still very troubled by the incident with Becca and this new guy. He hated him! He had to justify his rage somehow, but he had run out of ideas. If he knew where the guy lived, he would end this right now! But he didn't. Maybe he should have just gotten himself a room at the Hotel and smashed it up. Instead he decided to drive way out into the darkness of the night, far, far out into the wilderness, and turn himself loose. So he did.

Cassidy hadn't felt fear since the night he was attacked, and now that he knew his attacker, he was less than afraid of anything. He was what was to be feared now, he and his brethren. He thought of Patti. Imagine being in trouble, he thought, imagine calling for help, and the help that comes for you is scarier than what you were running from in the first place. Nobody knew when they called Patti for help what he was capable of. That's my problem, Cassidy thought, I know too much.

He pulled up beside the lake and got out of the car. He stretched and breathed in the air deeply. He listened intently to the sounds around him as they slowly faded until it was completely still and quiet. His presence in nature had suddenly caused all the wildlife to flee and grow quiet, even the crickets. He breathed in deeply again and then started to undress. He threw his clothes back inside of his car and shut the door. Then he looked up to the sky and closed his eyes. He balled his fists and stretched out his arms. He began to think back, and reflect on his life with Becca. He flinched, his nostrils flared and his breathing got shallower and shallower. He clenched his jaw and kept remembering. He started to grunt and roar, still he held his eyes shut tight and thought back to this morning, to that guy with Becca. Finally, he slowly began to lower his head and open his eyes. They were not his own. He was invoking the shift. He wanted to run and hunt and be fevered. From the moment he first became it, Cassidy had embraced the beast inside him, and now the man he had become wasn't far from beastly either.

He continued to shift, welcoming it on. He had become quite efficient at shifting. He could bring it on in mere minutes now. He was complete in about fourteen minutes. He let the shift fall upon him slowly, so he could savor its power. His back tingled and crawled as it stretched and cracked. It was a satisfying sensation, he thought, knowing he was so powerful! Once complete he threw his head back and roared up at the moon in the sky, and then he dropped to his hands and ran full on into the forest. Wildlife scattered all around him as he snapped and howled at them, and ran through the trees. He wanted to put his power to the test, and he soon had his chance. As he entered a large clearing, he ran square on into a giant grizzly bear. It rose to its feet as Cassidy approached and rose to his. This would definitely be an interesting challenge, Cassidy thought, and he smiled through his wolf-skin.

~~~~~~~~~~~*~~~~~~~~~~~

TWO WEEKS LATER . . .

M had retrieved The Founder and had been working feverishly on his newest diabolical plans. He was working on a new weapon for ensnaring the manimals, and he was planning on an ambush upon the fullest moon. It was only a couple of weeks until then, and he would be ready to capture the others. Until then, he would test his newest inventions on The Founder and vent his anger on the man by torturing him. Something, unfortunately, The Founder had become quite accustomed to over the years.

Likewise, the pack had been readying itself for the moon. Though they new nothing of M's latest plans, they new there would be trouble. The Founder had told them there would be trouble. But while Tad and Liam and Luke and Patti and Jessica were preparing, Cassidy was always gone, following Becca. He had been watching her and this new guy for days now. He was obsessed with it. He would watch from his car, and he would follow them on walks and he would peek into her bedroom windows. He certainly gave stalking a whole new meaning. Patti and the others simply could not avert him from it long enough to get him involved.

And Patti was getting worried. He had always worried about Becca being around Cassidy, and now he was far more dangerous and volatile. He had always been violent over Becca anyway, but now, he could really do some damage. Patti was afraid that in a fit of rage, Cassidy might shift and accidentally kill Becca. He knew he would never do it intentionally, but his new abilities made him even more unpredictable.

~~~~~~~~~~*~~~~~~~~~~

Luke had been helping Chloe get things back in order. He had been spending a lot of time at the Feed 'N Seed store with her, readying it for its Grand Re-Opening. It was a lot of responsibility for a girl of her young years to take on, but she felt she owed it to her mother to try, and she had plenty of support from Luke plus her other friends and their families. She would be fine.

After they spent a few hours at the store, Luke and Chloe decided to go back to her house. She had been able to return to it the week before, and she and Luke had been staying there together. She was still a little too freaked out by the house knowing what had happened there, to stay in it alone. So Luke, being the gentleman that he was, volunteered to stay with her. He figured it would free up some room at the cabin for Tad anyway, since he now had Jess there all the time, and it would give he and Chloe some more privacy too.

As they walked through the front door, Chloe had to stop for a minute. She dropped the bag she was holding and held her head. Luke quickly put his bags down too, and wrapped his arms around her. "Are you O.K.?" he asked her.

She kept her eyes closed for a minute, and then she looked up at him. "No." she said, "No, I can feel thum here." She whispered at him. She feared he would think she was having a breakdown or something.

"Feel them? What do you mean?" he looked at her confused, willing to believe anything she said.

"My Uncle, and Jared. They are still in this house." She looked worried. Luke could tell she believed it herself, "They haunt me still, victims of a violent death. They linger in this house! Will I ever be free of them?" Her voice was quivering. She began to cry a little. "Hold me."

He didn't know what to say. He wrapped his arms around her tighter and held her there in the doorway for a few minutes while she cried. It was going to be a lot harder for her than she had thought.

~~~~~~~~~~*~~~~~~~~~~

Tad and Liam were engaged in filming a sequence that would finish off their nature film. They would submit it to their benefactors later that month for editing. Being out in the field, studying nature, that's what they loved to do the most. The unnatural things they had become did nothing for them. They didn't embrace its freedoms as Cassidy did. They saw it for what it was, a curse, an intruder in their normal lives. At least that's the way Tad felt about it.

Jessica felt as he did. Although it had given her new insight as to the nature of the supernatural, it had also robbed her of her real life. The one she longed for and missed. She watched them from the kitchen window as they adjusted their cameras and got ready for a day out in the field. She had taken time off from school to try to figure this new thing out. She had to lie to her best friend. She was afraid of what would happen to her next. So far she had not transformed into anything, but her senses were a hundred times sharper, and her temperament and agility were through the roof. She no longer feared Cassidy because now she was the same. Now, she understood him.

She watched Tad as he jumped into the Jeep with Liam and drove away. What would she do with herself here all day? She picked up a magazine and plopped down on the couch. How boring, she thought.

~~~~~~~~~~~*~~~~~~~~~~~

As usual, Cassidy was parked outside of the bookstore. He sat smoking a cigarette and chugging black rum from the driver's seat. Lover boy was there again. Cassidy's blood boiled under his skin. He thought about following the man home a time or two and then decided to wait on killing him. He wanted to make a point with Becca, so she wouldn't try this again. He had told her he would never let anyone else have her, and he had meant it. He waited for the man to leave, and he watched as Becca kissed him goodbye and waved to him. His nostrils flared. He flung his cigarette out the window, kicked back the bottle again till it emptied and started the car. He whipped the car around in the road and punched the gas, letting out on the clutch all at once. The tires burned into the asphalt, leaving long stinking rubber marks on the road behind him.

He flew down the highway, full throttle, with the engine wide open. The needle on the odometer was bouncing wildly up and down on the 160 mark. He yelled at the top of his lungs as he shot like a bullet in his car down the long straight stretch of road, finally slamming on his brakes. The car screeched to a sliding halt. It slid for several yards before stopping, but before it did, Cassidy jumped out and fell to his knees in the road. He screamed and slammed his fists into the pavement violently over and over again until they bled. He yelled and roared and vented his rage all over the road. He was hitting the road so hard and violently that his knuckles and fingers were breaking. Still, he kept slamming them into the asphalt. Blood sprayed all over his face and shirt and the bones and ligaments in his fists cracked and shattered. Finally, he stopped and lowered his head to the ground. He was breathing hard and tears were flowing from his eyes. His rage had taken him over, but he did not shift. He didn't want to.

The car had rolled finally stopping in a small dip in the side of the road. After a few minutes, Cassidy rose to his feet and slung his hair back out of his face. Then looking out over the road with tears streaking his cheeks, he smiled. The vision in front of him faded in and out from color to black & white as his eyes adjusted for a shift. He looked over at his car, then down at his hands. They were crushed. He couldn't bend them to close his fists. Every bone in them was broken. He gritted his teeth together and flinched back the pain as he forced them open as wide as he could make them. They cracked as he stretched his fingers out to their full extensions. They were healing as he watched. He bent them back and forth until he could finally ball up his fists again. The scrapes and abrasions on their surfaces were the last things to heal. He watched them vanish. He hated that they disappeared. He used to love wearing the scars of his battles. It was like a badge he could flash at every body showing he was tougher than they were. It was almost sexy, he thought. He missed it.

He walked over to the Mustang and grabbed the front end. He heaved and growled and then almost effortlessly wrenched the heavy machine back up onto the road. Then he ran around and jumped in the front seat and cranked it up. He cut the wheel tight and let out on the clutch, spinning the machine around until it was facing the opposite direction, and then he bolted back down the road toward the cabin.

~~~~~~~~~~~*~~~~~~~~~~~

Patti had spent much of his time lately handling his police duties. There were tons of reports that had not yet been filed, and he had plenty of other things to handle out at the jailhouse. So he did. It was going to take him weeks to finish, as he had let things go for months. He had been so preoccupied with his new condition that he hadn't covered up the way he should. If he were to be investigated by the state police, he would have a whole lot of explaining to do. For the most part the small town had been quiet. The only shit going down, Patti had been a part of, so there really hadn't been too many calls for help, and the population was such that pretty much everybody knew everybody else here. Patti's vigilante behavior had brought what little crime they had here to a halt. No one wanted to fuck with him. He was doing a pretty good job by doing things his way. Everyone was happy.

~~~~~~~~~~~*~~~~~~~~~~~

Hannah had been helping out at The Golden Earring. She really liked being this close to Carlo, and she was still within range of Jessica too if she needed anything. To be honest, Hannah was real worried about her friend. It wasn't like her to lay out of school and she was acting very secretive too. Hannah knew there was something she wasn't telling her, but she didn't know what to say or do to get it out of her. So she decided to spend her free time and non-class time here with Carlo until she could figure it out. She wondered if maybe Jess was pregnant and just didn't want to tell her yet. That would be pretty big news though, and she found it hard to believe that her very best friend wouldn't tell her first. Whatever it was, Jessica was definitely different.

Likewise, Carlo had worried over his sister. He was supposed to take Hannah out for dinner and fun tonight but he just couldn't shake this overwhelming feeling of dread and doom. He knew it was over Becca. She was going out with this new guy tonight, and she seemed really happy here lately. He couldn't figure out why he was so worried, he just *felt* something was wrong all day.

Carlo had met the new guy and thought he was nice. He felt like Becca could handle herself with him. He never was able to get her to tell him or Hannah anything about the old boyfriend, or about what happened a few weeks ago that freaked her out so bad. He guessed he should just be relieved that she was moving on. He knew that she would eventually confide in him about it one day.

They finished polishing tables and sweeping up and then he and Hannah returned to his place to get ready for their night out. Carlo was certainly happy with his own love life. Hannah was terrific.

~~~~~~~~~~~*~~~~~~~~~~~

Tad had returned and crawled into bed with Jessica, while Liam took the Jeep and went on out to the jail to help Patti. He had promised him he would do what he could to help him get things in order out there. And Luke was helping Chloe box up Jared and Darby's belongings so they could donate them. Chloe had decided she was going to sell the house and the business. It was all too much responsibility for her, and besides, she just couldn't stand to be there. Especially now that she was sure it was haunted by her uncle and stepfather.

As they cleaned out drawers and boxes, Chloe ran across a few of her mother's things. It caused her to break down and Luke had to console her by rocking her on his lap until she passed out asleep. He laid her down on the sofa, and made sure the doors were locked, and then he returned to the bedroom to finish up where he had stopped. As soon as he entered Darby's bedroom, he heard a loud "BANG!" from the other room. He pricked up his ears and followed the sound. "BAM!" came another noise from the direction of Chloe's bedroom. He turned his head toward the noise and opened his nostrils wider to try to take in the scent of something. "BAM! BAM!" It came again. This time he was sure it was coming from Chloe's room. He followed it down the hallway and cautiously opened her bedroom door. "BANG!" Something hit the floor right behind the door. He reached around the wall and flicked the lights on. Then he slowly put his hand on the door and pushed it open.

When it opened his eyes immediately widened, for what he saw was other-worldly. Papers were flying around the bed like they were in a whirlwind and shoeboxes were flying out of the closet and landing against the floor with a "BANG! BAM!" The hairs on his neck were pricked up and he couldn't believe what he was seeing. After all the unusual things he had witnessed over the past few months, he was surprised to be surprised. If he existed as a werewolf, then why not ghosts too?

He was more fascinated than scared. He wanted to go get Chloe up but he was afraid it would be over if he turned his back on it. He walked inside the room and the door slammed shut behind him, and everything just stopped and fell to the floor. He turned and tried to open the door but it wouldn't budge, and the sudden stillness in the room was even creepier than the whirlwind. It was as though the ghost was looking for something in a fury. The room was a mess. Luke leaned down and looked through some of the things in the floor, nothing significant, really. Luke jumped up, his hair was being blown about his face by the force of the wind whipping up from behind him.

Luke stood, silently absorbing the incredible moment. Finally, a small flat shoebox was pulled from where it had lain underneath the dresser. The invisible entity seemed to have kicked it across the floor to Luke. It stopped in front of his feet. Luke reached down, picked it up and opened it. Once he did, everything stopped. He could feel the entity leave the room like a sigh. He returned his attention to the box.

Luke looked down inside the box and what he found was just as shocking as the ghostly encounter. There was parchment and candles and a dagger, and clips of hair, all wrapped up inside of a blood-covered velvet cloth. What was all this? He thought. He opened the parchment up and read the heading in a whisper, "Drawing down the Moon." He looked concerned as he continued to read it, it was a chant, an incantation, asking the Goddess for the power to over throw oppressors. It was witchcraft! Chloe had been begging the Goddess to rid her of her uncle and stepfather! She had cursed them!

Luke had been raised in a primarily Christian faith. He had never believed in any of these things until he had witnessed them for himself. Now he would never doubt anything again. He couldn't begrudge Chloe for her attempts at freedom. Her life had been little more than slavery. But he wasn't sure how to feel about this newest discovery. Had she actually summoned a beast to destroy the men that had abused her? Had he been one of them? Or was it just coincidence? Did Chloe believe she had done it? Maybe that was why she was so tormented, she was guilt-ridden. Or was she? It was all too freakish.

He put the items back into the box and carried it into the living room. He stood over her for a moment, trying to absorb everything that had just happened and trying to decide just how to confront her with this. He wondered if he should tell her about himself. Was now the time? It had to be. He reached down and nudged her. She stirred and stretched and blinked him into focus. What was he holding?

She sat up and suddenly it became obvious. The box! How had he found that? She didn't know what to say. She looked into his eyes. He didn't know how to ask. In another time this sort of thing would have scared him away, but now in light of his own secret, he was open minded and prepared. He sat down and put the box between them, and then he looked into her eyes and said, "You tell me about this," and then he paused and lowered his head for a second, then continued, "And then I have something to show you."

~~~~~~~~~~~~*~~~~~~~~~~~~

Would?

Cassidy had followed Becca all night long. He could hardly wait to rip into this guy she was with. How dare she sneak around on him? No man was better for her than him! He kept cool for the moment though, lying low in the shadows, he watched them eat dinner while he smoked a cigarette in the alley across from the restaurant. She really floozied herself up for this Jackass, he thought. In reality she looked positively beautiful and he knew it. Cassidy had never really appreciated what he had in Becca. Her Gypsy lifestyle had made her very accepting of whom he was. She also had a great understanding of his needs. She had never failed to please him. But Cassidy was wicked. He chose to be, and Becca had become sick of his arrogant behavior. She was tired of being man handled and mistreated by him, and she was sick of the violence he constantly absorbed. She also had recently become aware of his new affliction, and she could not be with a killer, let alone a cursed one. She had told him it was over many times. It was Cassidy that wouldn't let it go.

The man she was out with tonight was Chris, the guy she had met at the bookstore, and she found him intelligent and charming, and she hadn't said a word to anyone about him for fear of Cassidy finding out. She wasn't in love with him, but she could be one day. Her heart was still mourning Cassidy for now. She didn't know that Cassidy had been following her for weeks. He always followed her when he wasn't caught up in something else more devious. She should have known that. He used to follow her and harass her all the time.

Anytime he would catch some other guy flirting with her he would follow her home and give her a few smacks to the face. Sometimes he would follow the guy and give him a few too. She had forgotten how bad her life had gotten with him. But she hadn't heard from or seen him in a few weeks now, not since the confession in the bookstore, so she assumed he had finally decided it *was* over, and moved on to someone else. No such luck. Cassidy may not have been very nice, but he knew when he had a great girl, and he was *very* territorial. What was his once was his forever.

After dinner he followed them to the park. Becca and Chris walked for a little ways, and then they sat down on one of the benches in front of the pond, the lamps were trickling light onto the water, it was very romantic. Becca really could go for this guy. He was sweet and smart and very good-looking. He had dirty blonde hair and sparkling teal blue eyes. His smile was dazzling and he had those great dimples on his cheeks. He leaned in to kiss her. She let him, it felt good to be treated gently, and she *loved* the kiss!

It was as if Becca didn't care to be seen with him out here in the open, Cassidy thought. Wasn't she afraid she would get caught out here at night with some other man putting his tongue in her mouth? Cassidy clenched his teeth he could kill them both right now. But that's not what he wanted. He wanted to keep Becca for himself, and so he waited. It was almost unbearable for a man with his jealousy to watch this display. What did she think she was doing? He'd deal with her soon enough. He was going to make sure she didn't slip up like this again.

~~~~~~~~~~*~~~~~~~~~~

While Cassidy was stalking his ex, Hannah was out with Becca's brother, Carlo. He was every bit as intriguing as his sister and Hannah really liked him a lot. For the first time in her life she felt like she could fall in love. She and Carlo had been inseparable ever since she and Jess first arrived at the festival. Carlo was such a terrific guy, and Hannah really liked Becca too. Becca practically raised her younger brother Carlo. She had taught him how to be everything a woman loves in a man. It was a shame she wasn't such a good judge of that in other people, or she might have faired out a bit better than Cassidy. But Cassidy wasn't this bad when they first met. It seeped out of him gradually and by the time she got a taste of what he really was, it was too late. She had protected Carlo from him by never telling her little brother whom she was seeing. He got so angry when he would see the bruises on her, and she knew that Carlo could hold his own in a fight with any man. But Cass was no longer just a man, and Becca knew what he was capable of and so she kept her secret from her brother.

Hannah was really enjoying herself with Carlo. The restaurant he chose was this quaint romantic Italian place with low lighting and an authentic atmosphere. But all night long Hannah could tell something was troubling him. He wasn't his usual chatty, charming self. She loved to hear him talk. His accent was so Old World and mysterious. But tonight he seemed distant and distracted.

Actually, he had been like this off and on for some time now. Sure, he would smile at all the right places, but there was still something. She decided to ask him.

"What is it, Carlo? You've been quiet all night. Did I do something?"

He smiled and held her hand and kissed it. "Oh no, my love." He patted her hand, "You have actually brightened my day."

"Then what?" she squeezed his hand, "You can tell me."

He sat back in his seat. "My sister." He said, "We have always had this bond. I know when something is wrong and I just have this feeling. This sick feeling."

"Did she say anything when you talked to her earlier that gave you this feeling?" Hannah asked.

"No." He looked away for a minute then added, "No. I just *feel* it. You know?" he looked back to her.

"Well," she smiled, leaned in and held his hands to her face. "Why don't you give her a call before we leave here, or we'll stop by there and check on her on our way back to your place." She smiled slyly and rubbed her ankle against his legs under the table to let him know he *would* be getting her tonight.

He smiled back at her and leaned across the table to kiss her. "That sounds perfect." She had a way of making him forget his troubles.

Hannah smiled. She was proud of herself for handling that in a way that actually helped. She also couldn't wait to get back to his place. She had been longing for him all day.

~~~~~~~~~~*~~~~~~~~~~

Cassidy had watched them all night. With every kiss his anger swelled, and his blood was hot and boiling. He followed them all the way back to Becca's. He was not going to let this dickhead touch his woman. He wanted to give them enough time to get inside and get comfortable. So he smoked another cigarette. He must have inhaled a whole damn pack of them tonight. He would wait for just the right moment. Then he would settle this.

Becca still had no clue anything was wrong. She normally had a keen awareness of Cassidy's presence, but tonight she was caught up in the good feelings she was getting from Chris. She wanted to be with him, but now wasn't the right time. This was the first time he had been to her house. She didn't want to give him the wrong impression on their first real date, and if he were the sort of man she hoped he was, he wouldn't expect anything but a drink and a good night kiss. She offered him a seat on the couch while she poured them each a drink.

"This is it," she smiled at him, "Have a seat and I'll pour us some wine."

"Great." He smiled back at her with his dimples and made her blush. She handed him his drink and sat down. They got to talk and giggle for a few minutes. They were stealing another kiss when the door flew wide open. Oh God! Now she felt it! It was all too familiar! How could she forget to lock the door? Not that it would have made any difference to Cassidy.

They both jumped to their feet. Becca dropped her drink in the floor as Cassidy burst through the door and kicked it shut behind him.

"You really should lock your door if you're going to fuck another man, Sweetie." Cassidy snarled.

"Who the Hell are you?" Chris demanded. Becca had not told him about Cass yet, they were still getting to know each other. Cassidy cocked his head and looked at him like, excuse me? Becca ran between them, as Cassidy got closer.

"Cass, it's not like that! Please don't do this!" Becca pleaded with him.

"Oh really?" he said still glaring at her new suitor and still moving closer to him. His rage had built up all night. Actually, his rage had been building over this for weeks. He was positively maniacal. This would be over quick. He couldn't wait.

Cassidy came closer and Becca put her hands on his chest to keep him from Chris. But Chris didn't back down. He didn't know that he should. He asked again, "Who the Hell are you, I said?"

"You should be worried about *what* I am, Bubba." Cassidy smiled the same sadistic way that Becca was all too familiar with.

"Cassidy, please!" She yelled, "It's not like that. Please just go home right now!"

He looked down at her still pushing on his chest. "Do you really think I'm going to just go home and let this Jackass put his dick in you?"

"Why you son-of-a-bitch!" Chris yelled back.

"More than you know, my friend." Cassidy smiled.

"Cassidy!!" Becca shouted. Then Chris had something more to say.

"Wait just a God Damned minute! I don't give a shit *who* you are, you're not going to talk to her that way, and I think you should get your ass on home like she asked you."

Becca just hung her head and began to cry. She knew it was over now. Cassidy snarled and said, "Better tell him goodbye now, Becca. He's going home."

"Please," she cried to Cassidy, "Please just give me my life back!" But she knew it was no good, and she was right. He shoved Becca to the floor. The other man braced himself and got ready to swing but it was to no avail, Cassidy was far too quick for him to have ever stood a chance. In one fluid movement Cassidy immediately and quickly moved up to him and began pummeling him, one punch after another to the face. POW! POW! POW! He beat him mercilessly. Chris stumbled backwards and tried to block, but Cassidy kept them rolling.

POW! POW! POW! He was hitting him so hard and so fast the poor man had no time to swing back.

Becca begged and pleaded with him. "Cassidy, stop it!" she cried from her spot on the floor, "Stop it, please!" She feared Cassidy would kill him in front of her. Cassidy just kept pounding finally knocking poor Chris to the ground. He didn't stop, he got on top of the man and continued beating the Hell out of him. Blood was flying everywhere. Becca crawled over toward them; "Please!" she yelled, "You'll kill him!"

"Ya think?" Cassidy quipped as he continued to punch Chris in the face. Becca could hear the bones in the man's face and head crunching. He had stopped moving. Cassidy had beat him unconscious and almost to death. Becca wasn't sure if he was dead or alive. Tears streamed from her eyes. Cassidy stood up. Blood covered his fists and neck and shirt. He grabbed Becca up off the floor by the arm and proceeded to drag her to the bedroom. She was sobbing uncontrollably and slapping and fighting him all the way. "You Bastard!" she screamed. "Get away from me! I hate you!"

Cassidy picked her up and threw her on the bed. He didn't care how hard she fought him. She could have beaten him with a stick for all he cared he was going to have his way with her. He was going to make sure she didn't forget whom she belonged to. Becca scooted up next to the headboard, still sobbing she yelled at him again. "I hate you, Cassidy! Don't you touch me!"

"What's the matter, Becca?" he snarled "Don't you want me?" he took off his shirt and tossed it down. "Don't you love me anymore?" He undid his belt, pulled it off and whipped it loudly in the air, making Becca jump. It wouldn't be the first time he had whipped her with his belt. He tossed it to the ground.

"I did love you. Once upon a time." She cried. "Before I knew the beast inside you."

He sat on the bed next to her. He looked in her tear-streaked face. "Beauty is supposed to love her beast." He whispered and touched her face with his bloodstained hand, wiping Chris's blood all over her cheek. Cassidy was covered in it. It disgusted her and made her flinch.

"I don't love the beast inside of you." She sobbed.

"Oh, but you've *had* this beast inside you many times before." He smiled and leaned in to kiss her. She cringed and pulled away from him, disgusted. "Please Cassidy." She pleaded with him, "Please don't do this. I don't love you anymore."

"You are mine, God damn it!" he growled and he grabbed her face very hard. "You *will* have me!" He stood and slapped her hard across the face. She turned her head with the blow and cried, "Why can't you be like other men?!" she yelled at him, "You are brutal!"

He just stared at her and began taking off his boots. "Please Cassidy, don't." she cried. She knew it would do no good to run. He would take her in the front yard if he had to. She had feared him before, but tonight she feared him completely. She turned away from him and cried harder. She closed her eyes as he took off his pants. She had loved him. At one time she had found him beautiful. She had wanted to help him, to save him. But as the beast inside him grew, she lost more of the man she had hoped to save.

He pulled her down on the bed and held both of her hands in one of his. He pinned her to the bed by the wrists. He kissed her. She didn't open her eyes, and she tried to turn away. The metallic taste of her suitor's blood was in her mouth and she could smell it all over Cassidy. It made her sick and it seemed to excite him. He kissed her neck and licked and bit her. She used to love it when he did that. Now she could hardly bear it. But she had no choice. She had to submit. She feared what could happen if she didn't. She tried to convince herself that he must love her in his own way.

Cassidy groped her breasts and tore her dress away with his free hand. Her tears and crying weren't getting through to him. He wanted to dominate her and own her. The way he saw it this would mark her as his once and for all, and she wouldn't dare forget it! He huffed and growled and tore her bra open with his teeth.

She just wanted to get through it and get him away from her. She tried to remind herself that she had been with him many times before, willingly, and that at one time, she loved him. She used to love the feel of his mouth on her breasts. She tried to pretend it was one of those times, but the smell of her date's blood was everywhere. Cassidy had rubbed it all over her, and it seemed to arouse him. She couldn't forget that Chris lay half dead in her living room. It was all making her so sick. Cassidy was truly showing her the animal he had become tonight.

She could hardly move. He was pressing down on her with all his body weight. He was so strong. She kept her eyes shut tight and whimpered as he reached down with his free hand and ripped her panties off and pushed her legs apart. She just wanted this to be over. She readied herself for what was next. Cassidy moaned and growled and made unholy, animal-like noises as he forced himself on her. She thought she would throw up. The thought of the man who might be dying in the next room, and the smell of his blood all over her while Cassidy entered her made her nauseas. But that was only the beginning of worse.

Once he was within her, it all became more volatile. He began to change. She closed her eyes tighter and whimpered at the thought of what was happening. In her wildest imagination she could have never dreamed of what happened next. She could feel his breath on her face. He was so close. She opened her eyes and she screamed! The eyes looking back into hers were not Cassidy's! At least not the way she remembered them.

"Remember me." He growled. His voice was so raspy and frightening. She shook all over. Becca was terrified. She squirmed and tried to break free of him. His eyes were pale yellow and shining. The man she had once loved was gone from them. You couldn't even see the iris's anymore just huge glowing pupils. How was this possible? There was no moon out tonight. How was he doing this? He growled and held her tighter. She continued to squirm. He was shifting while he ravaged her. She tried to pull away from him, but he was far too strong. He was solid muscle. Her eyes were as wide as saucers as she watched in horror. He snarled and humped, and continued to change. He howled and his face stretched out to form a long snout full of razor sharp teeth. Becca was horrified! She could have recovered from the rape eventually because it was Cassidy, but her mind was not prepared for this. She let out a blood-curdling scream! He suddenly let go of her hands and quickly grabbed her hips so as to go into her deeper. She yelled out from the pain, and she grabbed his wrists and tried to free herself from his grasp, but he was too strong. He no longer had the hands of a man, but now had long furry fingers tipped with long black claws. Hair had come out all over him and he looked more beast than man now. Becca was petrified and the pain of his thrusts was unbearable. She cried and beat on his chest.

He thrust harder and harder. Pulling her closer into him. The feeling inside her was beyond description. His claws lightly scratched at her sides as he drew into her, but he was careful not to pierce her skin. She began to scream in pain and slap and hit him some more, but it did no good. He was unfazed by any of this. She screamed and punched his furry chest. He held her tighter, she thought she was going to pass out. She wanted him to just kill her now. He was almost all wolf now. Long ears; fur everywhere, long teeth and claws. She couldn't even scream anymore. He held her hips tighter, then howling he climaxed and the evil deed was done. When he withdrew from her she couldn't move. She lay there limp and beaten, unable to move, unable to scream. Her senses had been sent to the limits of what they could handle tonight. She would never be able to get that unnatural image out of her mind. She felt ruined for other men. She wanted to die. She could still feel him inside her. She guessed he had made his point.

He crawled off the bed and stood upright. Then he whirled around and stood there heaving and breathing hard staring at her. Becca had never seen anything like it before. She could do nothing but stare in disbelief at what she was looking at now. She hadn't realized he was so large and that he would stand on his haunches like that. He must have been seven feet tall! He looked animated. He looked exactly like a Gray wolf, only his fur was as black as his hair and his features were disproportionately longer in the extremities. But he still held the expressions in his face of the man he was hiding. She would have known him. He stared directly into her eyes and smiled that same sadistic smile through a wolfy exterior. If she hadn't believed him before, she had to believe him now. She also knew now for sure he was quite aware of his actions. He, frighteningly enough, was in control of his inner beast. He held up a long clawed finger to his lips and said, "SHHHH." Becca just couldn't absorb another thing. She finally mustered the strength to shakily pull herself up next to the headboard. She was sore and bruised all over. She could hardly breathe. Her heart, her mind, her body, her very soul had taken in too much. She collapsed. Cassidy threw his head up and howled long and hard. He had made his point. In his poisoned mind what he did was justified, and he had the right to take his woman when he wanted her. He walked out and returned to the cabin.

It would be a couple of hours more before Becca's brother and his girlfriend would find her and Chris, and save them from this nightmare.

~~~~~~~~~~*~~~~~~~~~~

The Boney Fingers Of Truth

Carlo was devastated by the state in which he had found his sister. He had known something was wrong all day. He couldn't have known what would happen, but he felt he shouldn't have left her alone. She wouldn't speak and she was in a sort of catatonic state by the time the paramedics arrived. The poor man in the living room was a few minutes from dead and beaten, quite literally, to a pulp.

Hannah was so sick to her stomach, she had to go outside and get some air. Here they were at dinner, having a good time, while poor Becca was being tortured. What had happened here? Where was the attacker? Who was the attacker? Hannah became frightened and returned to the house to comfort herself beside Carlo.

Patti had arrived and was filling out a report. He seemed very upset. Did he have some kind of lead already, Hannah wondered? He seemed to know something. She approached him and touched his arm, "Pat?" he turned and looked at her, "Do you know something?"

He looked even more distressed, and angry. His jaws clenched and tightened. He was feeling sick too. He couldn't believe what Cassidy had done. He knew it was Cassidy, this had his name written all over it, and his scent was still heavy in the house. Patti secretly had feelings for Becca. He had ever since the first time he met her. She would always have to call the station for help with Cassidy for fighting or hitting her or beating up somebody he thought was after her. Since he and Cassidy had to be brothers now, he had buried his feelings for Becca deep down inside of himself. But now they were coming up in his throat, and he wanted to kill Cassidy with his bare hands.

"Pat?" Hannah had lost him for a minute. She reminded him she was there, "Pat did you hear me?"

"Yes. I'm sorry, Hannah. No." he lowered his head and put his notepad back into his pocket, "No, I don't know anything yet." He walked over to Carlo and shook his hand. "I'm sorry, Carlo. I am so very sorry. I'll do whatever I can."

Carlo nodded at him and followed him out the door. He wanted to be in the ambulance with his sister. He stopped on the way out and in a fit of rage pounded his fist into the closet door five or six times and screamed until his hand was splintered and swollen, and the door had a huge hole in the middle of it. He took a moment to compose himself and then he gave Hannah his keys, his voice was shaking, "Here. Take my keys and follow us to the hospital." Hannah nodded and took them.

~~~~~~~~~~~*~~~~~~~~~~~

When Patti got to his squad car he let loose his rage. He beat on the steering wheel and cursed loudly at Cassidy. He would find him, and he would beat him senseless! Patti had never been this angry before. He couldn't control himself he was so overcome with emotion. He didn't like to see women get mistreated, and more than that it was Becca, and his feelings for her were beginning to resurface. He lowered his head against the steering wheel and cried a little. He was angry and broken-hearted and cursed.

He cranked up the squad car and spun it around in the gravel, and headed toward the cabin, he was sure that's where he would find Cassidy. He didn't want to give him any warning he just wanted to attack him. His anger burned inside him as he drove down the highway. He could feel the animal inside him trying to surface. It was hard to suppress it while he was this angry. His blood boiled and his eyes stung. His vision was going in and out of focus. He could feel the curse trying to overtake him.

It took him about twenty minutes to get out there from where he was, and he was holding back the beast inside as best he could. He wanted to save it up for Cassidy! He pulled into the driveway, and sure enough there was the Mustang. He jumped out of the car and had to brace himself against the fender for a minute. His guts were twisting with the shift. He dragged himself up to the front porch and kicked the door open. Jessica screamed when she saw him and ran into the bedroom to get Tad. Cassidy was on the couch. He turned and looked at the half-crazed Patti in the doorway.

Before the shift could completely engulf him, he ran over and sprung through the air grabbing Cassidy by the shoulders as he landed upon him, and rolled him off the couch and onto the floor. Cassidy held on to Pat's arms until they hit the floor and then they both sprung to their feet ready to fight. Patti's rage had invoked the curse and he was almost complete. Cassidy grinned that old sadistic way and waited for it, he knew what this was about. He could fight Pat with or without the shift.

Liam had heard the commotion and came running in through the back door, just as Tad was coming in from the bedroom. They were oblivious to what Cass had done. Jessica was terrified but fascinated, she had to see this and she couldn't believe what she was seeing. She couldn't look away. Patti was horrendous and beautiful all at the same time. What had set him off, she wondered? She stood behind Tad and watched with awe.

Tad kept her behind him. Until he knew what this was about he didn't want to interfere. There was no real danger of them killing each other. Cassidy provoked him further. "What is it, Pat? Come on! Come on!" he yelled. Cassidy lowered his head without loosing eye contact with Patti and tugged and ripped his shirt off. "Come on!!"

Patti growled and drooled and swung at Cassidy. Cassidy swung back and hit him POW! POW! in the nose. Patti snarled and roared at him. Cassidy could feel the shift peeking in his own blood, but he was much more skilled at turning it off and on than the others. He held onto his human form. Patti lunged and chased him. Cassidy was very quick. "I don't want to hurt you, Pat! But I will!!" Cassidy yelled at the beast, then he used one of the sofas for leverage and brought both feet up and over hitting Patti ONE! TWO! Right in the face.

Pat roared and stumbled backwards, he was so very angry! He came at Cassidy again, only this time he used all the strength in his legs to launch himself through the air and tackle Cassidy around the waist. Patti pinned him to the floor fast. It then became a power struggle, both of them pushing against the force of the other. Cassidy, although still in human form, was unbelievably strong. He pushed against Patti's hairy throat with his hands, finally letting go with one hand long enough to punch him in the throat with it. The beast retreated momentarily, giving Cass time to get to his feet. Finally, Patti had had enough, he lurched forward and grabbed Cassidy with both claws and threw him across the room, back first into the adjacent wall. The force knocked him out. Cassidy slid down the wall and slumped to the floor, unconscious. That was the only way Pat could have stopped him.

Now that the battle was over, Tad wanted answers. He grabbed a blanket off the back of the couch and waited for Patti to shift back. He was crouched on the floor facing Cassidy and panting and returning to himself. The sight of it all overwhelmed Jessica. It was incredible! It both fascinated and frightened her. She couldn't believe this was her life! Was this what she would become? Tad called over to Liam who was still standing by the back door, "Let's get him and put him on the couch." Tad directed him to help pick up Cassidy. They ran across the room and each grabbing an arm, pulled Cassidy's limp body over to the center of the room and put him on the couch.

Then Tad approached Patti and wrapped the blanket around him. He was still kneeling on the floor, and he was crying. He was overwhelmed with emotion. Tad whispered to him, "What the Hell is it, Pat?"

Patti took another minute to compose himself. He was still very angry, and then he stood and wrapped himself in the blanket and sat down across from Cassidy on the opposite sofa. He glared at him, not saying a word for a few minutes, tears still welling and then he took a deep breath and pointed to him. Tad stood with his arms crossed, waiting for some kind of explanation. Finally Patti began, "That bastard!" he spit and snarled and pointed at Cassidy, "He did something so vile tonight!" He was shouting uncontrollably.

Jessica stood next to Tad and put her arms around his waist as she listened to Patti. He was so emotional. They weren't used to seeing him like this. They looked over at Cassidy still out cold, and wondered what he had done for Patti to go after him like that. Tad had filled Jessica in on his violent history with Cassidy, and how her intuition about him had been spot on accurate. She knew it must be bad for Patti, who was normally pretty laid back, to want to kill him.

Patti continued to tell them the story of where he had been that night. About Carlo and Hannah, and not being able to tell them he knew who had hurt Becca, and finally about his hidden feelings for her. Something he had kept to himself for a very long time. Much longer than he had been friends with Cassidy. Back when they were just cop and criminal.

Tad and the others absorbed the information as they stared at Cassidy. They knew he had been obsessed with Becca for a long time now.

Especially ever since she rejected him in the bookstore when he told her his secret, and they had all noticed how sullen and deflective he had been when he arrived at Tad's a few hours before. But they never would have guessed he was capable of that level of cruelty towards Becca.

Tad didn't really know how to handle it. He certainly didn't agree with what Cassidy had done, but at the same time, they couldn't have decention among them. They were at war with their nemesis at the F.A.P.R. and they needed each other. Besides, Cassidy could cause a lot more trouble for them on his own, unmonitored.

Jessica was sick. She had known he was trouble from the get-go. Thank God Hannah hadn't gotten tangled up with him. Poor Carlo. He must be beside himself. She would have to go check on them tomorrow. But wait! She couldn't! She couldn't let them know that she knew anything about it. Damn! That's one more secret she'd have to keep from her best friend. She wasn't sure how much longer she could keep this up. But she had to.

~~~~~~~~~~~*~~~~~~~~~~~

THE NEXT TOWN OVER . . .

At the hospital, Carlo and Hannah were seated in the waiting room. Carlo was not handling any of it well. He was so hurt and angry. He was angry with the low-life that had hurt his sister, he was angry with himself for not checking on her sooner and he was angry with Becca for not letting him help her before it got this bad. He rocked back and forth on his heels with his head in his hands and cursed under his breath. Hannah wasn't sure how to help but she was there for him. She tried not to say too much, just be there, comforting him. She wrapped her arm around him and kissed him on the head. He lifted his head out of his hands and turned to her. Tears were streaming from his eyes, and he embraced Hannah and held her tight. She began to cry for him and held him, lightly rubbing his back with her hand. She would have never guessed a few weeks ago when Jessica first told her they were coming to this thing that she would have met someone like Carlo. She truly did love him. That fast, and Hannah was certainly not the type of girl to fall in love with anybody. She had always been a love 'em and leave 'em type, until now, and this new trauma had made her love Carlo even more.

Things had really moved quickly for Jessica as well. Hannah was really happy for her. It was just what she had wanted, for her friend to meet somebody to love her. Actually, Hannah had just hoped Jess would at least have a fling with somebody and lighten up a little. But this was even better. Tad definitely seemed to care about her. On top of that he was a real hottie, and a professional with a great career. Hannah couldn't ask for anything more for a friend who had been like a sister to her, her whole life.

This was all so sad. Hannah really liked Becca too. She had tried once before to get her to open up about this old boyfriend of hers and she just wouldn't.

Finally the doctor came into the room and Carlo jumped up out of his seat to greet him. "How is she? Eh, is she going to be alright?" Carlo bombarded the doc with nervous questions, he was just so scared, his sister was all he had. He became teary eyed again, "Please, tell me she's going to be alright."

The doctor put his hand on Carlo's shoulder both to comfort and to brace him. "Well," he began, "She still won't speak, probably a direct result of the trauma she encountered tonight. I am hopeful, however, she will make a full recovery, in time."

Carlo sighed with relief at the news. It wasn't great and perfect by any means, but it was hopeful. The doctor added some more, "We did a rape kit on her. She has clearly been assaulted. We'll have the results of that within about forty-eight hours or less. She has refused the D&C. That's a procedure that completely cleanses the uterus. Beyond that there isn't much else we can do for her right now, except make her feel safe and comfortable. I'll let you know when the results of the tests come back. Until then, you can go in and be with her."

"Thank you doctor." Carlo choked back his tears, "Thank you very much." Hannah put her arm around him and held him a minute after the doctor left the room until he had pulled himself together a little. Then they went into the room to be with Becca.

The minute Becca turned and saw Carlo she immediately put her hands to her face and cried. Tears jutted from her eyes as he ran to her and held her tight in his arms. He rocked back and forth and cried along with her. "I'll get him, Becca, whoever he is. I promise you. I will get him!"

Hannah could feel Carlo's rage from across the room. It was all about him. It was in the way he spoke through his teeth, the way he shook all over and the look in his eyes. She began to cry too, for both of them. It was terrible.

Carlo let go of Becca and held her tear-streaked face in his hands. He looked her in the eyes. "Please," he began, "Please, tell me who did this. Please, Becca. Help me to right this. You have to speak to me. I love you."

She only cried harder and then she laid back and pulled her feet up. Carlo was in agony over this. How would he do it without her help? How would he ever figure out who did this? He sat on the edge of her bed and hung his head. "I'll call your boss for you tomorrow. Don't worry. I'll take care of everything for you. Just please come around." He whispered to her. "Please come back to me."

~~~~~~~~~~*~~~~~~~~~~~

Back at the cabin, Patti had pulled himself together a little. He sat across from Cassidy and stared at his limp form lying on the opposite couch. Tad explained to him that it would only make their problems greater to cast Cassidy out at this point. He was far too volatile and hasty. He would be their demise. Patti agreed with disgust. He couldn't feel anything for Cassidy anymore. He stood up and wrapped the blanket around himself, and walked over to the kitchen cabinet where Tad kept all his liquor. He grabbed a half-empty bottle of Jim Beam and then he walked over to Cassidy and rummaged in his front pockets until he found his cigarettes. Patti didn't ordinarily smoke, but right now he just wanted the comfort of it.

The others watched as he did this and said nothing. Liam ran into his room and grabbed a pair of his jeans and brought them out to Pat while he was chugging back the booze. Jessica had to turn her head quickly as Patti suddenly dropped the blanket without warning and threw the jeans on. They really went through the pants, she thought. He kicked the bottle back again and walked over to the door and picked up his keys where he had dropped them.

He stood in the doorframe for a minute barefoot with the bottle and a lit cigarette in one hand, and then he half turned in Tad's direction and said, "I have to be alone for a little while. You can reach me on the cell phone if you need me." His jaws clenched as he finished, "But I really don't want to be around when that mother fucker wakes up. O.K.?"

"O.K." Tad answered solemnly. He felt for Patti, and it bothered him to watch Pat turn and go feeling like he did. Liam stood behind the couch Cassidy was lying on and stared at him for a minute. They both felt like traitors for not helping Patti fight or kill Cassidy. They didn't know how to feel, or what to say. Liam looked up at Tad. He knew they felt the same. Disgusted and troubled.

Jessica stood at Tad's side and glared at Cassidy for a minute or two. Then, without saying a word she calmly walked over to him and slapped him hard across the face. Then she turned on her heal and stormed out of the room and into Tad's bedroom, slamming the door shut behind her.

Cassidy was still out cold. He hadn't felt a thing. Liam's eyes got big at what Jess had just done. Then he looked at Tad and said, "She's getting really scary."

Tad just raised an eyebrow and cocked his head in agreement with the statement, and then he turned and joined her in the bedroom. They would all just leave Cassidy to wake up on his own. They would deal with it all tomorrow.

~~~~~~~~~~~*~~~~~~~~~~~

The next morning Carlo left Hannah asleep and made a trip over to the bookstore to meet with Becca's boss. He had called him the night before and told him she was in the hospital, and that he would be by the bookstore in the morning to explain. He was a very nice man. He had been good to Becca and he was very upset over what Carlo had to tell him. He would hire a temp until she felt like returning to work, if she ever felt like going to work again.

On his way back to his car, Mr. Whitehorse stopped him. "How are you, my friend." The old man gestured a wave at him from his seat in front of his shop. Carlo shut the car door back and decided to talk to him about Becca. Hopefully the old fella would know something that would help him find her attacker. Her boss had known nothing about him.

"Not so good today, Mr. Whitehorse. How are you?" Carlo answered, putting his hands in his pockets.

"What's wrong?" Mr. Whitehorse asked, hoping it had nothing to do with Becca. He was sad to hear that it did. Carlo filled him in on all the terrible happenings of the night before. The old man offered comfort, "Oh, Carlo. I'm so very sorry."

"Maybe you can help me, Mr. Whitehorse." Carlo began his interrogation, "Do you know anything about my sister's boyfriend? Or do you know of anyone who might want to hurt her?"

The old man sighed and looked down at the sidewalk for a moment then he stood and looked at Carlo and in a serious tone he said, "You had better come inside for a moment." He held the door open for the young man and motioned him inside.

Once inside the little shop Carlo was overwhelmed by the multitude of weaponry the old gentleman had. He looked all around him, astonished by some of the intricate and unusual pieces surrounding him.

"Come." The man motioned for Carlo to follow him to the back of the room. Where he stopped in front of an old trunk. He turned and looked at Carlo before opening it. "What I have to tell you may seem . . . a bit unbelievable. But you must trust me if you are to help your sister." Mr. Whitehorse made sure he had Carlo's full attention, "It is not a man you seek. Well, not entirely."

"O.K." Carlo said in a bemused sort of way. He knew that Mr. Whitehorse seemed a little off-kilter from time to time, but this really wasn't the time. This was very serious. "I shouldn't have bothered you, Mr. Whitehorse, I'll just be going." Carlo turned to leave, but the old man grabbed him by the arm, "Please," he said, "Hear me out. I promise I can help you."

Carlo decided to try to humor the old man out of respect. He knew he was in for a far-out tale. He got comfortable in an old chair and watched as the old Indian man opened the trunk and pulled back a black velvet cloth that revealed some unusual shining silver discs. He looked at them puzzled for a minute and then he reached down into the trunk and picked one up.

"Please," Mr. Whitehorse cautioned him, "Be very careful. The edges are very sharp, sharp as razors. "

"What are they for?" Carlo stood and asked him.

"They are for you." The old man answered as he took the disc out of Carlo's hand and returned it to the trunk.

"For me?" Carlo looked at him puzzled, "What do I need them for?"

Mr. Whitehorse slammed the trunk lid down and sat toe to toe with Carlo, "You will need them to slay the beast that plagues your sister."

Cold chills shot through Carlo. The old man was really creeping him out. As much as he wanted to wrap his hands around the bastard's throat that hurt Becca, in reality he knew it wasn't worth it to kill him. He was so ready to leave. He didn't need this, but he promised he would hear the man out, and now he was a bit intrigued, he asked, "What do you mean, Mr. Whitehorse? I can't kill anybody. As much as I would love to make the bastard pay for this with his life, I can't kill anyone."

"You will be doing him a favor." The old man began, "Now please bear with me. For what I am about to say, will shock you." He took a few steps back and sighed before telling Carlo what he had to say. "You are hunting a werewolf."

Carlo stood stunned by what the man had said. He was highly irritated and he didn't have time for Mr. Whitehorse's delusions and fairy tales. He tried not to become too angry with the old man, but he definitely let him know he was upset.

"I'm leaving now, Mr. Whitehorse. I can't believe you expect me to listen to this while my sister is in pain." He was getting very angry now. He paused and stopped himself from yelling at the old man any more. He put his hand out in front of himself and curtly said, "I'm going. Thank you for caring about my sister."

Carlo turned to leave and before he walked out the door Mr. Whitehorse said one more thing, "Carlo." Carlo stopped in his tracks but kept his back to the man, he couldn't look at him right now, but he didn't want to disrespect him. The man finished, "I know you are hurting, and I'm sorry I have offended you. But what I say is true. You ask your sister. She will tell you."

Carlo said nothing for a minute and he hung his head. Without turning around he said, "My sister can't tell me. She hasn't said a word since it happened. She can't and won't tell me anything."

"She is afraid for you. When she tells you, you believe her." Mr. Whitehorse walked over to Carlo and put a hand on his shoulder, "You will be back. And I will be waiting."

Carlo listened for only a minute more then, without another word, he walked out and left for the hospital. He had to admit, as ridiculous as it all sounded, it did stay in keeping with his sister's recent behavior. She was definitely terrified of something.

~~~~~~~~~~*~~~~~~~~~~

Bleed It Out

Patti sat inside his apartment for all the next day without talking to his blood brothers. He sat and drank whiskey and smoked and stared out the window. He turned his phone off and shirked his police responsibilities; he didn't care about any of it.

He was sitting on the couch in one of his stupors thinking back to when he had first met Becca. She had called him and the Sheriff to come out to her house because Cassidy had slapped her a couple of times over some guy that was hitting on her at work. Then he had run out after the man to beat the shit out of him. Patti remembered how she had looked. She was beautiful, she took his breath away, and she was crying so hard. Her face was red and swollen where Cassidy had laid a good backhand on her. It probably knocked her down. Cassidy was a good-sized man, and sweet Becca was delicate and beautiful.

Patti became emotionally attached to her at that very moment. He remembered how he had felt the pull in his chest. The Sheriff had to take the report from her because Patti was so entranced he was stuttering and making a fool out of himself. They ended up catching up with Cassidy a couple of hours later, but it was unfortunately after he had beaten the Hell out of the man he was looking for. He was smoking a cigarette and kicking the man's limp form when they pulled up.

They took Cassidy in and he spent a few nights in the jail for domestic abuse and assault, until Becca came down and bailed him out. The man he beat the Hell out of dropped the charges because he was afraid Cassidy would pummel him again if he didn't. Patti had fallen for her that first night, and he never could figure out why she had stayed with Cassidy as long as she did. She must have really loved the lucky hateful bastard.

He still didn't know what he was going to do about Cassidy or Becca or Carlo for that matter. He had to tell him something.

He finally decided to go to bed and sleep off the whiskey he had hammered down. Then tomorrow he would go up to the hospital and check on Becca.

~~~~~~~~~~~*~~~~~~~~~~~

At the hospital, Carlo was meeting with the doctor to discuss the results of Becca's rape kit and her overall condition. She still hadn't spoken and the doctor was puzzled over her test results. He pulled Carlo into one of the empty waiting rooms to talk to him.

"Mr. Mathers," he began, "I really don't know how to say this where it will make any sense, and so I'm just going to say it."

Carlo nodded and with a worried sigh he listened intently to what was being said. Hannah watched all of this through the big glass window in front of the room. Carlo looked so stressed. "Go ahead, doctor." He said.

"Well, the results from the rape kit were inconclusive."

Carlo crossed his arms and looked puzzled, "What do you mean inconclusive?"

"I mean what the lab found was unusual, and based on what they found we were unable to retrieve the appropriate D.N.A. evidence."

Carlo was still confused, and getting angry about it. "Just say what you are trying to say man!" He shouted, "I can't handle any more of this foreign language everyone speaks around here!"

"I'm sorry, Mr. Mathers," the doctor said calmly trying to ease him, "What they found was animal D.N.A., and that's all. In particular, it's some form of canid. It must have been tampered with. I'm very sorry."

Carlo's face went blank and then it turned white. He flashed back to his conversation with Mr. Whitehorse. Could the old guy have been telling the truth? No way! There is no way that could be true! He was staring blankly into space. The doctor nudged him, "Mr. Mathers. Mr. Mathers, are you alright?"

Carlo shook himself out of it. "Yes." He cleared his throat, "Uh yes. I will be fine. I just don't understand."

"Neither do we. I'm sorry. It is very strange. Maybe she can give you more answers once she recovers. Beyond that, we've done all we can do here." He patted Carlo on the shoulder and then left him alone to absorb as best he could what he was just told. Hannah came into the room once she saw the doctor leave. She put her arms around him and turned him around to face her. The look on his face frightened her.

"What, Carlo?" she whispered and put her hands on his face, "What is it? What did he say?" She looked into his eyes for the answers. He finally responded, "I don't want to talk about it right now, O.K.? I would just like to go in and see my sister now."

Hannah just nodded at him, O.K.," she said, and she pulled him up close and hugged him. "O.K."

~~~~~~~~~~~*~~~~~~~~~~~

Up on the mountain, M was torturing The Founder. He had discovered a new way of taming the beasts and he was testing it out on the old cavalryman. He had The Founder restrained to an upright table. Shackled at the wrists and ankles with chains and manacles. His shirt was off and he was still wearing his collar. It flashed and pulsed serum into him as usual.

The new device was a toxic spear. It was long and narrow, like an arrow without a tip; only it was sharply pointed and loaded with a silver serum that flooded out of it on impact. This way, even if it shot clean through them, it would still stop them. The weapon was only about ten inches long and could be discharged from a handgun-type of firearm that M had specially designed for it. Once fired, it could bring them very near to death without killing them, long enough for M to restrain them. It would only incapacitate them for a short while and then they would recover without flaw. Giving the poachers the necessary time to draw blood or capture them or inflict them with tracking devices.

The Founder braced himself as one of the new handguns was raised and pointed at him from across the room. The collar was removed and then they shot him. "PLING!" the dart made a strange pinging sound as it dismounted from the gun barrel and sliced through the air, striking The Founder with deadly accuracy straight through the chest, and lodging itself in the table behind him, pinning him to it while still inside him. He strained to breath as the low dose of silver crept throughout his system. He clenched his teeth and gritted back the pain involved. It was excruciating!

M smiled as he watched The Founder suffer and then slip into a limp trance-like state. It was marvelous! He quickly grabbed his chart and began marking down the results as his assistants loosened the restraints and pulled The Founder up enough to yank out and remove the silver shard from his back. He was curious to find out what The Founder had felt when it happened. He would just have to wait for him to wake up for that, though. And then he would test it again, only this time The Founder would be in his wolf-skin. M wanted to know if the dart would render enough silver serum to retract the shift momentarily or not. And there was only one way to find out.

~~~~~~~~~~~*~~~~~~~~~~~

As Carlo was leaving his sister's room with Hannah, Mr. Whitehorse was walking in. He had flowers and a smile for her. Carlo looked at him and without saying a word he nodded and the old man knew what he meant.

He nodded back and added a time to meet him. "Come by the store, after closing, tomorrow."

Carlo reached out and shook his hand, and then he and Hannah headed for the car. He just wanted to go back to his place for a rest. He was exhausted and drained and overwhelmed with belief in something unnatural. Hannah waited until they were in the car to ask, then she just had to know what was going on. Carlo hesitated after he started the car. He really wasn't sure how to tell her any of it. So he just told her. She almost wouldn't have believed him, but his exasperated explanation made a believer of her. She knew Carlo would not joke about this. But how could any of this be real?

~~~~~~~~~~~*~~~~~~~~~~~

Things had really gotten strange at Chloe's house the night before. While all of this debauchery was going on around the pack, Luke was unaware of it and dealing with his own situation. Chloe had been enraptured with the beast Luke had shown her. She was oddly enough turned on by it, and it was far more than pheromones. She was kinky weird, and Luke wasn't sure how to handle it. He had indulged himself in the passion she had laid upon him after he revealed his alter ego to her.

He must have been caught up in the sheer erotica of the moment, because he would never ordinarily have done anything so vulgar. But she had been so aroused and inviting, it was as if he were under a spell.

He rose up in bed and looked over at her lying on her stomach. A satisfied smile still clinging to her innocent looking face, and he questioned his own morality. He wasn't sure how to feel about any of this. His life over the past few months had been like some hazy dream. Part nightmare, part wet dream. What should he do about her? She obviously had more secrets than he really cared to know. Clearly she was no amateur at Witchcraft either.

He decided to put a little space on the issue and get dressed and head back over to Tad's and check in. Maybe his brothers would have the right advice. He just wasn't sure how to tell them about this, if at all.

~~~~~~~~~~~*~~~~~~~~~~~

The next day Patti got clean dressed and showered and bought flowers on his way to the hospital. Pretty little blue flowers. He chose them because they seemed soft, like her and he thought they would comfort her. He didn't call Tad and the others because he didn't want Cassidy to show up out there. He walked inside and took the elevator up to her room. She was sleeping when he arrived. He quietly walked inside and put the flowers on her bedside table. He took the opportunity to stare at her long and hard. She was so beautiful, he couldn't resist the notion to reach out and touch her cheek. He gently ran the back of his hand across her face, he touched her softly so as not to wake her. She was so soft and radiant. He brushed her hair back from her face and let his hand trail down her soft black hair. Then he stepped back and sat down. He was compelled to kiss her and he knew that would *not* be a good idea.

As he sat watching her, she began to stir. She slowly opened her eyes and stretched a little as she pulled herself up in the bed and tried to focus on whom was visiting her. Patti jumped to his feet and stood back and gave her a minute. He slowly came into focus for her. 'Oh, it's Patti,' She thought, 'How sweet of him to visit.' She had always liked Patti very much. He would always stutter and fidget whenever he was around her. She could tell he liked her. There was always something sweet and innocent about it, and she liked the way he made her feel. Something she wouldn't dare ever reveal to Cassidy.

He waved a little and came up closer to the bed. He wanted to comfort her and hold her hand, but he was afraid to. "I know you don't want to talk, Becca, and that's O.K. I just wanted to come out and visit you. You don't have to say anything."

She lowered her head to her hands and began to cry. She couldn't help it. She was so overly emotional and sensitive, and she knew he had to know who had done this. It ripped Patti's heart out. He hated Cassidy more and more. He clenched his jaw and then he finally reached out and held her hand. He kneeled beside the bed and put her hand to his forehead. He was fighting every urge to smash something. Then he made her a promise, "I'll fix this, Becca. I will. You don't have to ever worry about Cassidy again. I'm here now, if you'll have me."

Then he decided to take a chance and finally tell her how he felt about her. He hoped it wouldn't be too much for her, he just needed her to know before anything else could happen. He hadn't told anybody how he felt about Becca, ever. The Sheriff knew and used to tease him about it, and he was sure Becca knew, even though he never said a word to her before. But he was telling her now. He had to. He had to free his heart. He still didn't know what to do about Cassidy besides hate him, and he knew it would be a very long time before Becca would trust another man enough to touch her, if ever. But Patti didn't care he would wait, because he loved her.

~~~~~~~~~~*~~~~~~~~~~

After getting a bite to eat and visiting his sister, and letting Hannah talk to Jessica on the phone, Carlo decided it was time to go on out to Mr. Whitehorse's weapons shop and have a talk. He motioned to Hannah who was still on the phone, to hang up now. She had to make up an excuse to get off the phone. The two friends hadn't gotten to see much of each other here lately. Ever since they arrived in this town for that fair, it had been a crazy train ride, and Hannah didn't like not being able to tell her best friend about all this. It was still very hard for Hannah to grasp. But Jessica lived for this kind of thing. Once she was off the phone, they hopped in the car and headed out to the weapons shop.

It didn't take them too very long to get there, and once they pulled up out front it made Carlo's heart ache. He could barely glance over at the empty bookstore. But it gave him the strength he needed to go into the old man's shop and try to find a way to make it right.

They stepped inside and the bell on the door rang. Mr. Whitehorse walked out to greet them with one of the discs in his hand. "Hello." He smiled at them both "Come. Sit in the back of the store with me. I have much to teach you."

He led them to the back of the store where the trunk was. He had been polishing the discs. He handed Carlo the one he had just finished with. "Careful." He said, "As I said before, the edges are razor sharp. You really must handle them with this piece of leather, to protect yourself." He handed Carlo a piece of black leather to wrap around one side of it, so he could safely handle them. Hannah said nothing. For once she had no quips or puns or sarcasms. This whole thing was very frightening to her. She watched and listened in fascination to what the old man said and showed them.

"I've never seen anything like this before." Carlo said to him, "What is it?"

"It is a killing disc." Mr. Whitehorse answered, "I made them, long ago. They were designed specifically for killing werewolves."

"Have you ever used these before?" Carlo asked, intrigued.

Mr. Whitehorse lowered his head as if deep in a memory long suppressed for a moment, and then he answered, "Only once. When I was very young. The reservation on which my family lived was plagued by a beast like the one you now seek." He filled a pipe with tobacco as he told them his story. The lights were all turned down low in the shop and they were all seated on the floor in front of the large trunk, listening to him. It was like ghost stories around a campfire. He continued, "My brother and I decided there had to be a way to defeat the beast, and so we searched and hunted a whole season until we found one. After we discovered the beast's weaknesses, primarily to silver, we designed these discs and as this was my craft, I fashioned them out of pure silver. Not sterling silver, pure raw silver. They shine because I keep them polished well."

"Why not just use silver bullets, and shoot the creature? Like in the movies?" Carlo asked a pertinent question. The old man replied, putting his finger into the air, "Because. There is a chance that the bullet will cut clean through the beast and allow it to recover. It is not enough just to shoot it. The dose of silver contained in the bullet is too minute a dose to kill it. It might just render it pain and make it vengeful. Unless you are lucky enough to lodge it within the beast's heart or brain for a long enough time to kill it. Also, in order to get a good clear shot, you must be very close to it, this beast is lightning quick."

He made some valid points, Carlo thought. It was naturally more complicated than the fairy tales make it seem. After a moment more of thought Carlo decided to ask, "Mr. Whitehorse, what happened, you know? You said you had only used these weapons once."

The old man lowered his head again, drew on his pipe and then answered, "Yes, only once. I used them to deliver my brother from his suffering."

His answer sent cold chills down Carlo's back. He waited a long moment in silence before asking anything more, then he asked the obvious, finally ready to accept the truth of their reality, "Then how do you use them?" He held the disc through the leather and raised it up. "How does this work?"

"Ahh," the old man smiled, "This is fool proof. It will end the beast without failure."

"But why? I mean, how?" he asked again.

The old man smiled, pleased with the brilliance of his most honored weapon design, "Because. It is far too dense to go all the way through the creature, once this is lodged in the beast's flesh, it cannot pull it out, the sharpened edges ensure this. Within minutes it will assuredly die. The challenge is in the accuracy of your throw, and you must be quick as well."

"Pull it out? It has hands?" he looked worriedly over at the old Indian. "I don't know." Carlo was getting discouraged. This was all so unreal to him. How could there really be any such thing?

Mr. Whitehorse picked up on his doubt. He drew on his pipe and then read his mind. "You are wondering if what I say is true? You still doubt the reality of it all?"

"Well." Carlo hesitated, "Well yes, actually. But I have to believe now. After what happened to Becca. But I still am wondering." He stopped a minute and found it hard say what he was thinking.

"Go on."

"Why didn't it kill her? Why isn't she a werewolf too now? Why did it . . ." He stopped again, "Why did it defile her?" Carlo had to choke out the words.

The old man reached out and grabbed his wrist and looked him in the face. "Because it didn't want to kill her or make her one of them. It knows her. It loves her."

Carlo pulled back. He had chills all over him. Hannah was so frightened she began to cry. What did he mean? It was what Carlo had thought in the beginning, an abusive boyfriend. The one she was hiding from him! It had to be! He looked Mr. Whitehorse in the eyes. The old man nodded. "She knows him very well. He is a brutal man, territorial and jealous. As a beast, he is worse. He is mad. Unyielding."

Carlo was completely leveled. He stood up and put his hands on his head. Hannah didn't know what to say or do. This was weird and scary. She looked over at Mr. Whitehorse and he held her hand to comfort her.

Finally, Carlo spoke again, "But I thought they were wild, mad beasts, that knew not what they were doing. Isn't that what the fairy tales say?"

"That is not the truth of their nature." The old man explained, "Two things, nature itself and the nature of the man inside rule the werewolf. Though it bears a resemblance to an affliction, it is truly a curse. The soul becomes tarnished in a way that disturbs the man inside. It is old magic. You can treat the symptoms, but not the soul. The Gods devised it so, when devils began to medal with nature. Good and Evil ruled its inception and the Gods set the rules for its existence."

Hannah and Carlo listened intently; they were intrigued and horrified at what they were hearing. Mr. Whitehorse continued, "The change is biological, but the beast is a light and dark struggle for the soul. If the man within is sound of mind and strong willed enough, then he can control his actions while under its spell. If the man inside is tormented and mad to begin with, he gives way to its power and is consumed by it. Desensitized. It is not as in the fairy tales, you see? It is not that easily explained. It is instead complex and complicated as anything else in Heaven or Earth."

Carlo got chills again. This was creepier and scarier than any horror movie he had ever seen simply because it was real. He looked over at Hannah. She was terrified. She believed. Mr. Whitehorse could tell they were afraid. He offered comfort. "She will be alright, you know."

"Becca?" Carlo looked over at the little old Indian man.

"After he is gone, she will recover. Her heart will mend, in time. She still loves him, you know, but she loves you too, and she will forgive you for what you must do." He patted Carlo on the shoulder, "Now come. Follow me and I will show you how to use these." He pointed to the weapons in Carlo's hands.

Carlo and Hannah began to follow him out back of the store. Once outside, they crossed the parking area and into the little wooded lot adjoining it. The old man put on a leather gauntlet then picked out one of the discs and holding it in his right hand, he placed his finger through the slot in the center of it and heaved it back over his head. Then, in one quick fluid movement he whipped his arm and sent the disc slicing through the air landing it square on into one of the many trees on the lot. It was embedded halfway through its mass in the tree.

Carlo approached it both amazed at the old man's speed and accuracy, and at the efficiency of the weapon itself. He pulled on it and it cut him. It was lodged really well in the tree and the edges were, as the old man had said, razor sharp. Mr. Whitehorse and Hannah joined him, and the old Indian handed him a piece of leather, "Here," he said as he handed it to him, "Use this."

Carlo took the leather and wrapped it around the discs edges and pulled. It still wouldn't budge. So he propped one foot against the tree for leverage and heaved a couple of times, finally it gave and came out of the tree. He held it up and flashed its blade against the streetlights. It glistened with sap. The metal felt hot.

Mr. Whitehorse walked over and grabbed Carlo's forearm and looked him in the eyes. "Practice." He said, "Practice every day before the full moon. Shifters can change at any time. The moon really does not apply to that. But they are stronger and far more powerful when the moon is full, and that is when you should strike him down." Mr. Whitehorse paused for a minute then added, "There is more you should know."

Carlo looked at him very seriously. What more could there possibly be? "More?!" he asked apprehensively.

"There are more than one."

Carlo's eyes got wide. He looked over at Hannah, then back to Mr. Whitehorse, "What?"

"The one you seek is the darkest one. He has been seduced by his own power. Do not bother with the others unless they pose a fight, or you will be out-numbered quickly. You must go in and find the one you seek, kill him and get away."

"How do you know that? How do you know there is more than one? And how will I know which one to kill?!" Carlo was in a panic now. The thought of facing off with one horrible beast was frightening enough, but now there were more?

"I know there are others because I have seen them with him and their eyes are the same. They light from the inside. You will know one when you see it. From this point on, you will never forget, as I have not. You do not need to recognize the shifter you seek, he will know you and there will be no doubt. But you must kill him while he wears his alter-ego."

Carlo already had doubts. He still was having trouble wrapping his head around the truth of all of this. He sighed and looked down at the blade in his hand, "I wish I knew what he looked like."

Mr. Whitehorse looked upon him sympathetically for a moment, and then he said, "Come with me." He walked back towards the store and opened the back door. Hannah and Carlo followed him inside and all the way up to the front counter. He walked around to the cash register and reached down and picked a framed picture off the counter beside it. He looked at it for a minute, sighed and then handed it over to Carlo and Hannah. Carlo turned the picture against the dim light and he and Hannah looked at it. It was a picture of Becca and Cassidy arm in arm in front of the Mustang outside the shop. Carlo had seen the Mustang around town before, and he was sure he had passed Cassidy on the street a few times. He definitely remembered seeing him somewhere else too, but he just couldn't put his finger on it. But Hannah could. Her skin went cold. She suddenly burst into chill bumps, "Oh my God." She whispered.

Mr. Whitehorse nodded. He knew she had put it all together. Carlo looked over at her, "What is it, baby?"

"Oh my God, Carlo." She sat the picture down on the counter and looked into his eyes. "Jessica."

"What?" he asked confused.

"Tad and Jessica. This is their friend." She said in a panic, "This is the guy Jessica told me not to trust when we first met them!"

Carlo yanked the picture up again and looked it over once more, "Are you sure?"

"Yes!" she yelled, "His name is Cassidy. Jessica said he was bad news. Now I wonder," she stopped in mid-thought for a minute, "I wonder if this is why she's been acting so strange. I knew she was keeping something from me! Could it be that her boyfriend's a werewolf?"

"Yes." Came the answer from behind the counter, "And it may be too late for her as well." Mr. Whitehorse said solemnly.

"Don't say that!" Hannah yelled at him, frightened.

Carlo examined the photo for a minute more, taking in every detail, including the silver necklace around Cassidy's neck. Then he put the frame down and looked at Mr. Whitehorse. "I'll find him. Now I know where to look."

Hannah panicked even more, afraid for Jessica. "What about Jess?" she asked him.

He looked at her and held her hand, "It'll be O.K." he whispered and wiped the tears that started to run from her eyes, "We're going to save her." Then he picked up the discs and nodded to Mr. Whitehorse, "Thank you."

"Fear not when you do the right thing, Carlo." He answered, "Remember the cause, and strike true. Now you are the slayer. Trust in your weapons and the motive that drives you."

Carlo and Hannah had a lot to talk about on the way home. It was a lot to absorb. It all seemed like some kind of nightmare. They only had a couple of weeks before the full moon, and they both hoped for the best. But it was terrifying to know the truth of their problem, and what was more, now they knew about Patti too. Hannah remembered them all being together when she first met them. That's why he was acting so strange about Becca. He *did* know who had done it. Carlo was furious. He didn't want to give them any warning, and he wondered why Patti didn't do something about it. He had seemed truly upset over what happened. He had thought Patti was a good man.

As soon as they got back home, he immediately went outside and practiced throwing the discs. He would be ready. He would be ready for them all.

~~~~~~~~~~*~~~~~~~~~~

Killing In The Name Of

Carlo had been spending all of his free time between visiting with Becca at the hospital, working on the bar with Hannah, and practicing with the discs. He would be ready when the time came. He was keeping track of the days on his calendar, twelve more days and then there would be justice.

Becca still wasn't talking, but she managed to smile at Carlo when he entered the room. Patti had really made her feel better. Just knowing someone still wanted her after what had happened made her less discouraged by her future. Carlo leaned over and kissed her on the forehead. She hugged him. "You must be feeling better. That is quite a smile." He said as he pulled up a chair next to the bed. As he settled himself and prepared to say something, he noticed the beautiful bouquet of blue flowers on her bedside table. "These are pretty." He commented and he reached out to retrieve the card, "Who brought them to you, Mr. Whitehorse?"

Becca shook her head and still smiled not saying a word. Carlo pulled the card out of the envelope, "Can I read this?" he asked her, and she nodded. He read it out loud, "To Becca, please recover quickly. All of my love, Patti Leason." Carlo's expression suddenly turned black. He tossed the card onto the table and leaned in to talk to his sister. She was startled by his anger. She didn't understand it.

"Becca." He realized he had frightened her, so he held her hand, "I don't want you to see Patti Leason anymore." She looked at him confused and then she got angry with him. She pulled her hand out of his and plopped down on her pillow, trying to ignore him. How dare he tell her what to do? Patti was kind, and he was a friend, that's all. "Becca." Carlo tried to grab her hand and she pulled away from him again. "Becca listen to me. You don't understand."

She continued to tune him out. He stood up and put his hands on his hips and sighed. He decided to tell her what he knew. "Becca, I know about Cassidy."

She began to tremble all over. Her eyes got wide and she slowly sat up and looked at her brother horrified. He knew his name. How did he know? She slowly shook her head from side to side. He nodded at her. "I know what he is and I know what he did to you."

She began to cry. He immediately sat down next to her and held her. He felt awful for upsetting her again, and after she was finally smiling. But she had to know. In case he didn't make it back. She had to know she was still in danger. She had to know about Pat and the others.

"Becca, please." He begged her, "Please, you must understand." He pulled away from her so they could lock eyes, "Mr. Whitehorse told me about him, and he told me how to kill him. Patti is like Cassidy now, Becca."

She shook her head violently back and forth and began to beat Carlo in the chest with her fists. She was crying and hitting him as he tried to restrain her. He finally managed to grab her wrists and he just let her cry it out. She fell forward into his chest sobbing uncontrollably. She had never wanted Carlo involved because she didn't want him to get hurt, and she didn't want him killing anybody either, least of all Patti Leason. She couldn't believe it. She didn't want to believe it, but it made sense. The way he and Cassidy had suddenly become fast friends, and the way the Sheriff had disappeared. She should have known. But she hadn't really thought about all of that before now.

It was going to be harder for her than Carlo had thought. Maybe he should have just kept it to himself, he thought. But no, she needed to know so she could move on, and he didn't want her to second-guess Patti either.

He held her against him and rocked her. "I have to do it, Becca." He whispered, "Please, you must understand. I know you loved him, but I must end this. He will never stop. I am prepared, you mustn't worry about me."

They held onto each other for a long time. Just like when they were kids. Only this time it was Becca who was afraid and Carlo was the strong one. They didn't have to say anything else. Carlo was a good brother, and he loved his sister very much. And she knew that.

~~~~~~~~~~~~*~~~~~~~~~~~~

Patti had finally rejoined the others at the cabin. He hated Cassidy and he didn't want to be around him, but he knew for the other's sakes he had to. He walked inside and strolled right past Cassidy without saying a word to him, and started to set his duffle bag down on the floor. Cassidy sat on the sofa and lit up a cigarette and smiled sadistically at Patti. Then he spoke, causing Pat to freeze in the spot and seethe with rage. "She's my woman, you know Pat." Cassidy leaned forward on his knees, "I can tell you have this *"thing"* for her. But I can do with her what I please." Patti closed his eyes and tried to tune him out.

Tad had entered the room by this point and offered help, "Shut up, Cassidy. You've done enough damage. You've already lost your mind and your best friend. You can't afford to loose anything else."

Patti tossed his duffle bag down and exited the room. He didn't want to be anywhere near the bastard. He wandered into the kitchen and grabbed a coke out of the fridge and sat down at the table next to Liam. Liam could tell he was upset. "She'll be alright, Patti. All of this will pass."

"It will never be alright as long as Cassidy is still breathing, Liam." Patti said, and he slammed the coke can down onto the table and dropped his head to his arms. "I'm in love with her, Liam. I'm in love with her and I can't offer her anything. Not even hope. I'm no better than him." He sat up and pointed into the other room. "I'm the same loathsome beast he is."

Liam decided to just offer a sympathetic ear. He nodded and patted Patti on the back. Tad had joined them in time to hear what Patti had said. He offered his own opinion out loud, "You're a much better man inside than he is, Pat. Character is a choice. Don't forget who you were and who you still are."

Patti looked over at him and thought hard about what he had said. *That* was why Tad was leader.

It wasn't long before Luke had arrived at the cabin. He took a deep breath and prepared to tell his comrades about what happened with Chloe. He had hated to leave her without waking her, but he needed a little space. He was beginning to feel like a worse monster than what he already was. He was beginning to feel like a devil. And he didn't want to turn into Cassidy.

He walked inside and said "Hey" to Cassidy who was sitting on the couch grinning sickly and smoking as usual. He knew immediately that something must have happened. He almost wondered if Cassidy didn't already know about Chloe, the way he was smiling like a Cheshire cat. "Where's Tad?" he asked him.

Cassidy didn't say anything at first. He stood up and walked over to Luke and put a hand on his shoulder. "Did you ever do anything that made you feel sick later?" he asked him in almost a whisper.

It was a strange question coming from Cassidy, and an ironic one considering Luke's own current feelings. He answered him, "More than you know."

Cassidy just looked him in the eyes for a minute and let him feel him. Then the signature smile he wore slowly faded and he patted Luke on the back.

"I'm going for a drive." He said, and then he headed out the door. Luke listened as the Mustang roared down the driveway.

"O.K., that was weird too." Luke said to himself. Then he turned and entered the kitchen where he could hear the others. He hadn't seen them all in a couple of days. He walked over and hugged Tad, relieved to be around the only 'normal' he knew these days. Then he sat down next to Patti and took in the sadness on his face. He instantly knew something was wrong. He momentarily forgot about his own problems. "What is it?" he asked.

Liam looked over at him, but didn't answer. He looked at Tad, "What?" he asked again. This time he got an answer.

~~~~~~~~~~*~~~~~~~~~~

M returned the Founder to his quarters limp and bleeding. The poachers drug him inside and dropped him on his carpet. Then they slammed the cage door behind him and M personally locked it and checked it again. The Founder's blood spilled out onto the carpet. He was stunned. The new weapons M had concocted sadly enough, worked quite well. The man M knew these creatures too well. It gave him an advantage over them. He hardly feared them anymore. He felt invincible. Arrogant.

Professor Saunders had been following M around like a lost puppy. Ever since he was attacked he had been afraid to leave the safety of the facility. He wanted to learn more about M's rejuvenating serum. It had truly worked on healing his wounds, and he wondered why M wasn't more obsessed with working on that, rather than fooling around with trying to control these mythological beasts. He was driven by some kind of megalomania apparently, and he had even confided in Saunders that he had not revealed the results of the rejuvenating serum to his higher-ups yet. This was all very troubling to Saunders. He felt the serum should be developed post-haste.

But M was now only concerned with defeating the pack and harnessing them. He already had missions set aside just for them. The government was antsy in its desire to use their special prowess against their foes. M snickered a little under his breath as he looked upon The Founder's limp form. "Defy me again," he said, "and I will keep you hovering at death's door and never let you in." Then he turned to Saunders, "Come now, and let's look at your new manuscript!"

The two men had only been gone a moment or two when The Founder began to regain full consciousness. He tried to push himself up off the floor, but he was just too weak. His wounds were trying to heal, but the new toxin still within his flesh had slowed the healing action. His whole body hurt. Pain was not something that werewolves felt very often. Even a major wound would only barely ingest any pain sensation in them. But this new toxin contained heavy doses of the most lethal allergen a werewolf could encounter. Silver. He wanted to warn the others. But there was no way he could now. They knew something was going to happen, they just didn't know what or when. He hoped they would defeat this oppressor, and find a way to conquer this affliction. The Founder would have gladly given his own life to end this for them.

~~~~~~~~~~*~~~~~~~~~~

After a very long discussion, the guys decided to prepare what weapons they had. They wanted to be prepared for the coming moon. They had no idea there would be other parties interested in their destruction. Carlo would be a surprise to all of them. He had been practicing day and night with the killing discs. His weapons rivaled any that M could come up with. He had become quite proficient in their use, and he slung them with deadly accuracy. When the time came, he would not miss. He owed it to Becca.

The others were shocked to hear about Chloe's behavior, but Luke was even more surprised by what Cassidy had done. He knew he was malicious, but he didn't think he had completely lost his mind. It was obvious that he was mad. Luke told them about what he had said to him earlier. It was still no consolation to Patti though. His heart was bleeding.

Tad and Liam laid all the weapons they had acquired from the Feed 'N Seed and from the gun cabinet at the Police Station out on the great room floor. "We need to have these within reach. Easy access." Tad said as he picked up a lead pipe. "We have our sub-natural means, but it may not be enough against that Gortex. So far the facility has been able to subdue us quite easily. They know too much about us. We have no upper hand besides the fact that we know they are coming for us."

He paced as he continued, "We have discovered through our experience that we can use our hands as we normally do, even in our wolf-flesh. The plan has been that we would use that to our advantage. We need to practice handling all of these weapons. Only the large guns will help us. The shotguns, and that's only as men. When we are wolf-men, our fingers are too large and clumsy for gun handling, so we must rely on our other abilities, namely our speed, our senses and our agility. Also our strength and the ability to hold onto things like this." He slapped the pipe against his hand to demonstrate, and then he added, "We must not be captured."

~~~~~~~~~~~*~~~~~~~~~~~

Becca was feeling like getting out of bed finally. She put on her robe and slippers and picked up the flowers Patti had brought her and headed out the doorway. Her brother had told her that Chris was still in I.C.U., so she got on the elevator and rode it down two floors and stepped out. She followed the signs and arrows that directed her towards the Intensive Care Unit and walked down the hallway to the large glass doors that preceded it.

Once there she faced the desk nurse. The nurse knew who she was. She had been on duty the night they both were brought in. Becca had had to stay in I.C.U. the first night herself. The nurse looked at her with a smile and said,

"Oh, Miss Mathers. How good to see you're feeling better today!" She was a very pretty black woman, and she had the sweetest demeanor. It made Becca feel good to be treated so kindly. The nurse continued, "Are those for Chris?"

Becca nodded. "O.K.," the nurse said sweetly, "You just need to sign in here, and then you can go on back. He's in bed C."

Becca signed the form and then took the flowers and slowly approached the glass door marked with a C. Every step she drew nearer, her heart pounded harder. She was afraid to see what Cassidy had done. But she was thankful Chris was still alive.

She finally reached room C and looked in. His entire face was bandaged up, and he was on a respirator. Becca covered her mouth and lowered her head and began to cry. She felt weak and had to lean against the glass for a minute. She couldn't hold back the tears. They flowed so very hard from her eyes. She felt responsible. She was shaking and nearly dropped the flowers. Luckily the nurse had followed her for moral support.

"Here," she said, and she took the flowers from Becca, "He looks a lot worse off than he is, dear. Don't you cry, his doctor says he's doing quite well."

Becca sniffled and nodded at the nurse and took the flowers back. It was kind of her to say, but it was still no consolation because Becca had seen it happen. It was brutal and cruel, and it had scarred her. She would never underestimate Cassidy's capabilities again. She took a moment to recompose herself and then she decided to go in. She opened the door slowly and walked inside. The nurse held the door for her, "You can have ten minutes with him, honey, and then you'll have to go." Becca turned and nodded to her.

She approached slowly and as she looked upon him her mind began to flash and send her back to that night. She squinted and pushed out the flashing memory from her mind. She sat the flowers down on the bedside table and touched his hand. He was in an induced coma to protect him from the pain. She only wanted to stay for a minute and let him know she was there. She knew she could not be with him after this. They would forever remind each other of the horror that found them.

After a few minutes, she leaned down and kissed his head and then she turned and left to return to her own room, and her own recovery. She nodded to the nurse as she left the I.C.U. and took the elevator back upstairs. As soon as she stepped off the elevator, her doctor approached her. "Ah, Miss Mathers." He began, "I was just coming to find you. There is something I need to discuss with you."

She looked at him confused. "Follow me back to your room, please. I need to check your vitals, and then we can talk." He said calmly. Becca was scared. She didn't know how much more she could take.

~~~~~~~~~~*~~~~~~~~~~

Carlo rolled out of bed and got a quick shower, and then he and Hannah headed out the door and to the hospital. They didn't even eat breakfast. He had gotten a call from Becca's doctor before he had even gotten out of bed, telling him there was something he should know. So he and Hannah got moving as quickly as they could to get over there.

Once at the hospital and on Becca's floor. Carlo had the desk nurse page the doctor. It didn't take him long to arrive. He took Carlo aside and had a talk with him. Hannah watched from the other end of the hallway. She couldn't hear them, but she could tell by Carlo's body language that something was very wrong. He slammed his fist into the wall and then threw his head in his hands. The doctor patted his back in consolation and then left him alone.

Hannah immediately ran to Carlo and touched his arm. He flinched and turned his head. He was crying. "What is it?" she asked him, "Carlo?" she asked, "Carlo!"

He walked away from her without saying a word and opened the door to the stairs. Without looking back he ran as fast as he could down the flights of stairs until he was all the way outside. He looked up at the sky and yelled as loud and long and hard as he could, and then he took off running down the road. He had to vent his anger somehow. He would explain it all to Hannah later. The full moon could not arrive soon enough.

~~~~~~~~~~*~~~~~~~~~~

ONE WEEK LATER . . .

Everyone could feel the lunar pull. It was as if everyone's adrenal glands were supercharged by it. It wouldn't be long now, one more week. Their bodies were already beckoning the shift. Patti and Cassidy still were not talking. They were fighting the same cause but only this one more time.

Luke had decided Chloe was too much for him. When he had returned to her the last time, he had caught her performing some kind of love rites with a piece of his pants and a dead sheep. He had wondered if she knew the difference between Satanism and witchcraft. She had managed to seduce him again, however, and he found himself making love to her on the floor covered in sheep's blood. After that, he couldn't go back. She had apparently been into this kind of thing for many of her young years. Luke decided he had enough demons around him on his own without her summoning more. She wasn't happy about it either. He worried she might try something even more unholy to keep him. Sadly, it wouldn't take much, he was oddly intrigued by the whole thing.

Tad and Jessica spent a lot of their time discussing their options. They were definitely bound together now by this unnatural similarity. They already had felt connected from the first night they met, now they knew they could never be apart. Even if it all ended tomorrow, they had something between them now that would tie them together forever.

~~~~~~~~~~~*~~~~~~~~~~~

M had continued to torture The Founder. Daily he would get him and inflict some brutal experiment on him. It kept him in a weakened and delirious state, and it pleased the man M to do it. Every day The Founder would be returned to his cage and dropped on his carpet bleeding from some inflicted wound or poison in his system, and every day he prayed for death from whatever deity that would take him.

~~~~~~~~~~~*~~~~~~~~~~~

Carlo had contacted Mr. Whitehorse upon his request to retrieve some final instruction. Becca had been released from the hospital and the old Indian was going to be there with her and Hannah when it came time for Carlo to go. But today he was to visit the man at his store. Carlo walked in and found the old gentleman sitting behind the counter waiting for him.

"I'm glad you are here." He said to Carlo with a smile, "Come. I have you something."

Carlo followed him to the rear of the store, to that same old trunk in the back of the room on the floor. This time when he opened it, he removed the top shelf and sat it in the floor, revealing a whole new level of fascinating things underneath it.

"Go ahead." Mr. Whitehorse said as he pointed his hand toward the items inside. Carlo reached down and pulled out a black leather gorge'. It was what swordfighters wore to protect their chests and necks during duels. It was beautiful and Carlo was honored to wear it. It came down over his right arm as well and it strapped down to the leather gauntlet that covered that hand. It also covered his belly and back and buckled down the sides. He felt so medieval in the thing, but also so very cool.

The inside of it was lined with chain male and there were clips around the waist of it for his discs. "There." The old man said after helping him put it on, "Now you are a true warrior, ready for the field of battle. Worthy of the opponent you seek. You must wear this when you go. It will protect you."

Carlo didn't know what to say. He was overwhelmed by all the old man had done already. Now he had gone a step further. "Thank you." Carlo said and he placed a hand on Mr. Whitehorse's shoulder, "Thank you so very much, and wish me luck."

"You don't need luck," the old man smiled, "You have rage. But be careful. Life and Death bear no difference when you are dealing with what is in between."

~~~~~~~~~~*~~~~~~~~~~

The Beginning Of The End

It was time. The moon would be at its fullest tonight. All of the pack was restless. They didn't know when the attack would occur, but they were ready. So far it appeared that M's experiment with Jessica had failed, but not completely.

She had all the benefits of lycanthropy without the harsh shifting effect. She was faster, stronger and meaner, and she contained the unlimited self-healing powers the others did. But she was still incomplete, an even more unnatural hybrid than the werewolves themselves.

She and Tad were inseparable now. Their union in this unholy thing had bound them in a way that she couldn't explain to Hannah. She knew she would have to tell her, but how? Hannah would think she had let this place go to her head, or that she was playing a really big prank. If all went as hoped tonight, she would go and see her friend tomorrow, and try to explain.

Tad had all the weapons laid out and ready. Their shifting strengths would be at their peek tonight. They at least had that advantage. He worried about Jessica though. It would be hard to protect her while fighting the poachers, and he knew they wanted her as well. Without the ability to shift, Tad worried that she would be an easy target, and if they captured her, he also knew they would use her against him. He would have to keep her close to him most of the time.

The others were aware of this possibility as well, and were also going to keep close to Jess. They would have to take turns guarding her while trying to save themselves. It was not going to be easy.

~~~~~~~~~~*~~~~~~~~~~

Up on the mountain, M was already prepared. He had armed each of his poachers with protective gear and weaponry. Six of them had the newest weapon available, the toxic spear gun.

M had the soldiers lined up so he could inspect them. He tugged on and checked all of the suits and had his assistant make corrections where he felt they were necessary. Then he sat them down for instructions.

He paced back and forth in front of them and explained the importance of capturing the girl first. "Once we have the she-wolf, we have won!" He boasted arrogantly, "They will all submit when Thayer does, and he will quickly give yield once we take his woman into our custody. So that should be your primary mission."

~~~~~~~~~~*~~~~~~~~~~

From his cage, The Founder could sense the anxiety in the air. Even this many floors below the Earth's surface, he could still feel the lunar pull on his body, and he knew that tonight was the night M had been planning for. He had to find a way to help the pack tonight. He had to find a way out of here. He would have to wait until M was gone to try anything, but he already had a plan. When the woman comes to feed him tonight, he would be free.

~~~~~~~~~~*~~~~~~~~~~

Hannah and Becca were beside themselves with worry for Carlo. He had spent all morning arguing with them as they tried to convince him not to go. He was getting worn out with all the bickering and he needed to clear his head. He was thankful, however that Becca had begun to talk again. He just wished it had been for a better reason. Mr. Whitehorse was scheduled to arrive and stand guard over them at seven O'clock. Carlo wasn't sure if he could handle them until then.

~~~~~~~~~~*~~~~~~~~~~

Cassidy had been out by himself all night. As he had done so many times before, he had slept in his car by the lake. He knew the others would need his help tonight, and he would be there, if for no other reason than to unleash himself. So he stretched and yawned and took a long look out over the lake that had comforted him so many times, and he cranked his car. Unlike his brethren, he didn't feel he needed any preparation. He was a killer, and a seasoned one at that. He had honed his shifting skills into an art form and he was always ready for a fight. So all he felt he had to do was to show up. Not because he felt he owed them anything, but he had promised Tad he would be there and support the cause. Promises he kept, and Tad he respected. So he backed out and turned the Mustang toward the cabin.

~~~~~~~~~~~*~~~~~~~~~~~

Noon had come and gone, and the guys had all fed their bodies need for red meat. The proteins fueled their muscles growing need for regeneration as they slowly morphed throughout the day. Tad had discovered a lot about the shift while keeping a journal. He sat reading back through it, fascinated at the discoveries they had made through this experience. It truly was unbelievable.

The others didn't say much to each other. Patti was busy cleaning the shotguns and Liam was wrapping razor wire around a couple of the ball bats they bought. Cassidy, as usual, was drinking and smoking and thinking they were foolish to even worry about it. He looked over at Jessica and began to see what Tad found attractive about her. She could feel him staring at her from the adjacent sofa and she looked up from the book she was reading to take her mind off of things, and locked eyes with him.

He did have a lot of sex appeal, she thought. Then she quickly shook it off, remembering what vile things he had done. Damn pheromones, she thought! She knew if they were alone together for any good length of time sex would be inevitable. She would submit to him without rational thought just because her libido was so supercharged by the moon and all this raw animal heat was in the air. Something she would never ordinarily do, but it was like she was in heat when the moon was full. She and Tad had been going at it like rabbits, even in the midst of all this tragedy and stress, and she knew the males could pick up on it.

She could feel herself start to perspire and her heart began to get a little racy as she locked eyes with him, neither of them saying a word. He smiled slowly, the way he always did and her lips began to quiver. She had to look away! She was caught in this sexual tractor beam he had directed at her. What was he doing? What was *she* doing?! They were trying to prepare for battle, and here this maniacal rapist that normally disgusted her was arousing her.

He knew he could have her at that moment if he wanted her. It made him smile to himself to think that he could manipulate women in this way. But he really didn't want her at all; he just wanted to toy with her because he was bored and frustrated.

Finally Tad picked up on the energy in the room. He looked up at Jessica and then followed her gaze over to Cassidy. He was instantly infuriated. He threw his journal at Cassidy, hitting him in the chest with it and stood up. "Back off, Cassidy." He warned him. This quickly brought Jessica out of her trance. She was embarrassed. She jumped up off the couch and went straight to Tad's room and locked the door.

Luke, Patti and Liam all stopped what they were doing and looked over at Tad and Cassidy. Cassidy just smiled and lit another cigarette. "Just having a little fun, man. That's all, a little harmless fun. I don't want your woman."

Tad said nothing else, he just kept eye contact with him long enough to make his point. Once he was sure Cassidy understood he would kill him for it, he turned and went over to the bedroom door and knocked on it.

"Go away!" Jessica yelled at him.

"Jess, open the door. I don't need this today." He coaxed. He really wasn't angry with her at all. He knew what was happening to her. "Jessica." He spoke more firmly this time, and it worked. She opened the door and let him in.

~~~~~~~~~~*~~~~~~~~~~

It seemed to be the longest day Carlo could remember. He sat and watched the hands on the clock slowly roll by minute by minute. He was too anxious to sleep too nervous to eat and too exhausted to fight with his sister and girlfriend anymore. It was almost dusk and as soon as Mr. Whitehorse arrived, he knew it wouldn't be long before he would be face to face with a real life movie monster. The very idea of it sent chills down his back, but fear wouldn't stop him tonight. He had a score to settle, and Becca would get justice.

Becca had exhausted herself crying and pleading with Carlo. She had lain down on the couch and was sleeping peacefully when Mr. Whitehorse arrived. Carlo thought it was a blessing. He leaned down and kissed her head and petted her. "I love you, Becca." He whispered, and then he stood and faced Hannah. She was already crying, and she was too frightened to sleep.

"I want to go with you." She begged him, "Please. I can't stay here anxiety ridden and worried. I have to be with you."

"What? Are you crazy? No, Hannah, it is out of the question." He answered, "We've been over this a thousand times already today. It will be O.K., I will be back." He reached out and touched her face. She held his hand and cried. She knew he would not change his mind. So she nodded and hugged him tightly, and then she excused herself and went into the bedroom and closed the door.

Once inside, she put on her sneakers and picked up a dark blanket and then slowly opened one of the bedroom windows and crawled out. She closed the window back slowly from outside and then snuck around to Carlo's car and got in the back seat. She covered herself with the blanket and lay there quietly and waited for Carlo to get in. She was terrified of what she might see tonight, and she knew it was foolish to go with him, but Jessica was out there all alone with those creatures. Hannah didn't know fully what was going on with Jessica, but she knew her best friend needed her. So she stowed away under the blanket and waited.

~~~~~~~~~~~*~~~~~~~~~~~

M was excited! He felt victorious! He couldn't wait for the battle to begin! All the poachers loaded up in the Suburbans and Jeeps and followed M into the forest. They would lie low near the lake and wait for the full cover of night.

It wasn't long after M had left the building that it was time to feed The Founder. He roused himself and sat ready. He heard the sound of the elevator doors swing open and then he could hear the young woman's footsteps clicking as she walked down the long corridor. He breathed in the air deeply, he could smell the sweet aroma of her perfume. She was alone. Perfect, he thought. She finally came into view as he stood and propped his arms on the bars. The silvers contained within them stung his wrists a little. She smiled at him as she moved into the room. She was pushing his food cart. He was treated like an animal exhibit at the zoo.

The woman was beautiful. Her name was Maria and she was chosen specifically to taunt The Founder. M had chosen a woman that suited The Founder's taste and sent her nightly to torture him, by dangling her just out of reach. Of course she had no idea of this. She thought she had been chosen for this duty based on merit, and she rather liked The Founder, he could be quite charming.

"Good evening, Colonel." She smiled, and even the sound of her voice dazzled him. He wouldn't have harmed a hair on her head, even if he were free, except to satisfy her.

"Good evenin', darlin', what have you for me tonight?" he grinned back. Two could play at this game, and tonight the moon was in his favor. He knew she liked him, and he also knew he could tempt her. This was how he would escape. "And while we're at it, I think we are long past this Colonel business. Call me William."

She smiled and looked into his eyes, "Alright, William." He was a good-looking man. She had thought so from the first time she got this assignment. She could feel him watching her as she prepared his meal. The big flirt.

"Whatever is that insatiable scent you are wearin', my dear? Why it is positively drivin' me wild." He threw on the charm a little heavier than usual tonight.

"Now William, you know it's the same as I always wear. You've asked me before. It's Imari." She knew he was flirting with her. She looked forward to it every evening. He made her feel beautiful and desired. She really wasn't that afraid of him at all. In fact, she felt pity for him being tortured and kept like an animal. She turned to approach the cage. "Now, William, you can see I am unescorted tonight, so you are on the honor system with me." She shook her finger at him and he reached through the bars and grabbed her hands swiftly in his. It startled her and she jumped but she couldn't pull loose.

"Don't be frightened, Maria. I'll not harm you. I'm just so overcome with the aroma of you that I can't help myself." It was working, she stopped resisting, he could feel her body give in, "William!" she shouted as if in protest, but he knew better, he could smell her desire.

He held her close to the cage and wrapped an arm through the wide-set bars as best he could and around her back. She was trembling, but not from fear. She smiled and looked into his eyes as he whispered to her.

"You know, Maria, M has been denying me women for quite some time now as punishment. You know I desire you above all the ones he chooses for me. You have to know that."

"Yes." She whispered back, "I think I do."

"Now what harm would there be in you sneaking in here with me tonight? You know I wouldn't hurt you. Why, I couldn't hurt you. I can't even shift with this fool concoction around my throat."

The low cool tone of his voice was like an aphrodisiac to her. She could feel herself begin to give in. She was finding it harder and harder to resist him. Maybe he was right. No one would know, they were all involved in the capture maneuver tonight, and she did have the keys.

Before any doubt could set in he nudged more. "Kiss me."

"What?" she whispered. She had heard him but she was stalling, he was winning her over fast.

"I said, kiss me. Let me taste your lips and then you tell me if you'll not give yourself to me at least this one time." He whispered the perfect words just the right way. She closed her eyes and leaned into the bars and their lips met. She could feel electricity between them. She was intoxicated with passion for him. Ignited! She would not be able to say 'no' now. He let go of her to see if she would withdraw, she didn't. Instead she moved closer to the bars and put her hands to his face and kissed him passionately. When she pulled away, he coaxed her to come inside with him.

"Please join me in my bed, Maria. I desire not food this evening, only the attention of a beautiful woman."

Her eyes never left his. She trusted him completely. She was so excited she didn't care what the consequences were; she needed to be in there with him. She quickly took the keys from the table and began unlocking the gate. "Click, click!" The lock made a loud noise as she turned the key. His ears pricked up and a smile, much like Cassidy's, flooded across his face. Once she came inside, he had every intention of taking the keys and locking her safely inside, but he just couldn't pass on a beautiful and willing woman.

She fell into his arms and he slipped the keys right out of her hands. Then he lifted her chivalrously and placed her on the bed. Why the Hell not? After all, this may be the last time for him. Besides, he thought, he wouldn't want to disappoint her! He pulled the curtain and took his prize.

~~~~~~~~~~*~~~~~~~~~~~

Carlo pulled off to the side of the road not far from the driveway that led to the cabin. He turned off the lights and got out of the car. He was still unaware that Hannah was hidden in the backseat. She laid low and kept quiet. She would wait until he headed for the cabin before she got out of the car. She was terrified.

Once out of the car, Carlo fastened himself into the gorge'. He clipped the three discs to it and then kneeled down to say a prayer. "God in Heaven, please protect me that I might slay the unholy beast that defiled my sister, your daughter in God. Amen." Then he rose and before heading into the woods, he stood in the middle of the road and looked long and hard into the beautiful full moon in the sky. It would never look the same to him again. He took a deep breath and closed his eyes to prepare himself, and then he ran through the woods to approach the cabin from behind.

~~~~~~~~~~*~~~~~~~~~~~

Tad rose out of bed and began to shift. He had decided the safest place for Jessica, was to stay locked in his room. Then he and the others could do their level best to keep the poachers away from the outside. Since they weren't sure of their enemies' numbers, Tad had felt that would be the easiest way. Jessica slept while he shifted, and just before he was complete, she woke.

Cassidy had retreated through the kitchen and up the stairs to the loft where he could have full view of the cabin, as well as the advantage of surprise on any would-be attackers. He shifted from there and then sat back in his wolf-skin and waited.

Patti readied himself by the front window with the shotguns. He had enough rounds to take out quite a few of them right off the bat. He would suppress the shift as long as he could.

Luke and Liam had already shifted and armed themselves with razor wire ball bats and machetes'. They were ready. Patti looked over at them, standing there heaving and swaying in the low light, armed. It was a gruesome sight, animated, and frightening, even to him.

Jessica sat up in the bed and looked upon her boyfriend. She did not fear him. She knew he knew her. She pulled the blankets around her naked body and stood. She had to stand up on the bed to be eye level with him. He lowered his ears a little and looked her in the eyes. This was it; he needed her to be strong and smart. She understood she was to stay in the bedroom. She looked at him worried, whispered 'I Love You', and stepped off the bed and then opened the door closing it quickly behind him and locking it tight. Then she got dressed and crawled back up onto the bed and waited.

~~~~~~~~~~~*~~~~~~~~~~~

M's men were in position. He had twenty-five poachers with him, fifteen in Gortex and ten in ninja armor, and two medics. He figured five poachers per werewolf and he would grab the girl. There were twenty-five more ready at the facility just in case. He instructed them to have their weapons at the ready.

Carlo had made his way to the cabin. He had approached from the rear. He looked all around to make sure there were none behind him, and then he peered slowly into one of the windows on the back door. It was dark inside and he couldn't make out too much, and then he saw some movement across the room near the front door. He squinted to get a better look and then he saw something that sent shivers all down his spine. He made out the forms of two of the beasts. They were tall and standing upright on their hind legs. They kind of swayed back and forth slowly, evidently to keep their balance while they were standing still. It was true they were real! Carlo quickly moved and put his back to the outside wall and closed his eyes for a second or two and took a few deep breaths. Fear made him doubt himself, but only for a minute.

Suddenly something touched his arm and he jumped and had to restrain himself from yelling out. It was Hannah! "Please don't be mad. I had to come and help Jessica."

Carlo stood breathing hard and staring at her wildly for a minute, and then he got angry. He had never gotten angry with her before. She didn't know what to do. He yelled at her in a whisper, he knew the shifter's hearing was exceptional. "What are you doing here? Better than that, how did you get here?"

"I climbed out the window and hid in your car. I'm sorry." She whispered. He was still very angry with her. Now he had to worry about her too. He grabbed her hard by the arm with one hand and put his finger to his lips and said, "Shhh," with the other. Then he pushed her around so she could look through the window. Her eyes got wide and she took in a deep breath suddenly like she was about to scream, so Carlo quickly put his hand over her mouth and pulled her into him until she calmed down.

She was mortified! She wasn't sure what she was expecting, but that hadn't been the way she had imagined them! They were huge and gruesome!

Meanwhile, M's troops moved in towards the cabin, and three open air Jeeps rolled down in front of them with the flood lights on, lighting up the whole front yard. M stood astride the middle jeep and pulled out his megaphone. "Come out, come out, where ever you are!" he smiled as the words echoed and bounced off the walls of the cabin. Inside the manimals and Patti and Jess yelled out and held their ears. M continued to taunt, "Or I'll huff and puff and blow your house down! HA, HA, HA, HA, HA!" his laughter echoed through the megaphone.

Patti hollered at Tad from his vantage point near the front window. "There are a lot of them, Tad! But it appears they are all in front." Tad nodded and motioned for Luke and Liam to follow him out the back door. Carlo held Hannah's mouth and pulled her around to the side of the house as the manimals headed for the back door and came busting through it. He and Hannah cringed and turned their heads, and then they crept around far enough to get a look at what was going on out front. "What the Hell?" he whispered. "Who are these people?"

Suddenly, gunfire came from the front of the cabin. BLAM! BLAM! BLAM! BLAM! BLAM! Patti had fired the shotgun out the window at the poachers to provide cover and distraction for the others. Carlo and Hannah flattened themselves against the wall of the cabin again. Hannah tried not to scream. She was petrified. "I wish I knew how many there were." Carlo whispered.

"Five." Hannah answered, shaking.

Carlo looked over at her astonished, "How do you know that?"

"Because, I told you. We met them all that first night at the Festival, Jess and I. There were five men. I'm sure of it." She answered.

He glanced both ways quickly and then he grabbed her by the arm and ran towards the road to regroup. "Come on."

~~~~~~~~~~~*~~~~~~~~~~~

Maria woke up smiling and naked in The Founder's bed. The curtain was drawn around it and the lights were low. Suddenly she jumped up.

"Oh my God! I fell asleep!" She turned to see if he was there and quickly realized he was not. "Oh shit!" She jumped out of bed and quickly found her clothes and hustled out of the bedchamber. As she walked out, she saw the gate wide open with a note taped to it. He hadn't locked her in, and he had left the keys behind as well.

She grabbed the note and read it out loud, "Dearest Maria. I thank you for thoroughly pleasing me before battle. It took me back to a time before yours, my time, if only for a moment. I couldn't have you get into trouble on my behalf, so I have left you with a way out. Since I may not see you again, farewell. William." As a worried tear ran down her cheek, she couldn't help but smile and laugh a little. It was totally worth it, she thought, totally worth it.

~~~~~~~~~~*~~~~~~~~~~

Sport Before Dying

The Founder had made his way through the building. He had one more thing to do before he left forever. Remove the collar. He followed M's scent down the hallways until he found his office. Grabbing the doorknob and pushing firmly, he was able to bust the frame and push the door open without making too much noise.

As he walked in, Professor Saunders confronted him. Saunders was standing on his guard with a chair in his hands raised high above his head. "Why, Jack!" The Founder smiled, "I thought we were friends."

"You're no friend o,o,of m,m,m,mine." Saunders stuttered.

"Now Jack," The Founder purred as he lit up a stogie and calmly walked over and sat against the desk, "That's not very nice. You're hysterical, calm yourself."

"How did you get out? Wh, What are you doing in here?"

"I just came to get this." The Founder stood up and yanked the desk drawer open and pulled out M's keys, "I'll be going now. Of course, you have to keep quiet about this, or the next time we meet, I'll have to kill you."

"You can't kill me! You can't even shift!" Saunders yelled. The Founder stood flipping through the key ring, finally selecting a little square key with odd-looking divots around the edges, and ignoring Jack's comments. Then he cocked his head to the side and pushed the little key into the matching notch on his collar. Professor Saunders watched in horror as with one little click, the lights on the collar went out, and then with another turn and click, it hissed and the latch popped out.

The Founder smiled and grunted and closed his eyes as the collar fell loose and he was able to pull it from his neck. He tossed it onto the desk and rubbed the stinging holes left in his hide from the serum compressor.

He cracked his neck back and forth and then he lowered his head and opened his eyes. They were yellow! Jack Saunders began to edge his way around the walls of the room, trying to make his way out the door before William could catch him. The Founder smiled at him and let him go, before The Professor ran from the room he took one last glance back at The Founder. "Goodbye, Jack." The rumbling voice came from the man as he began to change.

Jack Saunders wasted no more time. He had had enough of all of this! He ran as fast as he could and made his way toward the garage. He grabbed a set of keys off the table and jumped in each of the Suburbans until he found the one that the keys fit and turned it on. Before he slammed the door shut he could hear the long blood-curdling howl of the werewolf just inside the building. "Screw this!" he said as he slammed the door and peeled out of the building and off the mountain. Once he hit the main road he kept going and didn't stop until he was out of the State.

~~~~~~~~~~~*~~~~~~~~~~~

Back at the cabin, Patti had managed to take out three or four of the poachers with the shotguns. The wolf-men had run through the woods and up and back around coming in behind the armed poachers. Carlo and Hannah watched with avid fascination from the side of the driveway, as the werewolves seemed to come out of nowhere and began taking on the soldiers. They moved so quickly and with such agility, Carlo wondered how he would ever conquer the one he hunted, and how would he determine which one that was?

Tad leapt up and back down and twisted the necks of two of the gunmen before they could ever even fire a shot. M ducked in his Jeep as Liam leapt through the air and swung at him, grabbing instead the windshield and quickly turning, swinging at M wildly with his claws. M was dodging the blows and screaming orders at his men to shoot. "Shoot him! Shoot him, damn it!" But Liam was too quick. That was one advantage the wolf-men did have, their lightning speed. They made very hard-to-hit moving targets. Luke came out of the dark cover of the forest swinging a machete' in his wolfy hands. It was a surreal vision to look upon. Carlo was overwhelmed.

Patti continued to fire the shotgun from the house. He didn't have to worry about hitting his brothers as they wouldn't even flinch from a

271

shotgun wound, so he fired continuously, moving the gun back and forth, taking out as many as he could before the moon's influence had drained him. He threw the guns down and stood up and looked into the loft. He could see Cassidy's black wolfy form in the darkness, sitting up there in the wingback chair like Satan on his throne, with his big yellow eyes glowing brightly. They regarded each other for a moment, and then Patti joined them in their sub-human state.

Carlo and Hannah counted three in battle. They didn't know what any of this was about, but at least they could use the distraction. Provided the one they hunted wasn't one of the three. They made their way back up to the cabin and just as they approached the side door, it flew open and out came one of the beasts. Carlo grabbed one of the discs and readied himself to throw it. Hannah screamed and quickly stood behind him shaking. Carlo and the monster made eye contact. They were only a couple of yards away from each other. The gruesome beast grunted and cocked its head from side to side, looked to the battle and then right back to Carlo.

Somehow, Carlo got the sense this was Patti. He didn't know *how* he knew and he didn't feel threatened, he just knew. Patti turned his head and looked back toward the house then slowly back at Carlo and nodded his great head. He knew whom Carlo was there for, and he was letting him know where he was. He felt that was the least he could do for Becca. Give her brother fair warning. Then he turned and bound away toward the poachers, he stood and roared loud and hard, and picking up one of the ball bats from the porch he began to pummel them to keep them back from the house.

Carlo and Hannah approached the door with great caution and opened it to go inside. They tiptoed down the hallway and looked back and forth for any sign of any open door or shadowy corner. They finally walked into the great room. It was such a massive room, and it was dark. This complicated things a lot. Hannah stayed close to Carlo's back and moved with him slowly into the middle of the room. They had to rely on their memories of the lay out of the cabin from the one time they visited Jess out here.

Cassidy had smelled them from the moment they reached the side door. He knew they were armed, he could smell the silver. He stayed still and growled a little under his breath. Carlo stopped. He had heard that. His heart began to beat faster and his hands were getting sweaty. He held onto the disc, ready to throw it as soon as he found that bastard Cassidy.

As soon as Hannah and Carlo moved underneath the loft, Cassidy stood up and balanced himself on the banister that wrapped around it, and then, almost gracefully, he jumped and dropped to the great room below. He was stealthy as a cat and made almost no noise landing despite his massive size. His blackness was good cover in the shadowy room. Carlo put his hand on Hannah's stomach and motioned for her to stay put as he approached Tad's bedroom door. He tried to turn it, but it was locked.

Inside the room, Jessica readied herself for a fight. Tad had armed her with a hatchet, and she was poised on top of the bed, ready to swing it at anyone who busted down the door. Her new and keener senses told her someone was in the cabin before Carlo ever approached the door. Carlo didn't push it. He decided to search some more.

As soon as he saw his moment, Cassidy snuck up behind Hannah and slowly reached around her neck and began to slide his wolfy hand down the front of her open shirt. She was petrified. She couldn't move, she couldn't scream. Her mouth was open but nothing was coming out. Cassidy growled under his breath again and smiled through his wolf-skin.

Once Carlo heard the growl; he whipped around quickly to see Hannah frozen and trembling where he had left her, and the grizzly figure of Cassidy in his wolf-skin behind her smiling. He was smiling! With his hand groping Hannah's breasts under her shirt. Carlo seethed with rage and raised the disc into the air. Cassidy chuckled in a rumbly way and pulled Hannah up close to him and held her there, and waving his other finger back and forth at Carlo, he grunted out, "Uh, uh, uh."

Carlo looked upon the monster's neck, and there was the silver pentagram necklace. He had remembered it from the photo Mr. Whitehorse had shown to them. There was no doubt now. This was Cassidy. Mr. Whitehorse was right Cassidy did know him. But now he had Hannah. How would he defeat him and not allow Hannah to get hurt?

"Let her go, you unholy bastard, and fight me for your crimes against my sister!" Carlo yelled at the beast. Cassidy purred and rubbed on Hannah more, squeezing her left breast in his wolfy hand. "Stop touching her!" Carlo was out of his mind. He had to calm down, he couldn't loose control or it would all be over.

"Carlo," Hannah trembled and cried, "Help me. Please." She was too horrified to move. From inside Tad's bedroom Jessica could hear what was going on. "Hannah?" That was Hannah out there! And Cassidy had her! She had to do something. She knew Tad had ordered her to stay put, but they didn't know about Hannah and Carlo. She jumped down off the bed and unlocked the door.

She opened it slowly. Carlo backed up trying to look at the opening door, not knowing what to expect, and still keeping Cassidy and Hannah in view. Jessica stepped out of the doorway slowly and into the moonlight coming in from the back door. She put her hand to her mouth and gasped as she saw her friend in Cassidy's clutches. Her worried eyes lit from within.

"Jess!" Hannah cried out, "What's wrong with your eyes? Why didn't you tell me?"

"I'm so sorry Hannah." Jessica started to cry. She lowered her head and cried for a second, and then all of a sudden she threw both hands around the hatchet and raised it into the air. She snarled at Cassidy and growled through her teeth, "You let her *go*, you fucking *PRICK!!*" Cassidy grunted and laughed and backed up into the darkness of the room with Hannah still in his clutches. Hannah couldn't believe it. She had never seen Jessica so vicious before. Their personalities had suddenly changed. Jessica's eyes flared and flashed in the darkness as she kept approaching and moving around to one side of Cassidy. Her new vision allowed her to see him perfectly well in the dark room. Carlo followed her lead and moved to the other side of him. He just needed one clear shot. Jessica had noticed that Carlo was brandishing a weapon, she only hoped he knew how to use it.

Cassidy pulled his hand out of Hannah's shirt and placed it around her neck. Jessica knew with one twist her friend would be gone. She had to think of something. She offered herself. "Cassidy!" she yelled, "Take me." She would have to really be clever to outsmart this evil genius, and she knew it. "I mean it. Take me." She lowered the axe to the floor and put her hands up and started to unbutton her shirt and looked him in the eyes. "You know, the way you wanted to this afternoon? The way *I* wanted to let you." She put on a smile.

He wouldn't fall for that alone and she knew it. She knew all he wanted was Becca. She needed to make him angry. She needed him to come at her. "Oh, I forgot, you only want Becca. But she doesn't want you anymore. Does she? You make her sick!" Jess could see it was getting to him, she could feel him now like the others, so she prodded some more, "That's right, Cassidy. She doesn't want *you* anymore," she lowered her head and whispered for dramatic impact and smiled, "She wants Patti now."

Jessica could see he was mulling it over in his twisted mind. He was really angry now but he knew it was a trick. She watched his hand on her friend's throat and waited for the right moment. He began to loosen his grip but he was no fool. Jessica prodded a little more. She wanted him angry enough to leap at her. "Just think of it, Cass. Patti's hands all over your woman, feeling her body, his tongue in her mouth." It was working he was seething with rage, both at the thought of it, and at Jessica for taunting him with it. Then she added the crowning touch, "And Becca letting him have her, again and again and enjoying it!" Suddenly he let go of Hannah and sprung across the room toward Jessica all in one fluid movement. He was lightening fast but Jessica was ready and equally as quick and Cassidy had forgotten that. He sprung at her and when he stopped and turned to grab her, she dropped to the floor in a split, giving Carlo the open shot he needed to strike, and he did.

Before Cassidy could reach to the floor for Jessica, Carlo slung the disc from his hip like a Frisbee. The silver blade cut through the air like a whip and landed in Cassidy's chest. Cutting his attack short and stopping him in his tracks. His arrogance had cost him. The metal instantly went to work coursing through his system. It was doing more than damaging him; it was an overdose of a lethal allergen. He growled and clawed at the disc trying to release it from his flesh, but the edges of it only sliced into his fingers. He frantically tugged and pulled at it. Roaring angrily, he finally retreated out the back door and up into the woods. He didn't get far before the full effects of the silver took over. It was stiffening his joints and muscles. Slowing his heart. He fell to the ground and stared up at the moon, writhing in the dirt and leaves that covered his deathbed. The same moon that was in the night sky when he began would be shining on him at his end. He would soon go into anaphylactic shock and die. It was over.

Back inside the cabin Jessica and Hannah were holding each other, and Hannah was crying. They couldn't stall long, however, because there was still a battle going on in the front yard. "Take care of each other." Carlo whispered, "I'll be right back."

"Wait a minute," Hannah grabbed his arm, "Where are you going?"

"I have to make sure it is done. I owe that to Becca."

"Becca wouldn't want you to risk that, and neither do I." Hannah pleaded with him. Suddenly, Jessica fell to the floor and gasped for breath. She clutched her chest and began to shake and tremble all over, finally passing out. "Jessica!" Hannah yelled and fell to the floor next to her. Carlo leaned down as well. "What is wrong with her?" he asked.

"I don't know!" Hannah was panicking, her best friend had just collapsed and was now unconscious on the floor! Suddenly it occurred to Carlo that it might have something to do with Cassidy. He handed Hannah a disc off his waist and kissed her on the head. "Stay here with her. You will be fine. Mr. Whitehorse says the others pose no threat."

"Wait! Carlo!" Hannah called to him but he was gone. He ran out the door and looked at the ground. He followed the trail of blood into the forest. It was dark and hard to see, but the moonlight was bearing light against the trail. Just a few minutes later Carlo spotted the form of a man lying in the moonlight in a small clearing. He approached the lifeless figure. It was Cassidy, the pentagram still dangling from his neck, and the blade still lodged in his chest. He was gone, his dark eyes staring up at the moon, its reflection still burning in them. Carlo took a leather swatch out of his pocket and dislodged the disc from Cassidy's chest, "That was for Becca. You brutal mother fucker." He snarled at Cassidy, and then he turned and went back to the cabin to protect the girls.

Out front of the cabin M's troops were taking a beating. The manimals had managed to avoid capture and serious injury. Except for Luke, who had fallen and the others didn't know why. He had convulsed and dropped unconscious to the ground. Tad was trying to cover him from his vantage point and still fight. If one was caught, they all were caught.

M saw the advantage at his disposal. He grabbed a toxic spear gun from the hands of one of his poachers and aimed point blank and pulled the trigger. The spear split the air with a quick, PLIMP!, and shot straight through Tad's gut. He threw his head back and howled and fell to his wolfy knees. M smiled from his perch in the Jeep. He was feeling very victorious now! Now he would rule them! He gave a signal to his men to hold their positions. He wanted to watch this. Tad panted and bled and pain surged through his entire body. "Prepare a collar!" M called out to his medics.

But just then an unexpected force came from behind M's Jeep and turned it over. Spilling M and the other men in the Jeep with him onto the ground. The figure roared loudly and then quickly sprung to action again, banking off of the bottom of the Jeep and up into a nearby tree and avoided all the gunshots fired at it. It was The Founder! The other wolf-men watched him in awe. They were not aware those abilities were even possible!

M pulled himself up and dusted himself. Some of his poachers dropped their weapons and retreated back into the forest. He screamed at the one's remaining, "Shoot him! Take him down now!!" M searched for his transmitter to call for more help. But before he could reach it Liam snatched it from the ground and crushed it. "Shoot them all!!" M screamed with rage, but The Founder suddenly dropped out from the top of the tree and landed with a crushing blow onto the top of another Jeep, and began plucking the poachers out of it, Gortex and all by the handfuls. He slung them several yards rendering most of them unconscious. The ones that did get back up retreated into the forest.

M looked around himself. He was slowly becoming out-numbered. He ordered his general guard to cover them and they settled slowly back into the remaining Jeep and headed into the forest in front of them. Plowing down small trees in their haste to get away. He intended to re-group and come back later with more poachers.

The Founder shook his big wolfy head and looked over at Tad, and Luke lying on the ground. He knew Tad would recover in a few hours, but he didn't know what to think of Luke. Tad lay panting on the ground next to him.

Finally Jessica had come two inside the cabin and her and Hannah and Carlo cautiously opened the front door. They could tell the fighting was over outside because it was quiet, but they didn't know what else they would find.

They stepped out onto the front porch and Jessica scanned the devastation for Tad. She looked to her right and saw him lying next to Luke injured. "Oh my God!" she yelled and ran past the other werewolves to his side.

"Jessica!" Hannah called after her, afraid to follow. It was quite a sight seeing Jess among some of her favorite beasts. None of them tried to hurt her, but Carlo and Hannah stood back, and Carlo kept his hand on the disc on his waist.

Jessica held Tad's big wolfy head to her breast and cried as she petted him. His breathing was so shallow. What had happened? He was bleeding. Suddenly behind her, Luke began to shake and cough and shift back into his human form. The curse was gone in him and Jessica now. The others looked upon one another and they knew what this must mean. Jessica confirmed it for them, "Cassidy is dead."

He was out of his misery now, and Becca would be safe. Carlo held Hannah by the hand and counted. There were still five counting Luke. Who had they forgotten? Hannah wanted to go over and check on Jessica, so Carlo held the killing disc in his hand and made sure they knew what it could do. "All of you!" he yelled, "Just stay back! This is how the blackest of you died, and I won't hesitate to use it again!"

They cautiously moved closer to Jessica, and then The Founder saw his moment. It was a way to save them all. He threw his head back and grunted causing Carlo to halt in his tracks and hold onto Hannah. "I mean it! I don't know who is who and I don't care! If you move I will finish you!" Carlo warned them again.

The Founder looked over at Tad and locked eyes with him. He let him know his intentions, and he said Ado'. Tad, breathing very shallow, reached out a clawed hand at The Founder. He didn't want it to be this way. He wanted to find another way. But The Founder knew there *was* no other way. He had spent enough time with this old magic to know that, and he was ready to go.

Without wasting another minute, he threw his head back and roared like a bear, the same way he had the night he had attacked and made them all, and turned his eyes toward Hannah. He really had no intention of hurting her, The Founder did not hurt women, even if they *were* trying to kill him, but he knew this action would cause the slayer to react, and so he charged.

It was as if it were in slow motion. Jessica and the others roared and collectively yelled "Noooo!!" But it was too late; Carlo reacted with lightning speed and flung the blade from his hip with lethal skill straight into The Founder's heart. He crumpled to the ground and closed his eyes. As he lay there dying, his mind began reflecting on when he was first turned. It was a cool foggy September morning. A thick mist had risen up over the battlefield covering up the bodies of the soldiers that had fallen earlier that evening. Colonel Jack stood surveying the carnage. He sighed and hung his head as he flung his cigar to the ground and stepped on it. Then he heard it, the low grumble of a very large beast. He squinted and blinked back the mist as he tried to bring it into focus. But before he could, it sprang out of the low-lying fog, taking him by surprise and ripping his throat out. It practically ran through him, and left him for dead. That was where his journey began, and this is where it would end, almost two whole centuries later. He didn't fight it. It was what he wanted. He would finally be free.

The others began to howl and whine and they lowered their heads. Carlo didn't understand. He did what he had to do. Who was this? Hannah ran over to Jessica and held her as they both cried. Hannah no longer feared the werewolves she just wanted to be with Jessica. She joined them in mourning as they looked upon the lifeless form of Colonel William Jack of the Confederacy. Freed at last.

Almost instantaneously at the point The Founder's heart stopped beating, Tad and Liam and Patti began to choke and gasp for air as their bodies expelled the curse that had plagued them. This ultimately seemed to be the only cure. They too were finally free.

~~~~~~~~~~*~~~~~~~~~~

ONE MONTH LATER . . .

M's backing support from the government had ceased, and his failure with the project had ruined his reputation as well. But he had found something in the woods that night, that he was determined to explore, and he would fund his own experiments as long as he could, hidden away at the top of the mountain.

Tad was able to buy the cabin and he and Liam finished their documentary. Jessica went back to school and would continue to work on her book as well. They were all going to meet the others tonight for a little get together at Carlo's pub, The Golden Earring. It would be the first time they had hung out together since the curse was broken.

As they each arrived Carlo let them in. He had closed the pub just for their special meeting. Becca was there with him. She worked with her brother now. She felt safer that way. Patti arrived first and as soon as he walked in he approached Becca, with his hat in his hands. It was the first time he had seen her since he brought her flowers in the hospital over a month ago. She looked at him without saying a word as Carlo stood watch. He had invited Patti for her, because she had asked him to, but he still wasn't sure how to feel about him. Patti reached into his pocket and pulled out a set of keys and placed them in her hands. She began to tear up before she even looked down, because she knew what they were. She looked at them and the tears flowed harder. It was the keys to Cassidy's Mustang.

"It's only right that you keep it." Soft spoken Patti told her. She looked up at him with tears flowing from her eyes and wrapped her arms around his neck and held him close to her. His heart was beating wildly through his chest. He closed his eyes tightly and wrapped his arms around her as far as they would reach and held her tightly.

Carlo lowered his head and smiled. He decided they would be O.K. and he left the room to give them a moment. After a few minutes of tears being shed, Becca pulled back from Patti's embrace and whispered, "Thank you." And then she fell into him and kissed him passionately on the lips. Patti was fulfilling the one thing for Becca that Cassidy hadn't, compassion, and that was enough to make her love him.

It wasn't long before Hannah and Jess and Tad and Liam and Luke arrived. Becca let them in and held the door open for Mr. Whitehorse, whom arrived last. The group drank and ate and laughed, and shared a bond forever with each other that no one else could understand. They would make a habit of these meetings, and promised to stay close to one another forever. Except for Luke. Now that he was whole he felt he needed to return home. He was an only child, and he would be the only family member to return from that last camping trip. He felt he owed it to his mother to go home. But he promised to visit at least twice a year. They would all miss him. He was still their brother.

They had buried The Founder on the land by the cabin and erected a monument in his honor. The epitaph read:

~Colonel William Jack~
Man of War & Founder of Beasts
We benefit from this gift we got from you . . .

They picked a perfect spot facing the lake. His memory would live on in them for eternity. He was an unlikely ally and an indefinable hero to them all. Tad would never forget him and he visited the grave frequently, usually in the presence of his wolf pack. While he stood regarding the grave, the pack would be just on the hill regarding him. For a short period of time he was one of them, and the pack nor Tad would never forget.

The month had come and gone without incident. Everything was as it once was. For a moment in time they had all been touched by something supernatural, and only in death would they know what the crimes of their half-life would bring them in the afterlife. That was another adventure for another time. This time had been surreal. All of them had been altered by it. Aside from becoming volatile killers, Liam had become a playboy, Patti had become an outlaw, Luke had become an occultist, and Cassidy had become a violent murderer. The only one whose nature didn't change was Tad. His nature stayed true to the very end despite the affliction he had been stricken with. Did it prove we have a choice? Maybe, maybe not.

~~~~~~~~~~~*~~~~~~~~~~~

The Rooster

ALMOST FIVE YEARS LATER . . .

The man M filled a syringe with serum and tapped it. Checking that his measure was correct. Then he proceeded to load the needle into Cassidy's arm. "Maybe, this time, my beauty." He hoped out loud. He finished administering the serum, and then picked up his medical chart and made a quick notation of the time and the dosage.

He had no sooner set the chart down and left the room when Cassidy's eyes popped open wide, like he had just awoken from a nightmare. He was confused and disoriented. He blinked hard a few times. Where was he? He was naked except for some kind of black shorts and he was strapped to a vertical table. He tried to pull on the restraints, but he was still too weak to move very much. He flexed his arms and clenched his fists and tried to look around. It was hard for him to focus in the bright light overhead, and the rest of the room looked dark. He could feel his strength returning, pulsing through him like electricity. He could hear his own heart beating, thumping loudly, building speed. He was having trouble remembering. He knew who he was. He remembered what he was. He felt the same, only like he had been in a hard sleep for a while. He thought he had died. Where the Hell was he? Maybe he *had* died. Maybe this was Hell.

M finally returned to the room. His heart almost stopped beating when he saw Cassidy awake. He yanked his glasses off and gasped. "Good Heavens!" He put the back of his fist in his mouth and just stared at Cassidy for a minute without saying anything else, and Cassidy stared back at him dead in the eyes as his species dictated, trying to retrieve some sense of the man in front of him. Finally M spoke again, "I can't believe it! I thought it would not happen. They said it was useless, but I never gave up on you! Oh, how you owe me."

Cassidy tried to speak. It was difficult at first, almost like he was drugged. He had to struggle to annunciate, "How . . . do I . . . owe you? I don't . . . know you."

"Oh, my boy!" M was so excited he could hardly refrain from laughing, "You, are a miracle!" M paced in front of him, "Your very existence will put me back on the map! You will be my crowning achievement! Much more powerful than The Founder! Yes! We will be unstoppable!"

Cassidy could tell the man was completely mad. His memory was coming back to him, however, and he did remember The Founder. He was a crass old bastard.

Cassidy choked and blinked and tried to re-animate himself further. "Untie me." He said to M. M replied, "In due time, my pet. You still have some recovering to do first, and until we come to some agreement, I would feel much more secure having you restrained. Especially in light of your violent past, if you don't mind."

"I do mind." Cassidy growled, "And you can tell me right now how *you* know *anything* . . . about *me*."

M was preparing another syringe, and couldn't remove the smile from his face. He was thrilled that Cassidy had regained consciousness; this would be a whole new beginning for him. The heir to his legacy was home! The prodigal son as it were, to M's reign. Cassidy reminded him he was speaking, "Hey, old man!" he growled, "I'm speaking to you! Who are you?"

M turned around and approached Cassidy with the syringe. "What the fuck is that?" Cassidy snapped, his wit and charm returning at full speed.

"This is just a little protein boost." M answered, dismissing Cassidy's aggressive demeanor, "Your body has been in limbo for so long, this is the only way I have been able to fulfill it's demand for this essential nutrient. And in light of your rapid return, I think an extra dose is necessary."

"What do you mean for so long?" Cassidy squinted as M injected him with the booster. "Where the Hell am I?"

"Now," M said calmly as he retracted the needle and picked up his chart to record the entry, "I will make things crystal clear for you." He pulled up a stool in front of Cassidy and began to explain, "I am M. I am the one who made you what you are. Well," he paused, "I am the one who hand-picked you to receive this gift. Your benefactor, William, is the one whom actually," he gestured with his hands, "Made you what you are. But, in essence I am the one responsible for your becoming a werewolf. I arranged the attack on you and your friend Mr. Leason in the beginning, and I was there at your end. You were dead when I got to you. It seems someone had stabbed you through the heart with some kind of silver-infused weapon and let you die. Shortly after, The Founder met his end, releasing the others from their curse, and ending my hard earned research on the spot. My backers, your Government, withdrew funding and any knowledge of me, or what I had done here. Leaving me with only a skeleton crew of dedicated staff, and my own money to fulfill my work. I brought you back here, to my research facility, revived you, somewhat, and for as long as my funding held out, I have worked to keep you alive. It has been almost five years."

Cassidy looked upon M in shock. "How long?" he whispered, "Years? How did you do this? *How . . .* have you done this?!"

"I retrieved your body from the woods, unnoticed by the others. When I got you here I gave you a transfusion of your own blood. Blood that I had collected from you over the course of time. I didn't know if it's healing properties would restore you to your former glory or not, but it was worth a try to me! You were the only chance I had left to save my life's work. I got lucky. Maybe I got to you quickly enough or maybe the bloods' power was greater than I had realized. Either way, it brought you back, but not completely. You have been in some sort of limbo state, much like a coma, until today. I have spent every waking hour of it by your side and I have all but drained my financial resources. But you are worth it!" M smiled again, proud of his evil genius, "You are worth all of it!"

Cassidy tugged on the restraints, "Let me go now. You've completed your work, cut me loose."

"Oh, I'm afraid I can't do that my friend. You are far too valuable to me now, and as I said before, you owe me. You will stay with me as The Founder did before you. You . . . are the heir apparent to my legacy of brutality, as it were, and we have much work to do yet." M told him, trying to gain control of his monster. But M wasn't dealing with The Founder, he was dealing with Cassidy, and Cassidy was no one's pet. He was certainly no gentleman, and he would not be domesticated. Not for any reason this man had to offer.

M stood up and tossed the chart down on the stool he had been sitting in, and began preparing the serum for a restraining collar. The cover of the folder flipped open to where Cassidy could read it. There was a photo of Becca pinned to the inside. Cassidy's criminal mind began to recharge. His clever kicked in. He would not be had.

"How is she?" he asked M, hoping to give him a false sense of comradery, enough to get himself released. Plus he was curious to know. He would be going to visit her as soon as he could get free of this madman.

M turned toward him and noticed the open chart, "Ahh," M sighed, "Your woman. That's right, you don't know." He smiled like a serpent. "She is doing well. Very well." M made sure he was looking at Cassidy when he added, "So is your son."

Cassidy had not been prepared for the last comment. He could feel his heart pounding, unrestrained within him. He looked over at the man. "What do you mean, my son?"

"Ahh, yes." M grinned, "Remember the violent act you bestowed on her the last time you saw her?" M looked over his glasses at Cassidy. It flooded back to him. The rape. How had this scientist known about that? M continued, "You sired a son." M gave it a moment to sink in, then he approached Cassidy and stood in front of him to finish, "I have been watching them closely all this time. Waiting for the signs to appear in the boy."

"What signs?" Cassidy snarled.

"You know, that he is . . . like you." M smiled over his glasses, "the blood I revived you with was tainted, you know. To answer your earlier question, it *has* fully restored you to the ultimate beast you were before you died."

"You stay away from them!!" Cassidy roared, pulling on the restraints. "I'll kill you before I let you turn them into one of your lab experiments!"

M laughed and returned to the collar. "That is why I have modified this device. It was enough to control William. But I have added a few extra precautionary factors just for you."

"Fuck you!" Cassidy snarled. He could feel the power in his body returning. He knew he would have the strength in a few moments to break free of his restraints. Then he would finish off his new 'friend'.

"You know," M added some more, "They are safe from me right now. I have no staff left to follow my research anymore. No more "poachers" to help me. My resources were tapped over a year ago and, sadly, I had to let them go. This building is powered with a solar generator that is why I use only what electricity I really need. I have to conserve. But I can't get close enough to the boy to test him because your friend is always there to protect them. In fact, I think if he knew I was still up here, he and the others would kill me." He chuckled.

"What do you mean? What friend?" Cassidy huffed.

"Why she is with your friend Patti now. Didn't I mention it before?" M smiled, pleased with how angry Cassidy was becoming. He felt taunting him would help release his inner 'beast', and accelerate the healing process. Since anger and violence is what fueled him before, M thought this would be a great way to test his strength. A tactic that always worked on The Founder. But M was forgetting this was *not* The Founder, and it was about to backfire on him. He had sealed his own doom.

With a sudden burst of rage, Cassidy let out a wall rattling "RRRAAAHHRR!!" and with one swift, fluid movement he pulled hard on the metal wrist straps and flexing his chest pulled his fists together quickly, and snapped and broke the chains from the table, and from his ankles. He stepped off the platform, free, with the manacles still locked to his wrists.

M hardly had time to react. He was not expecting Cassidy's strength to be super-charged like this. Those restraints had worked to hold him and many others in the past. But maybe by re-animating him, he had unwittingly doubled Cassidy's powers. He should have thought of this before! He rounded the supply cart and grabbed up the serum revolver and pointed it at Cassidy. Cassidy walked toward his captor slowly, only this time *he* was wearing the smile, in his signature sadistic way.

M's hands shook, his arrogance fading as he pointed the weapon at Cassidy. Though he tried to maintain the appearance of control, he had never been alone, one-on-one with his manimals before, and he was terrified. As Cassidy passed in and under the low lighting, his eyes flashed and refracted the light like an animal's. He tossed the supply cart out of the way and cornered M behind his own desk.

"You can't survive without my help, you know." M pleaded, "There are none like to you. You are a beast without a founder. The curse can *never* be broken in you! You are unique! A Superbeast! I am the only one who understands what you are, and what you are capable of!"

"Is that so?" Cassidy slurred, "If you're going to shoot me, you'd better do it now. I assure you, if there is one thing I do know how to do, it is survive, and I owe you nothing."

"Yes you do!" M argued, "Without me, you would be gone! Lost forever! Then you would never know your son!"

Cassidy moved with lightning speed and before M could pull the trigger and save himself, Cassidy was squatted up on the desk and had M's gun arm in one hand and his throat in the other. He twisted M's wrist until the gun fell out of his hand and to the floor. Then Cassidy crawled off the desk and with his hand still locked around M's neck he slid in behind him, got close to his ear and whispered, "What else do I need to know? If you value your creations so much, tell me everything. Otherwise, we can't be friends."

The man M decided he didn't have much of a choice. He had underestimated Cassidy's diabolical thought process. He was oh so clever and so very fast! M answered carefully.

"You are solitary . . . in this world." M trembled as he answered. He had never been in the grasp of his creations before, he did as he was told, but as fearful as he was, he still admired Cassidy's lethal attributes. He found him beautiful. "Your curse can not be ended by the death of your attacker . . . because he is already dead." He choked out the words, "You cannot kill yourself. No werewolf possesses this ability. You have . . . uncharted, regenerative capabilities, your strengths are double that of any werewolf I have *ever* studied. You cannot die, and . . . you cannot be freed of the curse . . . this time. You are man-made . . . in a sense. The only other person that remotely understands your nature is Professor Jack Saunders, and he has fled for fear of you, and your wrath."

"Where is Becca?" Cassidy asked.

"She and Leason live with your son . . . in a house with . . . a white picket fence near the park . . . in the center of town."

"And the others?"

"They . . . are here . . . at Thayer's cabin. Except for the boy. He has returned home. You need me Cassidy. We need each other. You would not be breathing if not for me! I saved your life!"

Cassidy's lip twitched and he said nothing for a second, then deciding he had said all he had to say he answered, "Nobody asked you to." And then with a sound like someone twisting a roll of bubble wrap, he quickly twisted M's head around on his shoulders, breaking his neck and killing him instantly. He let go and let M's body fall to the floor. Like The Regulators, M had met his end, by the sword he had dabbled with, by preserving the creature that would ultimately kill him.

Cassidy collected a few things before leaving. He picked up the chart and flipped through it more thoroughly, this time finding his pendant taped to the back cover. He ripped it out and put it on. It immediately stung his hide. "Now I'm back." He smiled. He saved the chart and checked out the other rooms. He searched around and found a locker room where he then found a t-shirt to throw on over his bare chest, and a pair of pants and boots that obviously must have belonged to one of the staff that used to work there. He stopped to check a wall chart and located the parking bay. He made his way there and helped himself to one of the many black Suburbans collecting dust in the garage. He got behind the wheel, and after a long glance at Becca's picture, he cranked the truck and headed her way.

Memories flooded Cassidy's mind as he descended the mountain. It had been so long, but everything looked as it did before he died. It seemed so strange to know that. He did feel truly invincible, but unlike before he wasn't exactly consumed with killing anyone. He was more curious about his young boy, and trying to reunite with Becca. He didn't really care that Patti had been taking care of them either. Before, he would have killed him for it. He passed by the entrance to the driveway to the cabin. He wondered what Tad would do if he walked inside and punched him in the mouth. The thought made him laugh out loud.

He followed a few familiar curves in the road and before long he was crossing the bridge, where under he had participated in the slaughter of those filthy Regulators. It seemed like yesterday to him. He wondered about Roy. He snickered again. The thought of the look on that man's face the night the pack attacked his camp.

Finally he was nearing town. There were a lot of little old houses around the main hub of town, and the park kind of centered it. He parked about a half a block away from the park, tucked the chart in his pants and stepped out of the Suburban. He walked down the sidewalk cautiously. All of his senses were heightened. He didn't want to be noticed yet. He was saving that up for later. As he got closer to the park he noticed a little white house with a picket fence. This had to be the one. He could hear laughter and loud voices coming from the little house's direction. He recognized Becca's laugh from within it. Yes. This was the one. As he got closer, he noticed a small child in the front yard behind the fence. He got a little closer still, ever cautious of his old friends inside the house. It looked as though they all were there. He could hear Tad and Liam's voices, as well as a couple of unfamiliar ones. He stepped up to the fence keeping eye contact with the boy. The boy just stared back at him.

Cassidy could not believe the truth that was staring him in the face. But there he stood, a four-year-old little boy with his eyes. He wondered what Becca felt when she looked at him. Cassidy would have known he was his even if M hadn't told him. He could feel it. And he could feel the beast boiling just underneath the boy's skin. He wondered if Becca knew that too.

The boy didn't seem afraid of him at all. Maybe he could sense the familiarity around them as well. Maybe Becca had told him something about his father. He had been such a bastard. It was only fair if she hadn't. Cassidy kneeled down and staring him in the eyes he talked to him, "Hi."

The boy answered back, "Hi." in the cutest of voices. Cassidy put his hand to the fence. "Do you know me?" he asked.

The boy nodded. It made Cassidy smile. Not in his usual way, but in a way he had once smiled at the boy's mother. "How do you know me?"

"Mommy's pictures." The boy squeaked, "You're Daddy."

It took Cassidy by surprise. He felt salt water sting his eyes. His heart hurt. He was unfamiliar with these emotions. This pain was a foreign sensation to him. He choked it back and asked more, "Yes. I'm, your Daddy. Do you know where I've been? Do you understand?"

The boy nodded again and said, "You were dead."

Cassidy fell off balance. He had to sit down. This was too much, and he still had to be aware of his past friends laughing and talking just inside the house. It took him a few minutes to regain his composure. He hadn't asked the obvious, he decided to now, "What did your Mommy name you?" he rephrased quickly, "I mean, what is your name?"

The boy pointed to his own chest, "Evan."

"Evan." Cassidy smiled, he liked the name very much. She had named him after Cassidy. Evan was his middle name. She did well. The boy was beautiful. But now was too soon to re-invite himself. Patti was taking good care of them for now. He leaned in and motioned for Evan to come closer. "I want you to give your Mommy something for me, O.K.?"

The boy nodded. Cassidy reached up and yanked the pendant from around his neck. It would be a way to let her know he would be back. "Give me your hand, Evan."

The little boy reached through the fence as he was told, and opened his hand out. Cassidy laid the necklace in his tiny hand and folded his fingers around it. "You put that in your pocket, and after I'm gone, you give it to Mommy, O.K.?"

Evan pulled his little hand back through and looked at it a minute. "Mommy's pictures of it." He said, "You wear it."

"What?" Cassidy asked confused.

"Mommy's pictures." He said again, and then he added, "Star on Daddy and a Black Car."

Cassidy had forgotten the Mustang! He hadn't even thought about it once. He looked puzzled and asked him, "You know my car?"

"Uh-huh." He nodded, "Mommy's pictures. I drive it."

"You drove it?" It took him a minute to think, and then he asked, "Do you know where it is?"

The little boy nodded and then turned toward the house and pointed with his little finger at the garage. "It's asleep."

Cassidy stood up. He was in shock; he smiled slyly as he got cold chills. So much had landed in his lap since this morning; he couldn't believe Becca kept his car! He looked over at Evan, "Can you show me?"

"Come on." Evan answered and he reached out to grab his Daddy's hand over the little picket fence. Cassidy held onto his hand, and carefully followed his lead toward the garage. He looked over to the house and could see Tad and Liam laughing and talking through the windows. Becca was there too, but her back was to him. He didn't want them to know he was there yet. Evan opened the fence gate and walked through it and over to the garage door. "In here." He told Cassidy, and he turned the knob and pushed open the door. The car was there. It looked the same as the day he parked it at the cabin for the last time. He touched it to make sure it was real. Then he opened the driver's side door. He could smell the leather cleaner. It looked good. Pat must have been taking care of it too. He had always admired the car.

Cassidy touched the seat and then slid inside and sat down. He closed his eyes and leaned his head back and took a deep breath. It was all coming flooding back to him now, who he was. What he was. Evan stood beside him by the door. "Are you going away now, Daddy?"

The boy knew he was leaving. It hurt Cassidy to hear him say that. He called him Daddy. He had just met him and he knew. They were already connected. He looked the little boy in the eyes and answered him, "Just for now. I *will* be back, Evan. I promise."

"O.K." Evan replied, "I tell Mommy?"

"After I leave, you give her the necklace. Remember?" Cassidy asked him.

The boy nodded, "O.K., Daddy."

Cassidy rubbed his head then leaned over and opened the glove box looking for the keys. They weren't there. He checked under the seats, not there either. He looked at Evan, "Where are the keys?"

Evan walked over to the workbench and opened a drawer and pulled out the keys. Then he handed them to Cassidy. Cassidy got out of the car and kneeled down in front of the boy and put his hands on his shoulders. "I will be back, Evan. Soon."

The little boy nodded and then quickly threw his hands around Cassidy's neck and held on tight, like he had known him his whole life. It took Cassidy by surprise, but then he returned the hug. He held the boy close and closed his eyes tight to block himself from crying. He could feel Evan's heart beating next to his. "I miss you." Evan whispered. Cassidy pulled back and told him to watch out while he opened the garage door as quietly as he could. "You go on back in the house now, Evan. Before your mother calls for you."

"O.K. Goodbye." Evan waved at his Daddy. Cassidy waved back and then got into the car and waited for the boy to go into the house. Once he heard the interior door shut, he threw the keys into the ignition and cranked the car. It immediately roared and rumbled. He knew it would be heard, he heard everybody jump to their feet inside the house. Then he backed it out of the driveway and into the road, and with one last glance at the little white house he let out on the clutch and let her rip. Within seconds he was out of sight.

The group of friends ran outside in time to see the Mustang roaring into the distance. Patti had Evan in his arms. Becca was hysterical, "Oh my God, Evan! Are you alright? Someone stole the car! It could have been you, are you alright?" She approached him and pet him.

"What happened, Pat? Who would do that with us right inside?" Tad asked him.

"I don't know who would be that bold around here. I mean we know all the neighbors." Patti answered.

"Who would do this to us?" Becca sniffled, shaken and Thankful they hadn't taken Evan and heartbroken over the loss of the Mustang.

"Daddy took it, Mommy. Don't cry." Evan said calmly.

Everyone fell silent. It took a minute to sink in. They weren't sure they heard him right. Becca looked shocked. "What did you say, Baby?" she asked him. Hoping she *hadn't* heard him right.

He reached into his pants pocket and pulled out the pendant and held it out to her. "He said give to Mommy. Here Mommy."

All the guys' eyes widened as they looked upon the medallion. Becca could feel herself go white as a sheet as she looked upon her baby holding that icon of her past, and she reached out with a shaky hand and took the pendant from him slowly. "Oh my God." She whispered. Patti set Evan back down and joined the others in staring at the pendant in stunned, speechless silence. They knew what it meant. It meant he was alive. What they didn't know was in what form? Where he was going and when he would be back? Becca looked at Evan, tears flowing from her worried eyes, "What did he say, Evan? You tell Mama right now, what did he say?"

"He said, tell Mommy I'll be back, and give to her." Evan smiled, "He's not dead anymore, Mommy."

Becca looked up at Patti and the others and then fell to her knees and began to cry hysterically. Carlo and Pat and Hannah helped her up from the ground and Carlo carried her inside. Tad walked over to Evan and kneeled down to him, "Come on, Evan. Let's go in now."

"I want to wait for Daddy." Evan sniffled.

Tad glanced up at Jessica and Liam, not knowing quite what to say. They returned his 'what now' expression. He decided to be tactful, "I know, baby, but your Mommy needs you right now. So lets go in now, O.K.? For me?"

Evan nodded and wiped his eyes as Tad picked him up to go back into the house. Before they went in, Tad looked back over his shoulder at Liam and locked eyes with him, "What do you think this means, man?"

Liam answered, like always . . . "The same thing you think."

THE END?

LaVergne, TN USA
14 February 2011
216417LV00002B/19/P